Missing

A DETECTIVE CASEY JANSEN NOVEL

MISSING

C. T. JORGENSEN

FIVE STAR
A part of Gale, Cengage Learning

Detroit • New York • San Francisco • New Haven, Conn • Waterville, Maine • London

LIBRARY OF CONGRESS CATALOGING-IN-PUBLICATION DATA

Jorgensen, Christine T.
Missing : a Detective Casey Jansen Novel / C.T. Jorgensen. — First Edition.
pages cm
ISBN-13: 978-1-4328-2723-6 (hardcover)
ISBN-10: 1-4328-2723-5 (hardcover)
1. Kidnapping—Fiction. 2. Mothers of kidnapped children—Fiction. 3. Single parent families—Fiction. 4. Family secrets—Fiction. 5. Psychological fiction. gsafd I. Title.
PS3560.O765M57 2013
813'.54—dc23 2013019135

First Edition. First Printing: October 2013
Find us on Facebook– https://www.facebook.com/FiveStarCengage
Visit our website– http://www.gale.cengage.com/fivestar/
Contact Five Star™ Publishing at FiveStar@cengage.com

Printed in Mexico
1 2 3 4 5 6 7 17 16 15 14 13

To Jim

ACKNOWLEDGMENTS

I am always amazed at how many people willingly give of their time and encouragement during the process of writing a book. In this case, as in so many others, I owe a lifetime of thanks to many people. To my brother, John Turnbull and to Ida Sansoucy, RN, MS, Transplant Coordinator, for their assistance with information and expertise generously given, I offer my most grateful thanks. They were not only gracious and encouraging, but maintained a sense of humor in the face of all my questions. All kudos go to them. Any and all errors are mine alone.

To my friends and fellow writers and readers, again, my grateful thanks. Kay Bergstrom, Janet Lane, Linda Hull, Leslie O'Kane, Carol Caverly, Cheryl McGonigle, Chris Goff and Alice Kober kindly read and commented constructively and patiently. And the Capitol Hill critique group and the MWA Rocky Mountain chapter critique group: Christine Goff, Bruce Most, Suzanne Proulx, Jedeane McDonald, Laurie Walcott, Piers Peterson and Marlene Henderson, all have my gratitude for their consistently supportive and always helpful comments, always given with a smile.

And certainly not least, thanks to my editor, Deni Dietz, whose insight and guidance was ever helpful. Also, many thanks to Diane Piron-Gelman, Tiffany Schofield, Nivette Jackaway and all the folks at Five Star who brought this book to life.

And most importantly, to my husband, Jim, my everlasting

love and gratitude for all the encouragement, humor and wisdom he gives me daily. Oh, and my dog, T-Rex, who sat at my feet for the hours it took to write this novel.

Chapter 1

Joe Canan stepped from his hotel, strode through the noise and exhaust fumes of the hundreds of cars that clogged Caracas on even the quietest nights, and cursed his chief engineer on the offshore oil rig for the trouble. Kurt Gomez was missing. He was either drunk or dead.

Caracas's violent crime rate might have dropped from four thousand plus murders in 2004 down to around one thousand this year, but even for someone like Joe, fit, tough and street-wise, there was always the chance of a mugging, or worse.

As he walked, Joe noticed a slender fellow with a backpack, jeans and hiking boots, following him. Joe tensed. The guy behind him could be some foolish American kid completely unaware that the incautious could end up one of the thirty or so people murdered that week. But far more likely, the guy was a spotter for one of the many gangs of teenaged thugs that roamed the night streets looking for an easy mark.

Joe was no easy mark.

Despite the street noise, he listened for a telling whistle or the scuff of rushing footsteps and kept his hand loosely fisted, checking doorways as he went. Caution paid. Always.

Fifteen minutes later Joe reached the building where Kurt lived when he was on shore leave, a three-story, ancient pink apartment building where urine stained the foundation and windblown litter crowded the entry. Inside, the black-tar smell of cheap cigarettes was as much a part of the walls as the disintegrating plaster. He climbed a short flight of stairs and knocked on the door at the dark end of the hall.

On the second knock he heard the soft slap-slap of flip-flops on the floor and a tentative rattle of a hand gripping the doorknob. "Who is it?"

Her voice was soft, almost a whimper, as though she knew and feared the answer.

"Joe. From the oil rig. Kurt's amigo." Amigo, boss, both were true.

"Oh."

There was a pause, then the sound of turning locks, flimsy metal on metal. The door opened just far enough for him to see a rounded face and a pair of soft, black-fringed eyes peering up at him. She was small, barely five feet tall, and her head probably came no higher on him than his chest. And it would have come no higher on the chest of his buddy, Kurt, the fuckup.

The light in the hall barely lit her face, but it was enough for him to see the yellowing remains of a black eye and a swollen, cut lip. Cold fury rose in his throat. "I'm looking for Kurt. Is he here?"

She looked down at the floor. "No."

"Drinking again?"

A child squealed and she turned, the door opening wider so that he saw past her into the tiny room, hot, stale and cluttered with clothing hung to dry. Dirty plates and old food wrappers covered the little dining table. Kurt made good money working on the rig, plenty for them to live well. When he wasn't drinking he was a hard worker and a decent guy, but—Joe had learned—put a bottle of rum in Kurt and he changed.

It was none of his business, but still it infuriated Joe. The kids made the difference. "Gambling again?"

No answer, but she blinked rapidly, confirming his suspicion.

"Where will I find him?"

She shrugged, a hopeless lifting of her shoulders. "I don' know. Maybe at the corner, in back of Rudy's place."

Rudy's place, a dive that hosted a mobile game of crooked poker. "Did he leave you any grocery money?"

Her head bowed, shamed. "No," she whispered.

Joe pulled out his wallet and peeled off some bills. "Here, use it for food for the children."

She didn't reach for it.

Thrusting it at her, he said, "It's for the babies."

Slowly she looked up and he saw her eyes brimmed with unshed tears. He pushed the bills into her hand and left, cursing Kurt anew.

He arrived at the alley behind Rudy's just as Kurt windmilled headlong out the door, a red-faced bouncer behind him, threatening, "Next time, I break your knees."

Kurt stumbled into the wall of the building opposite, bounced back and, turning, ended up facing Joe. Kurt's face was slack with the effects of alcohol, and maybe something else. "Wha—? Joe?" he slurred. "Wha' the fuck you doing here?"

"You were due on the rig two days ago."

Kurt straightened, pulled his face into a drunken approximation of a frown, rocked on his heels and muttered, "Leave me alone."

"You got a wife to take care of. Kids."

"Says who?"

"Listen, you fuckup. I'd fire your sorry ass if I had a replacement. I was counting on you. Doesn't matter how good you are, when you aren't there, you're no good at all."

"You calling me no good?" Kurt reared back, pulled a fist and fired off a wobbly blow.

Joe sidestepped, grabbed Kurt's fist, twisted it, and spun him around, locking his arm behind his back. "You're going to sober up. Now march. Your shore leave is over."

He frog-stepped Kurt down the alleyway, noting that Kurt wasn't really putting up a struggle. He was probably broke and ready to sober up.

Joe was at the mouth of the alley when he heard the telltale scuffle of feet. Dropping his hold on Kurt, he wheeled around, ready to defend himself, and Kurt if necessary. Instead, he saw two young thugs jump the lone man who had been following behind earlier. One yanked off his backpack, the second tripped him up and threw him to the ground. They both started kicking him. Shit. The guy would be a statistic the way they were going.

Joe thrust Kurt toward the relative safety of the building wall and launched himself at the attackers.

He grabbed the shirt of one, dragging him around to face him. Barely into his teens. A gang wannabe. Earning stripes, no doubt. Mean and vicious, but not yet a match for Joe. Joe's arcing uppercut caught the kid on the point of his chin. His head snapped back. He stumbled and fell, his head whomping heavily against the pavement.

Grabbing the backpack from him, Joe turned to see the second teen circling, arms stretched out as if inviting a dance. A wide tattoo blackened his face in a devilish mask. A wicked blade glinted in his right hand as he circled, looking for an opening.

Joe feinted to the left, raised the backpack as a shield, and lunged forward to the right. The knife struck the pack, hard. Joe rammed his fist into the attacker's ear, stunning him. The blade clattered to the ground.

The kid reeled, fell on his side, rolled and scrambled to his feet. Joe stomped on the blade. The kid, seeing his partner had run off, hesitated, then took off in the same direction.

The thugs' victim had crabbed to the side, and now stood warily. He was definitely the same American who had been following. Up close, he looked young, maybe in his early twenties, old enough to know better than to wander around at night alone. He had a couple days' sparse growth of beard and wore a ragged, sweat-stained T-shirt that said, "Get Even" in large black letters.

Joe held out the bag. "Your pack."

The young man straightened, stepped forward closing the distance between them as he took the backpack. Then, with no warning, he slammed his left fist straight and hard into Joe's belly. A right to his chin followed. Joe dodged a strong, driving left so that it glanced harmlessly off his cheek.

Throwing up his left arm in defense, Joe drew his right to punch. "What the hell?"

He outweighed his attacker by twenty pounds of pure muscle and topped him by two inches. And Joe was in far better condition. This guy was an idiot to attack. What was he, stoned? At the last minute Joe pulled his punch. The blow popped the guy's right shoulder, leaving his arm dangling at his side.

Panting heavily, the young man backed out of range. "I've—been waiting—six years to do that, you son of a bitch."

Joe eyed him, wiped a trickle of blood from under his nose, looked at it, looked back at the young man. The kid was pale, his eyes hollow. He might last seventeen seconds before he'd drop like a leaf to the pavement. The whole situation was absurd. He'd just saved this kid's sorry ass and for thanks he was assaulted.

Joe laughed. "Six years?" Shaking his head, he continued, "Well, you've done it now. Want to tell me why, before I pound you?"

"You don't even know who I am, do you, ass wipe?" The kid fumed. "You don't fucking care, do you?"

"No, I don't." Joe shook his head. "I don't know what you want, and I don't particularly care. But you hit me again and you'll be nothing more than hammered shit."

The kid's head sagged. He eyed Joe sideways, as though considering his next move.

Joe lowered his arm, but stayed alert. The kid was clearly angry enough to attack again. He was circling, but carefully staying out of reach. He tried to feint to the left, then drove his weakened right fist into Joe's forearm, easily raised in time to fend off the blow.

"That's it." Joe threw a right to the kid's chin and sent him to the ground. He gave him a few seconds to recover, then leaned over, grabbed the back of the kid's shirt and hauled him to his feet. He was lighter even than he looked, almost skin and bones.

Joe shoved him up against the wall of the building, next to where Kurt had obligingly sagged to the ground, his head lolling on a shoulder. The kid's knees buckled and he slid down like a bag of dirt to hunch next to Kurt. "Who are you?"

"Sam." He rubbed his chin, then his cheek as though checking to see if they were still there. "Sam McGrath."

The past rolled over Joe in a tidal wave. "Karin's brother."

Six years ago this stringy, washed-out kid had been healthy, starting city college, planning to be an emergency medical technician. "What happened to you? You look like hell."

"Kidney cysts." Sam's words slurred a bit.

Joe didn't catch it. "Kids shits?"

Sam sucked in a steadying breath, then said, "PKD, a kind of kidney disease, genetic. You won't catch it."

This had the feeling of a long story and Joe wasn't quite sure he wanted to hear it. "Bottom line, Sam."

Sam leaned his head back against the building. For a minute Joe thought he was going to pass out right next to Kurt and then he'd have two feeble suckers to manage. He nudged him with his foot. "Hey, Sam, wake up. Look, we've got to get moving. Out here, we're just begging for trouble."

"I'm okay. Give me a minute."

Shit, it was going to be a long dragged-out story. Those two thugs that scampered were likely to come back. With reinforcements. Joe thought about jerking him to his feet, but the kid's face was so pale he left him alone. "So what's with this disease you've got?"

"Polycystic kidney disease. Inherited it from Dad. It started early in me. Cysts form inside and outside my kidneys, grow big, burst and make scars. It's pretty well shot my kidneys. Hurts like hell when one of them breaks."

He drew in another deep breath and struggled to a standing position. "I'm better now."

Joe rousted Kurt to his feet. "Come on, Kurt. Walk."

They started down the street, Joe on the lookout for trouble. At night taxis didn't roam the city looking for fares. In fact, the cars doing the roaming were bandits, with guns. "Get a move on, guys. Talk, Sam."

"I found you here by using the computer. Came down yesterday."

Joe hadn't made any secret of where he was, but still it had been six years and a lifetime of experiences, oil and gas engineering, Iraqi oil fields, Colombia, now Venezuela. "So why now? Why wait six years?"

Sam continued without answering. "I got your hotel from the rig and followed you tonight. I heard you with his woman." He jerked his head toward Kurt. "You shit head. You're all over him for ducking out on his woman and you did the same thing."

Never. Karin was the one who'd dumped him. All those letters and he never got one back. Resentful, Joe put a rough hand on Sam's shoulder and squeezed, digging his thumb in until the kid writhed in pain. "Don't push me, kid."

Sam squared his shoulders. "I used to think you were a good guy, someone who would care about her the way she deserved, but you turned out to be a complete penis-breathed, elephant fuck, assh . . ." His knees started to buckle again.

Joe grabbed his arm, steadying him. "And you turned out to be a foul-mouthed ass. What do you want from me?"

Sam seemed to be having trouble answering. Finally he blurted, "I promised her . . . if she came back to Denver last summer . . . I'd never tell. But I couldn't let things be. And now Karin's—"

"Karin's what?"

"She doesn't know, but I think she's in for trouble."

"Why the hell didn't you tell her?"

Sam's head wobbled. "Because I'm a fucking shit, that's why. I was afraid she'd run and I'd never see her again. I'm listed for a transplant."

"Jesus H. Christ!"

Sam's next words came out slowly. "You gotta . . . go back."

To help a woman who wouldn't give him the time of day? Joe shook his head. "Why would I do that?"

Sam's eyes closed and his next words were barely audible, but Joe heard them like a thunderclap. "You've got a kid."

Chapter 2

Ammonia fumes filled the room.

Melanie Allen's eyes watered until she could barely see. She stopped scrubbing fingerprints from the wall in the living room of the little house and blotted her eyes. Three-fifteen in the morning. Sunday should be a day of rest and worship, only for her this Sunday wouldn't be restful, at least not yet.

Two things had come together. The private donor backed out and then she learned that Sam McGrath had gone off to find Joe Canan. Joe Canan was smart and tough. It all had to be done before he got to Denver. And that led to her decision.

Melanie rose from her knees and checked her watch. In a single, short hour she was going to do a terrible thing.

It had been almost easy to convince Karin Preston to let her five-year-old daughter, Haley, spend the night with Melanie's own daughter, Jennifer. Of course, Melanie had prompted both Jennifer and Haley to dance around, pleading and begging. Exhausted after a full day of work, Karin caved in minutes. A pushover.

The girls had been awfully quiet. Of course, they would be, but still she should check on them. The paper booties on her feet made little brushing noises on the wood flooring as she moved down the hall.

At the doorway to the little bedroom, she peered in. A bright bar of light from a cold, late April moon streaked through a hole in the heavy black shade and lay like a glowing rod across the two sleeping five-year-old girls. Melanie stripped off the rubber glove to cool her right hand as she listened to the rhythm of their sleep. Was it a little too slow?

Jen, her daughter, lay on her back, her soft, wavy hair spread across the pillow. Mellie felt the silky waves, smelled the bright shampoo smell. Even though she heard them breathe, she reached down to touch Jennifer, on the forehead to reassure herself the child was all right.

Next to Jen, Haley Preston lay curled on her side, her hands folded together under her cheek. It was fortunate she looked so like Jen, could be a sister. A wisp of her blonde hair lay across her mouth and puffed slowly in and out with each breath.

Haley whimpered in her sleep. Only five and a half years old, could she sense what was to come?

Melanie nervously tugged the rubber glove back on her right hand. The house was so quiet. Seconds later she heard the garage door rumble up and the truck back in. The engine cut, the door of the truck banged shut, the kitchen door opened and her husband's footsteps sounded in the kitchen. "Hey, Mellie!" he shouted.

She hurried down the hall to the living room. He was coming out of the kitchen, his sharp features tired, a can of beer in his hand. "Not so loud. You'll wake the kids."

He looked tired and cranky. He popped the beer open and took a long drink, then spoke, "What are you worried about? You said they would sleep for hours."

Melanie flinched at the sharp tone of his voice. Roger could get pretty edgy when he was tired. Trying to placate him, she said, "It's tricky giving kids a sedative. Too little, they wake too soon, too much and they never wake."

"Yeah, well, don't worry." He turned to go back to the garage, then stopped. "You aren't worried Karin'll show up, are you?"

"Not really," Mellie said. Nervousness made words pour out

of her mouth. "But, you know, I could see in her eyes, she felt guilty leaving Haley. For a moment I thought she was going to change her mind, but in the end, she just purely wanted an evening to herself."

Mellie knew she was talking too much because Roger's chin lifted and his mouth firmed into a single thin-lipped line, but she couldn't stop. "Karin said she'd come early in the morning, but I just keep thinking, what if . . ."

"No what-ifs, Mellie." Roger snapped his rubber gloves. "Just how early is she going to show?"

"She promised nine o'clock, but she'll probably come around eight. Still, we should hurry. I want to get out of here."

She looked around again, the room ugly in the shadowy light of the camp lantern Roger had set up. "I've done the living room. You could load the girls. I'll get the last of the stuff. You can finish with the vacuum soon as we're out. Be sure to reverse it so it blows out."

"You sure it'll work?"

She nodded. She wasn't sure, but this was no time to admit it.

Roger let out a long breath as he turned and left, his footsteps loud in the silent house.

Melanie nervously pulled her glove back on. There was so much to do still, and so little time.

The sound of glass shattering split the air. "Mellie! Get the broom. That damn bottle broke."

Mellie grabbed the broom and dustpan and hurried to the garage. She made herself slow down. Things always went wrong when she got nervous and now was no time for mistakes. Still, she was as nervous now as she had been that first day when she met Karin.

As she had planned. She'd stopped carefully in front of Karin's house and knocked on the door, pretending to need help. Karin barely opened the door, her hair falling across her face in wisps, her wide gray eyes wary.

Melanie knew why Karin was wary, knew a lot about Karin, more than almost anyone, so she acted real scared herself as she said, "I've got car trouble. My cell phone's dead and to make it worse, my little girl needs to use the toilet."

Karin almost hadn't let them in, but of course, taking Jenny along had done the trick. Karin was very careful, but because Karin was a good person, she would help a child.

As Melanie swept up the shards of turquoise glass, a strange feeling grew inside, making her almost sick. She had loved the little bottle. Karin had given it to her. A friendship present. The coil in her belly tightened, causing a sharp cramp. "It's kind of like a sign."

"It's no sign. I just dropped the damn thing." Roger scowled. "You're the one who said we had to do this. You better not be changing your mind now."

Why couldn't she just keep her mouth shut? "I was just thinking about things, that's all."

With an inward shudder, she dropped the sparkly glass into the trash bag. One little bit escaped and dropped to the floor. She kicked it into a corner. Karin would hate her forever. She blinked back a sudden burning in her eyes and wiped her nose on her sleeve. Maybe she would hate herself forever, too.

But she had planned for this. Planned it all carefully and now it had to be done.

CHAPTER 3

At eight-thirty Sunday morning, Karin Preston parked her car, got out and for a moment stood almost spellbound. Melanie Allen's house was a simple seventies ranch-style home, but with a swoop of roofing that went from a peak over the front stoop to above the front window, all with a series of gingerbread scallops along the front edge. Sunshine burst over the rooftop and for a moment transformed the simple cottage-style house, the dull winter grass and the whole scene into a frosty, sparkling treat. Almost like a fairy tale cottage, she thought as she hurried up the walk.

She rang the doorbell. She could hardly wait to get her daughter from the overnight. It was the first time Haley had spent a night away and frankly, Karin had found herself hoping to get a call saying Haley wanted to come home.

Last night when she came to pick up Haley she had been so tired after her troublesome last home health client, she'd just dropped on Mel's couch and groaned. The day had been awful. And good old Mellie had said, "Oh go on, have a night to yourself. You know Jen's been begging to have Haley stay. She'll be fine for the night. They'll have a ball."

A lifesaver. One stolen night to have some wine, maybe see a movie that didn't have animated characters in it, or just take a bubble bath. Karin had caved in moments. "I'll pick her up at nine tomorrow. Sharp."

Laughing, Mellie had said, "No hurry," and looked as

delighted as the girls were.

Karin grinned to herself. She had been chin-deep in a hot bath with a glass of wine and no five-year-old audience before she even ate supper. By God, it was great—right up to when the phone rang. She'd been so sure it would be Mellie saying Haley needed her, she was actually disappointed when she saw it wasn't.

Instead, it was Joe. Joe Canan. The disappeared man.

She had choked on the wine, spilling it into the hot water.

Six years and not one word from him, and that night, in the midst of all her peace and calm, he called. He didn't say where he had been all this time, or how he found her, only that he wanted to meet her, at their old special place. To talk.

She was still trying to catch her breath and refuse when he hung up. It annoyed her that the very sound of his voice had left her unable to utter even one word. She had spent years putting memories of him away, so she wasn't even sure she should bother to go see him.

Why did he want to talk now, after all this time? What had brought him back to Denver and prompted him to look her up? She climbed out of the warm water, telling herself she didn't need to bother with him. She did not have any obligation to him at this late date. But, of course, that wasn't true.

In all fairness, she needed to tell him about Haley, as in that Haley existed. And she was his. He needed to know that, even if he had been crystal clear about not wanting children. So she dried herself, dressed and reluctantly set out to meet him.

It took half an hour to drive to the little neighborhood café bar where Joe would be waiting, and each minute raised her level of dread about seeing him. Hundreds of thoughts crowded her mind, all of them undermining her confidence.

When she parked and got out of the car, the breeze had stiffened into a driving wind that lifted her hair off her neck and sent a chill down her spine. Although it was the last Saturday in April, a cold front had pushed down from Canada over the Rockies and would frost the fledgling leaves on the still-bare trees.

She walked to the broad windows of the café bar where light streamed out, her heart pounding more than she wanted to admit. Inside she saw Joe immediately. He stood at the front corner of the angled bar, one foot resting on the rung of a bar stool, looking damn good. He'd filled out some; his shoulders looked broader, his face a bit lined but appealing. Other than that, he hadn't changed much, but she had. A lot. She sure didn't feel like the cute little naïf she'd been before. She had two feet planted solidly on the ground now. And responsibility.

If she hadn't peered in the window, she would have gone in, but as she looked, she noticed the young woman at his side. Pretty, laughing, the girl leaned in to say something with a flirty little shrug and laid a hand intimately on his chest. Whatever it was, he'd laughed back. He still had that heart-melting grin that used to leave her breathless. And was now leaving this other woman breathless.

Six and half years ago Karin had fallen for him, loved him. That brought her Haley, which was good. But of course, by then he was gone, leaving only empty promises and no forwarding address.

Well, forget this! If he wanted to have a let's-get-back-together, heart-to-heart talk, why would he suggest a bar? Why not a decently quiet restaurant, without the girl?

So, yes, forget him. She wanted a husband and Haley needed a dad and someday she would find someone as wonderful as she had once thought Joe was. For now, she was an independent, stubborn, capable woman. On her own.

A cold passing breeze brought her back to the present. Karin stamped her chilled feet and pressed the bell again. Why didn't

Mellie answer the door? Was the bell out of order? She put her ear to the door and rang two short jabs. Two muffled chimes inside. They couldn't still be asleep.

She peered through the little window cut into the front door, but couldn't see a thing. Black paper or something covered it. She knocked, sharp raps so loud the sparrows in the tree next to the house scattered. But no answer.

Her chest tightened, anxious. This wasn't like Mellie. She was an early riser. She and Jen always arrived at Karin's by seven a.m. to babysit. Maybe there was a note.

Karin glanced around. No note.

Where were they? Why no answer?

She pulled out her cell phone and pressed in Melanie's number. No answer.

And no muffled sound of a telephone ringing inside.

Then a recorded auto-message spoke in her ear. "The person at this number is unable to answer. You may leave a voice-mail message after the beep."

She could barely speak as she said, "Melanie, it's Karin. I'm at your front door. I thought we'd all go for a cup of coffee, maybe." As hard as she worked to keep the anxiety out of her voice, she knew it had crept in with the ending "maybe."

Shaking, she tucked the phone away and ran around the corner of the house. The garage was locked. Maybe Mellie took the girls and went for doughnuts, or bagels. No, she'd have left the garage door open. Or maybe not. Mellie had said she had to be careful about stuff, because her husband was in the Special Forces, very hush-hush, so she wouldn't leave it open. She would keep it locked all the time. But if she'd gone somewhere and forgot to leave a note, then she'd have her cell on. Unless she forgot to charge it and the battery was dead.

Karin's teeth chattered from cold and nerves. Why did the house feel so empty? The breeze murmuring through the pine trees sounded low and mean.

The backyard. Karin ran around to the other side of the house. The fence gate was shut, locked and solid, standing six feet high.

Karin grasped the top of the fence and jumped. The edge of the fence dug into her fingers but desperation gave her the strength to pull herself up and see into the backyard. Winter bare and desolate. No toys. No sign of children ever having played out there. Not even a forgotten ball.

She glanced to the side, saw through the kitchen window. The countertops were bare. No coffeepot or mug stand. The little turquoise-colored bottle she had given Melanie was gone, too. She started to slip. Her jacket caught on a splinter. For a second she hung, then her arms gave out. With a ripping sound from her jacket, she dropped to the ground. Her hands stung from scrapes, a long sliver in her palm. She yanked it out and wiped off the ooze of blood on her jacket.

Where were they? Where had Melanie gone?

The neighbors, they would know. Someone would have heard something.

She ran down the path, down the street, a hundred yards to the old house on the corner. No lights. She ran up the porch steps. Banged on the door.

Banged again. No answer.

"Please," she yelled.

A figure approached, barely visible behind the lace door curtain. Old, slow, bent. An ancient woman pulled the lace aside.

"Please, open the door. Do you know if Melanie Allen left this morning?"

The old woman shook her head.

"Please, open the door."

"Go away. Nobody lives there. Not years. Go away." The

curtain dropped back in place.

The old woman couldn't be right. Mellie had been living there for months. Karin bolted down the steps and ran to the house across the road. As she started up the porch steps she saw the old newspapers, maybe seven or eight, piled on the porch, a couple even leaning against the door. No one home.

Her heart raced. *The police. I've got to call the police.* For a nanosecond her fingers hovered over the keys of her cell phone. If the police recognized her name—what then?

It didn't matter. Nothing mattered but Haley.

What could possibly have happened?

The furnace.

Oh, my God.

For a moment Karin's knees shook. Then she started running back toward Melanie's house.

If the furnace malfunctioned—they could be in there, sick from carbon monoxide poisoning. It happened all the time. A bad furnace, carbon monoxide. People sickened, even died in their sleep. There had been two cases of it in Denver this last winter.

A cold sweat broke over her forehead. Karin punched the emergency numbers on her cell phone, pressing the phone to her ear as she ran.

An efficient voice answered.

Words spilled out of Karin's mouth, one over the next until she realized she was sobbing and struggled to control herself. "Please, help me! I'm at six nine nine two Paradise Lane. I came to pick up my daughter from the sitter's and nobody's answering. I think the furnace has gone bad."

The cell phone slipped from her chilled fingers and bounced on the concrete front stoop. She grabbed it up, squinted at it. It still worked. Teeth chattering, she could barely hear the woman answer. "Double-check the address where you are, Ms. Preston.

We show—"

Panting, she said, "I'm looking at the numerals right now. Six nine nine two. Paradise Lane. The street sign is right at the corner. About a hundred yards down the road."

How could this operator not understand? "Send help. No one answers the door. I'm supposed to pick her up, but they're not answering."

Karin heard sobs again, her own voice.

"Detective Jansen is on his way. Now, I need you to stay calm."

"Would you be calm if it was your daughter?" Without waiting for the answer, Karin slipped the phone into her pocket, the operator's voice still chirping. She tore around to the side of the house where little Jenny's bedroom was.

A rock. She needed a rock. Beneath the old pine, she spotted a small stone. It would have to do. "Please, God, help me."

She grabbed the stone, felt it cold and hard in her palm, and smashed the window.

Reaching overhead, she whacked at the remaining glass until she had cleared the sill and the sides sufficiently to allow her to crawl in. A siren sounded in the distance, but she couldn't wait. Every second counted with carbon monoxide.

She gripped the window sill and boosted herself up, her feet scraping, pushing, scrambling, against the side of the house. Finally, she was balancing on her stomach on the sill. Throwing one arm ahead to break the fall, she plunged inside. Her hand hit first; her elbow folded with the sudden weight and smashed onto the wooden floor. Her forehead whacked down next, sending lights flashing before her eyes. After a moment, she rolled to a sit, then rose to stand.

She looked around, shocked.

The room was empty. No air mattress for the girls to sleep on. No curtains. Even the plastic covering the window for winter was gone. Dust covered the floor. Where had that come from? The narrow closet door stood open; not even a single wire clothes hanger hung from the rod.

Across the hall, Melanie's bedroom was just as empty. The shabby dresser was gone. The air bed, gone. The curtains that had hung from the cheap metal rod, gone. Rising panic filled her ears, drumming out everything. "Haley! Haley!"

Cradling her bruised arm, she rushed down the hallway into the living room.

Where was the furniture? Mellie didn't have a lot. A plaid couch, old and lumpy, and a television, a few other items. Now, the room was empty. There was nothing but the faint smell of dust. Dust lay in an even coat all across the hardwood floor.

Dizzy with disbelief, she bent and slid a finger across the flooring. She stared at her finger, smeared with a light coat of grit and dirt. It wasn't possible. She knew it wasn't possible. She would have noticed the floor, the dust. She wasn't the best of housekeepers, but she could *smell* this much dust. Someone had put it there. They had to. It had not been there last night.

But how could anyone blow dust in like this?

Rough hands gripped her arms. "Ma'am, you have to get out of here." A fireman clad in bulky gear leaned into her face. "Ma'am? You hear me? You have to go outside now."

"I have to find my baby. My baby is here." She stared, unable to drag her gaze from the empty room, crying, "I even had a cup of coffee in the kitchen. They were here. Look. There, in front of the window. Haley and Jen colored right there, at a little coffee table. Last night."

She wrenched free. "There, on the floor. There's a mark where they were."

He looked, but an expression of disbelief spread over his features.

"That dust wasn't there last night! It's new." She was babbling. Panic eating at her, choking her.

The fireman looked at her now, his grip on her forearm gentler, as though he was afraid she would break, yet when she tried to pull away, she couldn't get free. Even his voice was softer, sad. "Ma'am, you have to get out of here. We'll look for your child."

Pity. That's what she saw in his eyes. Pity and disbelief.

The fireman led, really dragged, her from the house and made her sit on the running board of the fire truck. An unmarked white car pulled up and a lean man in a worn leather jacket and eyes nearly the same walnut color came over to them. He and the fireman spoke as though she wasn't even there.

Finally the fireman turned to her and said, "Ma'am, this is Detective Casey Jansen, Ridgewood Police Department. He'll help you now." Then he leaned toward the detective, lowering his voice. "When we got here she'd broken in through a window at the side of the house. We found her in the living room, saying over and over, 'I've got to find my baby,' or something like that. I couldn't quite understand, she was crying so hard." He glanced aside, then added, "She may be a little—out of it, 'cause, you know, this place is covered in dust. Nobody's been living here, I can tell you that. Not for years. She doesn't believe it, though."

Karin jumped to her feet. "She's there! Haley's in there. I left her here last night." She tried to swallow the fright that choked her. "Detective, you don't understand. They're all in there. Tell these men they have to look again."

Shaking his head, the fire captain glanced quickly at the detective, an unspoken message of terrible pity. He turned to her, his gaze first boring into hers, then sliding to some space over her shoulder.

She had seen that shifting of the gaze before in her work as a nurse's aide. Good news was delivered with straight-on eye contact, but bad news was delivered at an angle, usually over the shoulder. As though it might glance off and soften the blow. She thought she might throw up.

Squaring his shoulders in his bulky fire jacket, he lowered his voice, "Ma'am, I'm real sorry, but there's no one in that house. There hasn't been anyone in this house for *years.*"

The detective spoke. "You looked through the whole place? Basement and all?"

"You betcha. Nothing. Nada."

"Okay, I'll take it from here." Detective Jansen's cheeks were pockmarked from teenage acne or a savage case of chicken pox that gave his features a rugged look. His cool, dark gaze traveled over her face, as though memorizing her features. "If you'll come with me, we'll let this man go on his way." He stepped back but held out a hand to assist her as he said, "My car is parked just over here. I have a few questions."

Karin looked from one impassive face to the other. They didn't believe her. They didn't believe she had left Haley there, they just saw the dust on the floor and that was that!

The detective's gaze dropped to her torn jacket. She looked down. A smear of blood from her hand stood out. His eyes narrowed. A glimmer of something flashed in them. Something she recognized, and her skin turned cold.

Oh my God, she thought. *It's happening all over again.*

Chapter 4

A kid, for God's sake. Unreal.

Joe Canan's first thought when he woke, even before he remembered he was in Sam McGrath's apartment, with his head pounding and his feet cold because they poked out the end of the bed covers. He was used to the warmth of the Venezuelan coast; the crisp high-altitude air in Denver felt good, but cold. He peered at the clock. Nine-thirty.

He rolled onto his back, kicking the covers over his feet and propping his head on his arm.

A kid. Karin pregnant. None of it seemed real. He remembered her from the last time they'd been together. She hadn't looked softer, or rounder. She hadn't even tried to talk to him, just listened and smiled. Hell, wouldn't she have told him if she were pregnant? That's not the kind of news you hide, is it? So, maybe it wasn't his kid.

Until last Thursday in Caracas, a mere four days ago, his biggest problem was finding and sobering up Kurt Gomez. Then along came Sam McGrath. Asking him to help a woman who wouldn't give him the time of day. Literally.

Joe shook his head. "Why would I do that?" he'd asked. But Sam couldn't answer. Joe had barely gotten him to the clinic before he collapsed.

It took Joe the rest of the day to get Sam settled in a hospital and then to arrange a flight to Denver. Sam would have to stay in Caracas until he stabilized.

Sam had been so adamant about the child and that Karin needed help. If it hadn't been so clear that Sam had risked his life to come to Caracas, Joe would have refused. But for Sam to travel when he was in that much pain was more than a little convincing.

And it cost a fortune to get an immediate flight back to Denver. And then, dammit, Karin stood him up.

He was coming all the way back here from bloody Caracas, taking his vacation time, making the extra effort, so why wouldn't she talk to him? He was coming all the way here to . . . what? To claim his kid? No, not claim the child. To see if it was his. Could he tell by looking? Would he feel some certain connection? God, he was thinking just like the kind of shithead guy he hated.

He threw off the covers and sat up. Well, if Karin wouldn't come to meet him, he would find her. It couldn't be too hard to find her address. Of course, it would've been easier if Sam had mumbled out her address instead of his own, insisting Joe stay in his apartment. Then he had slipped into unconsciousness again and Joe had to leave the hospital to catch a plane.

As soon as he got to Denver he'd called Karin, and for a long moment she was so quiet he thought she would refuse or hang up. Then she spoke, her voice throaty, hoarse and soft. She had agreed to meet him at the bar and grill where they used to go. He got there early, so she couldn't have come and missed him.

He should have confronted her over the phone, told her what Sam said, but he'd been surprised at his reaction when he heard her voice. She had sounded exactly the same six years ago, and for a minute he pictured the smiling girl from before.

In those days, she would laugh at his jokes even when they were feeble, agree to anything he suggested. Looking back on it, he saw she had boosted his ego at every turn, as if she would just fit to him. Whatever he wanted to do, she'd go along. She was young then. They both were.

Back then, she never would have stood him up. Clearly, that wasn't the case now.

One moment last night when he looked out the window of the bar, he had seen a dark-haired woman staring in at him and for a flash he'd thought it was Karin. But it couldn't be. Karin was a blonde. Her face rounder, smiling.

Still, he'd almost decided to go out to her when she turned away and waved at someone across the street. Not Karin at all.

He should have insisted on getting her address while he had her on the phone. He should have shaken it out of Sam back in Caracas, and he would have, if Sam hadn't been so sick.

Yeah, Joe thought. Go see the pretty, slim girl with the hair that curled on her neck. Whose smile melted him. Whose body was to die for. A sudden memory swept to his mind. They were in the park, sitting on a bench feeding squirrels, a breeze blowing her hair—a soft, reddish-blonde color—across her face, hiding her eyes. Her lips curved, laughing. "Whatever you want," she'd said. The moment was perfect. So perfect it scared him, and he had felt a little chill run up his spine. Today, in Sam's apartment, just the memory brought back that same chill.

Chapter 5

Karin's heart hammered against her ribs. Panic threatened to burst forth in yet another howl. She scrambled to think. She could not afford to let panic immobilize her and eat up time. Time was essential. The clock measuring out Haley's precious life had started ticking the minute she was taken. The longer her child was missing, the less chance she would be found.

The detective was filling out a form on his clipboard, a slim gold wedding band on his left hand gleaming dully as he wrote. "Your name, please? And your address and birth date."

"Ten forty-nine South Avery Drive, Ridgewood, Colorado. I'm twenty-eight." Could she possibly be only that old? She felt like she was a hundred.

"Why don't you start by telling me what happened here?"

The question sounded neutral, but she had seen the look on his face when he and the fireman glanced at each other. He was patronizing her and wasting time. "You already know what happened."

His expression was flat, assessing her.

Her cheeks grew cold. She knew the blood had drained from them, and that her pallor might even look like guilt to the police. It had before, six years ago.

She spelled her name. She could go through a lie-detector test on that one, because it was her name now. She had changed it legally from McGrath to Preston, her mother's maiden name, to make Haley that much harder to find. Karin had been an emotional mess, upset at being pregnant, at Joe who had left, at her father threatening to disown her. Her whole world had imploded. She'd been so frightened, she'd left the state so her baby would never appear in Colorado birth records.

Detective Jansen cleared his throat. "It's pretty cold out here. Let's sit in my car."

He waited until she followed him to his plain, white Ford Fairlane, opened the door for her and then went around the side and slid behind the wheel.

When she remained silent he said, "It's usually easier to talk in a warmer place. Now, so I get the details straight, start at the beginning."

The warmth did help. She knew she had to get his sympathy, but she also had to be careful. Karin forced the first words through her lips and then found they kept coming, almost unbidden. "Last night, at six o'clock I dropped Haley off with my sitter, Melanie Allen, for an overnight. Mellie's daughter, Jennifer, is nearly the same age as Haley, five and a half. Anyway, Mellie fixed us a cup of coffee. She makes dreadful coffee, always with cinnamon in it. I was a little nervous leaving Haley and I guess she thought it would reassure me. She spilled the box of cinnamon all over the counter and down the side of the stove, and just laughed."

"Was she nervous?"

He was listening. Did it mean he believed her? "I don't think so. She was just her usual cheerful self." But as soon as she said it, Karin wondered. Had Mellie been nervous, laughing so much? Had she on some level sensed disaster looming, or was that just a hindsight question, now that they were all missing?

"Was anything out of the ordinary?"

Was there anything strange? Karin thought a moment, then said, "No, no of course not. I wouldn't have left Haley if there was. I'm just trying to give you a picture of what happened. I thought you wanted all the details."

A cloud drifted over the sun, leaving the windows in Mellie's house darkened and blank, like dead eyes. A deep chill shook her. Where was Haley now? What was happening to her?

Shuddering, Karin remembered the child for whom the Amber alert was named. Little Amber Hagerman who was taken and killed. *Please God, don't let my Haley and Mellie and Jen be in the grip of some monster like that. Please!* She had to find them, had to find her daughter. "Don't you want a description of Haley? To send out an Amber alert?" The Amber Alert Program would notify all law-enforcement agencies, broadcasters, and transportation agencies of a serious kidnapping, but Detective Jansen was the only one who could issue it.

He nodded. "Let's stay with the story."

"You don't believe me, do you? If you did, you'd be asking about Haley. You'd call in to the station to put out the Amber alert. All you're doing now is getting me to talk, like you think I'm making this up. I need your help. We're wasting time!"

"Please, I'll get all that. Right now I want the big picture."

"There isn't any more to tell. I left Haley, went home, and when I came to get her this morning, the place was empty. Somebody came here and took them all away. Everything."

"You're saying they were kidnapped?"

She pictured Mellie opening the door. Mellie small, but wiry and tough. "Mellie would fight to the death anyone who threatened the kids." Karin looked the detective straight in the eyes, so he'd understand she meant every word. "She would never let them go. Someone must have taken them all away." Then she paused as a thought struck. "But there must have been more than one to get all the furniture as well."

"There's no evidence of a break-in, except where you smashed the window."

"Maybe Mellie was trusting and let them in."

"The fire captain told you that this house is vacant."

"It wasn't vacant last night when I left Haley here. Mellie's been living here for as long as I've known her."

"How long is that?"

Pitifully short, she thought. "Two months."

He seemed to weigh what he would say next. "You saw the empty rooms and all the dust this morning."

Karin saw the disbelief in his eyes. As if he was going over a mental checklist, totaling up points in her favor and against her. Mostly against her, she sensed from his cool detachment. That had happened before, too. But she was stronger now, much stronger. "Detective, I know this is hard to believe."

An involuntary flicker of his eyelids.

She pressed on. "I know the fire captain thought I was hysterical, maybe even delusional. But who wouldn't be hysterical? Wouldn't you? If you left your child for an overnight and the next morning she was gone? And the house looked as though no one had lived there for years?" She heard her last words come out in a desperate sounding high pitch, and regretted it.

His eyes narrowed, as though he mentally retreated from her. Her cheeks warmed. "I'm not nuts, Detective."

"I know this is difficult." His voice was too patient. "But I need their names, please, and ages and descriptions?"

She struggled to lower her voice to a normal tone, but her lips, stiff from panic, made her sound stilted. "Haley is five years old, blonde hair, gray eyes, average build, about forty-three inches tall, maybe forty-five pounds."

"Any distinguishing marks?"

"A little mole at the base of her thumb."

"Describe the other child, please."

"Jennifer is five years old too, and looks like Haley except she has blue eyes. They could be sisters."

"And your babysitter?"

"Melanie Allen. She's thirty-three, about five six, slim, dark-blonde hair, blue eyes."

He wrote carefully as she talked. "Do you work, ma'am?"

"I'm a home health nurse's aide. Premier Home Health Agency, four days and forty hours a week and as much overtime as I can get. You can call them. I've worked there for a year."

"Do you have family in the area?"

"No," she said, but she flinched and realized he had noticed the reaction.

He looked steadily at her. "I want to remind you it's important to tell the truth."

"No family in the area."

She was surprised at her sense of loss. Not for her raging father in his protective compound in the mountains, but for her calm, loving mother, dead eight years. And most of all, she realized with a jolt, for the loss of Sam and even Joe. Over a lump in her throat, Karin continued. "My only brother, Sam, left last Wednesday for South America. Said he was going backpacking."

"Dangerous territory, isn't it?"

"I tried to stop him, but he said he wanted to see Machu Picchu. He has serious kidney disease. He wanted to do this while he could." She leaned toward him. "Detective, none of this pertains to Haley."

"Did she inherit it?"

"No. She's fine. So am I. What's important is that you put out an Amber alert so people will be looking for her."

"We're getting to that. What about a husband? Haley's father? Is he involved?" Detective Jansen's voice seemed to soften as he continued. "Is this a custody problem?"

"I'm not married. And her father—hasn't been involved." Karin's voice dropped to an awkward whisper. "He, uh, doesn't know about Haley. He moved away before I could tell him I was pregnant."

Jansen frowned.

Karin hurried to explain. "He said he hated the thought of having a child, didn't want the responsibility. He was adamant. Then he left for the Iraqi oil fields."

"You never heard from him again?"

"No." Last night flashed before her eyes, and her mouth went dry. There was no way to fully explain to the detective and it would only delay finding Haley. "He lives abroad somewhere. I've told Haley he died in Iraq, because for me, he sort of did." He had to understand. "I've been on my own for years. I'm independent and I take care of my daughter and myself. There are worse things than being single."

"His name?"

"He's not involved. I told you that." How long had they been talking? She glanced at her watch and felt panic rising again. "It's been over an hour! Every minute is taking Haley farther away."

"What's the father's name?"

If she had to give up Joe's name, she could at least get something for it. "I want out of this car. I can answer questions just as well outside where there's more air."

He seemed to think it over, then said, "Name first."

"Canan, Joe Canan. And I don't know where to find him." Not a lie.

"You can get out."

The sense of release that came over her as soon as she stepped outside was almost exhilarating. For a moment, Karin considered running to her car, driving away and starting the hunt for Haley herself. But there was the Amber alert, for which she needed Jansen's cooperation.

The detective leaned against the fender of the patrol car, his expression veiled. "When was the first time you came to this house?"

Conscious of every ticking minute, she licked her lips, working to keep her voice calm. "Early February, nearly two months ago. We spent a Sunday together taking the girls to the park to play in the snow. Then we came back here. We did the same thing another weekend, on Saturday." Did he have children? Maybe if he did, he'd be more likely to believe her.

He nodded. Was that a good sign? "Did you come here afterwards that time, too?"

"No, we went to my house. She's really good with the kids and loves Haley, always asking if Haley can spend the night." Worry tightened around her chest like a strap, making her breath come in gasps again. "It seems odd now I hear myself say it, almost ominous, but it seemed so natural then. You don't think . . . ?"

"Go over that description of Melanie Allen again, please."

"Medium height, dark-blonde hair about shoulder length, long oval face, very slim." What else might he want to know? "She always wears jeans or slacks and sweatshirts, usually the kind with a hood and a front pouch."

"Eye color?"

Her wits were so scattered by fear, she had to think about it. "Blue, kind of faded blue. Sometimes she looks like she's been crying, her eyelids are sort of pink and kind of puffy. I guess she misses her husband. Mellie talks a lot about wanting more kids. I sort of got the idea she might have lost one once. She just loves being a mother and housewife." *Like I wanted to be. I'd have seen Haley take her first step, heard her first word, instead of a babysitter.* God, this interview was painful. So many things she hadn't thought about for so long.

"And her husband?"

"I've never met him. Roger's with the Special Forces on assignment. They moved a lot because he's with the military. I even asked last night if she'd heard from him lately."

That seemed to interest him. "What did she say?"

"That she couldn't talk about his assignments."

"Did you ever see any mail or anything from the military around her house?"

She noticed her hands were trembling and stuffed them in her jacket pockets. "No, but I wasn't here that much."

"Do you let Haley stay overnight often?"

"This was the first time. Ever."

"What made you decide to leave your daughter here last night?"

Karin glanced at the house. It looked brooding and empty. It seemed impossible it ever could have appeared warm and friendly. Even the detective looked disapproving, his mouth a grim line. How could he ever know just how much one night alone meant to her? If she tried to explain, wouldn't she sound like a selfish harpy?

And then there was Joe.

How could she explain that out of the blue, he'd called last night, the first time in six years? The detective wouldn't believe anything she said. And Joe didn't even know Haley existed yet, so he couldn't possibly be involved.

She plunged ahead. "Melanie—Mellie urged me to let her stay for an overnight. I thought the sleepover would be a nice treat for her. She doesn't get many treats on my salary." Suddenly impatient, she blurted, "Look, I know Melanie. She is a wonderful mother, absolutely dedicated. She's helped me out babysitting when I can hardly afford to pay her much. She does it because she's lonely. I'd never leave Haley with her if she weren't absolutely trustworthy."

His expression didn't change. "You said you came over early to pick up your child. Why? Were you worried about something?"

How could she explain that since the day Haley was born, she was afraid her child would disappear? How could she say that without sounding crazy, or worse, talking about why? *Because of Nicole,* she thought. Six years since Nicole vanished, and she still wasn't free of it.

She couldn't think of that now. Her breath caught in her chest, she whispered, "It was the first night we were apart since Haley was born. I got lonely."

He stared at her for a long time, but she held his gaze until he glanced away and asked, "Did you get references on Melanie?"

She winced before she could stop herself. "No, I just trusted her. She had car trouble in front of my apartment one afternoon when I was home. She came in. I let her use the phone, helped her locate a tow truck. We liked each other, we had so many similarities, and the girls loved each other instantly. When she suggested she could babysit Haley, I couldn't believe my good luck. My other sitter had just moved and this was perfect. You have no idea how hard it is to get good child care!" God, she was babbling now. Complaining about child care, for heaven's sake.

"So she suggested she'd come to your place?"

She pinched the skin on her wrist, using the pain to control her emotions. "Mellie said she didn't have much furniture because they moved a lot and she just left most of her things in storage . . ." Karin swallowed, feeling her knees start to shake. "I know what it's like to move a lot."

He looked down, giving her a minute to pull herself together, then asked in a soft voice, "What kind of car did she drive?"

"Chevy, pretty old, Impala, I think. White."

"License?"

"I think it started with CW." If she could just recall the license number it would be such a help, but her mind was so slow, nearly a blank.

The detective looked at her, waiting. He was using silence to make her uncomfortable, to make her talk. He must think she was holding back, she thought, and her heart did a double thump.

She looked at him, and realized in a far corner of her mind that his facial scars were from multiple cuts, like she'd seen on auto-accident victims who'd gone through the windshield. Would an accident in his past make him more sympathetic? She so needed his help.

He was still staring at her, speaking softly. "Who? Who would kidnap a whole little family? Why?"

"Maybe because her husband is in the Special Forces? Maybe they came to take Mellie, like a hostage. That would explain why she always wanted to come to my place. Maybe they'll leave the kids and just keep her. If you put out an Amber alert, someone will see them. Two little girls with blonde hair, hard to miss. Don't you see?"

The very thing she had feared since Haley was born had finally and terribly come true. Her child had been kidnapped.

And nobody believed her.

All this time she'd been so careful, but she never told about Nicole. Maybe if she had, if she'd warned Mellie. She clamped her lips shut, but the thoughts kept coming. Nicole. The court case. Herself a suspect. The threats, the notoriety. She'd been cleared officially, but that hadn't mattered. Not to Nicole's mother, anyway. But that was another lifetime ago. Wasn't it?

The more she thought about it, the less sense it made. A cold sweat broke over her brow.

Chapter 6

Melanie Allen shook with the kind of chills her mother used to say were caused by someone walking over a grave. That thought made yet another shudder run across her shoulders as she parked her car in front of the old house where Karin had a basement apartment. The street was Sunday-morning quiet.

Fear stirred in Mellie's gut. And her hands just wouldn't warm up, ever since last night when they left the house. Important that it was a Saturday night. Crucial. No government-type offices were open on Sunday. She had planned that especially.

She shivered again. She had to hurry, she told herself, yet she just couldn't get moving. Like her feet didn't want to go.

Karin would be at the Paradise Lane house now. Early, of course. Despite agreeing to come at nine, Karin would come by eight-thirty because it was the first time Haley had been away from her overnight. And Mellie knew just how empty and yearning a mother's heart was when her child wasn't with her. God, how well she knew.

Karin would be looking around, stunned, not believing her eyes. She'd be thinking she'd lost her mind, maybe, because there wasn't a single thing left from last night when it looked like a lived-in house. Even the walls had been scrubbed, everywhere the girls might have left a fingerprint. But the kicker would be the dust. Dust everywhere. That was the genius stroke she had thought up.

For an instant, she regretted the pain Karin would feel, and rubbed the goose bumps on her arms. Then she pulled her coat tight around her body and told herself she was a fool. There was no place for guilt or regret. She was saving her child's life. What she had to do now was go inside and clear the place as fast as she could, and not overlook a thing.

Roger had put different license plates on her car just in case someone came around while she was at Karin's apartment, but all the same goose bumps rose again. She craned her neck around before stepping out of the car. The street was empty; people were all inside on a still Sunday morning.

Already three minutes wasted with thinking. "So get going, girl." Roger hated it when she talked to herself, but the sound of her voice soothed her when she was nervous. "And I'm damn good and nervous now. Thirty minutes is all I need. Slide in, slide out, easy." She had timed herself before while she was babysitting. Thank heavens the kids had never noticed what she was doing.

She picked up the three black garbage bags and the little bundle, her heart thumping in her chest. Roger said the only one who could be trouble was Karin's landlord, Kenny, but he was lazy and never around, especially on a Sunday.

Biting her lower lip, Melanie got out and unlatched the car trunk with her remote then pushed it nearly shut so nobody would notice it was open. That way she could stow the bags more quickly when she came out.

She hurried up the sidewalk, careful not to trip on the uneven paving. She hated Karin's dingy basement apartment in the old house. The porch boards creaked so loud, she was sure the whole neighborhood would hear, but the front door opened easily. She stepped inside to the landing, where steps led up to the main floor and down to Karin's place. She listened briefly, but heard no one inside. There shouldn't be anyone there. Roger had rented the whole upstairs to make sure.

Silence.

The overhead lightbulb was out. Kenny was such a lousy landlord, he probably never planned to replace it. Mellie hurried down the steps to Karin's and unlocked the door. She stepped quickly into the living room, which was lit only by a little basement window.

Karin's apartment was shabby, but she kept it clean and tidy. She had moved so often, she didn't have much beyond the necessities. Melanie shoved two of the garbage bags in her back pocket and went to work. There were only two rooms, pitifully small and drab. She started in the bedroom, taking clothes from the closet, then the pictures from the dresser top. Then she rifled through the dresser, scooping Haley's things from the drawers.

The idea of being Karin's babysitter had paid off. She knew where everything was. And she'd had plenty of time to get Haley to trust her. All Mellie had had to say to Karin was that she loved to clean. And clean she had. Karin never questioned her. So simple.

Everything had to fit into the three big black bags because that was all she could carry at once. And Roger said she could risk only one trip to the car. Good thing she'd been able to get rid of a few things beforehand, though not enough that Karin would notice.

She filled the first bag and placed it by the front door, then shook open the second.

In the kitchen, she stopped for a moment, rooted to the spot. A small turquoise bottle, the match to hers that Roger broke last night, sat in the middle of the little table. Tears threatened, and she screwed her eyes tight for a second. She hadn't figured she'd like Karin so much. She hadn't anticipated this would hurt.

Twenty minutes gone. She had to hurry.

She checked the refrigerator, emptied the carton of milk, and put it and the jar of children's vitamins into the bag. Then she checked the upper and lower cupboards. She already knew there were no kiddy plates or cups in them; a week ago, when she learned this all had to go down, she'd stolen the little china cup with Haley's name on the side. She'd simply told Karin it got broken.

Karin never questioned it. So trusting.

It wasn't likely the police would dust this place for prints, but just in case she wiped an ammonia solution over the places she knew the kids had put their hands. Karin's place wouldn't be as clean of prints as the house, but clean enough to stall things for a few days.

Two days were all she needed, and maybe a third for good luck. Three days. Today, Monday, and Tuesday. Then it would all be over. They'd be gone.

The toy closet didn't take long. Melanie tied the top of the last bag and carried it to the door with the other two already set to go. Then she pulled a little bundle from the pouch of her sweatshirt. Two last things, the sweater and the photo, to guarantee they'd have enough time to get away, because a spring storm was forecast for the mountains.

Roger said the sweater was crucial, to make sure the police would hold Karin. He said they'd recognize the sweater immediately. Mellie had argued with him over the photo but he insisted, saying otherwise Karin might not recognize the sweater or worse, she might call the FBI. He didn't want her doing that until they were well away. Once they were long gone, he didn't care, of course.

She laid the Xeroxed photo on the kitchen table where Roger had said Karin would be sure to see it. *And the police, too,* Mellie thought. That bothered her. Even though she'd sort of doctored the picture, just leaving it on the table was too obvious. So obvious, they might start to believe Karin, and that would be disaster. Might as well scream *kidnap*.

Her gaze fell on a stack of phone books. Of course! If Karin decided to call the FBI, she'd have to look up the number. Quickly, Melanie slipped the photo into the government listings, and for good measure ripped out the page with the FBI listing. The sweater she slipped just under the edge of the double bed Karin shared with Haley.

Hefting the bags, she took a last look around and went through her mental list. Everything done, a perfect job.

A footstep sounded from the landing. The hair rose on the back of Melanie's neck.

Dammit!

Who was here? Surely not Kenny. He was the world's laziest slumlord. He would never come on Sundays. Besides, when she last talked to him, Kenny said he'd be out of town. She listened as the footsteps went to the back of the house.

She cracked the door. Three paint cans stood at the top of the stairs. A plastic tarp lay in front of the front door, the only way out of the place. Shit! Now what should she do? Fuming and frightened, she closed the door.

More footsteps overhead, and then the sound of something heavy being dragged from the front porch to the upstairs apartment. Maybe Kenny had hired someone to paint, someone who wouldn't recognize her.

No. That wouldn't be her luck. Kenny took care of his own maintenance, the little he bothered to do. Karin had to badger him just to fix a broken window in her place. So why was he here now?

When Karin first moved in, Roger had rented the upstairs apartment to make sure nobody else would be around to be a friend to her. Melanie had told Roger to wait before cancelling the lease so there wouldn't be any chance of Kenny trying to rent the place too soon, but he must have called anyway and cancelled for the next month. Stupid!

She peered out the crack in the door again. If she tiptoed up the edge of the stairs and took a huge step over the cans and the tarp, maybe—but she had these big bags. They were heavy. And awkward. She couldn't just leap over the stuff.

He came into view, his back to her. Definitely Kenny. *Damn!*

Kenny stopped, stretched, and snorted.

He did that a lot. Mellie had noticed it before. Every third word or so, he'd snort. He must have allergies. The other thing Kenny did was leer at her. His eyes always traveled to her breasts and stayed there. Even sweatshirts didn't discourage him.

She closed the door, careful to hold the knob so the latch wouldn't make a sound.

This was definitely bad news.

Had he spotted the car? If he recognized it, wouldn't he have come knocking on the door to talk to her? And how would she explain the bags?

A brushing sound across the hardwood flooring above, then footsteps back. She cracked the door again and saw him pick up paint cans, heard him take them upstairs and start toward the back of the house.

Now was the time. She stepped out, pulled the bags after her and shut the door. The lock clicked softly into place. Thank God she had the sense to oil the lock and hinges last week. She pussyfooted up the steps, hefting the bags and telling herself not to look up the stairs where Kenny had gone.

In spite of herself, she looked . . . straight into Kenny's eyes. *Dammit!* But all she said was "Oh, Kenny! You startled me."

He was standing halfway down the staircase. His gaze went straight to her chest. He noticed the coat and sweatshirt, and disappointment crossed his face. He dragged his gaze back up to meet hers and said, "Didn't expect to see you here today."

She pasted on the best smile she could and gripped the three garbage bags tighter. "I came to pick up a few things."

He glanced at the bags. "More'n a few, I'd say. You and her have a fight or something?" He shifted his weight to his other foot and started toward her.

"No, no." She edged out the front door onto the porch. "I just ran in for a sec." Roger would say she was talking too much.

"She there now?" he asked. "I need to talk to her."

"No, she's out now."

"Maybe you got some time to spare . . ." He let his voice drift.

Melanie knew what he was hinting about. He was always doing that. What was she going to do now? "Look, Kenny, I better go. Good seeing you."

He leered at her. "Don't hurry away on account of me."

"Gotta go now." She started toward the car.

Kenny was staring at it—suspiciously, like he wondered if something was wrong. Had he noticed the plates? Surely not. Kenny barely noticed anything beyond a woman's breasts.

Roger would be very angry about Kenny. She shuddered, but kept on walking.

CHAPTER 7

Karin Preston was hiding something.

Jansen knew it in his bones. She had that look, the furtive eyes. And her jacket was torn with a smear of what looked like blood on the front, as though she'd been in a struggle. There was something about her. Her body language, that was it. Her shoulders were bunched into tight, bony knobs beneath her flimsy jacket. That tension and the pinched line of her lips told him she was trying to keep from saying something. He'd noted this before in other cases where someone tried to hold back information, usually important, although not always. She leaned against the front of his car, her back to the chill breeze and he mimicked her body language a little to put her at ease, to keep her talking. The more she talked, the more likely she was to trip up.

She'd been jumpy, nervous, when she first started answering questions. After she gave her name, she'd calmed down as though she'd almost expected he would recognize her or know something about her. He'd run her name through his computer on his way there—routine procedure—but nothing had come up, not so much as a traffic ticket.

Karin Preston had a stubborn jaw and dark circles under her eyes, made more pronounced by the pallor of her cheeks. And her eyebrows were oddly dark. She'd penciled them in heavily and her hair had light roots along the part. He noted that because most women liked to lighten their hair, not darken it.

Until they were covering gray.

She was thin. A good meal would show in her stomach like an elephant in a boa constrictor. A week of sleep might fill out the hollows under her eyes and relax her frame. Jansen tried to imagine what she would look like if she were rested and carried another ten pounds, but the picture didn't help.

She leaned toward him, a breeze lifting her hair, streaming it across her broad forehead. Even pale and drawn as she was, he realized she was a good-looking woman. Earlier he'd seen panic in her expression. Now in its place he saw a haunting desperation that touched him. It made him uncomfortable, almost angry. If he let himself be swayed by her feelings, it could contaminate his thinking, his judgment. He knew from bitter experience the difficulty of discerning feigned from genuine emotion, especially if the woman was a good actress.

Karin Preston seemed intelligent enough to be very convincing. Emotions played across her face as though she were struggling for control. He wanted to catch her in a lie, find a significant change in her story. Lying was a tedious business and hard to keep straight, so he would ask tedious, unimportant questions that just edged on what she'd said before and he'd wait for the slip. He knew there would be one.

In a soft voice he said, "You were here and left your daughter—tell me what you saw when you were here." He reached into his jacket pocket and pulled out a tiny recorder. "I'll record what you say. That way I won't miss anything."

Her expression grew wary, like a cornered cat.

"The recording cuts down on repetition, keeps me accurate." He emphasized *me*. "You said Melanie was a good mother and housewife."

She surprised him. He'd expected her to protest. Instead, speaking in a hoarse whisper as though choking, she said,

"There's a smudge on the living-room wall where the couch was."

He had noticed the smudge the moment he saw the living room. "There's no way to date a smudge. It could have been here for years. What else do you remember?"

"Clean. The living room was clean when I was here, maybe a little dust here and there, but tidy. Melanie is a real thorough housekeeper. She even cleaned my place sometimes. This week she washed my windows while she took care of the girls."

Her house. The very next place he wanted to go. He could tell a lot from her house—depression, disorganization, mental confusion. She'd given him an opening. "I'll need to see where you live."

She looked at him, still wary, then leaned back, her gaze on the front window of the house and when she spoke her voice was a whisper, almost convincing. "That window, all the windows, were covered on the inside." Turning to face him, her gaze bore into his, direct and uncomfortable. "I never, ever, saw dust like that in there. How did it get there?"

Nice change of topic, he thought. He'd go with it for the time being. "What did you see in the bedrooms?"

She described them in detail, right down to the color of the curtains she maintained had been there and ending with a description of plastic covering the windows to keep the cold out. She was working hard to convince him with all this minutiae. So far, he was only convinced that she was good at producing detail. "Go on."

"The kitchen. This little turquoise bottle I gave her was in the kitchen window. That window wasn't covered, so the sun would shine in through the glass and light up the little bottle. She said she sometimes put a flower in it as a vase, but it was such a little thing, mostly she just looked at it. She said it made her feel happy."

He had to hand it to her, this woman was much more imaginative than most.

She was quiet for a minute, as though reliving the moment. Then she roused and continued. "And there was a coffeemaker, Mr. Coffee I think, on the other side of the dish drainer. I told you, Mellie spilled her can of cinnamon last night." Karin looked up at him, her expression bleak. "The whole kitchen smelled like cinnamon when I left Haley."

He starred the note about the spilled cinnamon. One thing he could easily check.

She pulled her coat tighter and wrapped her arms around her waist. "Haley's been . . ." Her voice dropped and she covered her face with her hands for a long minute. When she looked up, he knew from the horror on her face that she had at last accepted there was no one in the house. Or else she wanted him to think so. *Here it comes,* he thought. *The slip.*

Instead, she said, "You need to put out an Amber alert, statewide. Nationwide."

He could use that switch of topic, too. "I need a picture, a description of what she was wearing and as much information as you can give me."

She pulled her wallet from her bag and opened it, then stopped. "I . . . I guess I don't have a picture on me, but there are lots at home."

He could barely keep his expression flat. "Then we'll start at your house."

Her lips tightened. But she surprised him by saying, "Only if I can drive myself there."

She wasn't under arrest so he couldn't refuse, but it was suspicious and he noted her license number again, in case she tried to flee. "I'll follow right behind you."

"Detective," she said. "You don't need to worry. I'm not going to run. I'm the one who called you."

He nodded, irritated. He would have to follow up details, checking and rechecking. Tedious work, but it had to be done, and there might be nothing at the end of the search. Her background might fill in the picture, but most of all he needed solid information from her that he could verify, because so far as he could see, nothing was adding up. As his brother would say, it was all juke.

Chapter 8

Uncomfortable, Joe rose from the bed, pulled on his jeans and headed for the kitchen.

Last night he'd stopped at a grocery store for juice, bread and coffee. Now, thirsty, he pulled the juice bottle from the refrigerator and drank from it. He started a pot of coffee then tried Karin's cell phone several times, only to be told it was busy. Or there was no answer. She was probably reading her caller ID and refusing to talk to him.

She'd agreed to meet him last night, so what happened? Why hadn't she shown up? Car trouble? Maybe something came up and she couldn't reach him. She had been hopeless with cell phones before. In fact, kind of helpless, period. That had been good for his ego, but . . . He frowned. Smothering too, at times.

He poured coffee into a mug and stood at the window looking out over the Capitol Hill area of Denver, a place filled with turn-of-the-century homes, many now subdivided into apartments. Sam's place was the attic of a once-lovely old house and Joe could see straight across the city to the snow-covered and frozen Rocky Mountains.

The kitchen area was bare bones, a closet really, built into one wall, not even a curtain separating it from the rest of the room. Sam had referred to his place as an attic loft. *Attic* was the operative word.

He sipped coffee and returned to brooding. It really got him that Karin had never answered his letters, never taken even a minute to tell him she was pregnant. A kid! She should have said something. When did she think she'd tell him, when the kid graduated college? Or got married? Sweet Jesus! By God, he'd find her and settle this thing.

He scanned the rest of the room. Sam's desk. Tidy, with a picture that caught Joe's eye. Karin?

He went over to the desk. The woman in the photo looked like the one he'd seen looking in the window of the bar at him last night. Sort of. Probably Sam's girlfriend. Sam had always been so close to Karin, he probably chose a girlfriend who looked like her.

He picked up the photo, a snapshot taken up close, or maybe with a zoom lens. The woman's hair was dark and all wrong, and her face was much thinner than Karin's, but her eyes were the same. And her lips. She must be a cousin. And she was smiling down at a pretty little girl hanging on her, arms twined around the woman's neck.

He nearly dropped the photo. Surely not. His mouth went dry and a strange mix of feelings swamped him, leaving him determined to find Karin and the truth.

He tried Sam's top desk drawer, the one usually reserved for pens and pencils, paper clips and junk. Unlocked.

At the front of the drawer he found an address book. Nothing under *McGrath,* except someone named Zebulon, no doubt some other family. Finally under *K* for Karin he found her address lightly penciled in. Then he noticed a previous address crossed out, then another and another and several erasures. There were nearly fifteen addresses in all, not counting one at the Eberhards' where she'd lived when he knew her. And a name, Preston. Karin Preston. He choked. Married? She was married? Why the hell hadn't Sam told him? He wouldn't have come all this way if he'd known Karin was married. What the hell was Sam thinking?

What else might have changed with Karin besides her last name?

Oh, yes. A kid would have changed her some.

Then he noticed a notation, *Haley, at five years old. Happy b-day.* Five years old. He'd been gone, what? Nearly six years now. Not his. She'd be six years and some now. A feeling spread over him. Relief, followed by something new. Sort of let down.

He picked up the photo again. Five? This child couldn't be his. There was a missing . . . what, almost a year? Nine months?

Nine months. He sat down. Stared at the snapshot. Nine months? Oh.

He turned it over and slid the cardboard backing off. A scrawl on the back read *Merry Xmas, Love Karin and Haley.*

His hand shook. Karin, but with dark hair. Where—no, why—did her blonde hair go? A kid who had the same wide, gray eyes as Karin, and blonde hair. Haley.

Karin had seemed so straightforward, so honest. Hah! How wrong he'd been on that score.

He looked again at the child. This would take some thinking. Could she really be his? Or had Karin lied to Sam?

Could the trouble Karin was in be something to do with a husband?

One thing for sure. He was determined to find Karin and the truth, regardless of what it might be.

Chapter 9

Sunday traffic was light as Melanie Allen sped west on the highway, feeling the car engine work hard as the road climbed into the foothills. Thousands of thoughts, mostly of Karin, crowded her head, but the whole episode with Kenny bothered her. Had she calmed him down? Did he believe her? Worse, what would she say if Roger asked about him? That was what she had to figure out. What to say. *Don't want to get Roger riled up.*

Maybe she just wouldn't tell Roger. After all, Kenny always leered at her on the few occasions when he came around to pretend to work. He tried to look tough and important, but he'd never been a real threat to her.

The road was dry, but at the edges little rivulets spilled snow-melt from higher up on the hills. Already some of the snows were beginning to melt with the unseasonably warm weather.

The side road to the mountain house would be slippery and treacherous. Roger always parked under the old pine tree to hide the truck, and she would have to slip the car close to the mountain's edge to get past. Every time she had to do that she felt ill. Today maybe she would park out a ways and walk in.

Kenny's leering face broke into her thoughts again, the way he'd peered first at her chest, then at the bags she held. Of course it wasn't his leering Roger would be pissed about, it was the fact that Kenny knew Mellie had been in the apartment without Karin and left with three bulging garbage bags. Roger really wasn't going to like that.

Her stomach knotted up again at the thought.

She took the exit ramp, turned onto the frontage road and steered through the little village, passing the general store. The second road was the turnoff to the cabin. She knew the way by heart.

Roger would ask her how it went at Karin's. She played it uneasily through her mind. She would lie about Kenny, she decided. Trouble was, if he ever found out she had lied, he'd be real angry. She pictured him, all tense and scary, squinting straight into her eyes all the way through her brain. Could she hold it together?

Her cell phone rang. It would be Roger.

She swallowed, pulled to the side of the road. She couldn't drive and deal with a potentially pissed off Roger. He was difficult when she had both feet on the ground and if unease started rippling through her it would be impossible. She fished her cell phone from her purse, flipped it open, and held it just a bit out from her ear. She had a feeling Roger would be more than a little angry.

Roger's voice, rough and annoyed, shouted out. "Where the hell are you?"

She glanced at her watch. She wasn't that late. Roger was just worrying. Not a good thing. "I'm almost there, Rog. Why don't you check on the girls."

"Still asleep."

"You better wake them. I'm worried I maybe gave them a little too much of the drug."

"They're okay. Why're you late?"

She had to distract him. "Don't worry. By now Karin will have called the police. She won't want to, of course. She'll be afraid they'll recognize her. And of course they will, even though she looks older, thinner in the face. They'll put her name in the computer and it'll flash McGrath. Karin McGrath." She'd seen how it happened on television. "And then, the police will hold Karin, keep her maybe one or two nights, maybe more because she doesn't have bail money and that gives us time."

He sounded edgy. "I don't know, what if—"

"Hey, I'm counting on it. Don't worry. That's how it's going down." She closed the phone before he could say any more.

Forty minutes later, Melanie pulled into the side road, braked and studied the route up to the cabin. Fifty yards ahead, snow-melt and mud streamed across the treacherous ruts, hiding rocks that might rip the bottom of her old vehicle. Below, two trees leaned precariously into space, their roots exposed by the water eating away at the earth.

She could walk in to the cabin, but the water was deep at the bottom of the dip. Her feet would be soaked by the time she got through it. And she'd have to carry those bags.

Roger's truck had already gone through, but the truck had more clearance than her car. She hesitated and felt her nerves tense up, then eased the vehicle forward.

Damn, she hated this lonely place! At least they wouldn't be staying. Roger had promised they could drive tonight over the pass to Capstone. Then, if the weather was still clear, Roger would fly them out to Mexico. Just a few hours and they would be safe. Away and safe.

The thought emboldened her. She nursed the car through the water, edged along the narrows, then past Roger's truck parked under the old pine tree and up to the house. Sweating, she parked next to the van, the vehicle they would use to take the kids out tonight.

Shaking from the strain, she sat for a while just listening to the wind in the pines. Funny, she thought, how usually there were birds around, but just now, not a one. She wasn't fond of birds, but their absence felt like a slur against her, as if they somehow knew what she'd done and hated her for it.

She sighed, pulled herself out of the car and walked up onto the porch. The door was unlocked. No lights in the house. He must be using only daylight so the utilities wouldn't show they'd been there.

Inside, she saw Haley curled on the couch, her eyes closed. "Asleep?"

Roger nodded.

She frowned. "It's cold in here."

"It's warming up. I just started the fire. Don't use any paper in it."

Her temper flared. She'd seen the fake log in the fireplace. "I know. Don't want anyone to notice the smoke." What did he think, that she was an idiot? "I get it, Rog."

He stopped and turned, his face dark with irritation. "No, you don't get it. I'm doing this for you. You."

She crumpled under the weight of his blame. "I know. I'm sorry. You're right. It's just I didn't think it would be so hard."

"What's hard now?"

The edge in his voice and the emphasis on the word *now* scared her. "I just meant, I feel bad for . . ." At the last minute she nodded toward Haley. She'd actually been thinking about Karin, but any mention of her would probably make Roger go ballistic.

Roger looked at the child, still lying motionless on the couch, her coat covering her up to her neck. "Yeah, well, can't be helped, can it?"

"We fly out tonight, though, right?"

He scowled. "It doesn't look good."

"We can't risk waiting." Melanie felt panic begin to build. "We have to get out of here tonight."

"Yeah? Well, we can't fly in a snowstorm, Mellie, and Capstone is socked in right now. We'll rest tonight and go up tomorrow after the storm has passed."

"But there isn't time—"

"I can't set down the plane and take off again in that snow. On that landing strip, with the wind shear there, I'd just run straight into the mountain. We'll stay here tonight."

"But—"

"Don't start it, Mellie." His jaw was set and angry.

She swallowed. "It's just that we had it all timed . . ."

His eyes narrowed. "We built in the extra time, remember? That's why you left the sweater . . . you left it, didn't you?"

"Like you said."

He frowned. "Okay, then. I've got to get some sleep."

He got as far as the door, then turned. "How'd it go down there? Get everything?"

"It's all in the three bags in the trunk. She didn't have much." Mellie tried to smile, but it didn't come out well.

He squinted at her, his brows lowering until she could barely see his eyes. "What?"

"Nothing." She swallowed. When he looked like that, she couldn't tell him Kenny had been there. He'd start ranting on about how she'd messed things up and there'd be no peace. "Nothing. Just it was harder than I thought it would be. To get it all together and not miss anything."

"And?" Twin dark spots tinged Roger's cheeks.

"Like you said to, I gathered up all her stuff, left the sweater just under the edge of the bed."

"Not too far. They need to find it."

"They'll find it."

"And the Xerox? You got that there?"

She smiled. "I put it in the phone book in the blue pages where she'd see it if she tries to call the FBI."

He took a step toward her, menacing. "You were supposed to put it on the table. Nobody uses a telephone book anymore.

They just call information."

She stood her ground. "It was too obvious. They'd know somebody'd been there. And she'll use a phone book. I even turned the phone book out so she'd notice it." Roger was right, of course, but anger had grown in her belly at the way he was acting. Who was he to order her around? "Believe me for once. Drop it, Rog."

Roger scowled and pursed his lips, glancing out the front windows and across the valley. He wasn't fully convinced, but he seemed to have come to an end point. She waited patiently, knowing he'd either wind up and go at her again or he'd shrug and walk away. She hoped for the latter, but braced for the possible storm. Finally he said, "We'd better get some sleep. It was a long night last night."

She hesitated, looking at the sleeping girls, one on each end of the old couch. What he said was true; they'd been up all night and she was exhausted. Haley's cheeks were flushed and warm. She tucked a blanket around the girls, then turned and followed Roger into the back bedroom, relieved that he seemed to buy her story.

CHAPTER 10

Jansen pulled out his cell phone and called in a missing-child report, naming Haley Preston, five years of age, and ordered it sent statewide.

Since it was Sunday, there was a chance, although slim, that the media would be slow to pick up the report. A media blitz wouldn't help this case right now. Better by far to have the state patrol alert to a false alarm than to risk a kid's safety by not reporting a possible child abduction.

He chose to keep this bit of information from the Preston woman. Her story was too vague. Once she knew an alert had gone out, she might stop talking.

They were winding through Ridgewood's quiet, suburban streets lined with 1930s-era brick bungalows set so close that grass wouldn't grow between them. Preston's car turned and she drove past a tired strip mall, two boarded-up storefronts and a liquor store that probably did just enough business to keep the neighborhood complaining. Abruptly they were in an older, more run-down area with two-story brick Victorians, their porches sagging, their peaked roofs and fish-scale shingles in need of paint. Even the trees looked run-down and depressed.

He couldn't get past the fact that Karin Preston didn't have a picture of her kid in her wallet. Most mothers carried scores of pictures of their children, their pets and relatives. He still carried pictures of his wife and child, and they had been dead for six years. Six long, lonely years.

Jansen flashed on the memory: driving back from a weekend in the mountains to celebrate their anniversary and Margot's news. She was pregnant with their second child. A dark, moonless night. Margot beside him snored gently, little Brooke in the back, slept in her car seat. The car lights glared off a rain-slicked highway from a sudden downpour on the mountainside above. Rock, loosened by the winter freeze and thaw and the sudden shower, began to slide high above, unheard by the river of cars below.

No one saw the rush of water, rock and mud tumbling down the mountainside. One minute they were snaking sedately down the highway toward Denver behind an eighteen-wheeler; the next moment, the semi in front of them hydroplaned, braked, and slid. Jansen jammed on his brakes. He hit mud slick. Felt the sickening slide as his car shot straight toward the steel pipes that the semi was hauling.

He twisted the wheel, pipes looming. He stood on the brake. Yelled at Margot. "Get down!"

Too late.

Pipes shot through the windshield. One grazed his face. Ripped his scalp.

The car slammed into the back of the truck. His knees jammed into the dash. Jansen flew forward. His air bag deployed. Margot's was useless, ripped through by the pipes. The car whipped back and forth behind the trailer truck, hooked to it by the pipes, like the tail of a dying fish.

In one terrible moment, his beloved wife and darling daughter were both gone. His life as he knew it was over.

For three weeks he had lain in the hospital, his body healing, his mind numb with grief. Another two weeks in rehabilitation, until he checked out and left for the Caribbean. He started to return to normal after his brother dragged him to the Mississippi coast to work with him on his leaky shrimp boat. Finally, he was ready to come home. For the last year and a half he'd been working with the Ridgewood police department, trying to keep the memories at bay. He shook his head, pulling himself back to the present, feeling the familiar ache in his right knee. Most of his body had healed, but some parts of him never would.

Close behind Karin, he turned onto South Avery Drive and spotted the house numbers of the place where she lived. Karin parked in front of a shabby, one-story house set back from the street. She stepped from her car and pointed, indicating the house. Her expression was intent and grim.

He parked and followed her up the walkway, stepping carefully on the cracked, uneven paving, and came to a shabby wooden porch where two mailboxes hung, slightly off level. Only one had a label, *K. Preston.*

"Mine is the basement apartment," she said and opened the door to a musty-smelling landing. She descended several steps into a pervasive gloom; the overhead lightbulb was out. At the bottom of the steps she unlocked another door and let him into a cramped, semi-dark room. A slight smell of ammonia hung in the air.

Karin stopped as soon as she entered, sniffed, and frowned as though surprised by the odor. She shrugged. "The landlord must have cleaned upstairs for a new tenant."

"Nobody lives upstairs now?"

She shook her head. "It's been empty the whole six months we've been here."

The length of her stay in this apartment had just changed. Her lies were starting to show. Keep her talking, and more would follow.

The carpeting, laid over concrete flooring, had a threadbare path from the door to the love seat and to a little kitchenette. Karin flicked on a lamp, and he saw the love-seat cushions were worn and sagged in the center.

He noted the windows. Clean. She had said Melanie washed them. Of course, that wasn't proof of anything. She could have washed them herself.

In spite of the shabby furnishings, bright pillows and two poster prints of Monet paintings brought a bit of warmth to the room, a feeling of order and welcome. Maybe the apartment was a little too clean, he thought, remembering the light clutter of toys in his own home before. He pushed it to the back of his mind. He needed to concentrate on Karin now.

Karin moved quickly to a little side table, saying over her shoulder, "I keep all my pictures in this drawer." She opened the drawer and sucked in her breath, then pulled the drawer out completely and bent to squint into the drawer bed. "They're gone!"

She ran to a bedroom. Jansen followed. It was clearly hers, from the double bed and the bedside table covered with novels. "No," she murmured, staring at the top of a scratched, painted dresser. She wore a look of blank shock. "Her Easter picture—it's gone! Her stuffed animals—her folder of drawings . . ."

Jansen watched as she spun and yanked open the closet door. Pitifully few clothes hung from the rod, all adult-sized. "Where are her clothes?" she whimpered as she slumped against the wall.

Jansen noted the appearance of anguish, the graying of her cheeks. If it was an act, it was very, very good.

Abruptly, Karin straightened. "The laundry hamper! I haven't done a laundry. There are clothes in there," she cried as she ran to the bathroom. She bent over a lidded wicker basket and yanked item after item out, dropping them in a heap on the floor. All the clothing looked to be in her size range.

A bewildered look spread over her face. She looked up at him, her cheeks ashen, her eyes troubled and pleading. "They're all gone. All Haley's things."

She turned slowly around, scanning each item in the room as though it might change before her eyes. Was she avoiding his gaze?

Jansen was careful not to lean against the doorjamb. There might be prints to preserve. "You said she's five. Her school might have pictures."

"I haven't registered her for kindergarten. Yet." She spoke slowly. "Betty, my previous sitter, took lots of pictures of all the kids, but she moved out of state three months ago. I don't have her address."

How convenient, Jansen thought, and rubbed his chin. He was biding his time, wanting to heighten her anxiety. So far he saw no evidence of a child. Not a picture, not a scribble on the wall, not even a bed for the kid. The more he contemplated that, the more he had the feeling this place was as barren as the house where Karin claimed her daughter had been. In fact, here were the very items of furniture she claimed to have seen in that house: the couch, a low table, a bed, a lamp. The biggest difference was that here, there was no dust.

"Where did your daughter sleep?"

"We shared the double bed. My camera!" she said, and brushed past him back to the little living room. "I've got a digital and pictures on the memory card."

In the living room, she pulled open the closet door and stiffened. "My camera's gone! And Haley's extra mittens, her boots. Everything was here when I left this morning to pick her up."

There was no television, or anything that usually went with one. "Did you have a DVD player?"

She nodded, with a pitiful look. "It was just a little cheap one, but it's gone. All the discs, too." Pain was etched in her face. The expression looked so genuine, but she could have practiced it before the mirror. Her voice dropped to a near whisper. "There's nothing here. Just like at Melanie's. Everything's gone. They must have come after I left to get her. It's eleven now. That's nearly two and a half hours. Plenty of time to clear everything."

"Who? Who would do a thing like that?"

"I don't know! Whoever kidnapped my child!" She grabbed his jacket in both hands and shook him. "You have to believe me, you have to!"

Gently, he removed her hands, noticing they were slim and cold, and easily contained in his own broad, muscular palms. "Why would anyone take the time to steal all your child's things?"

"So you won't believe me." Her eyes, large and stormy, seemed to burn as she paused to think. "So you won't believe me and they'll have time to get away."

He looked around the depressing room. He hadn't succeeded in verifying her story. There was no evidence of a child. No pictures, no children's clothes, no crib, books, toys, not one child's item. She was right, he didn't believe her story. In fact, he didn't believe there was a child at all.

CHAPTER 11

Karin had heard the placating, phony calm in Jansen's voice when he asked why anyone would take a child's things. Now, she saw the speculation in his eyes. Saw him distancing emotionally from her. He didn't believe her. She had to find proof. Surely they'd overlooked something.

"Isn't there someone who could help you out here?" Jansen said. There was no hint of sarcasm in his face or voice, but Karin knew he meant someone who could testify she was telling the truth.

"You mean, someone who will back me up?" A moment's frantic thought gave her the answer. Of course. Why hadn't she thought of it before?

"All right! I can prove I've got a child." She pressed in numbers on her cell phone. "There's Doctor Wetford. He saw Haley once when I was afraid she had strep throat. He did some tests. He'll have records. Maybe you'll believe a doctor."

She listened to the phone ring, and to the click of the line when the call switched to an answering machine. "Doctor Wetford is out of town for the weekend, returning Monday morning. If you have an emergency, call . . ."

Karin grew colder with each word. After the beep, she left a message to call her cell phone as soon as possible; she needed him to verify he had seen her daughter. She rang off and said to Jansen, "He's out of town. Back tomorrow."

Jansen rested a hip on the arm of the couch. In a soft but

meaning-laden tone, he said, "What about your employer?"

She'd never told Ms. Voyers she had a child, but Karin called the number for the home health service and listened to the woman who had answered. "I'll put a call through to Ms. Voyers, but I believe she's out of town for the week. Can I be of help?"

Slowly, Karin closed her cell phone. "She's unavailable too," she said, and gave the detective Ms. Voyers's number.

"I'll try tomorrow. What about your neighbors?"

Karin closed her eyes. "I told the neighbors Hayley belonged to Melanie. And that Mellie was my sister."

"You certainly kept a low profile with your child."

"I've moved so often." Karin fell silent, thinking, *I kept Haley away from everyone except Melanie. I hid her from my landlord, didn't tell my boss, and I moved anytime someone started to get to know me. How do I explain this?*

Jansen's chin lifted and he looked almost down his nose at her. "This reads like you're hiding out. Do you want to change your story about this Joe Canan?"

That would be the easy way out, but it was a lie, and it sure wasn't fair to Joe. If she said anything about him being in town, it would implicate him in the detective's mind. Poor Joe, who didn't even know he had a child, would suddenly be a prime suspect. Karin knew what a nightmare that was. "I don't know how to reach him. And like I told you, he doesn't know he has a child."

Miserable, she looked up at Jansen. "The truth? The ad for this place said no children, no pets. I'd looked so long for a place I could afford and this was the best I'd found, so I didn't tell my landlord I had a kid. In fact, I lied and told him I let my sister come with her two little girls to stay during the day. I only wanted to keep Haley safe. I've always been afraid something would happen to her. These aren't good neighborhoods around here, you know that. And now someone's stolen her."

Jansen waited, giving her time. She knew he wanted her to change her story. But why should she? She had just told him the truth—most of it, anyway. "I know you don't believe me. I don't know what else to do."

"I don't see how you could keep a five-year-old child secret, hidden from everyone."

You move constantly, she thought. *You lie, you live on next to nothing, you rely on a few wonderful people.* She didn't give him an answer, figuring he didn't expect one.

"What about your family, parents, someone—"

"My only family is my brother Sam, and he left for South America a week ago. The only contact I have with him is through e-mail, and that only occasionally."

"Nobody else?"

"No," she said. She didn't mention her father or her uncle Zeb. *God knows they'd be no help. They'd probably accuse me of lying, or worse, like before.* "You have to put out an Amber alert." Her voice cracked with emotion. "Any moment they could be taking her out of the state, maybe out of the country. If you don't do anything, you'll be as guilty as the kidnappers, even more, because you didn't try to stop them!"

A flash deep in his eyes. Had she finally reached him?

"Please," she begged. "It's my child's life. You have to do something. If you won't issue the alert, I'll call the FBI. They'll know how to handle this."

He ignored her threat. "What about immunizations?"

Karin stared at the floor, seeing the little apartment as he would: the shabby, worn carpet, the faded and sagging couch, the general air of poverty. Would he listen better if her house were grand? She looked at him and knew it wasn't her poverty that kept him from believing her. It was the fact that there wasn't one single thing to prove she had a child.

Hiding Haley had been her success, and now it had come back to haunt her.

She shook her head. Of course she'd taken Haley for her infant immunizations, but that was in another state and records of them wouldn't be available until Monday.

Her chin rose in defiance. She licked her lips with a too-dry tongue. "I was going to take her for her preschool physical, but . . ." She faltered. "I just didn't have the money yet. I had to run up my credit card to pay my first sitter and I'm just getting that down. I planned to as soon as I was a little ahead."

"There are clinics that help with finances."

"I don't take charity."

"It's remarkable that no one in the neighborhood would have seen her at the grocery store or a hundred other places."

She felt faint, hardly able to take in his question. "Excuse me, my head's pounding. I'm going to get an aspirin."

"Before you go in the bathroom, may I take a look around in there?"

She nodded. He went into the bathroom and she heard him pull back the shower curtain, check the medicine cupboard, take a long moment, probably looking around. Then he emerged. "I'd like to look around the rest of your place."

"Go ahead."

She stood resolutely by the door. The aspirin could wait a few minutes longer. At least he was putting on a show of a cursory search. No search at all would have been a blatant admission that he didn't believe her. He probably didn't want to be that obvious. Finally, he finished and said, "You have only one way out of here?"

"Unless I crawl out a window. There are two of those."

His lips curled in a brief, nice grin. "And clean, too."

"I told you. Melanie washed them."

"You did."

She crossed the room quickly, headed to the bathroom and opened the medicine cabinet. Her hand stopped in midair. On the top shelf behind her aspirin bottle was an old bottle of children's Tylenol. Hidden because Haley liked the taste too much and Karin had been afraid she'd get into the cabinet and drink it. The kidnappers had overlooked it.

Triumphant, Karin returned to the front room and thrust the bottle at Jansen. "Here, look. They missed her Tylenol."

He looked at the little bottle, then at her. Was it pity she saw in his eyes? Her heart sank. If she screamed at him to convince him she was sincere, he'd think she was crazy, maybe hallucinating. And then no doubt he'd take her to the emergency psychiatric ward at the University of Colorado Health Sciences Center. All he had to say was that he believed she was a danger to herself or others. She knew the drill from working as a home health aide. They would release her, of course, but it would take precious time. Time Haley didn't have.

He was talking. "In cases where we have no picture, we ask that you come in and work with a sketch artist who can come up with a likeness we can use."

She recognized the move into the police station. There, he would have time to check records, maybe even fingerprints. She had to avoid that at all costs. She could not let the past catch up with her now.

He rose from the arm of the couch. Squaring his shoulders, he stepped close to her, clearly irritated. He must have sensed how frightened she was. "I'll give you a ride."

"No. I'll come on my own." She grabbed her bag and moved to the door.

"It would be better if I gave you a lift." He followed her, towering over her.

"No. I want to have my car there. I just need a minute to pull myself together." She dropped her purse and stooped to pick it up. From that angle she saw through the doorway into the bedroom. The edge of something pink showed from under her bed.

"Excuse me," she said and darted into the bedroom. She knelt and pulled out the pink thing. A sweater. A tiny, pink sweater.

She stared at the little garment in her hands. It was hand-knitted in soft wool, but not new. Dirt smudged the front, with some brown stains on the cuff of the right sleeve. It wasn't Haley's, had never been Haley's, but the sweater must have been left on purpose. It had to be important. Very important. Like a message for her, but she didn't know what it meant. Why would kidnappers take everything of Haley's and leave something that wasn't hers?

Something about the sweater nagged at her. A wisp of memory, gone before she could place it.

She heard the detective behind her, snapping on latex gloves. Reluctantly, she let him take the little garment from her, watching as he held it up for inspection. For what seemed like a lifetime he examined the little sweater, his eyes speculative slits. "Do you recognize this?"

She shook her head and focused on the little blue bunnies artfully woven into the knitted fabric. They hopped around the bottom edge. Exquisite, rabbit-shaped buttons fastened up the front. The buttonholes were carefully worked with what appeared to be silk thread.

She reached for the sweater. Jansen blocked her hand. "Look carefully. Tell me what's on the sleeve."

Her lips were numb from nerves. "I don't know. Maybe mud, or chocolate?"

"Or blood?"

"Blood!" she whispered, shaking her head slowly back and forth. "No. It can't be!"

He stared hard at her. "The stains are chocolate. You've seen this before."

"No!" She felt paralyzed, her hands dangling at her sides.

He turned the tiny garment around, studying it from all angles. "Talk to me."

She stayed silent, forcing herself to breathe regularly. That memory. What was it?

When he looked pointedly at her, she shook her head again. "I don't know why it's here. Maybe to make me look crazy, or guilty." The word *guilty* had slipped from her lips. His gaze flickered, and she knew she'd strengthened his suspicions of her. He was gauging every word she uttered. She had to be much more careful of what she said.

He spread the sweater out, examined the knitting. "Good quality cashmere. Handmade, I'll bet." He glanced around at the spartan apartment and added, "It's a very nice little sweater."

She nodded. Far nicer than she could ever afford for Haley.

Jansen continued to examine the little garment. Maybe he hoped she would break down and confess the whole thing was a charade. But it wasn't. Haley had been kidnapped.

Finally he spoke. "It's close to a toddler size, like maybe a two- or three-year-old. Small for a five-year-old, isn't it? What size is Haley?"

"She's size five or six." She watched him fold the little sweater gently and slip it into a bag he took from his jacket pocket. An evidence bag. She knew what they looked like, from six years ago.

The sweater. Tiny-sized, for a toddler. Two or three years old. It was all falling into place. The air turned cold. An odd panicky buzz started up in her ears.

Jansen spoke softly. "I think we need to get to the station and get started on that artist's sketch."

She felt light-headed. Her breath was coming too fast. The

hair on her head prickled in fear. The buzz in her ears grew louder as her panic mounted. Just like before. He was a cop. Cops hadn't listened to her before. They'd talked nice and polite, but they'd lied. They'd already made up their minds. And they'd kept her at the police station, then in jail overnight.

Jansen slid his pad and pencil into the breast pocket of his leather jacket. She shot a glance at his hands. They were strong and broad. They could grasp and hold her. That happened before. She couldn't go to jail. Couldn't. The kidnappers would get away. Haley would be lost.

"Miss Preston, are you all right?" He put a hand on her shoulder.

She flinched, her fists clenched.

His hand dropped to his side. "Miss Preston. Karin. Look at me." He peered at her. She focused on the tiny creases at the outside corners of his dark eyes, the small cut marks on his forehead and cheeks.

Through stiff lips she whispered, "What?"

"Are you all right?"

She felt a trembling in her chest, as if some frightened creature had escaped from it, freeing her to breathe again. "I didn't eat any breakfast. I was going to share it with Melanie and the girls. I get hypoglycemic if I don't eat."

He seemed to think for a long minute, then said, "I'd like you to ride with me. You've had a lot to deal with and you look shaken. I don't think you should be driving."

No way would she get in the car with him. "Am I under arrest? Charged with something?"

His lips thinned and his chin rose. He slid his hands into his jacket pockets, but miraculously he agreed. "All right. I'm going to take the sweater to my car now. Stay calm." He took a slow step toward the door. "I'll arrange for a sketch artist while you get ready."

He pulled a card from his pocket and handed it to her, his face unreadable. "You've got a cell phone, right? This is my number," he said quietly. "If you get a call, anything at all, call me. Now, I'll follow you to the station. You know where it is, right?" He stepped out the door, his footsteps sounding loud in the silence as he went up the stairs. And up the next flight. He was going to try to talk to Kenny.

Karin closed her apartment door and slumped against it. A trip to the police station? Oh, no. She had to figure out how to elude him. She heard him knock twice upstairs, then rattle the doorknob, then return to the front door and leave. It was so hard to concentrate. The little sweater kept coming back to mind. But time was passing. The most important thing was to get away from him, then figure out where to go next. She went to the kitchen and pulled out the telephone book, just in case she really did need to call the FBI. She'd just rip the page out and call from somewhere else, because they could trace her cell.

Inside the phone book was a piece of loose paper, folded in fourths. Slowly, she unfolded the sheet. A black-and-white Xerox of a photo: an elderly woman seated in a wheelchair, wearing a fluffy shawl, a small child clad in a light-colored sweater at her side and several blurred figures behind them.

Horror and a sense of aching loss spread deep inside her. "Oh, my God, no."

Karin's knees weakened and she sagged against the wall, the picture nearly slipping from her fingers. "Nicole," she whispered. Her mind raced with the implications. The sweater had to be Nicole Eberhard's. It was pure luck Jansen hadn't thought of the Eberhard kidnapping case, but it wouldn't be long before someone in the police department remembered. And remembered her, despite everything she'd done to hide.

If it was Nicole's sweater, the fact that it was found in Karin's apartment would bring suspicion on her again like a suffocating blanket. She would be a hunted woman . . . but for Nicole's sake, not Haley's. With no proof that Haley existed, no one would look for her. All attention would immediately turn to reopening the Eberhard case. The man who'd confessed to taking Nicole, an itinerant painter, had suicided and left a letter but never said where he'd put Nicole's body. Or even whether he'd killed her, only that he took her. Haley would be invisible. Successfully stolen.

Then she realized something else that left her breathless and shaking. It was so obvious, she wondered how she'd missed it.

If the sweater was Nicole's, in order to leave it, Haley's kidnappers must have had it. Whoever they were, they had to be involved in Nicole's kidnapping as well.

A cold sweat broke over Karin's face. Nicole Eberhard had never been found.

Chapter 12

Jansen walked slowly down the uneven sidewalk to his car, shaking his head. He was starting to change his mind about Karin Preston—not that her wild story was true, but that she believed it was. Her intense emotion and consistent, vivid detail testified to that. When she'd failed to find any photos, the baffled look in her eyes had been remarkably convincing. Her only slip had been the change in the length of time she'd claimed to have lived in her apartment. Three months versus six. He frowned as he considered it. A pretty big discrepancy. But was it a lie, or just a slip of the tongue that stemmed from self-delusion?

Her story fell apart when she tried to explain that she had a five-year-old child, yet in all that time no one had seen it or could attest to the kid's existence. The woman she worked for had no knowledge of a child, there was no school registration, her previous babysitter had conveniently moved and couldn't be reached, she'd lied to her landlord about the kid being hers. If he'd even seen the kid. At this point, Jansen didn't know. And there were no children's clothes, toys, pictures, not even a crayon drawing on the wall. He'd check with this Dr. Wetford, of course, but it wouldn't surprise him if that was a dead end, too.

He shook his head, unable to avoid the question: What if there's no child here at all?

And this little sweater was weird. Planting a garment that couldn't possibly fit a five-year-old made no sense, unless she hadn't meant for it to be found because she kept it to bolster her delusion. But chocolate on the sleeves, maybe to look like blood? He shook his head. This whole thing felt like a pathetic attempt to get attention.

But then, he had expected her to claim that the sweater was her daughter's from infancy. Instead, Karin had responded with denial. Not her daughter's. That was a little odd, a flaw in her story.

She claimed someone was trying to make her look crazy, but frankly she didn't need any help to look unstable. And there was that strange reaction as he was leaving. Although she'd claimed she was just hungry, the glazed look in her eyes reminded him of someone experiencing a post-traumatic stress reaction. He'd observed a few of those in his time. When he'd seen that terrible inward look in Karin's eyes, as though she was seeing something no one else could, he'd automatically reverted to a calming voice, visible hands, slow motions. Usually he'd seen this kind of response in male veterans, but with more women in the service, they were suffering from wartime horrors, too. Maybe her report of a missing child was the result of some trauma she'd experienced, or maybe a cry for attention or even a subconscious plea for treatment. And yet there was a certain appeal to her, a childlike quality when she looked straight into his eyes with all her feelings painted on her face. She clearly believed she had a kid.

In all, a very disturbing situation.

He slid into his car and glanced back at Karin's basement apartment in the dreary little house. Depressing. The kind of place he could see would drive a sensitive person nuts. Hell, maybe any person. As he watched, a man carried a sign out into the yard of the house next door. The sign read *For Rent.* "It'll be a while before that happens, fella," he muttered as he climbed back out of the car. "Hey," he called and approached the man.

"Have you noticed a child living here?"

The fellow shook his head. "I'm just posting a sign here, I don't know the neighborhood." He turned away.

Jansen looked at the innocuous little house in the dreary street full of barren yards. Once he got Karin to the police station, he'd keep her on the pretext of working with the sketch artist, maybe call the mental-health people for a consultation, and if that wasn't enough, he'd think of something else. By the time all that was done, they'd have enough solid information to know for sure what was happening and wrap this case up.

He called in to headquarters to see if the missing-child alert had gone out.

"The alert went statewide half an hour ago. They'd like more than just your brief description. They'd like a picture."

"So would I." *In fact,* he thought, *I'd like to think there's actually a kid.*

"Five years old, fifty-six pounds, blonde and blue-eyed isn't much."

"Tell them there's a mole at the base of her left thumb."

"That's it?"

"It's all I have. And if you get questions, don't give out anything yet. It's way too early."

Silence, then: "Is the mother coming in for a sketch?"

"Yes. Meantime, please start a search of mental-health records, social-service records and old police records, anything at all, on a Melanie Allen and a Karin Preston."

"Jansen, this all sounds hinky."

"Yeah, but aren't they all?"

Chapter 13

Karin stood at the door, listening, planning. She could not go to police headquarters, could not risk being identified. She'd be detained. And, if she were detained, even for an hour, she would never find Haley. Already too much time had elapsed.

So far her only break was the fact that Detective Jansen didn't think of Nicole Eberhard as soon as he saw the sweater. But soon he would, or at least as soon as someone at the station saw that sweater. They were bound to. There had been such a clamor when Nicole went missing. She closed her eyes. This break wouldn't mean a thing if she didn't get away from the detective now, before he figured out who she was.

Throwing her backpack over her shoulder, Karin took a last look around her little apartment. Twelve o'clock already, three and a half hours since she had discovered Haley missing. *Haley, where are you?*

She backed into the hallway, pulling the door firmly closed behind her, and turned. "Geez!"

Kenny Bristow, her landlord, stood atop a stepladder. "Changing the bulb," he said gruffly.

Her voice was shaky as she asked, "On a Sunday?"

"As good a day as any."

"Have you been here all this morning?" He never came around to fix things, yet he was here now, perched outside her door screwing in a lightbulb, a twenty-watt bulb, no doubt to save money on electricity. He was spying on her.

"Just got back." He stopped twisting in the lightbulb and frowned down at her. "Something wrong with that?"

So he had been here this morning. "I just noticed some of my things are gone and I wondered if you saw who was here?"

"Never saw nothing."

Karin wanted to scream. Instead, she stretched her mouth in the best reassuring grin she could manage and said, "Come on, Kenny. Someone was here. I just need to know who it was."

"Oh yeah?" He climbed down the ladder, stepping close to her, too close. "You talk so high and mighty, but I know better."

Karin realized anxiety was making her voice sound harsh, and to him, it probably sounded accusing. She tried to soften it. "Please, Kenny. I need you to tell me who you saw. And tell the detective outside that I have a little girl."

He looked at her hard for a long three seconds. "I didn't see nobody. I was upstairs, painting." He picked up the ladder and started toward the steps.

She went after him. "Kenny! Please, I need help. I left my little girl, Haley, with Mellie last night and now they're all missing, Haley, Mellie and Jennifer. I've got to find them. You have to help. At least tell the cop I've got a kid."

Backlit by the light from outside, his expression was impossible to read. "I rented to you 'cause you said you *didn't* have a kid. You swore you didn't have a kid. And I ain't talking to no cop. Period."

"Kenny, I beg you."

He moved to the top of the steps, distancing himself from her.

She tried again. "Look, Kenny, Melanie was my babysitter. She'd come here with her daughter to take care of Haley. And now she and Jennifer and Haley are all gone. I'm scared, real scared about it." Desperation pushed her close to tears. "Kenny, please. Would you at least call me on my cell if you see or hear from Mellie or Roger, her husband."

"She's married?" Kenny scratched the back of his head, his eyelids lowering speculatively, as though he was about to change his mind.

"He's in the Special Forces, so he isn't around much."

Kenny rubbed his chin, the whisker stubble snapping lightly. He appeared to be thinking. Karin's hopes rose. Then he dropped his hand to the ladder, grabbed and hefted it again. He started back up the steps.

Karin stepped forward, following him. "If you think of anything, you have my cell phone number. Call me? Please?"

He looked at her over his shoulder, his eyes mean and angry. "Okay."

"Will you talk to the detective outside now?"

"Shit, no." He lumbered on upstairs, out of sight.

She checked her watch and glanced out the front door. She saw Jansen open the patrol car door and step out, looking toward the house. Was he coming in for her?

He could have radioed in to headquarters while she was still in here. He might already have discovered she had been, probably still was, a suspect in Nicole Eberhard's kidnapping. She couldn't go with Jansen. She'd never get free again. She had to get away and stay away from cops.

She ran up the steps after Kenny, pushed past him, running into the apartment where he had apparently been preparing to paint.

Kenny yelled after her, "Hey, what ya doing?"

She slipped on a plastic drop cloth, staggered upright, and dashed to the kitchen and out the back door.

Chapter 14

Joe's first impulse was to set out straight for Karin's place and confront her. Face to face she would have to answer his questions, have to explain.

And he would see this child. The little girl he couldn't quite believe was his, whose wide gray eyes stared out of the picture at him and just about stopped his heart. A kid. He'd never wanted a kid, and here he was, drawn to this big-eyed, smiling child. And her mother, despite it all.

He stopped, his hand on the car door handle. Last night it seemed simple. Just come right out and ask: so, were you pregnant and why didn't you tell me, and so on. But, that was in a bar, no child present. Staring at him. Maybe even crying, frightened.

Turning, he walked down the street toward the wide expanse of Congress Park. Walking would clear his thoughts. The image of talking to Karin in front of this child made him rethink how he would approach her. He couldn't, wouldn't, frighten a child.

Whoever's it was.

And that, he thought, *is the issue.* He couldn't quite yet accept that this child could be his. At the same time, he realized with a sinking feeling, he couldn't deny it. When he'd had no picture of Haley, she had been a cipher, an unreality, but the sight of that wide-eyed little girl with her arms around Karin's neck had made her vividly real. He couldn't forget that face. In fact, he couldn't forget either face, Karin's so thin, Haley's so trusting and happy. It did something to him. But was it Karin who moved him, or that little child? Or the thought of two people suddenly looking to him to solve everything?

He shuddered. That was really it. Dependency weighed on him. Responsibility for himself was nothing. For Karin . . . he thought about that. Years before, Karin's helplessness had first drawn and then grown to irritate him. Always she had looked to him to make decisions. Hadn't had an idea of her own that he knew about. At first that was great. He'd never been in a situation where the woman looked to him for everything and he'd felt like a king, for a while. The last month or so, though, he'd begun to chafe under it.

"Where do you want to go?" he would ask.

She'd shrug, a smile lighting up her pretty face with its rounded cheeks. "Wherever you choose."

"No, you choose."

"Whatever you want is fine."

Yeah, it had become wearing. He'd even been a bit relieved when he left for Iraq. He still loved her then, but he'd known he wasn't ready for anything permanent.

At the park, he started along the path edging the grounds. Across the grass in a grove of pine trees he saw a swing set. And now, he wondered, was he any more ready to take on a family?

Walking had always been a time to think. Even as a child he had enjoyed rambling around, mostly along the creek side and into the foothills along trails in the parks and later up into the mountains. After his parents' deaths, walking in the wild areas and the national forests had been his salvation, the slow healing of his grief.

Now he strolled and thought as he passed the little playground. Two preschoolers were sliding down the little slide, shrieking with laughter. Did Haley play like this?

But if Karin had married, then what? If some asshole was

beating up on her or hurting that child . . . he let the thought go. The fact was, he didn't know one thing about what was going on. That was what he had to do now. Find the truth.

Back at Sam's apartment, Joe sat at Sam's desk, a pad of paper before him with a list of all the things he might to do to verify that Haley was his. Vital statistics was bracketed, because it was Sunday and the right office wouldn't be open until Monday. He went on the Internet, only to realize he didn't have Haley's birth date. Or even know where she was born. He searched under *McGrath* and *Preston* and turned up nothing. He even tried calling Sam in Venezuela, but they wouldn't let him through because he wasn't related and Sam was still in the critical-care unit.

Frustrated, he paced the floor. He tried to picture himself as a father, then tried to imagine how he would broach the subject with Karin. Maybe that was why she hadn't shown up at the Grille last night. She hadn't known what to say, either.

The caffeine in his system left his nerves jangled, his stomach hollow. Maybe he was totally off on the wrong track.

Karin had been devoted to the little girl she was nanny for around the time he'd left. What was her name? Madeleine? Victoria? Nicolette? *Nicky something,* he thought. Nicky-something Eberhard.

He pulled out the telephone book and looked up the name Eberhard. There were seven listings. He picked up the phone and started calling. Six denied knowing Karin. The seventh listened in silence until Joe mentioned Karin's name, then hung up abruptly.

Joe rose and pulled on his jacket. It was time to get some answers.

Chapter 15

Haley tried to open her eyes, but the light made her head hurt more. She closed them again, whimpering from the pain. She tried to put a hand over her eyes. Her hand didn't want to move.

Where was Mommy?

Mommy would help her. Mommy would lie next to her and rub her forehead until the pain went away. Mommy was warm and soft and smelled good, like flowers. Here, Haley smelled dust. Cold, dirty floor.

Slowly she let the light seep in under her eyelids a little at a time so the pain wouldn't stab inside her head again.

Her lips were dry and they hurt. Her tongue felt dry too, and big in her mouth. Like when she licked her teddy bear until her tongue was stuck all over with teddy bear fur. She couldn't seem to make any noise, even though she tried again.

Only her nose seemed to work right. Her nose could smell dirt and something else, sort of like medicine. Sort of like the clear stuff that looked like water but wasn't. It felt real cold when Mommy rubbed it on her back when she had a fever.

A high, uncomfortable sound rang in her ears, like when she was sick and her head was all stuffed up and she couldn't breathe right.

She peeked out from under her eyelids. She was lying on an old couch and she was cold. Where was Mommy? Her eyes were so heavy she could hardly keep them open. They went shut again. So sleepy.

"Mommy!"

The call woke Melanie. Had it been Jennifer or Haley? "Coming, honey," she replied and sat up, pushing her hair back from her face. It was nearly one in the afternoon; she and Roger had been asleep for less than an hour. She padded out to the living room, noting that the room had warmed up some so the deepest of the chill was gone. She stepped closer to the girls and peered into Haley's face. Her eyes were closed, her breathing regular as though she were still asleep, and her cheeks were flushed and streaked with tears as though she had been crying. Jennifer lay quietly, snoring gently under the blanket.

"You awake, honey?" Melanie felt Haley's forehead. Warm. A little too warm.

"I want my mommy," Haley murmured.

"She's at work right now. You feel okay?"

Haley's eyes opened. She looked around, then closed them again. "Sleepy."

Melanie sighed, anxious. She didn't like the redness of Haley's cheeks. Maybe she'd given the girls too much of the drug. She'd given Jen meds to keep her sleeping a bit longer several times before. Was Haley overly sensitive to the drug? She didn't want to hurt either one of them. And Haley had to be in good shape, for sure.

She went to the kitchen, ran water into a glass and took it back out to the child. "Here. Drink this. You'll feel better."

She pulled Haley to a sitting position and held the glass to her lips while she swallowed tiny sips. After a minute Haley slumped again, asleep.

Melanie felt her forehead. Was it slightly warmer? She shook her head. She was overdoing it, looking for trouble because she was really worried about Donny. Donny was the sick one. These girls were plenty healthy and strong. She picked up her cell phone and placed a call to Zeb, Donny's father. "H'lo? How's Donny doing?"

He sounded guarded, and tired. "He's asleep."

"But he's okay, right?"

"Yeah, he's okay. Why?"

"Just worried."

She could hear him breathing heavily into the phone. He always did that and it always made her uneasy. "I'm just, uh, just checking, that's all. It's hard to wait. Did you talk to Doctor Wetford today?"

He answered quickly, irritation grating in his voice. "No, and you aren't going to cither. I know you, you'll forget and use names and then you'll have blown the whole deal. You know what that'll mean. Now, settle down. Let it go."

"Give Donny a hug for me." Even to her ears, her voice sounded like a pitiful whine.

"Yeah, sure." He hung up abruptly.

Uneasy, Mellie checked her messages. She found and erased the calls from Karin, then sat down in the rocker to watch the sleeping girls. The motion of the chair and the soft sounds of the children breathing relaxed her. She was nearly asleep when her phone rang, startling her awake. The phone clattered to the floor and slid across the bare pine planking.

She picked it up, saw the caller ID and felt her shoulders tighten.

Roger called out sleepily from the bedroom, "Who's that?"

"Dunno," she lied and put the cell phone to her ear.

"Mel?"

Kenny. He sounded like he'd been drinking. Barely thinking, she pressed the off button. Immediately the phone rang again. This time she answered as quickly as she could to keep the ring from waking Roger again. "What?"

"I just had a visitor here."

"Where? What are you talking about?" she asked, but she knew even before he answered. Karin. Her breath came faster in spite of her effort to stay calm.

"Don't play dumb, Mellie. At the house. You know, where you took care of Miss High and Mighty's kid. The one you said was yours."

"She is mine. What is it? What do you want?"

"I'm pissed, Mellie. I got the idea something big is going on here. I don't like it when people lie to me. Treat Kenny Bristow bad and he never forgets."

Melanie walked to the front door and stepped outside. Better Roger didn't hear her just now. "What is it you want?"

"I might not have a friggin' big education, but I can put two and two together. First you're here, taking stuff from Karin, then she and this cop come by and she wants me to say one of your kids is hers. Begging me. Like she really means it. First time she ever talked nice to me and looked me in the eye."

Melanie heard a click and a hiss as Kenny popped a can or bottle of something. Beer, most likely; he always drank it when he was around Karin's place. She worked to keep her voice soft and said, "What did you tell her?"

"See, just let that cop try to come talk to me, I'll lie a thousand times. Saw him starting toward the house. I threw the deadbolt before he got as far as the middle of the walk. Wasn't no way I'd talk to cops. Not after what I've been through. Might be years ago, but I don't forget."

Could this man answer any question in two words? Melanie bit her tongue and let him continue. He was quicker when he wasn't interrupted.

"That cop was hammering on Karin's door, and I was standing by the window where he couldn't see me. I saw Karin streak across the front yard, backpack bouncing. Ran like Hell was after her. She was in her old car and gone before the cop got back up the steps and outside." Kenny laughed. "She was something. Made a chump out of him! A detective, too. I know that because he was in regular clothes, if you call a leather jacket regular."

"What'd you say to Karin?"

"Not a damn thing. She made a chump out of me as well, so screw her."

Kenny's words were slurring just a bit. He'd probably tossed back more than one beer before he even called her. "You there, Mellie?"

"I'm here. Just listening to you. What next?"

"It got me to thinking."

"What about?" Deep unease crawled in her gut. This might be a problem.

"People think they can look down on me, think they're smarter than me. I know. It was that way in school, too. And Marva, the old woman, she always thinks she knows best. Keeps all the money so I can't spend it. Well, see, I'd like to show her. And I figure you're on to something here. Something that could give me a little spending cash. Like say, enough to—"

"What are you doing?" Roger jerked the cell phone out of her hand.

Melanie swallowed. "It's Kenny. He's putting two and two together."

Roger's face turned to stone. He handed the phone back to her. "How much does he want?"

Melanie shook her head. "Hey, Kenny. The phone went out for a minute. Repeat what you just said. I didn't hear it."

Silence. Then, "Maybe you didn't want to hear it."

"I want to hear. Tell me."

"I need about forty thousand. That would keep me quiet, and

out of the country even. Mexico probably. Money goes a long way there."

"I don't have forty thousand."

Roger shook his head, walked to the railing and clenched it until his knuckles went white with the strain.

She heard Kenny slosh back his beer, then the clank of glass hitting the trash can. "See, Mellie, the way I figure it, Karin's got a bundle somewhere. She's that kind of woman. Refined, the kind that always looks away from me like I stink or something. I don't know why she's been hiding out here, but I figure she'll pay a lot to get that kid of hers back. Maybe both kids. Hell, I don't know but what they're both hers."

"They're both mine."

"Yeah, see, I don't believe you anymore, either. You and that old man of yours. The two of you are pulling a fast one. I don't really care about that. I only want what's due me. To keep quiet."

Roger yanked the phone out of her hand again, shoving her aside. His voice when he spoke into the receiver was tightly controlled. "All right. Let's talk, Kenny. We need to meet."

Chapter 16

Karin drove steadily away from her apartment, from the detective, from Kenny, from her life as she had known it. She had to find Haley and her only lead was the connection to the Eberhards. The little sweater. Her hands clenched on the wheel as she recalled the look on Detective Jansen's face, the suspicion in his expression. He hadn't seemed to make the connection to Nicole Eberhard yet. But then, she didn't either at first.

She should have thought of the Eberhards right away.

The night Nicole was kidnapped, Karin had put her to bed in turquoise pajamas with white swans Linda had embroidered on them. Karin's mouth was dry, the taste on her tongue bitter. When had she remembered the swans? How was she so certain now what Nicole wore?

The memory of Nicole came sharply to mind. Her chubby arms around Karin's neck, the sweet smell of her hair in the sunshine, her trusting violet-blue eyes and the fingerprint-shaped red birthmark on the inside of her elbow. Linda Eberhard had hated that mark and had it removed soon after Karin started working for the family.

She could see clear as day in her memory, Nicole toddling across the lawn of the beautiful house where the Eberhards lived in Red Oaks Estates. An older, established development with winding streets, Red Oaks Estates had wide lawns and charming starter-castles with three-car attached garages, many with living quarters over the garages for teens, or in the case of the Eberhards, for a live-in nanny. Karin had been so thrilled to get the job with Uncle Zeb's helpful recommendation. For nearly a year it had been perfect, because she was able to start on her nurse's degree.

All this had been radically different from Karin's family home. Her parents lived a spare, ascetic life in the mountains, firm in their belief that worldly goods brought evil temptations. Instead of harsh mountain terrain, the Eberhards' neighborhood shrieked stability, old money, comfort, and most of all, security. So when little Nicole disappeared right from her bed, the shock reverberated from one staid, alarm-outfitted home to another.

Karin had neither seen nor talked to the Eberhards since two days after the kidnapping when Linda, distraught over the loss of her only child, had turned from supporting Karin to blaming her. Later, she'd sent letters. Accusing Karin of complicity in the crime, threatening revenge.

Even now, six years later, recalling that awful morning made Karin bite her lip until she tasted blood. She had lived in the room over the attached garage, connected by a door to Nicole's nursery, which was next to the Eberhards' master bedroom. She always left the door open so she could hear Nicole if she cried.

That terrible morning she had woken with a start because she heard no gurgles or calls from Nicole asking to be picked up. No fussing. No thumping against the crib headboard demanding attention. Usually she would call out, "Kawi, Kawi." Grabbing a robe, Karin had hurried through to the baby's room expecting to see Nicole with her finger in her mouth standing at the foot of the crib.

The crib was empty.

Karin drove east across town into warming sunshine, the kind of day she would take Nicole to the playground. Except Sundays. Those were her days off. Secret days filled with sunshine and love. Those were her days with Joe. Joe, who didn't want children, so she hesitated to tell him when she thought she might be pregnant. Then he'd left for Iraq. Nicole was kidnapped a mere two weeks later.

And if she met with Joe now, what was she going to say? *Gee, Joe, a lot happened while you were gone. I had a beautiful child, she was yours and now I've lost her.* Or maybe, *you had a beautiful daughter, but I let her stay with the sitter and now they're gone.* Even if she met with Joe, he couldn't help. And what if he was like that detective, and doubted there was a child? How would she prove it?

A hollow feeling spread over her, slowly turning to anger. The kidnappers had not only stolen Haley, they had stolen Karin's life, too.

Karin turned in to Red Oaks Estates and went immediately to the right, down a winding street to the Eberhards' home. Clouds scudded low across the sky, flying to the northeast, the sun bursting forth after each one.

She drove past the Eberhards' three-story brick and half-timber Tudor with the wide front door, the gracious gables and side portico, glimpsed the room where she had lived over the three-car attached garage, and the nursery she and Nicole had occupied. Iron bars covered the windows, where before there had been none. That would not be the only change, she thought. A hundred yards down the street Karin slowed and parked at the curb.

This would be a tough meeting, but she had to confirm that the sweater was Nicole's and find out if it had disappeared with her. If it had, then the kidnappers had kept it all this time. They must be the same ones who took Haley. If the sweater hadn't been taken with Nicole, then Linda Eberhard had finally made good on her threats and had stolen Haley away.

Karin's backpack rested on the passenger seat. She pulled the

Xeroxed photo from it and stepped from the car. A cloud floated overhead, blotting out the sun as she walked the long hundred yards to the front door. *Please, let Edward answer,* she thought and shivered with a sudden chill.

The Eberhards had been solid people, kindly and trusting. Karin was counting on surprise and their ever-so-polite manners to get her inside. Once there she would have a chance to learn who had the sweater all this time and maybe even where the Xeroxed picture came from.

The doorbell sounded a deep, two-tone bong. Suddenly she wondered, did the Eberhards still live here? What if they had moved? As the tones died away, she heard approaching footsteps and a child's laughter. Nicole? Had Nicole been found and Karin had never learned of it?

The door swung wide. Karin gasped. A beautiful little girl, two or three years old, stood there. She was so like Nicole, it made Karin's throat ache. The same heart-shaped face and wide violet-blue eyes framed by wispy, dark hair.

Edward Eberhard's deep baritone cut through her amazement. "May I help you?"

Dragging her gaze from the child to Edward's light-blue gaze, Karin could barely speak. Mouth dry from anxiety, she stammered, "I . . . I have to talk to you. May I come in? Please?"

It wasn't what she had planned to say, it was just what came out of her nearly frozen lips. The curiosity in his eyes turned icy with dawning recognition. He stepped back and started to shut the door.

She threw herself forward, shoved a foot inside and planted a forearm on the doorjamb, pushing back. Desperation gave her strength. The door stayed partway open. "Please. Please, I have to talk to you."

The child at his knee clutched his trousers. He looked down

at her, forced a smile and said, "Cindy, go to Mommy, it's cold here."

As soon as the child was out of sight Karin said, "My child was kidnapped last night. I think it's connected to Nicole's kidnapping. I have to talk to you. Did Linda . . ." She could barely finish the words. ". . . take Haley?"

It was all wrong. She was alienating him, but she couldn't stop herself.

Edward glared at her as though trying to see into the recesses of her mind. "What kind of sick game are you playing?"

"It's no game. Please. Surely you remember how awful it was when Nicole was taken. And Linda's letters . . . you must have known about them."

His eyes narrowed. "I don't have anything to say to you. Go away. Leave us alone."

"No, wait!" She wedged herself further inside the doorway. "Nicole had a little pink sweater with bunnies on it, right?" The twitch of his eyebrows confirmed it for her. "Do you still have it?"

His lips barely moved as he said, "You know we don't."

"I put Nicole to bed that night in light pajamas, turquoise aqua with swans embroidered on the front. This morning I found a pink sweater, her sweater, left in my apartment."

Edward's face grayed. His lips were almost bloodless as he pressed them together, refusing to answer.

She had to make him speak. "I think your mother made the sweater."

His voice seemed to come from far inside him. "It was missing. After she was taken." He shook his head. "The sweater, her knit pants, shoes and socks, were all taken."

Hopelessness washed over her, smothering her like wet cotton. Not the Eberhards. The others, people she'd never met or even seen. "Linda blamed me. She threatened to take any child I had."

"Leave her out of this. Those letters were nothing, meaningless."

She could barely speak. "I didn't have anything to do with Nicole's kidnapping. I swear. Don't you see? If you don't have the sweater, it means the same people who kidnapped Nicole took Haley. My daughter."

"You've lost your mind."

Perfume wafted out on the warm air. She recognized Carolina Hererra, Linda's signature scent. Linda called out, "Ed? Who's at the door?"

His cheeks paled further. He called back over his shoulder, "Jehovah's Witness, hon. I'll be there in a sec."

He turned back to Karin, his voice low and harsh. "Leave us alone. Linda nearly lost her mind over Nicole; my mother suffered a second stroke and died. And you have the gall to come here and stir it all up again?"

Karin barely heard him. His mother suffered a stroke. Stroke patients went to nursing homes. Mellie had mentioned she once worked in a nursing home. "Was your mother in a nursing home when I was here?"

"Of course she was."

She knew of at least one in town. "Was it Oak Manor?"

A vein in his temple pulsed. "Go, now! If you ever come here again, even so much as drive by, I'll have you in court so fast you won't know what hit you. In fact, I'm calling the police right now. If you know about the sweater, then you're guilty."

She thrust the copied photo forward for him to see. "I found this picture this morning, too. Did you leave this in my apartment?"

His gaze fastened on the photocopy. "Where did you get that?" He grabbed for it.

She snatched it away, holding it behind her back. "You, your wife, Nicole and your mother. Was this picture your mother's at the nursing home? Or did you have it?" She held her breath, waiting for his answer.

His face seemed to grow thinner, haunted, his breath coming in quick gasps through parted lips. Muscles in one cheek spasmed. His glare seemed to burn her face. His hand twitched as though he could barely keep from reaching out to squeeze her throat. "Get out of here, before I strangle you."

Karin's hands shook as she walked back to her car. She had told herself Edward Eberhard might be involved, but seeing his reactions—his anger, his hatred and the guilt that swept his face—had shocked her. He knew something. He was hiding something.

Far-fetched as it was, the thought circled in her mind. Linda had threatened her in the past, but Edward could have engineered a kidnapping. He had money, he was smart and he was a planner. He wouldn't have been directly involved, though. He would have paid for it and covered himself very carefully. Who would he have found to do such a thing? And why? His had been the only moderating voice when Linda was so hysterical.

She felt a weight on her neck, as though someone was watching her. Karin turned and looked back at the house. The curtain in the window moved and her skin crawled. Pride and fury were the only things that kept her from running to the safety of her car.

Edward had reacted most strongly to the photo. It wasn't theatrics. Pallor was an autonomic response. He couldn't fake it. What had caused such a strong reaction when he looked at the photocopy?

Back in her car, Karin studied the picture.

The copy was grainy, but centered in the photo stood Linda,

the focal point, her luminous smile beaming out, her hand on Nicole's head. Linda's face was lovely, her eyes large and dark, her smile soft and warm, and at her knee, Nicole. Whoever took the snapshot had been captivated by mother and child. Next to them sat Edward's frail mother in a wheelchair. She had a wreath of silvery white hair and was wrapped in a fluffy shawl that looked expensive, hand-knit. Behind the chair stood Edward, his face younger, fresh, his hair tousled, his smile handsome. The only other person in the picture was a nurse standing a little apart from the group, turned slightly away from the camera, her face blurred.

Karin stared hard at the photo. What in these grainy images of his happy family had bothered him?

If Edward had left the sweater and the photo, he wouldn't have been surprised or shocked. He couldn't fake his grayed cheeks and nearly bloodless lips.

Karin frowned, holding the picture away from her, then upside down, then close, then back out, her gaze locked on one thing, the nurse's shoulders.

It wasn't just the shoulders, it was her whole posture. Sloped shoulders, very slim, standing hip-shot, one foot turned out. Dark-blonde hair caught back at the nape of her neck, her shoulders and bust rounded and full. The more Karin looked, the more certain she grew.

The nurse was Melanie.

Melanie could have known Edward, Linda, Nicole and Edward's mother at the nursing home. Confusion washed over Karin. Had Mellie and Edward been romantically involved? No, couldn't be. The police would have investigated that possibility, and there hadn't been a whisper of any relationship there. And Edward wouldn't arrange to have his own child kidnapped. No. No, it just couldn't be so.

Karin leaned back, resting her head on the seat.

What were the odds that Mellie would have even the tiniest connection to a kidnapping, twice? How could anyone be innocently involved in two kidnappings, unless . . .

Karin started to shake. Unless Mellie wasn't a victim.

What if Melanie was a kidnapper? The more she thought about it, the more she became convinced. Sweet, sweet Mellie was a kidnapper. Melanie, who had come so "accidentally" to her house some two months ago. She had set it up. That explained her furniture being missing. It wasn't stolen, she just took it along with Haley and everything else.

And Karin had trusted her with Haley. Had put all her faith in Melanie, who talked about how much she loved children. How much she loved Haley. How she wanted more babies.

"I've been such an idiot!"

All the people she distrusted, yet she never questioned Mellie, just believed she was a lonely woman with similar problems, raising a lovely child, wanting to give her child a safe, wonderful childhood, better than her own had been.

Karin closed her eyes. She had been so lonely. Had left herself open . . .

The picture implicated Edward, therefore it made no sense that he would have planned for it to be left at her place. If Mellie planted it to implicate him, that would explain his reaction to seeing it.

But Melanie couldn't have pulled all this off alone. Someone had to help her move the furniture, spray dust around somehow, and take the girls. If not Edward or Linda, or even the two of them, then most likely Mellie's husband, Roger, who was supposed to be away with the Special Forces. That was probably a lie, too.

Roger. Of course.

There were holes in the logic, but it felt right. And the one place she might get confirmation about Mellie and the Eberhards was the nursing home. Nursing homes kept records of patients and employees. For years.

Using her cell phone, she got the nursing home's number from directory assistance and called. A sweet but firm voice said, "I'm sorry. I cannot give out any such information. You'll have to call tomorrow and talk to Human Resources."

She closed the cell phone. "Like hell I will."

CHAPTER 17

"Ed? Who's there?"

"Be there in a minute, hon." Edward Eberhard stood at the library window quieting himself after watching Karin walk slowly down the sidewalk. This day that had started so peacefully had come unglued. Even the skies outside were darkening as clouds crossed over the sun, throwing mottled, uneasy shadows across the lawn.

The only thing he had wanted in these last six years was to forget Nicole's kidnapping, to keep Linda happy and to maintain the status quo. In the last six years he had put tragedy behind him, had seen Linda recover to nearly her former self, and buried the pain of losing a daughter. He had done well until Karin turned up and brought it crashing into his consciousness again.

"Ed! Where are you?"

Linda would see through him in a moment. He had to get control of himself. He was a super salesman, could sell folks things they never dreamed of wanting, hide his thoughts and feelings from all of them, but Linda could read him like a book.

So could Karin. He could feel it. She always had been able to see into his head with those frosty, gray eyes.

He had watched her walk away, unable to stop himself. In the second before he dropped the curtain, the sun perversely shone on Karin's head, glinting off her hair and creating a brief aura as though she was some kind of angel. Her slim body was stiff, her head high and proud above her worn jacket. Her gaze—straight, sure and piercing when she looked at him—had shaken him more than he wanted to acknowledge. He shuddered.

"Eddy, are you coming?"

Linda's voice drifted out of the dining room into the study where he stood sweating under his light cotton shirt, wondering how Karin had got hold of a copy of that picture. That rotten picture with Melody. Even in the picture he could sense her hovering presence. It was a cheap Xerox copy of the snapshot on the table in the living room, a reminder to him of Linda's suspicion that he and Melody had something going back then.

There had been two copies, one here at his house, the other with his mother at the nursing home. That one had disappeared. He hadn't thought about it for years, had forgotten its existence until Karin pushed the photocopy under his nose. The thought brought a fresh wave of sweat. The one time he had come close to having an affair had been with that nurse. Melody.

Linda's voice sharpened. "Ed?"

Any minute Linda would come find him. Working to keep anxiety from his voice, he answered, "A minute, dear." Then he winced, hearing his own words. "Dear" was a giveaway word. He only called her "dear" when he was upset.

Sit down. Look like you're at work, he told himself and turned from the window. He crossed the plush carpeting to his desk, dropped into his chair, and picked up a pen.

The picture. How did Karin get it and what did she want from him? Blackmail? But, Karin hadn't asked for money. Said her kid was stolen. But Nicole wasn't hers. Nicole was his kid. His and Linda's. Had Karin lost touch with reality? Maybe that was it. Maybe now she was breaking down. Linda had always believed Karin was somehow involved in Nicole's disappearance. Could she be right? And now, maybe guilt was finally getting to Karin?

"Edward?"

Linda stood in the doorway, looking at him with her dark violet eyes. Just like Nicole's, and like Cindy had now. An expression of puzzlement and something else crossed her face. In that instant he thought, *she mustn't know about Karin, or the picture. She'll get upset again.*

He shook himself and smiled. "It was just the Jehovah's Witness women. It's amazing to me how they persevere. I must have told them ten times not to stop here and they still come back."

Linda's chin rose slowly, "It's Sunday, Edward. You're not working and I was under the impression that Jehovah's Witnesses only come on Saturdays. So who was that young woman at the door? Her voice sounded familiar."

He shook his head, trying to give himself time to formulate an answer. He was usually a good talker, better at talking people out of returns than anyone in the firm. *Never give ground,* he told himself, *especially on a lie.* He frowned and leaned back in his chair. "She said she was from Jehovah's Witness. I should have known better. Don't worry, sweetheart."

"I'm not worried." She straightened, her expression guarded, and added, "I'm sure you'll take care of it."

What did she mean by that? She stood so still. Watchful. Scrutinizing him, searching for the truth. She was reading each movement of his eyes, his lips.

God, he was an idiot. The more he tried to protect Linda, the worse he made it. Linda was so subtle these days. He'd never fully understand her. Ever since she gave up all that society stuff and devoted herself to Cindy, she'd been different. Observing. And subtle. Just when he thought he had it all pegged, she'd pull something like this last: *I'm sure you'll take care of it.*

What did she know, or suspect? That picture had brought it all back. It wasn't even a flirtation with Mellie, nothing but smiles, a little conversation and a few fantasies. Well, maybe more than a few fantasies. The woman had a rack . . . but they'd never even kissed, so why was he so guilty about it? He smiled back at Linda and said, "You and Cindy are all my life."

Linda walked to the window, graceful and deliberate, and pulled the curtain aside. "Karin was at the door. Why was she here, and why won't you admit it? Are you afraid I'm going to melt down and go crazy? Is that it?"

"Of course not, dear."

Linda's shoulders stiffened. She turned back to him, her expression wooden. The bland stare in her violet eyes was worse than an accusation. An accusation would have triggered defenses. Her calm disbelief made him crumble. "All right," he said. "It was Karin. She told a wild story. She said she had a child who was stolen, kidnapped, last night."

Linda glanced obliquely at him, as though facing him directly would be too painful. "Why did she come here?"

"No idea."

"Of course you know." Her gaze bore into him. "If you would just trust me with the truth, Ed . . ." She broke off, then looked straight into his eyes again. "Tell me. Why did she come here?"

"Karin seemed to think I might know something about her child. I didn't even know she had one."

Linda didn't move. "I told you she had a child."

"I didn't remember."

Her gaze was piercing. "Yes, you do."

"Darling, I just didn't. She was so strange, I figured she had lost touch with reality again. Like when she had that little breakdown after Nicole was stolen."

"I don't recall any breakdown, only that she went home to the mountains. She always said she couldn't remember what happened that night. She said she was drugged. Of course, she had to be involved."

"The police investigated her, Linda. She had Rohypnol in her blood. She wouldn't remember anything."

"She could have given it to herself. That housepainter couldn't have operated alone. I don't care how innocent you and the police think she is, I will always believe she did it."

"Let's not talk about it."

"We never talk about it. Actually, we never talk about anything important anymore." Linda glared at him. "Do you know how I keep my sanity now, Ed? Do you? I blame Karin McGrath. Every day, I blame her. I hope she finds life a living hell because that's what mine became the day Nicole went missing. I don't know whether to pray for her return, for someone to find a body or for things to stay the way they are, with me never knowing. I don't know which is worse. I just know I have to blame someone besides myself."

"Darling . . ."

"Don't, Ed. Don't say anything. I'm perfectly sane."

"I know you are."

Hands on hips, she said, "I hope you know so, Ed. I truly hope so." She left the room, the light scent of her perfume lingering in the air, a rebuke.

He closed his eyes and flexed his hands. Oh, dear God. It was happening all over again. Would he, or Linda, ever stop aching for Nicole?

Nicole's kidnapping had brought his whole world down. He adored that child, just as he adored Cindy now. If anything ever happened to Cindy, he'd die. He couldn't bear that pain again, couldn't stand to see Linda obsessing again about Karin and Nicole. And the letters. God forbid Linda started writing more of those awful threatening letters. Thank God, he'd managed to intercept most of them.

He shrank deep into his chair. Linda had threatened Karin's life, and threatened to kidnap her child if she ever had one. No wonder Karin came here today.

This morning had been such an ideal Sunday, playing with little Cindy and seeing Linda healthy again. And then Karin came to the door and brought the nightmare back. He ground his teeth, stopping only when he became conscious of a pain in his jaw. Karin had brought disaster to his home before. He had to keep it from happening again.

Slowly, he pulled his keys from his pocket and unlocked the bottom desk drawer. The oaken case lay innocuously at the bottom. Inside, a Browning .38 nestled next to a loaded clip. His fingers trailed over the reassuring cold steel. He'd failed to protect his family before. This time he'd make sure he did whatever he had to do.

Chapter 18

It had taken Joe an hour to find Karin's apartment. Now he sat in the rental car and stared at the shabby house with the moldering porch, and wondered if this could possibly be the right place. She had been ready to graduate from nurse's training when he left. Karin should be able to live better than this on a nurse's salary, even repaying student loans.

Why hadn't Sam said more? How much had he carefully omitted?

What the hell was going on here, anyway? Last night he'd waited at the Grille for an hour and a half, thinking she'd show, but she didn't. He'd been disappointed, but mainly angry at her and at himself. He should have figured she'd never come. He should have dug up Sam's address book first thing when he got to Denver and just come straight here.

He'd had such mixed feelings when he first heard her voice on the phone. He'd forgotten how musical and warm it was. He hadn't been thinking quite right. The flight, fatigue, whatever, he'd just made the date and expected her to be there. Like when they were seeing each other before. He'd call, they'd meet and then spend the afternoon at the park or at his place. More often at his place. Just fun, pure fun.

Then the call came. The job. His chance and he took it.

Shaking his head, Joe stepped from the car, locked it and walked up the rough path to the porch. He saw two mailboxes hanging crooked, barely fastened to the house, only one with a name on it. *K. Preston.* Everything about this situation was more than a little odd. As if she were trying to hide. From whom? Him? Couldn't be. Beyond the first maybe twenty letters that she never answered, he'd stopped writing.

In Caracas, when Sam found him, Joe had been so shaken he hadn't really asked much. But why hadn't Sam said Karin was living in a slum neighborhood? What else hadn't Sam told him?

He shoved open the front door of the old house, noticed the grime on the walls, the dim lighting overhead, the pry bar at the foot of the steps heading down and a door with a cheap metal number 2 on it. He descended and knocked.

A kid! His kid, living in a place like this. He'd never have let a kid live here. Never. He didn't even know how to describe how he felt, his stomach churning, his breath quick.

He knocked again, hard and angry. No answer.

Overhead he heard footsteps. He climbed the stairs to the first floor and knocked on that door, which was slightly cleaner than the one for Number 2. A white calling card was stuck in the door frame. He pulled the card loose. *Detective Casey Jansen, Ridgewood Department of Public Safety.* A cop. He knocked again, louder, braced for trouble. This could be a drug den for all he knew.

A roughened voice called out. "Yeah, Roger?"

Joe pushed the door open and saw a lumbering, paunchy man holding a bottle of beer in one hand and a paint roller in the other. "I'm looking for Karin McGrath, I mean, Preston."

"Well, she ain't here." After a long pull on the bottle, the paunchy guy lowered it and said slowly. "So she's got another name, heh?" He snorted. "Mighta known. She lied about a kid, lied about her name." He paused as though thinking, then said, "So who are you, some kind of asshole on parade?"

Crossing the distance between them in one long stride, Joe grabbed the man's shirt, bunched it in his hand and yanked him upward. "I didn't come here to be called names. Now, where's Karin?"

"I don't have time for this crap and I don't talk to cops. Get out." He swung his beer bottle.

Joe knocked it out of his hand and walked him up against the nearest wall. "What's your name, fella?"

"Let go of me."

"Your name."

"Kenny. Kenny Bristow, now let go."

Joe pushed against him harder. "You've got to the count of three."

"You what, the kid's father?"

He felt like pounding Kenny's head into the wall. "Where is she?"

"The kid or Karin?"

"Don't get smart."

"I don't know. I ain't got time for this."

Joe wrapped his hand around Kenny's neck. "Talk, or you'll be hurting for a month."

"Okay!"

Joe released him slowly, ready to lunge at him if he tried to get away.

Kenny shook himself, glanced at his beer bottle spilling out on the floor and said, "She was here earlier, upset. Said her kid and her friend was missing."

Joe felt his heart skip a beat. "Missing? What do you mean, missing?"

"What're you, some kind of cop?"

Joe stepped in close again, menacing Kenny. "What did she say about her kid? I don't much like you, mister. You better talk."

Kenny looked sullen. "Don't need to get nasty. She said her

kid was missing, gone. Wanted to know if I'd seen her, or her friend."

Joe felt bewildered. "Whose friend? The little girl's? Karin's?"

Kenny's brow lowered. "Karin's friend. Never knew her name. Now, who are you?"

"I'm Joe Canan."

"Well, Mr. Joe Canan, when you find her, tell her the cop was mighty pissed when he figured out she'd got away from him."

Karin, running from cops? "Where'd she go?"

"Hell if I know. Just out the back door, running like a swarm of bees was after her."

CHAPTER 19

The Oak Manor Nursing Home and Rehabilitation Facility stood on a full city block, amid tall pine trees. The solid brick and white column entrance screamed Southern hospitality, although it was located in suburban Denver. The grandiose entry had always bothered Karin, though whenever she visited former patients she had never seen anything but the best of care. And the rehab wing was very new and impressive.

The receptionist, recognizing Karin from previous visits, waved her through. Karin went straight to the Human Resources Office in the far left wing, where it was located along with medical records. A light shone inside. She tried the doorknob. It turned easily. Inside, a faint scent of furniture polish lingered in the air.

She closed the door quietly and crossed the carpeted front office to the far door. The adjoining space appeared to be a conference room, no files, but a large wall display featuring the center's owner, Ethan Morgan. There were several photos of Morgan at ground breakings for different sections of the center. He was a rotund and balding man with an easy smile and a flair for publicity.

She moved toward the back rooms where medical records were stored. An upright vacuum cleaner and a trolley with cleaning supplies stood in front of a door marked *Files and Records.* Racks of medical records filled the room, with only a narrow walkway between them and three steel filing cabinets against the wall.

"Hey, there." A small, wiry woman wearing a blue lab coat with Oak Manor embroidered across the left breast pocket stepped in front of her, barring entry. Her identification tag said her name was Selma Ganz. "You ain't s'posed to be here."

"I need some help."

"I just clean here." Selma gazed upward, and Karin noticed the small, round eye of a camera. Without taking her eyes off the camera, Selma said, "Now you gotta git on out of here. This is s'posed to be secure." She pronounced it *see*-cure.

"My name's Karin. I only have a quick question."

Selma scowled, grabbed her arm and dragged her out the door. "If I'm going to talk to you, I'm least going to have a smoke while I do it."

Karin followed her to the rear door of the building. Selma stepped out, propped it open with a chunk of brick that lay nearby and quickly lit a cigarette, letting the smoke trail out in a thin stream from her nostrils. Then she glanced uneasily around the parking lot. Seeing Karin staring at the white van parked next to the loading dock, Selma said, "That's the pick-up wagon." She took a full draw from her cigarette, burning it a good halfway down. "They call it the ambulance, but it's a body car. Like this is a loading dock, but they call it the 'rear entry.' Don't want people to think their loved ones is coming in and going out like cargo, you know."

She took another draw on the cigarette and in a rush of smoke she said, "You gotta lotta nerve bustin' in there. Better be good, girl."

"It's important." And then Karin hesitated. How much should she say, or how much would she have to say, to get this woman to trust her? Maybe just start with Melanie. "Did you ever know a Melanie Allen? She used to work here."

Selma's expression hardened. "Maybe. Maybe not."

"Selma, it's important."

The woman considered her cigarette. "So's my job."

"Would money help?"

"No. I don' want your money. I want a good reason I should talk to you."

"My little girl is missing."

"Kids!" Selma's expression softened. "Don't I just know how kids run today," she said and straightened. "Don't know a good home when they got one. My youngest lit out when she was only fifteen, didn't see her till she came home a year later, scarred from drugs and carrying a kid herself. Then she wanted to live at home." Suddenly she glared at Karin. "I was so happy to see her. Took her in and helped her out. Money. Home. Thought she'd go straight." Selma stopped suddenly. "Lettie didn't go straight, of course. Still hurts."

"I'm sorry about that, Selma. But my girl didn't run." She swallowed, forced the words out. "Melanie stole her."

"Sweet God alive. You get yourself to the police."

"I did. They don't believe me."

Selma's eyelids lowered as she frowned. "They usually believe stuff about kids. Unless they're teens."

"She's five."

"You better explain this, girl. You're not making much sense to me."

"Melanie was my babysitter. I let Haley stay the night with her and her daughter, and when I got there this morning, nobody was there. I called the police, but when I went home to get pictures of Haley, all my girl's stuff, right down to photographs, winter clothes, toys, everything that was hers was gone. The detective doesn't even believe I have a kid."

Selma's gaze traveled slowly over her face. "Seems mighty odd, nobody would help you. You know, back you up, say yeah, you got a kid and all."

Karin felt her cheeks go cold. "I kept her out of sight. For safety."

Selma drew hard on her cigarette. "Why's that?"

"My family wanted me to give up the baby. I didn't agree."

"That don't make a lot of sense."

"My uncle is the sheriff in the county. I . . . I'd been in some trouble and I figured social services would think he was a better parent for my baby, so I ran. I lived out of state and haven't been back very long. And I couldn't get in touch with the doctor who's seen her because he's out of town. Until tomorrow, but that will be too late. Please, Selma, please help me. Tell me what you know about Mellie. I've just got to find her."

"My daughter didn't want her kid. Now I got another child to raise." Selma dropped the glowing cigarette butt on the pavement and crushed it under the scuffed toe of her shoe. "Don't know no Melanie. Was a woman named Melody used to work here, though. Off and on, as a private-duty nurse. The last I saw her was maybe a year ago."

Karin's stomach clenched. Another dead end? But the names were similar . . . Briefly, she described Melanie. Relief swept through her as Selma nodded. "That's her. Melody something. Don't remember what."

"You sure she wasn't working here last summer?"

"She left last year sometime. Said her husband didn't want her to work."

"Did she ever mention where they lived?"

"Nope. But she bragged a lot about him. Too much sometimes. Never did believe anyone who talked too much 'bout how good they husband was."

"Did you ever meet him?"

"Huh! He works here. Drives that van." She jerked a thumb toward the white pick-up van.

"That one? Right there?" Karin was stunned. "Melanie always said he was in the Special Forces and they moved around a lot."

"Don't know about any Special Forces and that." Selma straightened and headed for the back door. Over her shoulder she said, "I learned early not to believe much of what she said. Cute, makes you like her at first, then you re'lize she's nothing but a liar."

"And she never said where they lived?"

"Nope." Selma shoved aside the half brick she'd used to prop the door. She held the door for Karin and added, "I got the idea she lived somewhere in the mountains."

"Her personnel file would have an address."

Selma's face stiffened. Her voice was low. "They got cameras all over this place. You come tomorrow, see the clerk, Sally. She's pretty good."

"Mel could be clear gone by then."

"She's gone now. This job is my livin'. You know how hard it is to get jobs at my age?" Selma pointed to her graying hair. "I got a grandkid to take of."

"Please. Think of your grandchild, what if Mellie took her?"

Selma's head snapped around as she let the door slam shut. "I'd kill the bitch."

"So help me find her. My daughter's only five. And I know Mellie took her."

"Five! Same as my grandbaby. God in heaven! Wonder what she wanted her for. I knowed that girl was sneaky, but I never!" Selma hesitated, then held out her key ring. "Door on the left down the hall, use the notched key," she said in a hoarse whisper. "Look in the third file cabinet. You got four minutes while I run the cleaner out front in the hallway. Anyone comes, I'll bump the wall, but you'll be on your own. Keep your head down, away from the cameras. They just put those in. Don't know for sure if they're working yet. Best not take the chance."

She started the vacuum and turned her back to Karin.

The file cabinets were locked, but Karin found a key taped to the underside of the desk drawer. She tried it, and it worked. *Thank God for foolish secretaries.*

In the third file next to the bottom drawer she found paperwork on former employees as well as workman's compensation files. A quick flip through the A's turned up no one named Allen. Stomach knotting with tension, she searched again. This time she glimpsed a familiar face in a snapshot stapled inside one folder's front cover. She pulled the folder out. It was Melanie, all right. The folder was labeled *Alwyn, Melody.*

Karin jotted down the address and phone number listed, then looked hastily through the file.

As far back as seven years ago, Mellie had worked intermittently at Oak Manor as a private-duty nurse for patients paying for the service. Karin quickly copied down her Social Security number and birth date. Mellie was thirty-two. Person to contact: husband, Roger Alwyn, pilot. Forest Air, LLC, Atlanta, Georgia.

She flipped through some more papers. Mel had filed a workman's compensation claim for back strain from lifting. The name of the patient she had lifted made Karin's heart beat faster. Lucia Eberhard. Karin continued leafing through the file. Another workman's comp claim involving a private-duty patient and a back sprain caught her eye—not the name this time, James Galt, but his address. Paradise Lane. Galt was listed as the owner of Melanie's house.

A thump sounded against the wall. Karin wiped off the file, hopefully smudging her fingerprints in case anyone thought to look. Then she laid it on the chair next to the file cabinet and left the inner room. The outer office was nearly dark, except for the little light leaking in around the edges of the suite door.

Over the roar of the vacuum, Karin heard Selma's voice, loud and slightly irritated. "I came down here 'cause I saw some god-awful mess on the floor from installing those cameras. Knew Mr. Morgan woulda throw'd a fit if'n he saw it."

Silently, Karin turned the doorknob lock. Footsteps came down the hall, stopped outside the door, rattled the knob. Karin froze. The lock held.

Again, the doorknob jiggled. Then the footsteps retreated. Karin exhaled slowly, fearing her relief could be heard through the walls. More footsteps, then Selma humming loudly as she came closer. Finally her voice sounded through the door. " 'Kay."

Karin slipped out, pulled the door shut gently, listened for the lock click and said, "Thanks."

Selma nodded. "You owe me. Now git. Go back the way we came to the main corridor, go through the rehab unit. If you're asked, say you visited Gracie Long. Lotsa folks visit her, an' she's nuts, she'll never say nothin'."

Karin smiled and squeezed Selma's arm. "Thank you. I can't tell you how grateful . . ."

"If they come back on me, I'm saying you stole those keys."

"Fair enough."

Heart pounding, Karin hustled down the corridor to the Rehabilitation Unit. As she passed a patient on a gurney to the side of the hallway, his hand snaked out and wrapped her wrist in a drowning-man grip. "Help!"

Karin drew a breath to shout, then noticed the straps pinning him to the wheeled cot. He raised his heavily bandaged head, one eye covered, the other wide and pleading. "Help me!"

His voice was familiar. She looked more closely at his face under the wrap of gauze bandages, then gaped. "Johnny Ray?"

He was the last home patient she had seen just last Wednesday. Astounded, she asked, "Johnny, what happened? Why are you here? Why aren't you home in your trailer with your sister?"

The one eye visible appeared vague and unseeing. "Hit me, made me fall. I wanna go home."

"Who hit you?"

He moved his head minutely, indicating no. "The man. Tall."

She knew his head injury left him prone to blaming someone whenever anything went wrong for him. She didn't know whether he was telling the truth about being hit, or making it up to explain a fall. His grip was painfully tight. "Let go, Johnny." She kept her voice calm and reassuring. "I'll try to help you, but you must let go of me."

His head rolled to the side, the bandage sliding up to reveal a large, ugly bruise on his head where his hair hadn't fully grown in after his accident. His focus sharpened, as though he was concentrating. His long, thin fingers still circled her wrist, but he loosened his grip a little. Blood flowed back into her hand, her fingers tingling uncomfortably. "Johnny, let go all the way now."

A puzzled expression crossed his face as though he hadn't realized he was gripping her. Slowly his fingers relaxed. "Sorry."

Karin moved quickly out of his reach. "Johnny, I have to go now, but they'll help you get better here so you can go home again."

A lock snapped back and the door of the staff room on the other side of Johnny's gurney opened. An aide stepped out, saw Karin and instantly looked embarrassed. "A little emergency," she said by way of explanation. "I hope you weren't worried."

"He says someone hit him and made him fall."

The aide shook her head. "I know he says that, but his sister said she thinks he fell by himself."

Anger and fear filled Johnny's eyes. His face crumpled, child-like, and he sobbed, turning his head to the wall. "I'll die here."

Rubbing her wrist, Karin stayed out of his reach. "Why is he here?"

"He's in for rehab. They think he can make progress with intensive therapy."

"I didn't think he had insurance coverage for inpatient rehab."

The aide shrugged. "Guess they worked something out."

"Amazing, great." She turned to him and said, "Johnny, I can't stay now. You'll get better here. And this person will help you."

Selma watched until Karin disappeared from sight. Then she walked steadily on down the corridor and out the back door where she'd done her smoking. The dented van was still there. That thing gave her the creeps.

Curious, Selma peered in the van's rear window. Empty, except for a cot to haul the poor patients in from their homes. Like that poor Johnny Ray boy just brought in Friday. And they used it to haul the poor old dead patients out to the crematorium. That Roger drove it all the time. Selma stood still for a minute, feeling a crawling sensation on her neck. She peered in the window again. The cot blanket was wrinkled. Had that creepy Roger been sleeping in there?

What should she do? He could have been listening in on them. Would it matter? Selma ran her rough hand over her face as she tried to remember all they'd talked about. Back inside, she dragged the vacuum cleaner to her closet, trying to think. Would he have heard her agree to let that woman into the office? Didn't know about that, but he sure could have heard her talking about Mel, the little snake. Dammit.

Her boss, Mr. Morgan, was a good man to work for, but he expected people to follow the rules. And he didn't like people gossiping about staff and patients. She shouldn't have talked to that woman Karin, but hearing about that little girl being taken made her mad. And she really didn't like that Melody. The snot.

Selma rolled her shoulders. She shouldn't have let Karin into the office, either. They'd find out. They always did. Like when that young man got caught in the back, sneaking around the drug closet and they'd seen him on the cameras. *Cameras.*

Selma approached the ward clerk's desk, ran dust cloth over the counter and sidled up close to the clerk, a woman she'd known for several years. "Sheila, I seen plaster dust on the floor here and there. Are they putting in more cameras everywhere?" She kept on wiping down the surface, pretending the answer didn't matter.

Sheila looked up. "Just over the doors to drug cabinets, and a couple other places. Why?"

"Just wondered if there was messes I missed. You know Mr. Morgan. He won't like a mess with that award ceremony for him tomorrow. Could get me in trouble if I miss something."

"Yeah, there'll be people all over this place in the afternoon."

"I s'pose the cameras are working now in his office and all."

"They were just installed Friday, haven't got them working yet."

Relief blossomed in Selma. So much so, she decided she'd ask a few more questions. "You know that man, Roger, drives the patient-pick-up van?"

Sheila nodded. Selma continued. "Did you see him come in this afternoon?"

"Never saw him. Why?"

Selma shrugged. "Just thought I saw him. Thought it was kinda odd 'cause it's Sunday."

"And it's time we got back to work, Selma."

Selma returned to her cleaning closet, muttering to herself. She felt a little reassured, but not much. What if Sheila missed seeing him?

She examined the hallways for cameras. Nothing. Then she walked toward the back door where she and Karin had entered. Yep. A camera, a little one up high, watching the operating-room door. Mr. Morgan called it the treatment room, but it was an operating room in her mind, because it had a table and all the complicated stuff a doctor in an ER would use. Of course, they probably had drugs in there too, so the camera would be to make sure nobody stole them. Still, she didn't like that room. Gave her the creeps, it did.

CHAPTER 20

Joe found the Eberhard home in Red Oaks Estates more easily than he'd thought he would, even though he and Karin always had met elsewhere. Karin had always appeared so open and simple. No complications with her. She was working on a degree in nursing, got along well with her brother Sam, and seemed just perfect. Maybe a little dependent. Not the kind of person who wouldn't tell him she was pregnant, wouldn't tell him they had a kid.

Dammit, he went from being eager to see her, to being so angry with her. That she could have a child, his daughter, and never let him know was unforgivable. She wasn't the person he'd thought she was. She was deceptive. Last night she'd agreed to meet him and then never showed. Dammit, feelings like this were awful. Was he happy to have a child? Sad? Trapped?

Had his own father gone through these feelings when he was born? Maybe this kind of turmoil was behind a lot of behavior that he'd never understood and had resented.

Frowning, Joe parked. There was another aspect of their relationship to which he'd never given much thought. Karin hadn't mentioned much about the Eberhards, though she had talked readily about Nicole, clearly loving her dearly. And she had shared Sam, her brother. But she never talked about her parents or other relatives. Sam had once said something about Karin not getting along well with her father and uncle. *And I never took the time to ask her.*

As Joe walked up to the house, he noticed how comfortable and settled the place looked, as though it had been solidly there for years. He didn't know much about flowers but he liked the way the little yellow and purple plants lined the walk and ran around the base of the evergreen bushes. His mother had planted those one year when he was in grade school. Pansies, he thought they were called. Seeing this home, he understood why Karin had said it was lovely living there.

Then he caught sight of the bars on the upstairs windows and the burglar alarm sticker on the door. Maybe it wasn't as settled and secure a neighborhood as it looked.

He rang the doorbell. It was a long shot that Karin would still be here. Little Nicky would be in elementary school now, but there might be another child. In any case, he hoped the Eberhards would at least know where Karin was.

He heard the lock being turned back and the door opened.

A lovely, slim woman with dark hair stood in the doorway. She had the same remarkable violet eyes that Karin had described Nicole having. Clinging at her knee was a little girl with the same dark hair and violet eyes. She ducked behind her mother as the woman looked at him with a cool, appraising expression.

"Mrs. Eberhard?" he said.

"Yes?"

Her guarded manner threw him off-balance. "I wonder if I could talk to you and your husband for a minute, about Karin McGrath, or Preston, as I think she may be now."

The woman's expression hardened. "I don't think so." She started to shut the door.

"Please, it's very important." Joe lifted his hands in an imploring gesture. "I've been away for years. I never heard from her. It's important that I find her."

For a long moment, Mrs. Eberhard seemed to be thinking.

Then she asked, "What did you say your name was?"

"Joe Canan. I'm, or I was, a close friend of Karin's. Maybe you remember my name. I sent letters to her here."

Her eyes narrowed. "I can't help you. I haven't seen her since she left here."

"When was that?"

She didn't answer, but looked quizzically at him. "If you're here to upset me, you're succeeding."

"I certainly don't want to upset you. I've been out of the country for years. Six years, in fact. I really need to find Karin. I'm hoping you can help me."

"Before I talk to you, I need to know when you left Denver. Exactly what day?"

That was odd. The day? He remembered it vividly. "A Thursday, June tenth."

"You can prove that?"

"I have a passport stamp showing I entered Iraq on June twelfth. I don't have it with me, but it's available."

She stared hard at Joe, seeming to size him up, then surprised him by swinging open the door. "Maybe you'd better come in."

She led him into the living room, indicated he should sit on the couch and seated herself in a chair set at a careful ninety-degree angle away. He sat, uncomfortable, in the deep cushions. Despite their luxury, the room was cold, the decor formal. Satin window coverings in precise folds dropped to the floor. The furniture, all very nice, was placed carefully at right angles. Linda Eberhard arranged her legs and lifted her child up on the chair next to her. "You may call me Linda and you may tell me when you decided to return to Colorado."

Despite her attempt to appear relaxed, she was tense. He tried to disarm her. "I really appreciate you taking the time."

She waited, so he began. "I was in Caracas where I've been working for the last four years. Before that I was in Iraq. I'm an oil engineer. Last Thursday, Sam McGrath, Karin's brother, came to me in Caracas. He'd been backpacking in Peru and came over to find me. He was sick, very ill with some kidney problem. He said I had a kid and little else because he collapsed. So after I got him into a hospital, I came here to find Karin and find out what this business about a child was."

She was holding her little girl on her lap, but while her hands caressed the child, her gaze was riveted on his face.

"I flew in yesterday at three o'clock, phoned Karin and arranged to meet her last night, but she never came. This morning I found that she's gone under the name Preston and had numerous addresses. I went to her apartment and was told that the police wanted to talk to her and that she ran from them."

He leaned forward. "None of this sounds at all like the woman I knew years ago. I found a picture of a child with Karin but she never told me she was pregnant. I don't know where the name Preston came from. I just want to find out what's going on."

He waited for a response, thinking that it looked as if Linda had shrunk in the chair, her shoulders dropping forward as though the starch in her spine had softened.

"Mrs. Eberhard, please help me here."

"You left the country then, two weeks and two days before my Nicky was taken out of the bedroom where she slept."

Thank God he was sitting down. "Kidnapped?"

Her eyes brimmed with tears.

"I . . . I'm so sorry to hear." Time seemed to stand still for a long moment. Kidnapped. Two weeks after he left. Joe thought he could feel her despair. "I'm so very sorry to hear all this. You must be devastated."

She nodded, a tear escaping down her cheek. "Karin slept through the whole thing. We woke when she knocked on our door saying that Nicky was gone. I know tests came back showing that she had been drugged, but Karin had to have been involved. She must have drugged herself so the kidnappers could get in and get away."

"She couldn't have. She talked about Nicole all the time. She adored her."

"That's what we all thought." The little girl was curled on the chair, almost asleep while Linda crossed her arms, clasping each elbow with a hand, so tense the tendons showed nearly white against her already pale skin. "I haven't seen Karin since two days after my Nicky was kidnapped."

She looked away from him, her gaze traveling to a window, then to a small framed photograph. Finally she turned back, her hands clasped together, her knuckles standing out. "And you should know I continue to blame Karin."

Dumbstruck for several seconds, he struggled to comprehend what he'd heard, but it just didn't make sense, no matter how hard he tried to believe her. He was certain to his core Karin would never be involved in such a heinous crime. He nearly said it aloud, but Linda Eberhard's face was so torn with grief he clamped his lips shut. When he spoke, his voice was ragged from the effort. "Was she charged?"

"Detained briefly. Then a man who had been painting the trim on the house was found dead, suicide, and a confession letter with him." She looked at him. "The police were convinced. I wasn't. And I told her so when I wrote her."

Poor Karin. How she would have suffered. "And the name Preston that she's using?"

Linda shook her head. "I don't know. I suppose she took it to hide behind."

"Do you know where she went, after?"

Linda looked at him, her mouth a grim line. "Back to the mountains, I heard. Back to her father."

The father she didn't get along with, he thought. She must

have been desperate for somewhere to stay. "And when you wrote her, you sent your letter there."

She was still looking at him, but she wasn't seeing him. Even her voice sounded far away. "To her father, Zachariah McGrath, in Capstone. It's a small town. I'm sure they got to her."

"And the letters I sent to her here?"

"I don't know." Linda looked away from him, across the room again. "I was ill."

"Perhaps you saw them."

Her brows rose. "Or they were lost in the mail."

Not likely! It was entirely possible she'd destroyed them.

The room was so quiet for the next few moments he could hear the gentle snores of the little girl, now curled up like a kitten. Linda seemed detached from everything, eyeing a small framed photograph seated on the mantel.

He'd have given anything to stand and stretch his legs and break the heavy pall in the room, but he feared she'd ask him to leave and he still had questions, so he said, "That's a lovely photo."

Linda rose, careful not to disturb her sleeping daughter, and went to it. She picked it up and with her finger stroked the face of the child in the photograph. Looking at the picture seemed to loosen Linda's control because she began to speak more easily. "It was taken just weeks before Nicky disappeared."

"May I see it?"

He noticed as she handed it to him that her hand trembled, despite her seeming calm. "What a beautiful child." He smiled gently. Angry as he was at the treatment Karin had received, he felt a great sadness for Linda Eberhard's terrible loss. "I appreciate you sharing all this with me."

"Nicky was just two and a half that day and we went out to the nursing home to visit my mother-in-law. It's a snapshot really."

"And that would be your husband?"

"Yes."

He pointed to the woman standing next to Linda's husband, only partly visible and turned slightly away from the camera. "Who's that?"

"Mother Eberhard's nurse." Linda looked toward the doorway and stiffened. "Ed! What are you doing?"

A slightly older version of the man from the picture stood in the doorway, holding a pistol aimed straight at Joe's chest. His eyes were furious. "Who are you? Why are you asking my wife all these questions?"

Joe answered quietly, soothingly. "I'm trying to find Karin McGrath, er, Preston."

"Well, she sure as hell isn't here, so get out."

Linda stepped toward him. "Ed, what is the matter with you and why do you have that gun?"

The child roused and whined. "Ed, you've frightened Cindy. Now put that thing away."

Ed waved the pistol, indicating Joe should move toward the front door. "Go. Now."

"I'm going. But for the record, I didn't come here to cause trouble."

"I don't tolerate people upsetting my wife. Get out and don't come back." Finally he glanced at Linda. "Stand away from him. Get behind me. I'll protect you."

"Ed! He isn't threatening." She protested, but moved as he'd said. "Put the gun down. He'll go."

"You bet he will," he said and stood back, again waving the pistol.

"Oh, Ed. Stop it. You're the one who's upset."

Joe was on the threshold, Ed Eberhard behind him. "Go," Ed said. "Like I told Karin this morning, you come around again,

I'll have your ass in court so fast you won't know what happened."

"She was here?" Joe blurted as he stepped outside. "Why did she come here?"

"She said someone took her child, just like Nicky." The door slammed in Joe's face.

Chapter 21

Karin drove steadily, sticking to quiet side streets where traffic was at a minimum. The breeze was so chilly, not even many children were playing outside. Could Haley hear the wind wherever she was? So much time had gone by. Where was she now? *How could you do this, Mellie? I'll kill you.* Karin realized she was pressing harder on the gas pedal, going nearly fifty. She slowed, forced herself to loosen her grip on the steering wheel and breathe deeply.

It was already three-thirty in the afternoon, seven hours since she first rang the doorbell at Melanie's house. Seven hours could take Haley out of the state in any direction. And they were probably out of that house in the early hours, while it was still dark. That could put them almost a thousand miles in any direction. Nervous sweat chilled her forehead.

She turned into the street listed in Melanie's personnel file. The house number didn't exist. The closest possible corresponding number was a weed-blown vacant lot. More of Mellie's lies.

She parked and called directory assistance for the number of Forest Air Company in Atlanta. No such outfit. The nursing home couldn't have checked references. Or if they did, it would have been a simple matter to set up people to vouch for Melanie. And her husband.

Disgusted, Karin called Jansen's number, then wondered how much she should tell him. For so long she had kept secrets, but now with Haley stolen, everything changed. Maybe it didn't matter whether she kept her secrets anymore.

Her call was answered by voice mail. Relieved, she left a message telling Jansen where he could find a file on Melanie at the nursing home, along with her birth date and Social Security number. Let him run them down. No doubt they would all prove false, too.

What next? It seemed every single possibility was drying up. Karin's eyes stung. She brushed at them fiercely. No time for despair. She had to get Haley back and to do that she had to find Mellie. So where next?

She had only one idea. The house on Paradise Lane.

The police officer said there was nothing in the house, but surely there was something Mellie had overlooked. No one could be perfect at clearing things away.

A block from Mellie's house, Karin parked, fished a flashlight from the glove compartment, and got out, locking the car behind her. The air cooled noticeably as the sun slipped behind the cloud bank over the mountains.

A mere seven hours ago she had come here to pick up Haley with no inkling of how her life would change. Or how she would change. In those few hours old habits had come alive. She had been secretive since Haley's birth, but now she was outright furtive as she took the tire iron from the trunk of her car and shoved it under her jacket.

At the corner she scanned the street. The only two houses on that block of Paradise Lane were both darkened. Each was at least a good football field's distance from Mellie's house with trees and scrub oak separating them. Even with the tree branches bare of leaves, neither of these neighbors had a good view of Mellie's house. Unless they were actively snooping, they never would have seen lights or cars. It couldn't have been a more perfect choice.

Karin passed the house on the left. It still had the same piled newspapers on the porch. Walking toward Mellie's house, she kept her pace moderate, trying to look casual. The breeze rustling the winter weeds mocked her, dry whispers that blamed her for letting Haley stay overnight with Mellie. Despite herself, her step quickened as she approached the evergreens that sheltered the house. There had to be something inside that would lead to Haley.

The window she had broken was boarded up. Panting lightly, Karin slipped behind the overgrown juniper bush at the other side of the house, tire iron in her hand. She stopped beside a basement window barred with rusty strips of iron. The security bars were loose, only pressed into place. Stooping for a closer look, she found a semicircle of glass had been cut out around the window lock. Was someone already inside? Clutching the tire iron tightly, her nerves taut, she muttered to herself, "This is how you got in here to use the house, right Mellie?"

Her hand shaking, she pulled the security bars aside. The noise of the window scraping as she pushed it open sent a chill across her scalp. She froze, listening for a sound that would tell her someone was inside now.

Hearing nothing, she stepped into the leaf-filled window well. Still holding the tire iron, she sat down and slid feet first halfway inside, then turned over and lowered herself to the basement floor with only a minimum of scraping. A flood of dry leaves came in with her, rustling and crackling along the floor. The window dropped back into place, not quite closed.

Once inside, she flicked on the flashlight, playing the beam around. She was in a laundry room with a large wash sink and a dryer vent sealed off with plastic. The electricity meter and the main electric circuit breaker hung on the wall to the side of the space where an automatic washer and dryer would stand. A flip of the main circuit breaker switch would provide electricity to the house. How idiotically simple.

Everything she thought she knew about Mellie was proving false. She didn't even know for sure how long Mellie had actually lived in this house. The first time Karin came here was just three weeks ago, in the morning. All this time Mel could have lived somewhere else, coming here only when it was absolutely necessary to convince Karin she lived here. It would easily take a few weeks, maybe a month or two, before the power company became suspicious about the electric current usage.

"My God!" she whispered as a memory came to mind. Haley had even said they pretended living in different houses. What other hints had there been that she'd overlooked?

Sobered, she moved through the room to the doorway, listening for any sounds. A creak sounded overhead, as if from the living-room floorboards. She froze, listening. Little sounds, birds, rustles, the rub of a tree branch against the roof, came from outside. She shivered. It was a well-built house with thick walls, sturdy flooring and an occasional creak.

Holding the tire iron close, she moved to an under-the-staircase closet. It held only a dusty roll of wallpaper and several ancient paint cans marked with white drips down the sides. Farther along, she came to a small furnace room. She ran her hand across the metal side panel of the furnace, feeling for warmth that would indicate a pilot light was burning, but the panel was cold.

She passed an empty storage area and a partially finished game room with wood paneling and linoleum floor tile. A surprising amount of dust covered the floor, showing traces of large footprints, possibly left by the firemen and policemen earlier. So much dust. No wonder they assumed no one had been here recently.

Her heartbeat drummed in her ears as she tiptoed across the room, putting her feet in others' footprints. She climbed the stairs to the kitchen and into the bright light of day.

"Stop right there!"

She froze, her throat so constricted she couldn't speak.

"Hands up where I can see them."

She raised her arms shoulder height, the tire iron held so tightly in her fist, her fingers locked from the tension.

"Drop the tire iron."

The tire iron fell, clanging down the stairs, end over end, to the basement floor.

"Now, come up the last step and over here. Nice and easy. No sudden moves. Keep your hands up where I can see them."

She recognized the voice. Slowly, Karin moved to the center of the kitchen, two questions in her mind: *Does the detective know who I am now? Will he arrest me?*

Detective Jansen lowered his service pistol and then holstered it, resting his hands on his hips within easy reach of the weapon. He glowered at her. His stance was wide, as if ready to spring. "Now tell me why you ran from me and didn't show at the police station."

She could almost feel handcuffs on her wrists. She tried to read his expression. His eyes were narrowed, suspicious, and angry, but she saw no knowing glint in them. Was it possible he still didn't know who she was? Her words sounded stilted when she spoke. "I could tell you didn't believe I have a child. You didn't believe anyone was here last night and you had no intention of helping me. You were just . . ." She caught herself for a moment and then said, "You were just humoring me."

"Breaking and entering is a crime."

"The security grate was only pressed into place and the window pane was cut out at the lock. Someone got in here before me and left the window open. I just came in an open window."

He shook his head. "And in here, you're contaminating

evidence—"

"This isn't an official crime scene because you don't believe a word I've said," she interrupted. "And there's no yellow tape prohibiting entry." She took a quick breath and continued. "I know you don't believe me, but Mellie's not a victim. She took Haley. And there has to be something here to prove it. She couldn't have been so thorough that she removed every single thing. She must have overlooked something."

"Earlier you said Melanie was kidnapped, too. You're changing your story."

"It took me a bit to . . ." *Careful,* she thought. "I left you a message. Melanie once mentioned she worked at Oak Manor nursing home. She was a private-duty nurse, for a Mr. Galt. I remembered you said a Mr. Galt owned this house, so she would know this house was empty and could use it. Mellie would always come to my place. You've seen my place. Forget the dust, because it wasn't here before. Would you come to my place when you could be here instead? And when I think back, she was kind of uncomfortable both times when I was here. She'd laugh too much, apologize too much for having so little furniture. I thought then she was embarrassed, but now I know she was nervous. So I figured there might be something here she was hiding."

Had she said too much? Talked too fast? Cops noticed stuff like that. She drew a long breath to calm her nerves. "Like I said, I left a voice mail."

He rubbed his chin as though he was mulling over what she'd said. Then: "Is there anything you've left out?"

The Eberhards? Nicole? The other kidnapping? Joe Canan? She stifled a shudder, then hesitated, remembering the house last night, Jennifer's delight, seeing Mellie's smiles and the coffee they shared. "Cinnamon. She spilled cinnamon last night when she made the coffee. You can still smell it."

Jansen's chin lifted as he sniffed at the air.

Karin waved her hand at the kitchen. "She spilled it on the counter next to the stove and just laughed about it, but now I think she was really anxious, because she didn't want anything left that would indicate she'd been here. All this, the missing furniture, the dust, all this is a setup to make me look like a nutcase."

Jansen's expression was thoughtful. "It's a lot of effort just to make you look . . ." He let the sentence drift off, as if avoiding the word *crazy*.

"It worked, though, didn't it? You aren't looking for my daughter, are you? You don't even believe I have one."

He was quiet.

"Mel and I sat right there last night."

Speaking softly, Jansen said, "The table, the counters, the stove, even the knobs on the cupboard doors, all are covered with dust."

"True." Then Karin pointed. "But there are no cobwebs in the corners. No dead spiders or flies. All this dust, wouldn't you think there'd be dead flies too?" She moved over to let Jansen inspect the kitchen window that looked out on the dreary backyard. "And look, there's dust on the sill, but no layer of grime on this window and no cobwebs there. It was clean when I was here, and the only window in the whole house without a cover over it. I think she cleaned it so she could watch the kids playing outside."

Karin grabbed the sleeve of his jacket and practically pulled him into the living room. She opened the drapes, letting in the late afternoon light. "See? There are cobwebs and crusty dead things in these corner crevices. There's long-term grime on the window pane. And look at these." She gestured at the tiny pinholes in the sides of the wooden window sashes. "Mellie fastened plastic covers on these windows. She claimed to be saving heat and would laugh like she was embarrassed. So, like an idiot, to be polite, I never asked any questions." She watched as Jansen inspected the pinholes, then the room. "She wasn't preserving heat, she was preserving cobwebs. She had to have planned this for months." Karin looked into Jansen's dark, disbelieving eyes. "I liked her. I needed a friend so badly I didn't question anything."

He didn't respond, but at least he was listening.

Karin turned on her heel and went through the hallway to the bedrooms. "It's the same here. Plastic sheeting covered these windows, too. What a setup."

She went to the cord hanging from a rectangle in the hallway ceiling. "Here's a drop-down ladder." Stretching, she grasped the cord. She expected Jansen to protest, but he was quiet. Steel screeched as the ladder lowered and clunked to the floor. Moving easily up the wooden steps, Karin climbed into the dry, still attic air and stepped onto the one board that spanned the beams. She looked around, taking in the bare roof rafters, the joists, the drifting cobwebs, the smell of dry wood and dust. The entire space was empty.

Jansen, who'd come up just behind her, scrutinized the raw, unfinished beams and joists. "Cleaner here than down below."

"Don't you find that odd? Maybe this is where they got the dust for downstairs."

They retreated down the ladder and returned to the living room. How had all the dust got there, Karin wondered. It lay as though it had been painted on. "I'll get you, Mellie," she muttered through clenched teeth and turned away.

Jansen followed her to the garage. A dry, piney scent filled the air. The garage floor was clean, except for an old worn broom leaning against the wall by the steps and an oil stain in the middle of the wide cement floor. Again, a light layer of dust covered everything and showed footprints presumably left by the firemen.

She stood carefully on the bottom step down to the garage floor not wanting to leave a print of her own. And then she noticed one smaller, narrow, feminine print near the bottom step. Half a footprint, actually. She pointed. "There! No one leaves one footprint unless they stood here, one foot on the floor, one on the lower step, and somehow blew the dust in here." She held out her foot, clearly larger than the print. "It has to be, because there were only men out here earlier and no man would leave a print as small as that."

"Blew the dust in?"

"They did something. Had to. It just wasn't here last night."

He shook his head.

She flashed the beam of light around the ceiling. The overhead, exposed beams were clear. The unfinished wood walls held only occasional rusted nails driven into the studs, presumably to hold tools. Nothing, not even a crumpled paper, left to show where they went.

So far, Melanie had only overlooked two things. No dead spiders in the kitchen window and half a footprint in the garage. Karin shook her head, feeling desperate. Melanie had been very, very clever.

Jansen's silence wasn't reassuring. Frustrated, Karin stepped back up to the doorway into the kitchen. "The kitchen was Mellie's favorite room. Something has to be here."

Once more her gaze took in the sixties-style breakfast nook with the built-in seats and table. The tippy table. "The girls bounced on the seats. Mellie's purse dumped over, spilling everything. She absolutely scrambled to pick her stuff up. I wonder what she was covering up?"

Jansen put a hand on her shoulder, moving her aside. He knelt and pried at a tiny white edge of something peeking out from under the back corner of the table pedestal.

"Mel shoved something under there once," she said. Not daring to hope, she watched as he pulled at the strip of white. A bit tore off. She lifted the table by one edge to take pressure off that corner.

Jansen gently eased out a matchbook. Over his shoulder she saw *Moose Lake Bar and Grill, Moose Lake, Colorado.*

Bitter disappointment. She dropped her head in her hands while Jansen bagged the matchbook. *The seat.* Again her hopes rose. "Mel's spilled purse . . ."

Jansen jerked the booth seat loose, then out. Inside, amid toast crusts, mouse turds, dust and a pencil lay a smudged and half-torn business card. Jansen picked it up, turning it over. It read *Melody Alwyn. Surgical Technician. Dr. Wallace Wetford.*

"Mel, a surgical tech!" And for Dr. Wetford. What did that mean?

Jansen put the card into an evidence bag, pocketed it, shoved the vinyl seat back into place and turned to her. "Surgical nurses usually don't do private-duty nursing."

"You still don't believe me!"

His cell phone rang. Watching her, he put it to his ear. Surprise crossed his face. His gaze flashed to her face.

He knew! Someone was telling him about Nicole. Karin's breath came quickly, fear rising. Would he arrest her?

Jansen turned away and stepped toward the living room as though to muffle the conversation.

Karin spun and raced out the kitchen door to the garage, then to the rear door leading to the backyard. The doorknob twisted easily. The hinges made no noise. Oiled. Recently.

She sprinted into the yard. Six-foot board fencing surrounded it and weeds sprouted from the straggling, unmowed spring grass. On the far side a doghouse sagged against the fence.

Jansen's shout broke the air. "Karin! Stop!"

The doghouse roof groaned as she scrambled up onto it and threw herself over the fence.

Chapter 22

Jansen's bad knee slowed him as he ran through the house to the front door in time to see Karin emerge from the stand of scrub oak and sprint across the neighboring yard. She rounded the corner and ran to her car. He was too far behind to catch up to her. Frustrated, he saw her pull away even before he reached his own car, his knee throbbing, a leftover that rehab hadn't remedied.

He'd almost begun to believe her when his brother's phone call distracted him and she bolted. He'd even thought how similar the name on the business card was to the Melanie Allen Karin claimed had kidnapped her Haley. He had almost bought the whole thing and then she ran. Where would she go now? Her mental illness was escalating. At least, he thought, there wasn't anyone in imminent danger right now. And her apparent need to keep him involved meant at least she would recontact him at some point, probably within the hour.

He turned back to the house, thinking. In his experience even the mentally disturbed worked from some bit of logic and reality. This house was significant to Karin for a reason.

Surrounded by pines, the house sat on half an acre of land at the end of a cul-de-sac that backed onto a private holding of several acres. A solitary place, no one would be able to see into it or even notice lights if the windows were covered. He believed her that the windows had been covered at some point in time, but she could have done that. Probably did. Neighbors were far away, but light in the windows would show when the trees were bare.

Tucked away as it was, the house wouldn't be easy to find. Not a place she would easily have stumbled onto, so something led her here. Maybe she lived here once, perhaps as a child. Would she turn out to be related to the Galts?

A hunch had brought him back to the house. He had figured she fled from him because she couldn't describe a child she didn't have, and that she might return to the house thinking there she would "see" the kid.

Certain things stood out in his mind. First an infant sweater, conveniently found, then a business card, and the tiny holes in the window sash. The business card could be genuine and Karin could be telling the truth, or she could have put the card there herself, making up the spilled purse in order to "find" the card. He'd have it checked for prints, of course. Against that, no child, no toys, no clothes, most of all no pictures and nobody to say there was a child. The chances that she was telling the truth were very slim. All the same, he was uneasy. Long shot or not, there might be a child, and he was glad he had put out a police alert on Haley.

The back door of the garage had opened with no drag of broken leaves, no groan of disuse from the hinges. They were clean and recently oiled. Had someone else done that, or had Karin, perhaps on previous visits, perhaps when she left the card?

The house appeared to have been well maintained. Except for the dust, it could have been inhabited recently. In fact, he thought, it was only the dust that made it seem so very deserted. Who were James and Emma Galt, he wondered, and how were they connected to Karin? If he was right, there would be some thread that tied them together. He would have to check if there was a caretaker or an estate executor for the Galt property.

His cell phone rang. Caller ID indicated it was Detective Frost.

Frost's voice boomed through, laced with excitement. "Casey, you won't believe this. That sweater you brought in? That's Nicole Eberhard's."

Jansen nearly choked. "No!" That child had been kidnapped six years ago.

"The sweater was one of the details we never gave out to the press. It was part of an outfit missing from the house when she was kidnapped. I'm surprised you don't remember. Six years ago—oh man, I'm sorry. I forgot. That's when Margot and your little girl were killed. Happened while you were . . . away. I'm sorry."

Jansen shook his head, clearing the memories. His thoughts jumbled ahead. If Karin had been involved in the Eberhard kidnapping, could the Galt house be the place where little Nicole was held? The hair on the back of his neck rose at the thought.

Assuming Karin had been involved in the Eberhard kidnapping, then today—six years and some months later—she came to this house and claimed a child was kidnapped here. Was it simply guilt or had a specific event triggered this?

So excited he was nearly shouting, Frost said, "Say this Karin's involved. Could be a guilty conscience. Maybe a subconscious confession."

Even though he'd just had the same thought, Jansen frowned. It was still only speculation. "You're jumping ahead."

And then he thought, *she started on this path, this confessional,* but even as she called attention to the place by claiming a carbon monoxide poisoning, she had managed to bring multiple people tromping through the house and contaminating evidence, including himself.

What if the Galt house *was* where little Nicole had been held?

If Karin somehow knew it was vacant and available . . . his breath came quickly now. For that matter, if the property were tied up in a disputed or complicated estate, it was possible it would have been maintained with utilities on.

Frost was still going on. "Karin was a nurse's aide. She could have been assigned to the Galts."

True, Jansen thought. And just now, had Karin come back for something, maybe a scrap of evidence that would confirm Nicole had been here six years ago? It would all have to be checked out.

Perhaps, driven by guilt, she revisited this place because Nicole had been here. Karin could have come to the house more than once. Maybe she even drank coffee in the kitchen. By herself. Perhaps Nicole was still here. Buried. Guilt could have driven Karin to revisit the grave! "Frost, we need a thorough data search on the Galts, when they died, what property they owned—oh, and who their relatives are, were."

"You got it."

Jansen's heart beat faster. He felt hyperalert. "And we need a forensic team out here to the Galt house. Tape it off, check for hairs, prints, everything."

"I'm on it. I'll put a rush on it."

"Have them consider the whole yard as well."

"You thinking the Eberhard kid could be there?" Frost's voice climbed another register. "You know what this could mean?"

"It means everything has to be done exactly right. No bending rules, no sloppy work, no assumptions! And no press. This needs to stay under the radar for now."

"Right."

Jansen rang off. To clear this case, the satisfaction would be—he wasn't sure what, but the lift in spirits he felt at the prospect was distinct and immediate.

For the first time in years he felt completely alive.

CHAPTER 23

Kenny Bristow's heart thudded as he saw a lean, narrow-faced man coming up the walkway to the house. So this guy, who walked like he was trying not to leave footprints, was Roger. Kenny hadn't really believed Mellie had a husband. She'd seemed so friendly, smiling as if she really liked him. At least, at first she did, but she'd lied right through her teeth and it made him mad. The thought gave him a tight feeling under his ribs. He clenched his fist and swung his arm to work out the irritation.

Well, whatever little racket they had running, they wouldn't make a fool of him. He'd get his share now, or he'd spill everything he knew.

Roger's feet clomped heavily on the porch. Then he knocked on the door to the upstairs apartment with hard, sharp raps.

Scratching his ear, Kenny hesitated, wondering if he should have met Roger at a bar or somewhere else with people around. But people had ears and someone might see him getting paid off, and that wouldn't do. It was better to keep this private.

Still, he waited until Roger knocked again before he went to the door, unlocked it and pulled it open, his gaze traveling over the man who was Mellie's husband. Roger was a thin, narrow kind of guy, not broad like Kenny. His head was thin too, with ears so flat against it they could have been nailed on. Kenny stepped back to let him in.

As Roger walked in past him, Kenny measured him with his

eyes. Roger was only about two inches taller than he was, 'bout five eleven maybe, with longer arms, but Kenny outweighed him by about thirty pounds. He rocked forward a little onto his toes. It'd be a pretty even match, if it came to that, he thought.

Roger kept swiveling his head around. "You alone here?"

"Course. Think I'm stupid, or something?"

Then he thought maybe he shouldn't have said that. Roger's eyes had a way of darting all over the place that made Kenny uneasy.

Roger grinned, easy-like, shrugging in a kind of jerky motion. "Just making sure."

"You brought money?"

Roger tilted his head and frowned. "Now Kenny, it's a Sunday. No banks are open on a Sunday, so I thought we'd just talk this thing through. Get an idea of what's going down, what's required, all that kind of stuff. I figured you were a businessman, owning property and all that."

Kenny nodded. It was true. He owned this house and another that he and Marva lived in. He pushed out his chest a little. It was nice to have someone recognize him for a businessman.

Roger smiled, kind of slow. "I figure maybe a beer would help things out a little. You got any?"

Kenny didn't like the idea of sharing his little stash. "Maybe we'd better do business first."

Roger's narrow head moved slowly up and down. "Okay. Looks like you're ready to paint." He walked to the far side of the long living/dining room. "You've got a tarp all rolled up here."

"Just gettin' started when I saw you got here."

Roger put a foot against the rolled-up tarp, then leaned down and pushed it open. "Figure I might as well lend a hand, since I'm interrupting your hard work."

Kenny wasn't sure about this. Those words sounded a little

like the teasing he'd had in high school years ago, but Roger had the tarp nearly unrolled, covering the whole floor. He looked at it a minute, then tugged it toward the kitchen so the edge fell at the doorway.

Roger dusted his hands. "There, now I don't feel so bad interrupting you. So, should we go to the kitchen, then? Do a little business?"

Kenny just stood a moment like he was considering saying no. He didn't want to look like he was easy. Wasn't good business. Besides, he didn't quite like the way Roger was taking over. And he didn't feel so comfortable going to a smaller space. There was something about Roger that made him want to keep a good distance, but he didn't refuse, he merely went slow.

Roger walked ahead into the kitchen, his arms swinging loose at his sides, shoulders relaxed. "You got a nice little place here, Ken."

He'd made a little emphasis when he said *Ken*. Was it sarcastic? Maybe it didn't matter. He liked being called Ken instead of Kenny. Kenny sounded like he was some kid, slow and kind of stupid. So maybe he'd go by Ken after this. He squared his shoulders and followed Roger into the kitchen, his unease fading. "Yeah, not bad."

Roger went to the back door, opened it and stuck his head out. "Pretty good porch with a little fixing up. That gate work?"

"Works good." Kenny opened the refrigerator and took out his last two bottles of beer. "Want a brew?"

Roger turned, slow and thoughtful. "Thought we were going to do business first."

Kenny shrugged. "Guess there's not much to decide. I just need to be cut in. Not a lot, you know, the forty thousand like we talked about. Should be chicken feed for you."

Roger frowned. "Nothing is chicken feed to me, Ken. It's all important. See, I'm not making money on this deal. This is just to help Mellie out."

"What do you mean?"

Roger lifted his chin. "What'd Mellie tell you?"

"She said she had twin girls and used this place to take care of them. But I figure she was babysitting Karin's kid. See, I knew Karin had a kid when she signed up here."

"You were just being a good guy letting her rent this place?"

Kenny didn't like Roger's tone much, but he figured he'd ignore it for now. Get the money thing settled, then he could work on attitude. "So when you gonna have the twenty thou?"

"Let's talk about this. What did your wife say about Karin renting this place with a kid?"

Kenny shook his head. "Hell, I don't tell her everything. She don't know about the kid. Hates kids. Dogs, too. No way she'd rent to anyone with kids or dogs."

"So you just upped the rent a little and let Karin stay here?"

Kenny nodded before he realized. He kind of regretted doing that. "Let's quit the questions here. When are you going to get the money?"

"So your wife—"

"Marva."

"So Marva doesn't know about the kid. Just you."

"Yep."

"And she doesn't know about this little deal of ours then, either, right?"

"Right. And that's the way it'll stay."

"How are you going to keep that a secret from her?"

"That's my worry." Kenny drained his beer and tossed the bottle into the trash bin with a loud clank.

Roger got up and wandered over to the sink, set his bottle down on the counter, turned and faced Kenny, leaning back against the countertop. "Well, see, it could be my worry too if she found out, Ken."

"She ain't going to. I'm not planning to stay here all that long, see."

Roger picked up his bottle and took a drink. Kenny noticed he hadn't taken much out of it. If he wasn't going to drink it, he could have said he didn't want it. Kenny wished he had another.

Roger pulled a paper out of his jacket pocket. "Okay. You're going to have to agree to never say a word to anyone and I want your signature on that."

He slapped the paper down on the table along with a pen.

It was three pages of small print and Kenny had a sudden concern. "I'm not signing a thing until I read it."

"Figured you'd be pretty smart about it. Go ahead. It's a standard contract. Take your time."

Kenny leaned over, putting both hands on the table to steady himself. He'd barely started reading when Roger moved over close to him and leaned over, pointing to the bottom paragraph. "See this here?"

Kenny looked hard. "Yeah?"

"This is the real important part, Ken."

Kenny felt Roger move, felt a light breeze on his head and then a crashing pain at his temple. Then another blow and another. Then nothing.

Chapter 24

Karin's hands were slick on the steering wheel and adrenaline pumped through her veins. She glanced in the rearview mirror, but saw no one there. Now that Jansen had connected her to Nicole, whatever help he might have been was gone. Now he was as good as an enemy. She was on her own.

She had barely reached her car when she got a text message. From Kenny. *Info 4 U.*

She could hardly believe it. Kenny was coming through for her. He must have remembered something, or relented once he thought about it. A kidnapping was serious, but even if he had decided to help out, Kenny couldn't be trusted completely. The queasy feeling in her stomach was a mixture of fear and fury. She'd have to be careful. Very careful.

She would approach the house from the rear. She parked mid-block around the corner from her apartment, got out and entered the alley that ran midway through the block between the backs of the houses. Hugging the edges of the alley, she picked her way along, using overgrowth and the garages in various states of disrepair for cover.

At the age-blackened back gate to her own building, she lifted the iron latch handle slowly, to avoid the scrape of rusted metal. The gate creaked as she stepped into the yard. She halted momentarily, listening, then closed the gate softly, surprised to see the house shut up. Kenny had appeared to be planning to paint, so she had assumed he would have the windows and doors opened for ventilation.

Uneasy, she collected two baseball-sized rocks from a pile of river-smoothed ones, one of Kenny's many unfinished projects. Still nervous, she picked out a smaller, palm-sized stone and dropped it into her pocket. Hefting the two larger ones in her hands, she eased along the side of the house, ducking beneath the window ledges, until she came to the front door. Again, she was surprised to see the door closed. She quietly opened it and wedged it wide, using one of the larger rocks as a prop.

Inside, a heavy odor of fresh paint filled her nose. So Kenny was here, or at least had been. For a minute she considered calling out to him, but the silence worried her. The smell of must rose from the basement where her apartment was, a dank smell, unpleasant.

The second stair tread to the upstairs apartment creaked, the sudden sound seeming so loud she froze with her foot midair to listen again. Her heart beat faster. Had she also heard a footstep? Four more steps and she reached the landing. Silently she turned the doorknob, found it unlocked and pushed the door open. She propped it with the second rock, in case she had to leave in a hurry.

She stepped into the living room. The smell of drying paint filled the air. In earlier years this might have been a light, airy room with its high ceiling and broad front window. Today the shade was drawn down to the sill, so that the room was cast in a half gloom. Midway along, an arch divided the room into living and dining spaces. Near the far wall a paint roller lay in a shallow pan, with a can of paint open next to it. Kenny must have just finished and decided to take a break.

She looked down the hallway to the kitchen, where a thin light streamed out. The house was hauntingly still. She pulled her car keys from her pocket and positioned them so that one poked out between her fingers. Already, she realized, she was thinking differently.

"Kenny?" Her voice echoed in the large, empty space.

She walked toward the kitchen, her footsteps loud on the wooden floor. Two steps into the kitchen she stopped, her breath caught in her throat. Kenny lay on the tarp, motionless. Nearby she saw beer bottles piled in the trash bin. Drunk? Asleep? "Kenny?"

She stepped closer, knelt and shook his shoulder. Then she saw blood pooled beneath his head. "Oh, my God!"

A swish of fabric. She glanced over her shoulder. In the fleeting second before a nylon-clad arm snaked around her neck, she saw a ski-masked face. One arm circling her throat, her assailant jerked her to her feet, nearly wrenching her head from her shoulders. Her back tight against him, she felt the rise and fall of his chest. With her free hand she grabbed at his forearm, trying to pry it loose. Her fingernails ripped across the nylon of his jacket.

His fingers dug into her skin. He clenched her wrist, twisted her arm up behind her. Propelling her in front of him, he steered her out of the kitchen, into the living room. His free hand came up in front of her, blood-covered.

She tried to twist away. He jerked her arm upwards. White hot lightning shot through her elbow and shoulder. She bent forward to ease the pain, then reared back to undo his hold on her twisted arm.

He loosened the hold. She straightened. He tightened his forearm across her throat and squeezed until lights flashed across her eyes. With her free arm she scratched at his hand, then his face. Her nails grated against his skin through the loose knit of the ski mask. He jerked out of reach, his arm pressing mercilessly on her throat. Her lungs heaved for lack of oxygen. She sagged, fumbling for the stone in her pocket. For a crucial second his grip loosened.

Using her weight and surprise, she twisted away from him, her hand with the stone flailing at his head. She landed a solid blow to his skull.

He snarled and lunged. She jumped back. He caught her arm, swung his other arm back and slapped her hard across the face.

The floor seemed to tilt, then spin as her knees gave way. He yanked her to him, his forearm clamping again across her neck, but she had gasped in a deep breath of air. The pressure of his arm on her neck sent lights flashing across her eyes again. He pressed tighter and tighter. "Drop the damn stone!"

She gripped it harder. She'd seen too much. He'd never let her live.

She clasped her hands together over the stone for added strength, then slid her torso sideways and jammed her elbow into his solar plexus. When his grip loosened, she twisted the other way, jamming her other elbow deep into his stomach. Still close to him, she stomped his instep, then slid out of his grasp and faced him as he bent forward.

Hands still clasped, she rammed them upward, catching his jaw. His teeth clacked shut. His head snapped back.

Her foot slipped. She dropped to one knee as pain shot up her leg.

Despite the pain, she rose and spun away, dodging through the living room, his footsteps thundering behind her. She made it through the front door and jumped down the four steps, but lost her balance and reeled against the wall.

It gave him just enough time. He grasped her jacket and wrenched her toward him. She jammed her fist, thumb protruding, straight toward his eye.

At the last moment he jerked back, falling against the wall. Her fingernails caught the tender skin under his eye, tearing down his cheek through the face mask. He recoiled.

She lunged at the front door. If she could just get out before he caught her again.

A stunning blow landed on the back of her neck. Pain and flashes of light blinded her. She tumbled back, toward the steps to the basement. Barely keeping her feet under her, she grabbed the banister.

He swung. She ducked. His fist glanced off her shoulder, spinning her around. Then she stumbled down the steps toward her own apartment. *Only one way in or out,* she thought. But at least she could put a door between them.

Four steps down, she reached her door and twisted the knob. It was open. Someone had been in there. No matter. It was her only chance.

She flew inside, but he reached out and grabbed her coat, pulling her back toward him. She swung at him, but somewhere she had lost the stone. Her hand swept the side of his head.

A hard muscular arm circled her, crossing her mouth and nose, cutting off her air. Choking her again.

She jammed an elbow into his ribs. He grunted but maintained his grip. Her lungs fought for air. She tried to drop to her knees, hoping the sudden weight would pull her free. He tightened his grasp.

Lights flashed again as the pressure of his grip increased. His arm covered her mouth. Suffocating her. She worked her mouth open. Bit down, hard. Her teeth sank into his flesh. She tasted blood.

He howled in rage and pain. His arm jerked away.

Staggering, she backed up, aimed and kicked as hard as she could. The toe of her shoe slammed into his kneecap.

Groaning, he dropped to one knee.

She lunged into her apartment, slammed the door and threw the bolt lock. Panting, she dragged the love seat in front of the door. It wouldn't stop him, but it would slow him down.

Silence. What was he doing?

A crash against the door. The flimsy wood cracked, but the lock held the door frame in place. For the moment. The love seat held. She raced to the bedroom.

Another blow to the door. She heard wood splintering.

She grabbed a towel, wrapped her hand and smashed the bedroom window. She scraped the shards away as best she could and boosted herself out. The window frame snagged her jeans. She heard the door tear away from its frame.

Adrenaline surged through her veins. She yanked at her jeans. The worn fabric ripped free.

His fingers closed around her foot. She kicked. Her heel drove into his face. He grunted and lost his grip. She rolled away from the window up onto her feet. Sheer fear drove her out the back gate past a white van. She raced down the alley. She was nearly at its mouth when she heard him behind her, his feet pounding in the loose gravel.

CHAPTER 25

Joe's head was buzzing after seeing the Eberhards. He drove back to Karin's house reeling from what Edward Eberhard had told him, and thinking maybe he knew now why Karin had moved so many times. The Eberhards clearly still blamed her for Nicole's disappearance. It was a wonder she even went by there. She must be truly desperate, as desperate as he was feeling right now at the thought that Haley had been kidnapped just like Nicole. Amazing, how he could feel so devastated over this child he'd never laid eyes on, hadn't even known of until four days ago.

He turned into the alley behind Karin's house. A white van blocked the way. He braked and started to back out.

A woman raced toward him, terrified. Karin!

Behind her, a man stepped into the alley, raised his arms and aimed a handgun at her.

Karin dashed past his window and threw herself behind his car just as a shot rang out. Joe ducked. He could just see through the rear window that Karin was safe, at least for the moment.

Joe popped up, saw the gunman fire again. Behind him, the windows of a car parked across the street exploded, sending glass crashing to the pavement.

Karin was still behind his car. He couldn't back up. He'd run over her.

What the hell was going on? This wasn't Caracas, crime

capital of the world. This was Ridgewood, Colorado. And someone was trying to kill Karin.

He risked a glance at the gunman and saw him dodge sideways into a yard.

Karin was up and running again, across the street now. Joe threw the car into reverse and peeled out of the alley. He stopped, thrust open the car door and chased after her on foot. "Karin, wait."

She stumbled and fell hard. He reached her side, pulled her to her feet and held her tight to him. "Run. To the car."

Her eyes round with surprise, she hesitated only a moment, then followed his direction. Once safe inside the car, he pulled her tight into his arms. The feel of her body, the scent of her hair, almost overwhelmed him. "Oh, my God, Karin. It's been so long."

At first she pulled away, murmuring, "Joe, so much has happened."

"Don't talk now, just let me hold you." A moment's hesitation, then she melted into his arms.

He glanced over her head. Down the alley, the van was moving. It could come around. *I could spend a lifetime holding her.* "We need to get out of here."

They drove several blocks before he pulled to the side of the street and parked. "Come here. Let me hold you just a little bit longer. Then we'll talk."

"Oh, Joe." She reached for him.

A few minutes later, he said, "What was that all about?"

She pulled away, shaking her head, facing away from him. "I found Kenny, my landlord, dead. Then this guy attacked me. I think he was the killer. I got away and ran . . ." Then her nerves took over and her teeth chattered so hard, she couldn't talk.

Joe pulled out his cell phone.

She grabbed his arm. "Wait, I'll call."

"You're in no shape to. We need to get an ambulance there."

"He doesn't need an ambulance. I know what dead looks like. He's dead."

"That man was trying to kill you."

A siren sounded in the distance.

"No!" She shook her head violently. "No! Joe, hear the siren? They've already been called. Some neighbor must have done it. Please, trust me on this."

Karin was shaking, he realized. Whatever was going on now, she was in very bad shape. Pale and sick-looking, with a reddened handprint on her cheek where the gunman had struck her. The sight made Joe want to find the guy and pound him, but right now he needed information. He figured he'd be more likely to get it if he slowed down. "Karin, I don't know what all is happening, but I know we have a child, Haley. Sam found me in Caracas and told me before he collapsed."

"Is he all right?"

"He's okay now. Haley is the one I want to hear about. Ed Eberhard said you accused them of taking her. Has she been kidnapped?" He started pressing in numbers. "You talk, I'll call the cops."

"No!" She grabbed at his hand, knocking the phone to the floor. "Don't call the cops. They'll hold me and I'll never find Haley."

"So she *has* been kidnapped."

Karin's face was twisted with grief so deep she couldn't cry. "I let her spend the night with Melanie, my friend, her sitter. When I went to get her this morning, the house where Mel lives was empty. Full of dust."

"Did you call the police then?"

"Of course! I thought maybe the furnace was bad and they were in there dying. So I broke a window and went in, but it was empty." Karin was panting so hard, she could hardly speak.

"The firemen came, the detective . . ." She gasped. "Joe, the house was empty. They *all* said it had *always* been empty." She grabbed his jacket. "They didn't believe me."

He took her hands in his. "Easy there. Just tell me what happened next."

She pulled a hand away and swiped at the hair falling into her eyes. "The detective said he had to have a picture of Haley to send out an Amber alert. The one in my wallet wasn't there, so I took him to my place and . . ." She gasped. "All Haley's stuff was gone. Every bit of it. Every picture. All her clothes. Even her toys." She sniffed. "And the detective looked at me like I was crazy. He didn't believe I even have a kid."

"*We* have a kid."

She shook her head, barely keeping back sobs. "Joe, this is all my fault. You should just go away while you can. This is a mess. And it's not your problem."

"The hell it isn't! Haley is my child, right?"

"Right. She is."

"Well, I don't know why you didn't tell me you were pregnant, but I do know now that Nicole was kidnapped and you were in a hell of a mess back then."

"They blamed me. And I was there. I slept all through it. But honest, that one wasn't my fault."

"I know. I know. Linda Eberhard told me someone confessed."

"They still blame me." She looked up at him with an expression of crushing desolation he'd never seen before.

"I know, but what's important now is to get Haley back. And to do that, we need to call the police."

"No, that's what I've been trying to say." She put her hands on either side of his face, her gaze boring into his. "At first, Detective Jansen didn't realize I was connected to Nicole's kidnapping, because I changed my name. But now he does.

And if you call them, he'll keep me and question me about Nicole, because he doesn't believe I have a kid. I couldn't prove it to him."

"Okay, slow down. Honey, I found a picture of Haley at Sam's apartment. That's where I'm staying. So we can call the police now. Karin, they can help. We can't do this by ourselves."

"No. No. No. They'll hold me. And I know who took her. I do. The same people who took Nicole, took Haley. I know, because they left Nicole's sweater. It was supposed to trap me, and the police were supposed to recognize it, but the detective didn't and I got away. But if you call them, they're going to put me behind bars. And Haley will never be found. Just like Nicole was never found."

She was close to hysterics. Almost screaming. If he called the police now, and if she was right and they held her, he knew she'd never forgive him. And he'd never forgive himself if Haley was lost forever.

Joe brushed her cheek with his finger. She was so pale, so shaky. "Okay. Take it easy. Let's do this. We'll go to Sam's place. You can get some food in you. We'll get the picture and we'll make a plan."

She felt on the floor until she found the phone. "Okay, I'll hold the phone."

"No." He took it from her. "I won't call, but I keep my phone." He started the engine and pulled out. "You have to trust me, Karin."

"I did, once."

He steered into a side street as a squad car raced past. "That's not fair. I wrote you. I tried to contact you. I even went on the Internet. You just evaporated. I don't know how, but you did."

"I didn't get any letters."

"I know. Linda Eberhard destroyed them." He hesitated, then said, "I waited for you last night."

She sighed. "Not my finest moment. I started to come inside, then I saw you were with someone, and at that point, I thought it was going to be some kind of social visit and decided that was no place to talk about, uh, everything. All the changes. So I left."

"I wasn't with anyone."

"It looked like you were. And I just wasn't up to making small talk. Too much has happened. I've been through too many changes."

"You were the dark-haired woman I saw outside."

She nodded without speaking.

"This morning I was going to just call it all a bad idea and then I saw the picture of you and Haley. So I rifled Sam's desk and found his address book and decided I'd go looking for answers. You weren't home, so I went to the Eberhards hoping they could tell me where to find you. And you're right. A lot has changed, we both have. But I wasn't with anyone. I was waiting to see you."

"Like I said, not my best moment."

He was hit with a terrible thought. "Did you leave Haley with the sitter to meet me?"

"No." She sighed and closed her eyes. "I left her because I was so tired from work and because Melanie begged to have her stay and I trusted Mel. She's the only person I allowed myself to trust, and I was so, so wrong."

"We'll get Haley back. We're almost at Sam's. Do you really believe the Eberhards are behind Haley's disappearance?"

"Ed would be capable of planning it, and they knew Melanie because she was his mother's nurse at Oak Manor. He got all pale when I showed him a photo that had her in it with them, but he never would have taken Nicole. He adored her. He was a wonderful father. He was really shaken about the sweater. I think he was just terrified to see me. They've got another child now, and I don't know, maybe he even still thinks I was part of Nicky's abduction."

Joe glanced at her. Her face was ashen. "Better stick your head down. You look like a ghost."

"I'm okay." Still, she put her head down. "After I left the Eberhards, I went to the nursing home and found their old employee files. The woman I talked to said Roger still works there. And he's a pilot. So I figure the two of them could plan to fly out of here."

And may have already, he thought with a shudder, but he said, "Why would they take Haley? Ransom? It's not as though you're wealthy." He pulled to the curb across the street from Sam's apartment.

Karin opened the car door. "I have no idea why. Just that Melanie always said she wanted lots of kids. Or maybe Ed just planted the idea in Mel's head."

"But why would her husband go along with that? It doesn't make sense." They mounted the steps to the old Victorian and Joe unlocked the door.

"It doesn't matter why. Haley's gone and Mel took her. I have to find Melanie. Every single minute counts if I'm going to get Haley back."

"We are going to get her back." But as much as Joe meant it, he hadn't a clue how they would do that. To him, it seemed the only chance they had of finding Haley was through the police, but it was clear Karin wouldn't be convinced. They climbed the stairs to the third floor where Joe unlocked and opened the door to Sam's attic apartment.

She crossed the room and sat heavily on Sam's ancient couch. "Could I have a drink of water or juice?" Her face had grown even paler than before. "I haven't eaten since this morning."

"I've got some juice and crackers." He also brought her a couple slices of bread and butter. She ate and drank slowly, as though she was trying to give herself time to think. Her hands still shook.

He sat down beside her on the couch and gently brushed the edge of the reddened handprint on her cheek. "That man, the one in your house, he hit you."

"It was an awful fight. I just barely got away by running downstairs and locking him out. I shoved the love seat against the door and crawled out a window." She looked at him with a crooked smile. "I'm getting good at running away."

"It's not funny. I'm thinking the man you were running from could be Melanie's husband."

She nodded. "I think so." She sagged against the couch back. "Who else could it be?"

She looked at Joe. The misery in her expression struck him like a punch in the gut, leaving him nearly speechless. His voice was a hoarse croak when he spoke. "He nearly killed you."

"Well, he sure has bad aim. He only got the windows in my car."

"And you got away." He didn't say it, but he thought, *how could that be*? She didn't have the strength to fight off a male. And, now that he thought about it, the shooter had shot at that car when he could have hit her as she ran.

"At first, I thought Kenny was asleep, maybe passed out, because there were a lot of beer bottles and cans in the trash barrel, but when I got close, shook his shoulder, I saw the blood. It was awful. So much blood." She glanced at her knee.

His gaze followed hers. Blood stained the torn knee of her jeans. This was deep, deep trouble.

She stared at him, eyes wide, lips bloodless. She looked like she was in shock. "You shouldn't have come. You should leave now, while you can."

The scent of her hair filled his nose and for a moment he flashed on the memory of those sunny days six years ago. How had so much changed? "Why didn't you tell me you were pregnant?"

"How could I?" She knotted her hands in her lap. "You had said more than once that you didn't want children. Still, I was going to tell you, but that day you had just heard about the job and I wasn't absolutely certain I was pregnant at the time. This was the job you wanted so badly. In Iraq with that company. Your big opportunity."

He stood. "Tell me about Haley."

"I don't know if I can," she said. She spoke haltingly at first, then words poured from her as she described Haley playing, learning, loving. "She's beautiful."

He examined the picture. "She looks like you, except for her hair."

She nodded, her hair falling forward over her face, revealing lighter roots. "I darkened mine."

All her moves, the changes of address in Sam's book, her dyed hair, all very clearly said, she'd been hiding. "You've been hiding because you've been terrified that Haley would be kidnapped, just like Nicole was."

"I know it sounds crazy, but Linda Eberhard threatened that if I ever had a child, she'd see to it that I suffered just like she did. I've told myself over and over that she was just ranting because she was so devastated, but all the same, I have lived with that nightmare." She looked up, her eyes wide and dark. "And now it's happened."

Joe reached for her, wrapping her gently in his arms. "We'll get her back. We'll make plans and we'll find her, but right now we need to tell that detective about Kenny."

She nodded. "I'll call. I'll talk to Jansen, I have his number, but I'm not telling him where I am. They'll just put me in jail."

Chapter 26

Jansen had waited until the forensic crew arrived at the Galt house, and then he started off toward Karin's apartment on a hunch that she would circle back to her home base.

As he drove he ruminated over the idea of Karin as accomplice versus Karin as mastermind of the Nicole Eberhard kidnapping. She intrigued him. She was smart, she was cunning, she was obsessed, she had to be. Whether or not she had a child, she herself had slipped through six years of life like a shadow, leaving almost no trace, which was nearly impossible with modern computer networks. How had she accomplished that?

Where had she come from? He had tried to place an accent when she spoke, but he couldn't detect one. No Southern softness, no Chicago twang, no Oklahoma slips, no Texas drawl, so she could be from the Midwest, or she could be from Colorado.

Obviously she had changed her name. Her age he guessed at thirty, maybe as low as twenty-eight. He hadn't picked up any signs of previous prison exposure. No jailhouse tattoos, no speech patterns from the cell house, no harshness from prison treatment, not even a hint of sociopathic slickness.

In fact, while he was talking to her at the Galt house, he'd been almost convinced she was telling the truth, that this Melanie had lived there, and she'd had coffee with her. And, the cinnamon detail had been really convincing. Of course, looking back, she could have put it there. She must have, in fact.

He'd called the home nursing service, and after some effort reached the owner and got confirmation that Karin had worked for them, was considered a very good worker, but the director had no information about a child. So she'd told the truth about her work, but she could be very good at fabricating, using truth to support her lies.

The more he thought about her, the more he was convinced she could have planned the earlier crime and now could be caught up in guilt. Something could have happened to trigger remorse over the kidnapping of little Nicole. Something which now was driving her to relive the crime, by claiming to have a child of her own. It was odd that she wasn't claiming a child of the same age as Nicole when she was kidnapped, two and a half. She was emphatic that this child was five and a half, not even as old as Nicole would be now.

Whatever had started this claim of a child, the whole thing was unusual, a confession of sorts. What if this wasn't the first time she claimed a child was missing, or for that matter, what if she was responsible for even more child abductions? He called in to Frost at headquarters. "Hey, look through other missing-child claims, go nationwide. We may be looking at the tip of an iceberg here."

Frost's voice was excited. "Holy shit, I'll get right on it. Do you know what this could mean?"

"Yeah, but keep in mind, this is all speculation."

"Sure."

"Seriously, Frost, this is all speculation. Not a single word to anyone. That could be devastating for the family and for finding that child."

"Right. I'm on it."

Jansen rang off, uneasy. As exciting as the prospect of wrapping up the Eberhard case was, it had to be handled carefully. And right now Frost sounded a bit over the top. That could mean mistakes. Frost was well meaning, but he had a tendency to go too fast and overlook things. If Jansen was right about Karin Preston, she would continue to escalate until someone or something stopped her. That meant he had to stop her before anything dire happened.

Jansen's cell phone buzzed. He peered at the screen, saw the caller ID and put the phone to his ear. "Where are you, Karin?"

"I just came from my house. I went to see Kenny Bristow, my landlord, but he was dead in the kitchen. And someone attacked me and tried to kill me." Her voice was shaky, almost a whisper, as though she was shocked, or frightened.

Jansen smacked the steering wheel with the heel of his palm. He was right about her, but she was escalating much faster than he'd anticipated. The question was, had she really killed someone, or was she imagining this, too? Jansen pulled out his backup cell, called headquarters and said softly, "Frost, get to Karin Preston's place." He left the line on the backup phone open so he could be heard. *Whatever I do,* he reminded himself, *make sure she thinks I believe her. Anything less and she'll think she has to do something even crazier to convince me.*

Into the cell with Karin he said, "What happened? Tell me everything, every detail you can remember."

"Kenny texted me, so I went home. I thought Kenny had decided to help me. He seems to know Melanie."

"I'm on my way to your place. Wait for me."

"I'm not there anymore."

"Where are you?"

"Forget that. Listen!" Her voice was stronger now, her breathing more even. "Half an hour ago, maybe an hour, I went into the upstairs apartment. Kenny was lying on a plastic tarp in the kitchen. I thought he was drunk, but then I saw all the blood. He was dead."

Jansen turned right at the corner. "Keep talking." Then,

reminding himself to be sympathetic, or sound like it, he added, "Are you okay?"

Silence, then, "Of course not. How okay can I be when my child has been kidnapped?" She was quiet for a moment, then said, "At first I thought he'd passed out. I knelt down. There's blood on my jeans. I think it's Kenny's. Then this guy grabbed me. I thought he'd kill me and I fought back. I finally got away from him, got down to my place and got out a window."

"Can you describe him?"

"He had on a mask." She paused, then said, "I think I scratched his face through it. And I bit his arm. Drew blood, even. He's tall, skinny."

"Eye color?"

"Blue, I think. Dark hair."

"Clothing description?"

"Jeans, black nylon jacket, boots. Black boots. They were muddy."

"Do you think this is tied in to your daughter?"

"Kenny saw Mellie there this morning. And he's just the kind of guy who would try to blackmail her."

Blackmail. That was a leap of logic. How did that come in, unless she had been blackmailed by this man and had killed him to silence him. Thoughts racing, he said, "Did he try to blackmail you, too?"

"No!" Her voice cracked. "I'm telling you exactly what happened."

Jansen doubted that. There was no way a slender woman such as Karin could get away from a man who was larger than she was, even a skinny guy. What had really happened and what was she imagining? "I'm trying to help you. I can't find your daughter unless you cooperate with me."

"I am cooperating! You don't even believe I have a daughter. Do you believe anything I've told you so far? If you really want to do something useful, put out an Amber alert on Haley and go into the upstairs apartment and find Kenny's body. Then maybe you'll believe me."

"Why didn't you tell me about Nicole Eberhard?"

She hesitated. Then, voice low and soft, she said, "I knew this would happen. I knew as soon as you stumbled onto Nicole, that's all you'd think about. That's what Melanie wanted, planned on. They figured you would get so excited about reopening Nicole's kidnapping and maybe finding her, that you would hold me, believing Haley doesn't exist. They'd have all the time in the world to get away." Her voice caught, then she continued softly, "I'm paying the price for keeping my child secret from everyone. Mellie played on that. My Haley has been kidnapped by the same people that kidnapped Nicole. I don't know why they took her, but Mellie's the criminal here. Not me. They murdered Kenny and they're trying to kill me. And I have to find Haley, before they kill her! Please believe me. Please help me."

"Wait, don't hang up."

But his screen showed the call ended. He felt ill. Her charge that they would focus entirely on the Eberhard abduction struck home. And if she was telling the truth, then another child was in the worst danger.

Jansen drove down the side street and spotted her car. Its front side windows were blown out in a pattern consistent with gunshot through the driver's side. She hadn't mentioned that. He pulled up in front of Karin's apartment house. The front door stood open, propped with a round stone.

Frost's patrol car rocked to a stop right behind Jansen's. The two ran to the house, mounted the porch and peered inside. No one.

Frost tried the upstairs inside front door. Locked.

Downstairs, the lightbulb was broken out. Jansen's flashlight illuminated Karin's door, splintered, broken inward. "She said she saw Kenny upstairs in the kitchen, dead. Says she was attacked there, fought back, ran down here, locked out her attacker and escaped through the window."

Frost peered down. "Think we need backup?"

"No. Better assume there may be someone injured inside."

Frost tried the doorknob. "Locked."

"Let's try the back," Jansen said. He pulled on gloves as he followed the footpath along the side of the house, noting the ragged weeds and then the broken glass from Karin's basement window. The shards lay in the dirt; the window had been broken from the inside out, not the outside in.

At the back of the house he stopped to examine the back porch steps. Turning toward the alley, he noted the grass on the edge of the narrow paved walk. It was crushed, as though something had been dragged over it recently. Something heavy.

He pointed it out to Frost, then tried the gate to the alley. "Unlatched. Possible blood smear here. And here's a bit of black plastic caught on a sliver at the side edge." He touched it. "It's heavier weight than the usual black plastic trash bag." Glancing at his fingers, he said, "No apparent blood."

Frost already stood on the steps to the back porch. "Porch is unlocked." He went in. "The house door is open," he called.

Inside, three beer bottles topped the trash barrel in the kitchen. The little breakfast table stood askew from the wall. "There's a dent in the wall there. Careful. A likely blood smear on the center floor. She could have wrapped him and dragged him out."

Jansen pulled out his cell phone and snapped pictures. They wouldn't do as evidence, but they were fine for his personal records.

In the living room, Jansen flipped on the light switch. Two thirds of the way to the front door, he saw a stain on the wooden floor. "Blood there."

"She said there'd be some. What do you think?"

"Looks like a smear stain, like someone slipped and dropped a knee in it."

Frost tucked his flashlight under his arm. "Doesn't mean she didn't slip, but maybe she slipped when she dragged him out. How big is this woman?"

Jansen frowned. "Not big enough to lift a dead man." He turned. "Notice something?"

"Not much. It's pretty clean in here."

Jansen pointed. "There're the paint cans. Paint roller and a roller pan. But no drop cloth or plastic sheeting."

Frost pulled out his cell phone. "She could have killed him on the plastic and dragged him out. Plastic slides pretty easy. I'll call for forensics."

"Yeah, and have them run a computer search on Kenny Bristow."

Downstairs Jansen pushed open the broken door to Karin's apartment and thrust his head inside. Karin's tattered love seat angled away. It could confirm forcible entry, certainly looked like it.

Frost at his side said, "She could have staged this. Anyone who pulled off the Eberhard kidnapping could plot all this with ease." He glanced around. "There never was a ransom note on that case. Maybe she just wanted a kid and then something went wrong and the child died. You're thinking that she might have taken some other kids too, right?"

"You're jumping way ahead. I'm just trying to cover all possibilities. Nothing is for sure yet. There's even a possibility she's telling the truth."

"Huh, not damn likely, is it? First there's a kid, then there's no evidence of a kid, now she reports a murder and there's no body. Just a few maybe-blood smears, and maybe a missing paint tarp."

"Don't jump to conclusions, dammit."

Frost shrugged. "If it looks like a duck."

"Just get some pictures with that phone of yours." Jansen played the beam around on the floor, letting it rest on a thick, iron crowbar lying against the far wall, as though flung there. He moved forward, flashing the beam ahead. *She did have time,* he thought. *She could have staged all this before she went to the Galt house.* All the same, he too took pictures.

Frost whistled. "Forensics will be up all night here. They're not gonna be happy."

Jansen examined the room before moving farther in. "No overturned furniture, don't see blood on the carpet. Other than the door and the misplaced love seat and those papers on the floor, there's not much sign of a struggle."

Stepping carefully, Jansen moved across the floor to the bedroom. This door also was smashed, then shoved aside to allow entry, as the front door had been, only this time her dresser had been used to block the door. Or at least it appeared that way.

"Seems she went out the window all right," Frost said.

Jansen scrutinized the carpet. Thin, worn, with no pad and no apparent blood. He stooped to feel it. Dry. No chemical scent, no cleaner. He crossed the room to the little window she had broken out when she left her house. Large shards of glass lay outside on the ground. Smaller bits were scattered inside on the floor. He stepped closer. Several threads adhered to the side of the window as though Karin's jeans had snagged as she crawled out.

Frost stretched his back. "Frankly, I don't buy all this. I mean, how could she get away from her attacker? If he'd just killed a guy, wouldn't he just kill her right off? All this drama . . . I think she staged it."

Jansen drew a deep breath. "There's another possibility. Suppose the rest of the people involved in the Eberhard kidnapping found out she's talking to us. What do you think they'd do?"

"I'd say they'd do their level best to shut her down, any way they could." Frost glanced around. "Maybe she'll do us a favor. Draw them all out into the open."

CHAPTER 27

Mel rocked slowly back and forth in the rocker, liking the sound of the creaking. She was exhausted and rested her head on the musty old head cushion. The only other sound in the cabin was the soft slumbering noises of the girls nestled on the couch. Both of them had been upset with the move. She had spent at least an hour rocking them both and had barely been able to get a breath for their weight on her lap.

She smiled at the thought. It felt so good to have two little children in her lap. The smell of their hair after their bath and shampoo was sweeter than any perfume she ever smelled. At one time she had wanted a whole bunch of children. Now if she could just have these two and Donny, or at least see Donny and hold him, she would be happy. To do that, she had to keep Haley healthy and happy. Kids who weren't happy got sick. She knew it from experience.

If only Haley wouldn't keep asking for Karin. She would sit so quiet, looking at her little hands, twisting her fingers, then all of a sudden there'd be tears streaming down her cheeks and she'd ask for Mommy. "Your mommy's at work, hon. She'll come tomorrow, I think. You be brave," Mel would say, but the tears kept coming.

Her cell phone buzzed. She'd turned it to vibrate so the ring wouldn't wake the girls. "Yes?"

She recognized Zeb's hoarse voice immediately and asked, "How's Donny?"

"He's not so good, but holding. Did you get everything?"

"Yes. Haley's here. Sleeping. For a five-year-old, Haley sure is a determined little thing. She wasn't even comforted by her toys. Real stubborn. And quick."

He laughed.

Mel felt a pang of resentment. He thought it was funny. "She's smart like her mother. She wouldn't take the grape juice with the sleeping medicine in it after one little sip. Like she knew something was in it. I had to put it into a milkshake to get it in her."

"You be careful. That girl has to be in tip-top shape. Can't risk anything."

"I know. But you remember your promise. I get to see Donny again. Hold him. Talk to him. Regularly, right?"

"You do your part, I'll do mine."

"But Donny's okay, right?"

"He's holding."

She rang off and tiptoed into the bedroom to check on the sleeping girls.

Jen was flat out, her hair shining in the moonlight that streaked in the window. Haley was curled up, her little fist in her mouth. Mellie frowned. It wasn't good to keep using sleeping medicine on her. She'd have to think of something else soon.

Her breath quickened at the thought Haley might have caught cold, but she seemed better now. Her breath came and went clear, no sound of sniffles or coughing.

Mel pulled on a sweatshirt and went back out to the rocker in the living room. The gentle back and forth motion calmed her.

Headlights turned into the upper lane from the highway. Roger, coming home finally. She was glad Roger would be home, even though he was jumpy and that always made him harsh, even angry. Her mind was too busy to sleep and her nerves felt like they'd been peeled raw. She wanted company.

In the living room she waited for him with lights turned real low and the curtains drawn shut. At least Roger had put in dimmer switches so she could have a little light. In daytime she didn't have to always keep the windows covered. There wasn't a soul around to see in here, but at night the light could be seen for miles. Roger said so.

"Hey babe," she called out softly as soon as she heard Roger on the porch steps.

He came in, his shoulders drooping. Even his voice sounded tired. "Hey. Girls asleep?"

"Yeah, took a while. Haley acts like she knows what's up. Makes my skin shivery."

"She doesn't know. You don't need to worry about that kind of stuff."

"You should see the way she looks at me now. Like she can see inside my brain or something."

He dropped onto the couch, stretching out his legs. "Don't worry about it."

Mel sat down beside him, nestling under his arm, feeling the beat of his heart. Regular. Comforting. She looked up at his face and frowned. "You got a nasty scratch on your cheek, right there, so close to your eye." She examined the mark on the side of his face. "Where'd you get that?"

She started to touch it, but he brushed her hand aside. "It's nothing." He ran a hand over his face. "You look like you're at a funeral or something. Cheer up. You're bringing me down."

She tried to smile, but now her heart felt heavy. "I know we had to do this, but I don't feel good about it. I know I should. But if someone were to take Jen, I'd be wiped out. So I know Karin feels . . ." She didn't want to say *desperate,* so she hesitated then finished with ". . . bad. She'd feel real bad."

She also didn't say she wished she could've left a note for Karin to explain why this had to happen. Of course Karin would still be upset.

Mel thought about the little bit of blue glass she'd kicked into the corner of the garage. She shouldn't have left it. Karin might find it and think she, Mellie, broke the bottle on purpose. At the time she'd thought it might be a sort of sign of apology, but it was a mistake. Of course it didn't matter anymore after everything she'd done, taking Haley and all, but the thoughts kept twisting around in her mind until her stomach cramped and she wanted to let out the worry by talking about it. But she couldn't talk to Roger about that. He'd come apart. It would mean an hour lecture on being careful, not getting caught, going to jail, and on and on. All the stuff that made her really sick to think about. She looked at Roger. "We have to do it."

"Yeah, well, we're not turning back. You wanted this, you got it."

"I know, Rog." She hesitated then asked, "Did you see Kenny?"

He was quiet for several minutes, then stretched his arms overhead. "Had, uh, a little meeting with him. Karin went to the nursing home this noon. Any idea why she'd do that?"

Mel frowned. She sensed Roger had skipped topics too fast, but she didn't want to interrupt for fear he'd just say "never mind" and go all huffy and silent. So she said, "What'd Karin do there?"

"I'd just parked and was going to take a quick nap in the back of the pick-up van—"

"No! Not on that cot!"

"It's clean. Selma came out for a smoke and right after her Karin came out. That's how I know she was there." Roger got up and went to the kitchen. Mellie heard him pop a beer.

Now she wondered, how did Karin get away from the police?

She could barely keep from asking, but she knew she couldn't and bit her lip until Roger came in, leaned against the wall and took a long draw on the beer.

Selma, Mel thought. *How'd Karin think to go to the nursing home and find Selma?* Had she mentioned Selma? No, she didn't think so. "So, could you hear what Selma said?"

He nodded. "Said you were a bitch."

"The old cow! Selma couldn't keep her mouth shut if it was sewn that way. No wonder her girl lit out all the time, with Selma sour as poison. Did you talk to her?"

Roger looked at her funny. Sometimes he got this expression like he was thinking, *Is she nuts or what?* Only he never said anything. He just drank his beer.

"Well, Selma's got a mouth on her. You think she'll figure out something?"

"No."

"But you talked to her?"

"I went to find her, but she was gone. Went by her house a couple times, but no one was there. I figure I'll find her tomorrow."

"You'll talk to her, right?"

That look crossed his face again, then he said, "Kenny's more of a problem than Selma. Seems you made an impression on him."

An uneasy coil tightened in Mellie's stomach. "What're you talking about?"

Roger straightened. "I'm talking about Kenny knowing you and calling up and threatening to talk to the police if he didn't get a bit of the money he figured was coming our way."

The nasty feeling came again, like a poisonous snake in her belly, winding up to strike. "What are you going to do?"

"Nothing, now."

"But what if . . ."

"He won't."

Pain struck her stomach. "Rog, what have you done?"

Chapter 28

Roger brushed Mellie's hand away. What did the woman need? A road map? A written confession? Of course he'd done stuff. And he'd been helping a few of those old folks at the nursing home along their path, too, but Mellie didn't know about that. Or his extra cash in the box down in the basement. She didn't know about all the little extras he'd done, like whacking Johnny Ray and making it look like a fall, then telling Doc Wetford that Johnny Ray'd be a good rehab candidate. Even Wetford didn't seem to notice. Like Mellie, the doc didn't want to know.

Roger felt like he was going to explode, but he had to keep that kind of stuff inside. "Mellie, nothing's easy. You can't get a kid like you're shopping at some big box store."

"Yeah, but . . ." Mellie sucked in a deep breath, then let it out with a shudder. "I just didn't think it would be like this."

"What do you mean? What did you think?"

Mellie blinked. Her mouth opened and her lips worked but no words came out. He didn't like it when she acted scared of him, but how the hell could she act so . . . so fuckin' dumb sometimes? She did this same damn thing over that house-painter when they took Nicole. Looked all shocked and stupid when she knew exactly what was going to go down. Pissed him off.

She lived in this fantasy world all the time, like she was some kind of innocent kid and didn't think evil, but she sure as hell could think up things when she chose. For God's sake she planned this whole thing, or said she did.

He always sort of wondered about that. Like, she wasn't any mental giant, but she came up with all this stuff. She was making him mad, and he worked to calm himself, otherwise he might just say more than he should. Better she didn't really know everything. He had to shut her up. Do something that would put it back on her. "We're doing this for you, babe. You wanted it."

"I know. I need it for Donny."

"Right. And you remember that while people want what I do, they don't like to think about it. You know that."

"Yeah, but Karin—"

"But nothing!"

"But we planned to frame it so Karin would be held for questioning, maybe a day or two. Like happened with Nicole. I figured she'd fold like last time. I didn't plan on her snooping around." Mellie turned to him, her eyes wild. "Karin's all right, isn't she? You said she'd be all right."

"She's okay."

"She's really okay, right? We've got to keep her alive, you know. In case."

"I know."

He could barely keep his stomach from jumping when he thought about how close he'd come to killing her. He had only wanted to rough her up, scare her. Then he near killed her 'cause she went ape on him. Who'd have thought she could fight that well.

"Rog?"

"Yeah?"

"Do you remember that old lady lived on the corner from us? I've been worrying—"

"What?"

"You think she knows anything?"

Roger's gut tightened. He'd spaced out about the old woman completely. He looked at Mellie, her pale face, her worried mouth. For someone who couldn't stand to know any of the grim details, she sure had a way of bringing up things that had to be taken care of. "Why'd you ask?"

"Just thinking."

Dammit. She was doing it again. Coming up with stuff. Stuff for him to take care of. Problems for him to solve. That was the real trouble. Mellie was thinking. "Mellie, damn, don't think anymore. Talk about something else."

Get her busy so she wouldn't ask any awkward questions. She could get squeamish, no matter how bad she wanted this. "Get me a sandwich, will you? And another beer."

He watched her walk to the kitchen, head down, still thinking. Get her talking about the kid. She could go for hours. "Hey, talk to me, tell me about how Jen's doing."

It worked. She started in and he tuned out. Some people needed white noise, he just needed Mellie yapping on and he could begin to think. He stretched. His shoulders ached, his back hurt. Tomorrow. He'd take care of that one hanging thread. If Mellie hadn't mentioned the old woman, he'd have forgotten all about her.

This job was a mess. Nothing going right.

At least the Kenny problem had been fixed and he'd make some cash off him and off that Johnny Ray kid. Enough to leave this place and retire. Mexico. The beaches. No—Brazil, no extradition.

Karin was something else. Tougher than he'd expected. Six years ago she'd been a mouse, this time a rat. Sniffing after him every step of the way. He hadn't planned on that, either. What he had to do was figure out where she'd go next. And if she didn't stop getting in the way, he'd fix her too, even if they had said not to. Screw them and their "insurance."

He wasn't doing time for this. All he had to do was this last job and collect the money and they'd retire. He hadn't told Mellie yet, but she'd go along. She had to. Forget Donny. That kid wasn't his, was it?

He heard Mellie go down the hall to the bedroom to check on the girls, then come back fast.

"Roger, she's running a fever! I thought she was just sleeping, but I can't wake her up."

"Give her an aspirin, she'll be okay. Jen's a tough kid."

"It's not Jen, it's Haley!"

Chapter 29

Karin felt her strength beginning to return. She watched Joe pace the floor of Sam's little apartment. One emotion after another had crossed his face as he tried to understand all that had happened in his absence.

"So Melanie and her husband have taken two kids." He paced the floor. "If they would take two, they may have taken more."

"Oh, my God."

He stopped, struck by an idea. "Is there any chance that her child, Jennifer, is really Nicole?"

"No, Jen's only five, and Nicole would be almost nine now," Karin said, shaking her head. "Also, Nicole had very unusual violet blue eyes and dark hair. Jen's eyes are pretty, but they're light blue. And she's a natural blonde."

"Hair color can change."

"Eyes can't."

Joe started pacing again. "What's the chance that Jennifer is a kidnapped child? What if Mel took Jennifer too? Maybe she took Nicole and something went bad. Then she took Jennifer, too? Maybe she collects kids."

"Stop! We can't start imagining all kinds of horrors or I'll go off the deep end. We have to focus on getting Haley back."

She was right. He opened Sam's desk, got a pen and a pad of paper and said, "Write down everything you remember from Melanie's personnel file and anything else you can think of that maybe she mentioned about places. Places she either lived or worked. And then a listing of everything she said about her husband. Where he worked, what he does. That sort of thing. While you're doing that, I'm going for food. You're still white as a ghost and shaking. Once you have food inside you, you'll have the strength to help me find Haley. And the listing will help with making plans. We can divide up the tasks."

She started to protest, then said, "There's a Thai place down a block." She looked blankly at him for a second, then she realized she was starving and said, "Green curry with shrimp and fried rice."

"I saw the place." He grabbed his jacket, stopping in front of her to shrug it on. "Don't let anyone in while I'm out. Whoever attacked you is still out there. And I don't want anything to happen to you."

His hurried footsteps echoed as he ran down the stairs.

As soon as she heard the downstairs front door slam shut, Karin went to the front window where she could look out on the street. She watched Joe's easy, muscular stride as he turned down the sidewalk toward Colfax and the Thai restaurant. As she was about to turn away to start working on the list, she saw a man step out of a parked car and approach Joe. Joe waved him off and started to walk again, only to have the man reach for him.

Worried, Karin watched. Joe, shaking his head, pulled away from the fellow. Then they both turned and Karin got a glimpse of the stranger's face. She gasped. She knew him all too well. He was one of the policemen who had tried to build a case against her six years ago. Officer Frost.

Her phone rang. She pulled it out. Joe. His voice, loud and insistent, came through clearly. "She's not up there. I don't know where she is."

Below she saw Joe, the phone in his hand, not at his ear. He was trying to warn her.

Frost's voice, "Let's go see."

"Do you have a search warrant?"

She saw Frost slap a paper into Joe's hand.

They were going to come upstairs. Karin's head felt light. She glanced around the stark little apartment. Her jacket lay on the couch. Joe's car keys were on the kitchenette countertop beside a folded newspaper.

Desperate, she threw on her jacket, took the car keys and ran to the back window where an old wooden fire escape barely clung to the side of the house. It led down to the yard behind.

She tugged at the window. It was painted shut.

The downstairs front door slammed. Joe. Again, trying to warn her.

She heard their heavy tread start up the stairs.

Grabbing a knife from the kitchenette, she ran to the window and jammed it into the cracks of the sash, cutting and prying to loosen the dried paint. The paint popped, allowing her to shove the window up.

She crawled out, then pulled the curtain partially across and pushed the window back down as best she could. It stuck, leaving a half-inch gap. There was no time to work for more.

She slipped and slid down the old staircase, hearing the ancient weathered wood creak and groan with each step. With her every movement the fire escape groaned and bumped against the side of the house.

The last eight steps stopped about six feet above ground level. She dropped. The jolt of hitting ground ran up her spine. She shook herself and ran across the street to Joe's car, praying Joe would keep Frost busy and away from the window.

The remote unlocked the car, and she slid in and keyed the ignition. As she pulled away, she glanced up at Sam's window. Frost's nose was flat against the pane. He was yelling, and she thought she knew what he was saying. Still, she smiled.

Joe had warned her. He must believe in her. She was no longer entirely alone.

Chapter 30

Joe had stalled as best he could, hoping Karin would have time to get out onto the fire escape. Then he'd hoped the old half-rotted wood frame wouldn't collapse under her weight.

Once inside the apartment, Joe stood in front of Sam's desk and palmed the photo of Karin and Haley. He had no doubt the detective would take it as soon as he saw it. He knew now just why Karin was so paranoid about the police. Detective Frost had clearly decided Karin was his ticket to a promotion. He had nearly said as much outside.

From downstairs on the street they heard the roar of a car engine.

Frost ran to the front window and yelled, "You fucking let her get away." Furious, he spun away from the window and glared at Joe. "You'll pay for this, asswipe. I'm arresting you for obstruction of justice." Frost's face was reddened and blotchy from anger, his voice harsh as though choking on each word. "I'll need to see that passport of yours, too. So you'd better get that out, bud."

"I think I put it in the desk." Joe shuffled things on the desktop, then said, "No, I guess it's in the suitcase." He crossed to his duffle and slipped the photo deep inside the folds of his clothing as he lifted out his passport and handed it to Frost.

Frost flipped through the pages, squinting at different stamps, scowling at the fine print. He slapped it into Joe's hand and snarled, "Bring it along. You'll need it for identification."

The detective stomped across the room to the closet, yanked open the door and peered inside. He checked the bathroom next, then came back into the main room and caught sight of the back window. He pointed at the open half inch. "Well, well, look at this, Sherlock. She went out the window. Bet you're surprised."

Joe shrugged. "I opened it this morning. It's an attic apartment. Gets hot up here."

"Look, asshole, you seem to think this is some kind of joke. But your little friend is mixed up in all kinds of trouble." Frost bunched his fist and smacked it into his palm.

Joe despised men like Frost, men who used their supposed authority to intimidate and bully. Frost was not a tall man, but he had thick shoulders and obvious trouble holding his temper. It wasn't hard to see how a young, frightened Karin would have been intimidated six years ago by his manner.

Joe stepped back, wondering how much information he could get from Frost. "You have some reason to be on her case?"

Frost flexed his biceps, visible even under his sports jacket. "Bet your life I do. You ever heard of the Eberhard kidnapping?"

"I've been out of the country."

Frost moved to Sam's desk and stirred the contents of the pencil drawer. Joe had left it open, hoping Frost would be distracted by it. "See, that was six years ago, maybe six and a half. I was on that investigation. That friend of yours was the kid's nanny and she claimed to be drugged. Way I figure it is, she drugged herself, so the kidnapper could get in and take the kid."

Joe wondered just how talkative this detective might be. The guy seemed like the kind of blowhard who enjoyed shooting off his mouth. Joe did his best to sound intrigued, draw him out. "So she didn't take the kid herself."

"Not herself. This painter had been there a couple days before. He blew himself away, leaving a note that said he did it. But I always figured she was in on it. You could tell. First off, she was too upset. I mean, who gets that upset about someone else's kid? Then she just sat like a rock and wouldn't talk. I figure there was more than just her and the painter. We didn't find any link between them, but . . ." He trailed off with a shrug.

"But she wasn't charged."

"I told the DA she was guilty as sin, but he wouldn't make a case after the confession letter."

"If there wasn't a link before, what makes you think she's guilty?"

"I said we couldn't find the link, couldn't prove it."

Joe hoped to goad him into more talk. "Maybe it's not there at all."

"Oh, there's links there. She's guilty and I'm going to prove it. You'd better wise up. See, today she calls and says a kid was kidnapped out of this house that's been empty since the owner went into a nursing home and died. Same nursing home old Mrs. Eberhard was in before she died. And your friend Karin is a home health aide and has been at that nursing home to see people. See all the connections? That's when you know something's going on." Frost shut the pencil drawer, opened the side drawer and rifled through the papers.

"You were the lead detective on the case back in the day?"

Frost laughed. "I was in on it from the beginning."

"So you found the child's body?"

"That's what I figure we're gonna find. The way I see this is, she was never the only other one in on the snatch. But she's the weak link. See, she called in a kidnapping today and there's no kid. Then she called in a murder and there's no body again. So, what do you think that means?"

He said it like he already knew the answer, but Joe replied

anyway. "I think it means someone took the body away."

"That's one possibility. But I don't think so. I think she's feeling so guilty about that old kidnapping, she's breaking down. She's acting the whole thing out again."

"And this is going to lead you to what?"

"The rest of the gang. She's the bait. The others'll need to stop her. We'll get them all."

"That's pretty complicated. I thought crazy people had trouble doing complicated things."

"This woman is smart crazy. She'd have to be to plan that Eberhard nab."

"There must have been a ransom for the Eberhard kid."

"Painter killed himself before he got to it."

"And he never said anything about where the kid was?"

"Nope. He was real vague in the letter. Not too smart, if you know what I mean."

"Yeah, guess I do. You saw the letter?"

"In a manner of speaking. His writing wasn't too good." Frost turned away from his search of Sam's desk. "I figure she's going to lead me right to the whole nest of them. Let's go."

"Are you really arresting me?"

Frost flexed his shoulder muscles. "Obstruction of justice, boyo."

Chapter 31

Jansen, relieved that Frost was finally somewhere else, was in the apartment above Karin's place waiting for the crew to finish their evidence collecting. They had completed photographing and were working the blood evidence and some smears on the steps leading out the back of the house. Jansen waited until one of the crew straightened. "What do you have?"

"We got blood spatter on the wall, real fine spray. And a bit on the floor but it looks like someone tried to clean that up. Couldn't really say there was a murder here. That bottle, if it had been mostly full, would have been a pretty lethal weapon, but it's been wiped. I think we'll get some blood off it at the lab, but out here, can't see much. There's beer sprayed around, you can still sort of smell it.

"There's blood in the living room, a smear like someone fell or slipped on it. Can't tell. If there was a vic, he was probably wrapped in plastic, or on a plastic sheet, could be the painting tarp, 'cause there isn't one here and there would have been one. We found some of it caught on the back gate and a small piece in the alleyway. Vic could've been wrapped and dragged out, put into a vehicle and taken away."

"Can you tell how long ago?"

"Nah," the tech said, and shrugged. "There's a smaller footprint in the living room. Woman-sized. Too small, I'd say, to be able to drag a body to the alley and boost it into a trunk or truck bed." He rubbed his face. "You find out who owns this dump?"

"Belongs to a Kenny and Marva Bristow." His cell phone rang, and he answered it.

Frost's voice came through, loud and proud. "I got a Mr. Joseph Canan cooling off in the holding cell here. He obstructed me getting Karin Preston. Thought you'd want to know."

Jansen caught himself shaking his head and turned away from the technician. Frost's thoughtlessness could screw the whole case. "What did he do?"

"He stalled around and let her get out the window. I think he warned her some way."

"Well, treat him decent, just get the basic information and keep him until I get there. I'm going to run by Bristow's, then I'll be in."

"Right. Got it."

"Don't let him pump you for information."

"Trust me. Never."

"See if you can get him to let you record the interview."

"Good idea."

Jansen knocked on the door of the Bristow home at seven o'clock that evening. Marva Bristow greeted him at the door, wrapped in a worn, green chenille robe that struggled to contain her bulk. The robe was tight enough that the ribs in the fabric stuck out, making her look like a large, green tomato worm.

As Jansen identified himself, he noticed she held a large wrench down at her side and shuddered inwardly. Whatever would lure Kenny home to that?

"I heard you on the porch, I thought maybe you was Kenny," she said and stepped back to let Jansen in.

"We're still looking for him. You haven't heard from him?"

"No, but I'll bet I will tomorrow." Scotch whiskey fumes

emanated from her. "He'll be in jail somewhere sleeping it off. He's got a problem with beer. Have a seat." She waved at a couch along the far wall, then dropped her considerable weight into a sagging chair.

"Thanks." Jansen sat and pulled out his pad. "You say he has a drinking problem?"

"Tries to stay off it, but falls now and then. Then I have to bail him out. Used to think he'd get over it, but I've pretty much given up on that idea. He's just a binger, that's what." She laid the wrench on the end table and picked up a smudged glass. "Would you like a drink?"

"No thanks, ma'am. Still on duty. You told the officer when you called in that Kenny usually does his drinking at Willie's Bar. Do you know if he ever goes to the foothills, to a place called Moose Lake Bar and Grill in Moose Lake?"

She chewed on her lip. "Don't remember anything like that. He don't drive too much anymore. Not too far, I mean." She looked uncomfortable and busied herself with a large slurp of scotch.

Jansen made a note to check on Kenny's driver's license status.

He left Marva a short time later, none the wiser about what had happened to Kenny Bristow. Back at the station, Jansen found Joe Canan comfortably settled in the smaller interviewing room. A quick replay of Frost's recorded interview made it very clear that Joe had nicely controlled the whole thing and now knew everything they knew about the Eberhard case and Karin Preston's call to the station. Worst of all, Frost didn't have the least idea he'd been played. No wonder the original case was never solved. Frost alone could have screwed it by the same need to talk and make himself important. Jansen looked out into the main room where Frost was blabbing to the girl at the desk, getting way ahead of the facts. Some day that man would get into real trouble. "Frost!"

He came in as Jansen was turning off the tape. "What do you think of the interview?"

Jansen tamped down his irritation. "I think Joe Canan ran the interview. Did he give you any trouble about the recording?"

"Nah, easy."

"Did he ask for a lawyer?"

"Started to, then said he'd wait to see you first."

Jansen worked to control his anger. Of course Joe Canan waited to see him. Frost went on a talking jag and no doubt Canan decided to assess the strength of the police work.

Frost threw himself into his desk chair and put his feet up on a pulled-out drawer. Jansen, barely able to keep from kicking the man's feet down, asked, "Did you get Mr. Canan's passport?"

"Yep." Frost tossed it across the desk to Jansen, who flipped the pages.

"It says here he left the country before the Eberhard kidnapping."

Frost nodded. "Yeah, but he came back yesterday afternoon."

"Yes. So what are you thinking?"

"I'm thinking he came back to shut her up. Didn't want her to squeal to us."

Jansen drew in a long breath, calling on all his patience. "And how did he obstruct?"

"He walked real slow, fumbled his key in the door and made a lot of noise so she'd know we were coming and go out the window of the apartment."

"Did you see him signal her?"

"No. But he made noise."

"Did he call to her?"

"No."

Exasperated, Jansen blurted, "What were you thinking?"

Frost sat up, indignant. "I think I just got one of the gang. He helped her get away."

"Well, I think you brought in the only person who couldn't be a part of the crime. We've got to kick him loose. We can't arrest on obstruction because he made noise."

"But he's smart. He still helped her get away. We're talking the Eberhard case. We could be finding this kid's body."

"We can't arrest him because he's smart."

Frost smacked his fist into his palm. "That's the trouble with justice."

Monday morning, Jansen woke early, his sleep troubled by images of a dark-haired little girl. The Nicole Eberhard kidnapping had brought back his loss six years ago.

As he sat in the kitchen with a glass of warm milk, he realized again the loss of his family had left him sensitive to child cases. The Nicole Eberhard case especially, because it had occurred while he was still hospitalized after his horrific accident. He wanted that poor child found and everyone who helped in that horrible job proven guilty. And he wanted it proven beyond any doubt. No one, he promised himself, no one would walk away from this one. Around five a.m., Jansen gave up on sleep, showered and ate. The possibility of solving the Nicole Eberhard case made his blood race. If he could just keep the reins on Frost.

When he arrived at headquarters, Frost was at his desk, trying to locate Karin's brother, Sam McGrath. Coffee in one hand, phone perched on his shoulder, Frost waved and hung up as Jansen lowered himself into his chair. "Got something for you. That business card you brought in? My buddy, the data miner, didn't find anything for Melanie Allen but did find tax records for Melodie Alwyn, licensed surgical technician. She worked at Oak Manor Life Center seven years ago. She seemed to drop out after that, but she exists."

Uneasy, Jansen scratched his chin. One more thing in the short list of things Karin had claimed were true that now checked out. "I suppose Karin could have picked the name up when she was visiting one of her patients."

Frost nodded agreement. "Also, I've checked with Mrs. Bristow. Kenny still isn't home. Now she's sure something dire happened to him. So I've got another idea."

Jansen looked at him. "Of course you do."

Undeterred, Frost continued. "Karin told the truth, partly. Kenny attacked her and she fought back and injured him. In which case, maybe Kenny's still alive somewhere, hurt and afraid to go home."

"Why wouldn't he go home?" Jansen asked, and then pictured Mrs. Bristow with her scotch and her wrench. Stupid question.

Frost shrugged. "Mrs. seems to suspect he was having an affair. In fact, Mrs. Bristow says she'll kill him when he gets home."

"Did you tell her we were concerned and found traces of blood at that place they own?"

"Just said we were concerned." Frost slurped his coffee. "I placed calls to all the area hospitals, they haven't seen him."

Jansen picked up a complaint form lying on his desk and eyeballed it. "Did you see this?"

Frost shook his head. "I don't read your mail."

Yes you do, you just overlooked this one, Jansen thought, but he said, "It's a complaint about Oak Manor Life Center. This woman claims the nursing home is killing people. They go there. They die. No one comes out alive, she says."

"Yeah, well, it is a nursing home. Ethan Morgan is getting a citizenship award today for running a first-class place, or maybe it was yesterday, I don't remember. Something like that always brings out the loonies."

"The complaint's from an Emma Wilson." Jansen flipped through his notebook. "Emma Wilson's a neighbor to the Galt house, where Karin Preston says her kid was stolen." Jansen looked up. "You talked to her yesterday, didn't you?"

Frost leaned back, grinning. "Yeah, but she can't see very well and is so deaf, I don't think she heard a word I said. I told her we were looking into a missing-child complaint. She ranted on about kids taken by perverts who have been made crazy by the chlorine in our drinking water. Said it's a communist plot." Frost reached toward Jansen. "Give it to me. I'll run by Oak Manor, check out Preston's claim about files on this Allen babe, have a laugh about old Mrs. Wilson's complaint with Ethan Morgan and then I'll go reassure the old gal."

Frost made it all sound like a joke, but Jansen sensed it was Frost's way of trying to take a load off him. A pity offer, because he thought Jansen would have trouble handling a nursing home after his accident and rehab years ago. Jansen hated when Frost did that. Besides, if Frost didn't listen to this woman before, he wasn't likely to listen this time. "Nah, I can do it. I want to find out why a surgical tech would work in a nursing home." He tossed the rest of his messages on his desk. "I put in a call to Missouri and Kansas vital statistics and human services, just for good measure. They should be getting back to us this morning. Call me when you hear."

Frost nodded. "Two to one they won't have a thing on Karin Preston. I'll bet she's an alias queen with an AKA listing two pages long. I'll call Judge Hitchcock and start a warrant on her."

Jansen rose and had started out when the phone rang. It was Missouri vital statistics. He jammed the phone against his ear to cut out the surrounding noise of the office. Finally he would get some hard answers. Missouri would absolutely confirm that there was no Haley Preston.

The feminine voice at the end of the line was breathy and measured. Careful. "I think I found what you're looking for, Detective Jansen. A midwife report. A child born at home five years and two months ago to a Karin P. McGrath. Baby was a female, five pounds five ounces, healthy. Is that what you wanted?"

His heart hammered in his chest. Karin Preston hadn't lied. He didn't want to hear there was a child. It threw all his theories into chaos. "Does it give the mother's address?"

"Um, yes, here it is. The Lively Inn. You know, that's a motel in a pretty raunchy area of Saint Louis. I think it burned down a couple years ago. Or maybe it was torn down. But in any case, it isn't there anymore."

"Is there a father listed?"

"That line is blank. We try not to allow blanks but there's a notation here that when the officer went out to confirm the birth, Karin McGrath and the baby were gone. The motel manager confirmed they had been there, said she was quiet and left early in the morning, paid cash for the last day."

Chapter 32

Karin woke, stretched her arm across the bed feeling for Haley. The pillow was cold. *Oh, my God!* She rolled off the bed, stood for a moment disoriented, then remembered. Monday morning. *Haley's missing! Have to find her.*

She had spent hours the night before on the phone in the motel trying to convince the airlines to tell her whether Haley had been on a flight out of Denver International or Colorado Springs. Only after she had gone out to DIA, located a sympathetic person at the baggage-handling computer and let her assume it was a parental kidnapping situation had she been able to convince her to scan through the computer. No child of Haley's age had flown out that night.

Then she had finally slept. Now her eyelids were puffy and her eyes sore from tears in the night. One thought filled her mind: *Where is Haley?*

Dr. Wetford would be back in town by now. Not only could he attest that she had a daughter, he knew Mellie. He had worked with her, so surely he would know where to find her.

Monday morning. Would she be blasted all over the news?

Karin grabbed the remote control, turned on the television and saw live coverage of flames shooting in the air. The local news led with a story about a huge fire in north Denver, with injured firemen and two casualties. Buried at the very bottom of the exciting segment was Karin's story. The perky blonde newswoman mentioned Karin by name, stating she had reported a child missing, then had disappeared. The police were looking for her. Nothing more. Nothing on Kenny. Implication: Karin was a nutcase who needed to be rounded up. A grainy photo of Karin, evidently taken by Detective Jansen on his cell phone, flashed on the television. She had to move quickly.

Last night she'd paid cash for the room and before going to sleep she'd cut out the bloody patch on the knee of her jeans, frayed the edges to look worn and scrubbed the toes of her shoes until they no longer showed bloodstains. Karin showered under the hottest water she could stand, and within fifteen minutes of the newscast she had dressed, slicked her wet, shoulder-length hair back into a bun and left the motel, clutching the bloody scraps of denim in her hand.

She pulled out of the parking lot and drove south away from the motel, even then hearing the warble of a siren. She didn't wait to see if it was heading for the motel. She drove several blocks, threw the denim scraps out the car window and steered to an ATM where she withdrew two hundred dollars, her entire savings.

Once she was sure she was safely away, she purchased a fast-food breakfast from a drive-through and headed back toward Ridgewood. On the way she called Dr. Wetford's office from her cell phone. "I'm trying to locate . . ." She caught herself just before she said *my child's medical record,* and finished with ". . . Doctor Wetford, my auntie's physician at Oak Manor. He saw her a month ago."

The receptionist spoke firmly. "You'll have to speak directly to the doctor." She hesitated, then said, "He'll be at the Oak Manor Life Center for rounds this morning. You might try to catch him there."

"Thank you. I'll do that."

"What was your name? I'll make—"

Karin disconnected without answering.

Mornings were Haley's time of day. She habitually rose early, snuggled briefly with Karin, then slid from the bed to play with her toy stuffed turtle. Haley's face, lit with an impish smile, rose before Karin's eyes. Where was Haley now and what were the kidnappers doing to her? What was Mellie doing? All the terrible stories of buried kidnapped victims, injured children, came to mind and fury burned Karin's throat as she drove through the Monday morning traffic.

Using side streets, Karin arrived at Oak Manor Life Center in little more than half an hour. As a precaution, she parked in the employees' parking lot in back, next to an incinerator and partly hidden by a large, rusty truck.

The same white van she'd noticed before stood at the back door. She peeked in the window. It was empty, the cot made, the blanket pulled taut. She shuddered thinking Johnny Ray probably came to the nursing home in the thing.

Today, the back door to the building wasn't propped, so she had to wait until someone came out. In barely five minutes a rounded little housekeeper bustled out carrying a large black trash bag, which she dropped beside the incinerator. Karin followed the woman back inside.

The woman objected. "Hey, you can't come in like that!"

Karin grinned. "Selma told me I could. It saves a lot of time and I've got to get to work. I just wanted to check on . . ." Who? For a second her mind went blank. Then: ". . . Johnny Ray Alders."

"I don't care what Selma said. You can't do that."

"Okay, look, after this I'll go in the front, but I just want to see Johnny, and I'm real late this morning."

"Don't do it again."

"Promise." She started down the hall.

"Hey!"

Heart thumping, Karin stopped and turned, poised to run.

The woman was shaking her head. "Johnny got moved this morning. He's in the hospice unit now. Not doing so good."

Hospice. Why had Johnny Ray gone downhill? Intracranial bleeding from the fall was possible, but unlikely, unless he was on a blood thinning medication. But surely he should have been rushed to the hospital. "Okay, thanks. Do you know if Doctor Wetford is here yet?"

The woman glanced away, then back, her expression suddenly guarded. "Oh, he'll be in the hospice wing."

The woman's emphasis on the word *hospice* puzzled Karin. "Does he have a lot of patients there?"

The woman moved away, her shoulders stiff. "Quite a few."

"One more thing, is Selma here today?"

The woman shook her head. "Selma didn't show. In fact she forgot to check out last night."

Karin's heart crept into her throat. Somehow, she managed to sound calm. "You wouldn't know her address, would you?"

The woman hesitated, clearly reluctant to say.

"I'm a visiting nurse, that's how I know Johnny Ray and some of the other patients here. I just want to make sure Selma's okay."

It took some fast talk and a quick flash of her home health identification, her thumb half covering her name, but Karin finally got Selma's address. The woman still looked uncomfortable. "You don't tell anyone I told you, right?"

"Right. I never saw you and you never saw me." Karin walked briskly down the gleaming tile floor of the wide hall, to the heavy metal fire doors separating the hospice wing from the rehab wing. She pressed the automatic door opener, heard the pneumatic doors whisper open and stepped into a place of unnatural calm. The doors to the rooms were all nearly closed, the nursing staff evidently attending to the patients.

As she walked along the hallway, Karin was surprised to see

how many of the names she recognized. At least three were patients she had known from past assignments to provide them home health services.

Mrs. Crowley, only forty-eight years old, had suffered a debilitating stroke from which she never fully recovered. And Mr. Adelmyer, sixty-five, diabetes. And Kitty Berger, eighteen years old, a closed-head injury with a thoracic level spinal cord injury, from a car accident. Kitty had been recovering well, despite having some memory problems and being paralyzed from her chest down. What a shame she ended up in hospice. So young.

Karin found Johnny Ray in the last room, pale, barely breathing, the bruising on the side of his head swollen, purpled and ugly. The fall had been far worse than Karin had realized. "Johnny, do you hear me? It's Karin Preston, your nurse."

His eyelid twitched, but there was no other sign that he heard her.

Footsteps. She turned. Dr. Wetford stopped at the door to Johnny Ray's roomette. He said, "My receptionist said a young woman might be looking for me. Would that be you?"

"Yes, Doctor. I need your help. My daughter is Haley Preston. I'm the home health nurse for Johnny Ray and a number of patients who are now here. A year ago I was here visiting a patient and when I mentioned to you that my daughter was sick with a bad sore throat, you offered to see her, as a professional courtesy. All I need is for you to confirm that you saw her."

"I'm very sorry. I see so many people. I don't recall seeing her."

Desperation made Karin want to scream at him that he had to remember Haley. How many children did he see, for God's sake? She forced herself to say calmly, "For a test for a strep throat infection."

He continued to shake his head.

Karin's breath came more quickly. "I brought her to your office on a Saturday morning. You did some tests, gave us some samples of medicine and then on Tuesday you called and said to discontinue the meds because she didn't have strep."

He winced, looking truly sorry. "I just don't recall, but I'll be glad to check my records." He smiled. "I'm sorry. My memory's not quite what it used to be. If I saw her, there will be a record, I assure you."

Not what she'd hoped for, but it might be enough. "Thank you, I appreciate it. You see, she's missing. In fact, she was with Melody Alwyn, who used to work for you. And Melody also worked here. It's complicated, but I need you to confirm that you saw Haley. A Detective Jansen will probably contact you today."

He looked shocked to hear Haley was missing. "Sorry to hear about your daughter."

"Thanks. I appreciate it," she said. "What happened to Johnny Ray? He was doing well when I saw him Friday, then yesterday I saw him here."

Dr. Wetford's brows rose. "You saw him Friday?"

"I'm his home health aide."

"I see." Wetford nodded, his lips pursed. "Yes, sad case, really. Doing fine, then had a bad fall sometime early Saturday morning. His sister said he sometimes wakes in the night and wanders a bit. She thinks he fell from the front steps and hit his head on a rock."

"He told me that someone hit him. I was surprised to find him here, instead of maybe an emergency room."

"Yes, well, he was a prime candidate for rehab. Falls like that are dangerous, but with a bit of strengthening we'd hoped he could avoid them. You were here yesterday?"

"I was hoping to find you, and ran into him in the hall." She looked around, uneasy. "It's kind of sad. So many of the patients

I used to have on my caseload are here." She looked back at him. "I thought you were a surgeon."

"This is my pro bono work, my personal charity you might say. Now if you'll excuse me, I have a lot to do this morning. I'll check my records as soon as I get back to my office. You can refer the detective to me there." He walked away from her without waiting for her response.

"Wait! I'm also trying to find your nurse, Melodie Alwyn."

He stopped, turned and looked at her. "She hasn't worked for me for years. Now, I must get to my patients."

"But where . . . ?"

He raised his hand. "Call me at the office this afternoon," he said and stepped into a patient's room.

Karin started after him, then stopped in the hallway, telling herself to calm down. Badgering him wouldn't help. Discouraged to the point of desperation, she left by the side door. As she walked through the visitor parking area toward the back lot where she had parked, she heard her name called.

A small young woman in jeans and a heavy jacket stepped from an ancient red Toyota and waved at Karin. Johnny Ray's sister, Sissy. Karin waved back and Sissy's face lit up as she ran toward Karin. "Oh, I'm so glad to catch you. They called me this morning about Johnny Ray. The nurse said he's sinking." She looked as though she'd just finished a night shift. Her worried eyes were blurry, reddened, and her hair barely held back by a scrunchy. "Do you think he's going to die?"

Karin wished she could say no. "Did you ask if he should be transferred to the hospital?"

"No." She shook her head as tears sprang to her eyes. "I don't have money for that. He don't have insurance and I already paid as much as I can. There's just no more."

"Then how can you afford to have him in this place?" The words slipped out, sounding rude and unfeeling. "I'm sorry, that was so rude. I didn't mean it that way."

Sissy waved her hand. "It's okay. It's true. I couldn't afford this place ever. It was Doctor Wetford got him in with no charge, because Johnny Ray had a lot of promise for recovery. So, I had to put him in here. Johnny kept losing his temper, he put a hole in my wall, and last Thursday he hit me." She pointed to her cheek where Karin noticed a healing bruise.

"I thought he was doing better. He looked okay Friday when I saw him."

Sissy kicked at a stone on the pavement. "I know you left those forms for me to fill out for him to maybe get insurance, but then Doctor Wetford made this offer—I thought this would be better for him. I wouldn't have admitted him here, but then I found him early Saturday morning. He had a terrible fall sometime in the night and just laid there until I came at about six and I said to myself, that's it and I called Doctor Wetford's assistant. Johnny Ray hollered when they took him. It was awful, Karin. I couldn't even watch him go, but I thought he'd get better here. Now I feel so bad."

"It's a terrible bind for you," Karin said and patted Sissy's shoulder. Of course Johnny would protest leaving his trailer. He was fiercely independent.

Motion at the front of the building caught her attention. A white, unmarked, four-door Ford pulled up in front and parked. Detective Jansen, wearing the same dark leather bomber jacket and a fresh pair of chinos, got out of the car and walked with just the slightest limp to the front door of the Life Center. Karin moved out of his line of sight.

Had the detective said good-bye to his children this morning? Did his wife make him breakfast? Did he have any idea how hard it was to live as a single parent? These thoughts flew through her mind as she watched him. At least he was following up on her call yesterday. Had he found Kenny? And the blood spot on the floor? She moved around the car to a spot where she wouldn't be easily seen from the windows of the nursing home. "Sissy, I hate to do this, but I need to get going."

"Sure, I understand," she said, but she looked hurt.

"I'm in kind of a jam. The cops want to talk to me and I don't have time for them right now. I'd appreciate it if you didn't say anything."

"Dang!" Sissy stared at her. "Well, I know about jams. Johnny's been in one or 'nother for years now." Sissy made a sad little grin as she shrugged. "I guess I can handle that. For all you've done for Johnny. I sure hope things work out for you. I know you tried to make Johnny well, but like Doctor Wetford said when he came that day, it just wasn't to be."

Karin stopped. "Doctor Wetford made a home visit?"

"Not him actually, his assistant came to see me last week, before Johnny fell. Said Doctor Wetford thought Johnny might have a chance in rehab and did I want to admit him."

So many questions, but Haley came first. Still . . . "Sissy, what did the assistant look like?"

She shrugged. "Tall, kinda old, maybe forty. Nice hair, though."

"His name?"

"You know, he said, but I don't remember. I was so upset that morning. Johnny'd had a bad night and all."

Karin glanced toward the nursing home. Any minute Jansen could come out. The thought of him looming over her, possibly cuffing her wrists, gave her a case of terrors. "Thanks. I hope he gets better," Karin said, but Sissy had turned away and was heading inside.

All the leads Karin had were shutting down and every hour that passed took Haley farther away.

But there was one more possibility.

Chapter 33

Jansen arrived at the Oak Manor nursing home, determined to find Ethan Morgan and talk his way into records, but when he inquired, he was told Morgan wouldn't be in that morning. The clerk in Human Resources politely shook her head. "It's a rule. No subpoena, no records."

Judge Hitchcock had irritably refused both the subpoena and the arrest warrants. With no body, no crime other than breaking and entering of a vacant house clearly left untouched, the judge simply said, "Make a case and I'll sign it. This is not a case."

"Sally," Jansen said, having glimpsed her name tag. "I know that a woman named Melanie Allen or Melodie Alwyn or some variation of that name worked here in the past. I'm just trying to clear up a little question."

Her expression softened, but she still shook her head. "I can't do it. It's a very firm rule."

"I don't need to read her record, just verify there is one. Maybe I could step inside the record room and happen to see it?"

She crossed her arms over her chest as if to say, *Over my dead body.*

Maybe, Jansen thought, *there's another way to get at the information.* "Does Oak Manor employ surgical technicians?"

Sally glanced uncomfortably away, blinking rapidly. "We don't, but—" She glanced around the room as though checking to see who else might be in earshot. "Uh, Doctor Wetford has a surgical nurse who assists him." She chewed on the inside of her cheek. "Is she, uh, in trouble?" A hopeful little smile played at the corner of Sally's mouth.

Jansen didn't answer.

She capitulated. "Oh, hurry up."

He stepped quickly to her left and peered inside the record room. In her message, Karin had said she left Melanie's workmen's comp file on a chair with several others. But the only chair he could see was empty.

"Maybe there were some files on that chair?" He pointed to it.

She looked at it, her head shaking slowly. "You know? That's weird. I mean, they were just left out there. I filed them when I got here. They were all workmen's comp files. I don't remember one for Melanie Allen, though. Not one 'A' at all. I would remember because we keep all those files in the bottom drawer." She frowned. "How'd you know there were files on that chair?"

"I got a tip. From the person who left them there." He looked through the files in the bottom drawer. No folder for Melanie Allen or any other variation of her name.

Jansen drew in a breath. Karin must have broken in during the weekend. Either she saw the files on the chair or she left them there. Or she made the whole thing up. "Is there another place where you keep old terminated files?"

"No."

"You didn't happen to notice whether someone was in here over the weekend, did you?"

"It's locked on weekends."

"You look uncertain."

She shook her head slowly. "It shouldn't be possible, but my desk looked different this morning when I came in. I don't think Selma was here, and she's always careful not to touch anything, but it still just seemed different, you know what I mean?"

"I've seen cameras around."

She smiled. "Wouldn't you know? They've got them in, but they're not working yet."

"Who would have access to your office?"

She hesitated, then said, "Just the cleaning people."

"Doctor Wetford does rounds here in the mornings. Where would I find him?"

"You might inquire in the hospice unit. He's there a lot."

Jansen started out of the office. At the doorway he stopped and turned back to Sally. "What's the arrangement for doctors accessing medical records? They get here pretty early, right? And you must have a consulting physician for the patients."

She cocked her head. "Of course. While some of the docs follow their patients here for a while, they almost always turn them over to Doctor Wetford."

"Doctor Wetford would have a key to the records office here, then. To get records and such, I suppose."

Sally's eyes went round. "Hmm, yes, he does have a key."

Jansen found Dr. Wetford bending over the bed of a patient named Johnny Ray Alders, a young man who appeared to be in the last stages of life, with a large nasty wound on the side of his head. On the far side of the bed stood a young woman. Her tear-streaked gaze was locked on the doctor, and her shoulders were hunched as though trying to fend off bad news.

Dr. Wetford's heavily jowled face was solemn. His eyes were hooded and the sizeable bags beneath them gave him the look of a morose basset hound. "He's sinking, Sissy. There isn't anything more we can do."

"It's so fast," she said softly. "He was doing so well before his fall."

"Blood clots happen when we least expect them."

Jansen edged in closer. Obviously this was a poor time to interrupt, but time was passing, and he couldn't afford to wait through a long treatment conference.

Wetford seemed to sense his presence and turned, a frown creasing his broad forehead. "I'm in conference here. Would you wait outside, please?"

Jansen held up his badge. The young woman Wetford had called Sissy looked frightened. Jansen worked to sound gentle. "Excuse me, ma'am, I need to ask the doctor here a quick question."

She nodded and stepped back, as though that would give them some privacy.

"Doctor," Jansen started, then stopped, his gaze on the charts in the doctor's hand. "Did you have to pull those charts from the records room?"

Wetford frowned. "These are the bedside charts."

"I see." Interesting that he lied about it, Jansen thought. "I'm inquiring about someone I believe you know. Ms. Karin Preston."

Sissy sucked in her breath.

Jansen heard it and glanced her way. "Do you know Ms. Preston?"

"She's Johnny Ray's nurse. She's a real good person."

Dr. Wetford stepped forward, as though trying to shield Sissy from the questions. "What do you want to know?"

"Ms. Preston believes you treated her daughter, Haley, sometime last year."

Dr. Wetford's gaze flicked to the ceiling. "I told her this morning when she was here that I'd check my records, but I haven't had time to do that."

"Do you remember seeing the child?"

"No."

Sissy spoke up timidly. "I remember her talking about her little girl being sick. Several months ago. The first time she came to see Johnny, we spent some time getting acquainted and she mentioned a child then."

"When was that, can you be more specific?"

"It was after his accident the end of September. He was in rehab for six weeks. Then about a month later, maybe the end of November, Karin came. He had another nurse before her, but she quit. Johnny was difficult. Karin always seemed to know what to say to keep him calm. He liked her. He'd actually do his exercises for her. And take his medicine. That made a big difference in how he acted."

Jansen looked hard at her. "Did you ever see a picture or see the child?"

"No."

Jansen turned to the doctor. "How do you know Ms. Preston?"

"She works for a home health agency with whom I have a lot of business, so I'm familiar with her name."

"What's been your experience with her as a nurse?"

"She's a nurse's aide, actually. She's quite good as far as I know. She's had some very ill people to deal with, many of whom ended up here, in fact."

Sissy spoke up. "She's real dedicated. She even visited Johnny here yesterday. She was real surprised he was so sick after how well he'd been doing at home. Course, that was before he fell." Tears welled in Sissy's eyes and brimmed over onto her cheeks.

Jansen nodded, wishing he had words to heal her emotional wounds, and for his own, for that matter.

Wetford moved to the lavatory and washed his hands, drying them thoroughly on paper towels. "I have to be going, if you don't have anything more, Detective."

"How long have you been the consulting physician for Oak

Manor Life Center?"

Wetford frowned. "I believe it's been about seven years now. I had cases here before that, but signed on as the consulting doc seven years ago September."

"Would you know a patient by the name of Eberhard? Our records indicate she was hospitalized here at the time."

"Eberhard? The name's familiar, but I don't remember—oh, yes I do. That's the name of that tragic kidnapping. Michelle wasn't it?"

"Nicole."

"Yes, Nicole. Terrible thing. They never found her, did they? I think I do remember an Eberhard woman here around that time, but again I'd have to look at records to be absolutely sure."

"Do either of you remember what time Ms. Preston left here today?"

Wetford's brow lifted, an eyebrow shrug. "I have no idea."

Sissy shifted uncomfortably, then finally said, "No."

Jansen was at his car door when his cell phone rang. Frost's voice came through. "Hey, Casey, forensics have been through that house on Paradise Lane on their knees. Only thing they found was a bit of turquoise glass in the garage by the back door."

Turquoise was the color of the bottle Karin had said she gave Melanie as a gift. "Is the piece of glass clean?"

Jansen heard him rustling, then silence.

"Yeah. Didn't notice before, but yeah, brand new clean."

CHAPTER 34

Time was running out. The longer Haley went unfound, the less chance she ever would be found. The very thought of it made Karin's mouth go dry. She had to see if Mellie's neighbor could give her any clues as to where Mellie had gone. She drove to Paradise Lane, careful to park on the cross street with the car pointing away.

Karin mounted the three porch steps and knocked firmly on the door. At the third knock a pair of rheumy eyes peered out at her. Then the locks rattled and the door opened slightly. A taut chain held it at two inches. "What is it?"

Karin's throat tightened. "I'd like to talk to you about the people who lived in the house down Paradise Lane."

"Are you from the police? You don't look like police. They never come, even when I call them. Nobody comes to talk to an old woman. So, who are you?" The woman's brows drew together and the expression in her eyes grew sharper. "Wait a minute, I know you. You're the one who says her kid was stolen."

The lie Karin had planned died on her lips. She nodded. "Please, help me. Nobody believes me."

"Don't believe you, huh? I know what that's like. You're in a pack of trouble."

Karin nodded again. "No kidding. Saturday night I left my daughter with Melanie Allen for an overnight and in the morning when I came to pick her up, no one was there."

"Why did the fire truck go down there?"

"I called them. I thought maybe Melanie and the girls were overcome by monoxide poisoning." A flicker of expression in the old woman's face made Karin hopeful. "Please, I need your help. You know something, don't you?"

The old woman's gaze dropped to Karin's clothes, then traveled back to her face, her expression softening as she peered into Karin's eyes. "You'd better come inside."

The elderly woman closed the door just enough to unhook the chain lock, then swung the door wide and stepped back to admit Karin. "I've got to be careful. Someone messed with my door a while back." The woman closed and relocked the door. "Come on in the kitchen."

Like Karin's great-grandmother, the woman looked shrunken from her original size. Osteoporosis, Karin thought automatically. She'd seen it so often in her elderly patients. Also like Karin's great-grandmother, this woman wore a faded housedress covered by a full cotton apron, all topped with a large maroon sweater that sagged away from her bony frame. The garment had once been very nice, but now the tattered sleeves bagged at the elbows and were rolled at the wrists as if it had belonged to a large man in the past.

The smells of stale meals and mothballs filled the living room, which was just plain cold. Karin suspected the old woman was trying to save on her heating bill. Shuffling in her worn house slippers, she led the way to the kitchen, where sunshine warmed the room and a teakettle simmered on a gas stove. The woman pointed to a chair with a tabby cat on the seat and said, "Shove her off. She's been there long enough."

Karin urged the animal to the floor and sat, unsure of where to start. "Thank you for letting me come in, Mrs.—uh—"

"Wilson. Emma Wilson. My husband, George, has been dead for years now." Mrs. Wilson pulled two cups and saucers from the cabinet, then said, "I just made a pot of tea. Do you take milk and sugar?"

"Plain, thanks. What did you notice at the house?"

Mrs. Wilson set a cup of wickedly dark tea in front of Karin, then perched on a chair and eyed her. "I already told the police I didn't see anything. So, why did you come to me?"

"You're my last hope. What did you see?"

The woman straightened her napkin, her teaspoon, smoothed her apron, then said softly, "It's nice to talk to someone who listens. I don't get much company anymore. Outlived all my friends, you know."

"Mrs. Wilson, I don't want to be rude, but I don't have much time to find my daughter."

"Oh, of course. Forgive me. You must be worried sick. Let's see. Maybe three months ago I saw a truck go there and back up into the garage. I thought it was one of the Galt family come to get something. Didn't think about it a bit. Then, early Sunday morning while it was still dark, I heard a truck come down the street. I can't be sure it came from there, but I thought so at the time. Seemed odd."

"Did you see what make or color it was?"

"Don't know one truck from another. It might've been white."

"Did you ever see anyone at the house?"

"Once or twice I thought I heard a car, but in the mornings now I sleep in. And I don't hear like I used to. For that matter, I don't see all that well either. Except up close, like you and me. Once I thought I saw a light from there, but it couldn't be. Old Jim Galt's been dead a year now and that place has been empty for at least two years."

"Did you tell the police this?"

"The young fella that came to my door didn't have much time for me and I figured it wouldn't make any difference. It wasn't till I heard on the television that you said you'd lost a kid that I thought well, maybe I was wrong to think that."

"When did you hear it on the television?"

"This morning, eight o'clock news."

"And you still let me in?"

"Well, I thought maybe you were the police since I called them, but then I've called them before and they don't listen to me. Nobody much needs me anymore, but you looked like you needed a friend."

"The police don't believe I have a child. When they went inside the house, they found it was full of dust. They kept saying the house has been vacant for years, but I know Melanie lived there and it wasn't dusty last night when I left my daughter there. I think someone blew dust in there somehow to make it look like no one had been in there in ages."

Mrs. Wilson folded and refolded her paper napkin. "Could have used one of those old-style vacuums. Electrolux. Canister vacuum. Don't see them anymore, but I've got one. Used to be you could reverse them. Used to advertise you could paint with them. I did that once—painted the basement laundry room. Didn't paint too well, but it could work to blow dust." She sipped her tea. "Galt was an ornery old cuss. He could be a wonderful gentleman sometimes and other times he was mean and nasty. Had a wife, Emma, same name as me, but she left him years ago. Never had kids himself, but he had money. Don't know where he left it, though. The family's spread all over the countryside, still fighting over his estate and his other properties he always talked about."

Karin felt her pulse pick up. "Other properties? Where?"

"Arizona, I think, and somewhere up in the mountains west of Denver, up Cold Creek Canyon, maybe. Don't know more specifically. County clerk could tell you. Years ago Emma Galt used to talk to me a little. She said it was real lonely up there."

"Did he go to the Oak Manor Life Center nursing home?"

"Sounds right. I know he was so mean no one ever visited

him." Mrs. Wilson's head tilted to the right. "Lot of kids get snatched these days, ever wonder why?"

From the corner of her eye, Karin thought she saw a shadow pass across the side window, but by the time she glanced that way there was nothing visible. "I don't know," she said and suddenly felt very sick.

A knock sounded at the door.

Mrs. Wilson got up. "Oh, maybe that's the police come, finally. I'll be back in a minute."

Police? Anxious, Karin rose and moved to the back door, unlocked and cracked it so she could bolt if necessary. She heard Mrs. Wilson turn the front door locks. "Yes?"

A small scream.

Then the sound of the chain lock breaking and glass shattering as the door burst open.

Karin ran, her legs pumping, driven by adrenaline coursing through her arteries. She had to get away. A shot rang out. Pain seared her left arm. She gasped and glanced over her shoulder. No sign of the shooter.

She passed a backyard without a fence and glanced over her shoulder. Her pursuer wasn't in sight. She rushed across the backyard, through the narrow space between the two houses and into the front. She knew the adrenaline rush would only last so long, then shock would take over and the shakes would set in. She had to find safety before her legs gave out.

Two houses farther on, a thick clump of overgrown juniper bushes crowded the front lawn. Her knees shaking, she stumbled forward until she reached the thickest bush. She threw herself under the low-hanging branches. A spider web wrapped her face and the scent of dusty, crushed juniper filled her nose as she fought to catch her breath.

For several minutes she lay wedged under the bush, trying to stifle the sound of her ragged breathing so she could listen for telltale footsteps. A car turned into the street.

She shrank farther back under the branches and watched it approach, then pass on by. At the corner it slowed, then peeled away. Was this the attacker?

Once she was sure he was gone, she forced herself up, eased off her jacket and looked at the wound. It wasn't deep or even serious, really a graze, but it hurt like hell.

Mrs. Wilson. Karin pulled her cell phone out of her jacket pocket and flipped it open. She thumbed in the numbers for Jansen, listened as he answered, then said, "Get to Emma Wilson, Mellie's neighbor on the corner of Paradise Lane. Someone, I think Roger, Mellie's husband, just broke in and attacked her. He shot at me and grazed my arm." She broke off before he could respond and turned off the phone again so it couldn't be traced.

She closed her eyes. She kept hearing the sound of glass shattering, the door smashing against the wall. The memory of that dear old woman who had been kind to her brought hot tears to her eyes. Mrs. Wilson was surely injured, maybe even dead, and it was her fault. She'd led the attacker there.

Why hadn't Roger shot her in the back and killed her as she ran? Aside from Joe, everybody else she'd had contact with seemed to have been murdered. Except maybe one.

Selma's place turned out to be a tiny, square house with a small porch, two windows and a door facing the street, much like the houses children in first grade draw. Except there were no flowers by the doorstep. The yard was dry, the grass struggling to survive. Whatever else Selma was, she wasn't a gardener. Karin knocked, then leaned against the porch post, her head spinning.

Selma opened the door. "What're you doin' here?" Her gaze lingered on Karin's face. "Damn. You look sick. You'd better come in here."

"It's only a graze wound." Karin stepped forward, the floor tilting. Selma grasped her around the waist and led her to a slip-covered couch. "Sit here." Then she sat down opposite on a tired-looking chair whose seat had a permanent hollow. "What happened to you and how'd you find me, girl?"

"Someone attacked a woman I was talking to, then tried to kill me. I think I need some bandages."

Selma's eyes rounded. "And you came here? Bringing that no good trouble to me?"

"I wanted to warn you. We have to hurry and get out of here."

"We? What's this *we* business, girl?" As she said it, Selma ran her hands along the tops of her thighs, rubbing them as though trying to reassure herself.

"You need to get out of town. You have to get your granddaughter and stay somewhere for a few days. Everyone I've talked to gets hurt. I'm afraid you'll be next."

"God in heaven."

"I tried my friend Joe, but he didn't answer and my phone battery is about to give out." Karin shook her head to clear it, but the dizziness came in waves. "I need to use your phone to reach Joe. He'll help me."

"It's right there." Selma pointed to a wireless phone propped on a charger. "I'll just pack a few things while you're calling. When you're finished we'll get out of here. I'll fetch my granddaughter from school."

Karin reached into her purse and pulled out some cash. "I know you can use this."

Selma looked uncomfortable. "I ain't taking your money."

"Your little granddaughter can use it. And you may be in a motel for a while. Don't go to a relative. You'll just be hauling trouble there. Go to a Holiday Inn or something. It'll be safer."

Selma hesitated, then took the money and shoved it deep

into a pocket. “I won’t be a minute,” she said and left the room.

Karin pressed in the numbers for Joe’s cell. On the third ring his voice came on, loud and firm. “Hello?”

“Joe, it’s Karin.”

“It’s good to hear from you, Mom. What’s up?”

“Are the police there?”

“Yes, I’m fine and I plan to visit soon. Just as soon as I can.”

“Okay, let me talk. I’ve got this lead. Mel’s neighbor said Mr. Galt had mountain property. I figure since Melanie used his house down here, she might also use his mountain place. That might be where Haley is.”

“And where is that?”

“I don’t know, but, it should be public record.”

“Okay. I love a good picnic. What should I bring?”

“I’ll meet you there. My phone is about dead, so I’ll leave it off and check it in a half hour. Did you have a hard time with that detective?”

“Uh, okay, I understand you on that. Love you, Mom.”

Karin’s mouth went dry. “Uh, see you soon.”

Selma dropped a canvas rolling suitcase by the front door. “I worked for that ornery old Mr. Galt for a while too.”

“Do you know where that mountain cabin is?”

“Don’t know the address, but I can tell you how to get there. I had to drive his damn self up there several times.”

Chapter 35

Jansen parked his car in front of the Eberhard house and stepped out into the warming sun. He was hoping to catch Edward Eberhard before he left for work. A slow look around at the wide, manicured lawn, complete with stately trees and ivy climbing the brick walls, left him feeling almost smothered with the too-perfect appearance. He'd been in police work long enough to view perfection with a high level of cynicism. Could this family have stifled the investigation, perhaps to get out of the spotlight?

The forensic team had found no trace of Nicole in the Galt house, or in the backyard so far. Jansen drew in a deep breath and rang the bell, listening to the subdued chime inside.

Little feet clattered on the other side of the door. The knob moved slightly, as if a small someone were tugging at it. Then heavier footfalls and the door swung open. Jansen saw a lean, angular man whose stance was defensive. Edward Eberhard, he assumed.

Jansen introduced himself and said firmly, "We need to talk. About Karin Preston."

Eberhard's expression hardened. "I'm due in my office."

"You should call your office and tell them you'll be late."

Eberhard seemed to consider a protest, then briskly stepped aside, saying, "Why don't we go into the library?" He bent to the pretty child at his side. "Go to Mommy, Cindy, this is business."

As soon as the little girl clattered away, he led Jansen down the hall to a book-lined room on the right. He seated himself behind the imposing mahogany desk, and Jansen saw him pinch his trousers to maintain the pleat. A nervous gesture, Jansen guessed.

They waited in silence. Jansen remained standing, and idly noted that the books on the bookshelves appeared to have been arranged by height and color.

A slender, dark-haired woman, cheeks pale and expression guarded, appeared in the doorway, the child at her side. "Who is it, Edward?"

Eberhard's eyes closed briefly. "Detective Jansen, this is my wife, Linda."

Her face lit up, at once hopeful and apprehensive. "You've found Nicole? She's all right?"

"I'm sorry, Mrs. Eberhard." Jansen shook his head as he spoke. "We haven't located your daughter. I've come with some questions about your former nanny, Karin Preston."

Her expression closed, as if she had turned off all inner lights. "I want to be a part of this discussion." Jaw set, she turned to the little girl. "Go see Melissa, honey. Mommy and Daddy need to talk business."

Eberhard looked uneasy, but said nothing. The child protested briefly, then departed.

Linda Eberhard sat on the leather love seat at the far end of the room. Edward reluctantly left his desk and went to sit beside her. Jansen took a side chair and purposefully relaxed his shoulders to defuse the tension in the room. "When was the last time you saw Karin Preston?"

A brief pause, then Linda spoke. A little too loudly, as though she felt defensive. "She came by here yesterday and spoke to Edward. Why are you here now?"

"Why did she come here?"

Edward answered slowly. “She had some story about her child having been kidnapped. She said a sweater had been left at her apartment and she wanted confirmation that it was Nicky’s.”

Linda turned to Edward. “You didn’t tell me about the sweater.”

Edward put a hand on her knee. “I didn’t want to upset you, dear.”

She glared at him, then turned to Jansen. “If she has the sweater, it proves she was in on the kidnapping.”

Jansen asked patiently, “Was it your daughter’s?”

“Yes,” Edward said.

So Karin had been right to think the sweater was to slow down the investigation. It galled him that the tactic had worked. Jansen spoke again, quietly but carefully. “What else did Karin ask about?”

Edward’s voice was hostile. “She had a copy of a photo that had been my mother’s. She asked if Mother had ever been at the Oak Manor nursing home. I told her she had.”

“Do you know anyone by the name of Galt?”

Edward blinked. “No.”

“Did you know Karin was pregnant when she lived here?”

They both shook their heads, a little too quickly, Jansen thought. “Did she ever mention to you, or introduce you to, a man named Joe Canan?”

Linda frowned. “She was going to school, taking care of Nicole, and she had hardly any time off. When she wasn’t here, she said she was at the library, studying. I didn’t know she had any friends, male or female.”

“No hint?”

Linda looked down at her hands, which were twisting in her lap, and quieted them. “None.”

“But you came to know the name. After Karin left here.”

Linda drew in a deep breath, squared her shoulders and said, "Yes. Letters came for her. That name was in the return address. I know I shouldn't have kept them, but I wasn't quite rational at that point. I blamed her." She raised her chin and stared at him, a haunted expression on her face. "Because I couldn't stand to blame myself."

Edward covered her hands, squeezed them gently. "It's okay."

"No, it isn't really." Linda's voice was low and husky with emotion. "We thought at first that she was wonderful. Karin came here looking fresh and innocent, she seemed earnest. She wormed her way into Nicole's heart, and won our trust."

Edward roused. "We're not naive people. We both have good educations and we're not fools, but she fooled us. She's a consummate actress."

"You advertised and interviewed and checked references?"

Linda nodded. "Of course. I still have her application."

Surprised, Edward turned to Linda. "I thought you burned it."

"I changed my mind. I thought maybe one day it would be useful."

"May I see it?" Jansen asked.

"I'll get it before you leave. I can tell you exactly what's on it," Linda said softly. "Karin P. McGrath. Her references were two former teachers in her high school and her uncle, Zebulon McGrath, who was the sheriff of Capstone County. They all gave her glowing reports."

Jansen made a note of Karin's uncle's name. "Did she include a photo of herself?"

"No."

Edward shifted, the leather love seat making little creaking protests in the silence of the room. "Maybe we should have looked into her more, but it didn't seem necessary. And she seemed so perfect until . . ." He trailed off.

Linda chimed in. "So we trusted her and gave her more and more responsibility. I was pregnant again, overcommitted to my projects and sick much of the time, and when she offered to sleep in the room next to Nicole's nursery so I could sleep at night, I was delighted. I never, ever thought it might be her way of moving even closer, making the whole plot work."

Edward rubbed a hand over his chin. "We were under a lot of stress at the time. My mother was ill in the nursing home, Linda was suffering the worst morning sickness, I was under huge pressure at the office . . ."

"He was hardly home is what he's saying. Our marriage was a mess, quite frankly."

Edward's cheeks reddened.

Jansen noted the obvious tension between the two. "Is there anything you can think of that you might not have mentioned before?"

Edward shook his head. Linda took a deep breath and said softly, "Well, I never mentioned it, but at the time I was worried that Edward had perhaps been involved briefly with a nurse at the home where his mother was."

Edward looked stunned. Jansen perked up. "Would you know the name of that nurse?"

Edward shook his head. "No, it's been too long. I can't recall."

"I can," said Linda. "Melody Alwyn."

Also known as Melanie Allen, Jansen thought.

"There was *no* affair," Edward said. "It was entirely in your head. I never—" He stopped and looked at Jansen. "I think this is enough now. I don't want my wife upset with all this."

"Edward," Linda cut in, firm and sharp. "Since Nicole disappeared you've been a model husband, you've done everything you could to protect me. Now you have to stop. I'm fine. I'll always grieve for Nicole, but until I know for sure otherwise, I'll believe she's alive. I'm not being emotionally unstable, I'm being her mother." Her eyes filled with tears. "I'll always be her mother."

She turned to Jansen. "I'm convinced Nicole is alive. Because I believe that, Edward worries that I'll go over the deep end again, but I won't." Her eyes held a smoldering intensity that made starkly clear to Jansen why Eberhard was worried about his wife's mental state.

Turning back to Edward, she said, "You must stop trying to protect me. If you don't, it will be the end of our marriage."

Edward shifted on the couch, causing a flurry of leather creaks. "Karin said her child had been kidnapped. Is it true? Is that why you're here?"

"It appears so."

Edward bowed his head. "Oh, my God." He looked up, his cheeks pale. "You don't think we would do such a thing, do you?"

"Did you? Did you set it up?"

"No. I'm not a perfect man, but I try to be a good one. I would never kidnap a child. And I did not have an affair."

Linda's chin rose. "Your mother noticed something and told me that was why she insisted her nurse be changed."

Edward closed his eyes, shaking his head. "Mother was paranoid. You know that."

Linda looked at him with a mixture of pity and sorrow, then turned to Jansen, her expression calmer. "So what else do you need to know?"

There were so many connections between the Eberhard kidnapping and the kidnapping of Haley Preston. He listed them to himself. The little sweater left in Karin Preston's apartment; the nurse, Melanie Allen, or Melody Alwyn, whichever she really was; Karin herself. Something else nagged at him, though at first Jansen couldn't put a finger on it. Then it came to him. "Do you know a Doctor Wetford?"

They looked at each other, surprised. "Yes," Edward said. "He took a birthmark off the inside of Nicole's elbow. He was Mother's doctor at the nursing home. He's a surgeon, but he does pro bono work at Oak Manor. A fine fellow. He charged us almost nothing."

Another link between the cases. "Do you have anything of Karin's here?" Jansen asked.

Softly, Linda said, "Only her old mail." She leaned toward him. "You can't imagine how desolate it is to have your child taken. We—no, I—had to blame someone." She seemed to be pleading with him to understand. Her eyes were smudged and purple like summer thunderclouds moist with unshed rain. "I never saw anyone so loving and tender and patient with a child as Karin was. That's why I trusted her in the first place." She looked down at her hands clasped in her lap and continued in a near whisper, "If Karin didn't take Nicole, if she was innocent, then I've done a terrible thing."

"Linda, please," Edward murmured.

She glared at him. "Stop it! Don't hush me up!" She turned back to Jansen. "When those letters came for her, I kept them, even though I knew she was at her father's and I knew her address. Instead, I sent her hate mail. I wrote horrid things. I said that if I ever heard she had a child, I'd steal it from her, just like she stole Nicole. I know the housepainter was blamed, but I thought she had to be involved." Two tears trickled down her cheeks. "If she didn't do it, who did?"

For all their rage toward Karin Preston, Jansen didn't believe the Eberhards had a hand in Haley Preston's kidnapping.

He checked messages on his cell and found one Karin had left, saying she and Mrs. Wilson had been attacked. He called for an ambulance and ran red lights and siren to Paradise Lane.

He found Mrs. Wilson on the floor of her living room,

crumpled and bleeding, but clinging to life. Kneeling at her side, he asked, "Did you see who did this?"

Her nod was barely perceptible. "Young man."

"Do you know who he was?"

He couldn't tell from her mumbled answer whether she said *no* or *Joe*. "Was there a young woman here?"

"Karin. Nice girl."

The ambulance crew arrived and took the old woman to the hospital. Jansen watched them leave, two questions uppermost in his mind. Who attacked Mrs. Wilson? And would Joe Canan, who had been out of the country for six years, turn murderous for his old sweetheart?

Chapter 36

Melanie stood on the mountain cabin's porch looking out over the broad valley, fatigue weighing on her shoulders. She should pack and leave, but for the moment she needed to think. Inside the girls were watching a DVD, quiet at last. She had held them both for seeming hours, trying to console Haley, who was morose and weepy, asking for her mommy. It left Mellie feeling sick at heart. She hadn't counted on caring so much when she planned this.

She hated this mountain cabin. The stale wood-smoke smell that hung in the air inside, the creaky floors, and most of all, the isolation. An hour and a half out of Denver, sitting at about nine thousand feet, it might as well have been hundreds of miles away. She could yell her head off and not one of those silent, dark trees would respond. Nothing would. Nobody. It left her too much time to brood.

God, what a mess life was, she thought and took a long drag on her cigarette.

As clear as yesterday she remembered the day she went to Donny's father to get Donny back. When she said she'd made a mistake and needed to keep Donny, his face had twisted in fury. "No, you crazy bitch!"

This from the man she had thought loved her. The pain of that memory gripped her so hard she sank down onto the rough wooden step and felt again the crawly sensation in her belly and nerves, tying themselves into knots.

She had adored Donny's father. He had said he loved her more than anything in the world. He vowed he would stand by her, divorce his wife and marry her, she only had to let him have the baby first. He took her child and gave it to his wife. Then he tossed Mellie aside like she was nothing, saying she had no claim on the child anymore. He had everything: money, power, a ready-made home. She'd believed him, that she had no chance of keeping her child. No rights to Donny that she could enforce. She'd had no way to fight him.

A tear left a cold trail on her cheek. It stung, then itched. She wiped it away with the back of her hand.

When she planned to take Haley, only Donny had filled her thoughts. Donny and how sick he was, how he would die if she didn't do something. No matter what it cost her, she would go through with it for Donny and the chance for him to live. But the emotional price was far higher than she had thought it would be.

The silence of the mountain stretched away, almost a drumbeat in her head that said she was a bad person. No matter how hard she tried to defend her decisions, the silence sounded a relentless tattoo. *Bad. Going to Hell. Bad. Going to Hell.* And now she had added kidnapping Haley to her list of sins. But to do nothing would have meant allowing her own child to die. So what was the right thing?

She glanced in through the window at the two blonde heads. The girls were playing with a rag doll, and one of them was twirling in an old office chair. Haley. Mellie felt a twinge of anxiety, but there was no turning back now. The path was set once she decided in favor of Donny. And how could she not decide for him? How could she turn away from her own child's needs?

She crushed out her cigarette, scattering the last shreds of tobacco and shoving the filter tip into her sweatshirt pocket. So far her life had been a series of shitty decisions. Why couldn't she at least feel good about this one thing that had seemed so right three months ago?

The silence of the mountains brought back memories so sharp they sliced her heart and left her oozing useless hot tears. It was the first time she had cried in years. It felt bad, like maybe it would be real hard to stop now that she'd started. She gazed out at the open space, the valley below, the pine trees dark and dour. Above the pine trees hung a faint yellow haze. Pollen. Ominous and choking. She sighed and looked at the porch railing. Two perfect handprints, hers, showed in the pollen dust. Quickly she stood and wiped them out with her sleeve, and then realized she would have to wipe the cabin down for fingerprints.

Roger had left earlier, muttering to himself like he did when he was upset. He hadn't told her what he was thinking but she figured he didn't like her being so attached to Donny. Didn't like Donny much either because of the heartache it gave her when she was missing him.

She had tried to explain her feelings to Roger, but he didn't understand. It was different for a mother, and especially for her. She had promised herself repeatedly that she'd be a good mother. Not distant, like her own. Yet here she was, distant from Donny. But now he needed her and she had a chance again to see him. To hold him and smell his hair and feel his heart beat against hers.

"Mommy!"

She turned to see her daughter in the cabin doorway, frightened. "Yeah, Jen, what is it?"

"Haley's puking."

Melanie ran inside. She went to Haley and held her close, cooed to comfort her and wiped her face with a cool, damp cloth. "It's all right sweetie. You just got dizzy from twirling in the chair." She said it with all the comfort she could muster, but deep inside she was worried. Haley had to be okay. She couldn't be sick, she just couldn't, but her cheeks were flushed and her forehead hot.

Once Haley settled down and slept, Melanie stood by the door. Her gaze flitted around the living room from couch to rocking chair to an old framed picture of Custer's Last Stand hanging over the fireplace mantel. She hated that thing. Custer lay dying on the ground, arrow in his chest and blood all down his shirt, his head propped on the body of yet another slain cavalryman. Nobody should have all that gore in their living room, she thought. Old man Galt was just plain cruel. No wonder his wife left him.

She took out her cell phone, punched in some numbers and pressed it so tight to her ear that it hurt. The ring tone was faint, the poor connection here at the cabin just one more negative. Finally Roger picked up. "I'm telling you she's sick, Rog. What'll I do?"

"How sick? She's got a temperature?"

"No, but she threw up. She's got a headache and stomachache. It's not serious for her, but it will mean a delay. Donny is too sick. We can't use her if she's got something, even a little cold."

"You better call."

"Rog, what if . . . if Donny can't have the surgery . . ." Her anxiety choked her. She walked back outside to the porch where the girls couldn't hear her talking to Roger, couldn't hear the strain in her voice that even she recognized as fear.

"You still there?"

"Yeah. I just keep thinking about Donny."

"Quit it, Mellie. I told you. Get her some medicine and get on with it. Don't worry about that old bitch at the store. I've got to go. I'm flying out now with a delivery."

"But you'll be back this afternoon, right?"

"Yeah, around two. Look, clear the cabin and head on up to Capstone. You can stop at a store and get whatever you'll need. Leave the cabin clean as you can. When I come back I'll fly straight back up to Capstone instead of Denver."

She could hear stress in his voice and the whine of jet engines in the background. He was trying to talk softly and sound supportive, but she couldn't stand it. "Okay," she said and flipped the cell phone shut.

After a few minutes, when her heart rate slowed down, she turned and looked through the window. Jennifer and Haley were on the floor playing dolls, Haley's cheeks paler, but still too rosy. Her eyes were a bit too big in her face and gave her an elfin, unworldly look, as though she wasn't quite alive.

Mellie shuddered. Haley mustn't be sick. She couldn't be.

She reopened the cell phone, speed dialed and listened as the phone rang on the far end. When she heard Donny's father answer, she spoke immediately. "How's Donny?"

"Hold on. Have to move to the next room."

He must have been at Donny's bedside, she thought. She heard a door shut, and then he came back on. "Donny's got to have the surgery as soon as possible. So when are you coming? What the hell is the holdup?"

"No holdup. I'm leaving the cabin as soon as I get it cleaned up."

"How's the kid?"

Mellie felt fury burst forth. "She's a little girl. She's got a name. Haley."

"Dammit, how is she?"

"She just threw up, probably nerves. She's pale. Possibly coming down with something. That's why I called. There may be a delay."

"No. Can't be."

"It's not good for Donny if she's sick."

"The medication will protect him."

"But she won't make it through."

"You don't get it. We're looking at Donny here. Donny. And we've got Karin for backup."

"Wetford said he wouldn't use her."

"He'll do exactly what I tell him. He's got no choice in this."

Both of the girls had fallen asleep and Melanie was nearly finished wiping down the deck when she heard a car motor. She always heard the motor before she saw the car; the stone walls of the mountain made sound echo.

She tossed the wash water over the edge of the deck and shoved the dirty rag into the emptied bucket. Maybe Roger's flight had cancelled.

But he would have called. And he wouldn't have had time to get up here. Now she recalled, he'd said he'd fly straight up to Capstone, so this couldn't be anyone she wanted to see.

Uneasy, she went inside to the kitchen and pulled a knife from the drain board. Roger had sharpened it just last night after she complained that the tomatoes wouldn't slice easily for his midnight snack. She slid the knife into her hoodie pocket and walked out onto the front porch. "Hello?"

A man with thick shoulders was stepping carefully through the rushing stream that ran over the rutted road. He waved.

"What do you want?" she shouted. "I don't get company up here."

"Would you be Mrs. Galt?"

For a nanosecond, her heart stopped beating, then resumed double time as though she'd just run up the side of the mountain. "No. I'm a guest here. You can stop right there."

He waved a wallet at her. "Police. Detective Frost, Ridgewood PD."

"I don't need police." She held her ground. "Don't come any closer."

But he kept on coming, only stopping when he was a bare six feet away. A sneaky grin grew on his face. "I remember you."

Melanie felt her stomach turn cold. This was real trouble.

He laughed then, big and proud. "Just a few questions for you, *Melody Alwyn.*"

The man could ruin everything. She knew it the moment she saw that damn grin. She gripped the handle of the hidden knife and said, "Well, you'd better come inside."

CHAPTER 37

Where the hell was Frost?

Jansen went straight back to the office after seeing Mrs. Wilson off in the ambulance and found only an address scribbled on Frost's desk pad. He tried Frost's cell again, but got no answer. The clerk shrugged and said, "No idea. You know what he's like when he thinks he's on to something."

"You'd think he would leave a message for me."

The clerk smirked. "Not you. You got his job. He still resents it."

"Well, if you hear even one syllable from him, shout."

Where Jansen had worked before, there would have been a war room with staff filling out a time chart, adding information as they got it. In Ridgewood, it was Jansen, flip chart paper and a marker.

Jansen stood in front of the sheets he'd taped up and added "attack on possible witness."

One sheet of paper held the Eberhard time line, starting with Nicole's disappearance and ending with Karin McGrath living in Capstone with her father and at the end, the apparent suicide of the painter who had worked temporarily for the Eberhards. This man, an itinerant worker with no previous record, had left a note confessing to the crime, but in very vague terms. Basically he said he was sorry about Nicole and he didn't mean to do it. No hint of where her body might be. At least one officer, now retired, as well as the district attorney had questioned the validity of the note.

On the second sheet he had started with Karin's meeting Melanie Allen and included Joe Canan's arrival, Haley's kidnapping, Karin's contact with the Eberhards, the disappearance of Kenny Bristow, and Karin's meet-up with Joe Canan. To that he added the nursing home contact with Dr. Wetford and Sissy Alders and finally the attack on Mrs. Wilson.

He was left with a swarm of questions, all centering on Melanie Allen. It seemed that she had purposefully met Karin Preston and got to know her as a babysitter. Melanie had known the Eberhards from the nursing home. Yet six years ago she had flown under the radar. Her name never appeared in Nicole's case file. Never. It was looking like a very big omission. Mr. James Galt, who owned the house where Karin said Melanie lived, was also a patient at the same nursing home. Melanie had worked, maybe still worked, for Dr. Wetford as a surgical nurse. Dr. Wetford had removed a birthmark from Nicole Eberhard. Yet he too was not in the case file. And Dr. Wetford had seen Haley Preston for possible strep and tests.

That was a lot of linkage.

And there was another loose connection, Zebulon McGrath, Karin's uncle. He had been—and still was—sheriff of Capstone County, a county that ranged over the high Colorado peaks. Mostly vertical territory, some two and a half to three hours' drive southwest from Denver. Pretty scenery: rock, trees, mule deer, mountain goats and a few ghost towns left after the silver mining played out. The largest town was Capstone, population two hundred fifty souls in the summer, maybe one hundred in the winter.

Karin had run there after Nicole was abducted. What were the odds Karin would go back there now? Jansen pressed in the sheriff's number.

The phone was picked up on the third ring. Jansen identified himself and said, "I'm calling about a Karin McGrath. I understand she's a niece of the sheriff."

"I'm temporary here, sir. The sheriff isn't in just now. His kid is pretty sick, you know. But I'll tell him you called. He'll probably get back to you from home. He keeps track of stuff real good, even if his kid is sick."

Jansen left his cell number, then called the first of Karin's other references on her application to work for the Eberhards. Might as well fill in the blanks of Karin's life while he waited for the sheriff to call back.

A pleasant-voiced woman answered. She was hesitant to talk at first, but with a little urging came forth. "Well, there's not much to tell really. Karin didn't have too many friends in high school. She came from a strict family and wasn't allowed to go to after-school activities, although I saw her at a few football games and I heard that she and her brother would sneak out some. It was kind of sad she had to do that, really. She was a good kid."

That had all been in the old case file. "What was her family like, beyond being strict?"

"Their father, old Zachariah McGrath, runs a private religious compound, sort of a retreat. The kids from there come to town sometimes, always well-behaved, quiet. Don't ever buy much. Someone once told me he had an underground shelter for them all because he believes the end of the world is just around the corner. I understand he's pretty sick now, a kidney problem of some sort. I heard her brother has the same thing. He's been gone a long time, too, but their uncle is here in town. Sheriff McGrath. I see him from time to time."

"Do the children from the compound attend school?"

"Not since Sam and Karin were here. I guess Zachariah decided public school was too wicked. They're all homeschooled now. We never see them much. Just a couple of girls once in a while."

"Do you know them?"

"Capstone's a small place, out of the way, and those kids stand out. The two girls I've seen are always in long dresses. A little too long."

Jansen flashed on the cults he'd heard of in deep southern Colorado where girls were kept and married off at an early age. "Any of them ever come to the clinic up there? See a doctor for anything?"

"Nope. You thinking of early pregnancy and such? Not that I heard. The last time the doctor went in there was back when Karin's mother was ill with cancer. After she died, I heard Karin left for school down in Denver. She only came back one more time. That was when that little baby was kidnapped and she was sort of blamed. I can't believe she had anything to do with it. She wasn't that kind of person. One of my best students, ever. If she said something, you could depend on it. Oh, wait. I said there wasn't any doctor, but there is one, only he doesn't doctor anyone here, just the patients he brings in to recuperate."

Jansen rubbed an itch on his nose. "He wouldn't be a Doctor Wetford, would he?"

"I don't rightly know. Hardly ever see him, except when his plane comes in."

"You've been real helpful, thank you."

Jansen placed two more calls.

Wetford, he learned, had practiced most of his career in Missouri, retiring to Colorado after his wife died following a lingering illness due to diabetes and kidney failure. A transplant surgeon by training and years of experience, Wetford had a well-known clinic in Mexico where he performed numerous transplants for people who could afford to pay to bypass the system in the US.

Jansen stretched. Why would a skilled, proficient transplant surgeon act as physician consultant to a nursing home? A place where Melody Alwyn, also known as Melanie Allen, a surgical technician, had worked as well. Jansen glanced at the charts he had taped to the wall and phoned the county clerk's office. "Alice, my friend, tell me if Doctor Wetford has property outside Denver, maybe in a town called Capstone."

"Well, that wouldn't be my county."

"I know, but I also know you're a whiz on that computer."

"Give me a minute."

He heard the click of keys and then a few minutes later she said, "Bingo. Capstone. Listed as a commercial property, used to be a medical clinic, so probably still is."

Jansen noted the address and said, "Great. I've got one more for you. James and Emma Galt. They had a place in Ridgewood, and I'm betting there's a mountain cabin."

A few clicks of the keyboard and a minute later she replied, "Got a place on Paradise Lane and another in the mountains. Got your pen ready?"

"Sure do."

He noted Galt's mountain house address. It was the same that Frost had jotted on his desk pad. So that was where he went.

The clerk shouted at him. "Call, Jansen."

Hoping it was Frost, Jansen switched to the other line. "Jansen here."

It was Sheriff McGrath, who bypassed the niceties. "Haven't heard anything from Karin in years. I'll call if I learn anything." He hung up abruptly.

A minute later, another call came in. "Detective, this is Sissy, Johnny Ray's sister. He died. I gotta talk to you. I tried to call Karin, but she didn't answer. I don't know who else to call, but you."

Another person Karin had contact with, now dead. "What happened?"

"See, in order for Johnny to go to the rehab for free I had to sign some papers." Sissy drew in a deep shuddering breath. "I thought he'd be all right or I wouldn'ta done it. Johnny Ray's brain was damaged, but all the rest of him was good and strong. So he shouldn'ta died. He wasn't that sick when he went there, just a behavior problem. And now when I asked to see him, they wouldn't let me see Johnny. The nurse looked all upset, too. And I wanted to tell him good-bye. But here's really why I'm so upset. They won't let me see him. It's my fault see? The papers at the bottom said if he died, his organs would be donated to those who needs them." Her voice dropped to a hoarse whisper. "Could they've killed Johnny?"

Wetford, the retired transplant specialist, was Johnny's doctor. Jansen clenched the phone. "Where is Johnny's body now, Sissy?"

"They took him to the crematory to burn him."

The Morgan Crematorium was a bleak, utilitarian-gray building sitting on three acres of ground that grew sparse grasses, sage and not much else. Jansen pulled his car in the drive, noting the driveway went on around to the back of the building. Delivery door, he thought.

He knocked on the front door. No one answered, but he could see the faintest rise of heat waves from the chimney. Following the cement drive around the building, he came to an open garage door.

A slightly built man in his mid-forties with earbuds stuck in his ears stood in front of a large concrete-brick block, like a small building inside the bigger building. Unaware of Jansen, he gazed intently at a control panel on the front of the block. Most obvious were two large, circular temperature gauges. One was at zero, the second rising slowly. Beneath them were time monitors and further control dials.

Jansen stepped inside, expecting a thick stench laced with smoke and heat, but the air in the room was cool. No scent of burnt flesh, only a faint odor of warm metal and the low background roar of fast-burning gas jets. Beyond the two retorts that Jansen judged were three to four feet square was a long metal counter, bolted to the wall. At the end of the counter stood a barrel holding metal scrap, rods, melted bits, and wires. With an inner shudder, Jansen recognized a leg brace. The metal pieces had come through the cremation and were pulled out of the ash before it went into a round container that looked to him suspiciously like a grinder.

He dragged his gaze back to the control gauges. The left-hand, closer gauge indicated temperature. It was rising slowly. On either side of the control panel were wide metal doors, the left one shut, the right one raised and apparently empty. Beyond, in the far area, stood a couple of thick cardboard cremation boxes on gurneys.

The man turned, jerked out the earbuds and shouted, "Hey! You shouldn't be here."

Jansen held out his badge. "Need a word."

"Nada. I gotta get the next one ready to go. I'm jammed up." He turned his back and reached toward the closest gurney.

"Who's in there?" Jansen asked, nodding to the closed retort.

The attendant looked over at his clipboard. "I can't tell you that."

Jansen tapped his badge. "Tell me here or we go downtown."

"You got a warrant?"

Jansen pulled out his cell phone, pressed numbers and spoke into it. "Judge, I got a situation here."

"Hey!" The attendant waved. "I'll talk. I don't have time to shut down."

Jansen folded his phone. “Name?”

“Mrs. Alessie Wells. She just went in, not due out for three hours.”

“Then you’ve got time to talk some more.”

Grumbling, the attendant gestured to a door in the wall ahead. Through it, they were away from the noise of the fans. He stopped at a metal desk. “Okay, what do you want? You saw, I got a lot to do, so let’s get it over.”

“How many of the bodies in there came from Oak Manor?”

The attendant leaned over his desk and activated the computer. After a minute he answered, “Two. One at ten this morning, one ’bout an hour ago.”

“I need the doctor’s name and the patients’ names.”

“Anna Fenway this morning. Doctor Wetford. Johnny Ray Alders this afternoon, also Doctor Wetford. He’s the next one to go in. All of them have papers in order, all signed off. I am careful about that. Nobody goes in without papers.” He looked up at Jansen. “Wetford signs off on nearly all the Oak Manor patients.”

“How come Alders goes before the morning case?”

He shrugged. “Rush status.”

Why would it be a rush if everything was in order? “How many others do you have in there?”

“Three in the cooler. Been a lot of dying lately.”

“Print me a list of the people, where they’re from and their docs. Make it back two months.”

“I can’t do that.”

“Try real hard or I’ll send a crew out here and this place will be shut down for a week while we inspect it.”

“I run this place by the rules.”

“Just print out the list.”

Scowling, the man printed a list and handed it to Jansen.

The list was only for one month, but a quick scan revealed

that Oak Manor and Dr. Wetford were important clients of the crematorium. Jansen folded the sheet and tucked it into his inside jacket pocket. "Now let's see inside the Alders box."

The man shook his head. "Nope. He's got all his papers. You can't just bust in here. These people all come with their paperwork in order. All the permits signed legal from family and people responsible. It would take a warrant and you're not going to get one, not with the paperwork in order. Guarantee it."

Jansen placed a call to the district attorney, who confirmed what the attendant had said. "Depends on the paperwork. Most likely they're completely legal. The only way you get a stay is if you can show there is a crime involved."

Sissy had said she signed for Johnny Ray to donate in the event that he died. So, with all the papers in order, cremation would ultimately be legal. Unless he could prove that there had been a sale and profit from the donations, there could be no charges. No warrants. "Hold those two off," he told the attendant. "A stay is forthcoming."

"No, sir. Those papers are in order. I'm not waiting on anything that might not come after all."

Rage burned at the back of Jansen's throat. He cast around the room and caught sight of another box in the far corner. "What's that?"

The attendant shrugged. "Found that box here this morning. Waiting on paperwork."

Jansen frowned. "Does that happen often?"

"Not usually. Sometimes, though, a guy gets here, unloads the body and then realizes he don't have the paperwork."

"Open it."

The man's shoulders sagged. "Hey, I don't do that."

Impatient, Jansen pulled at the lid. It was snug, but not fastened, just awkward and a bit heavy. "Help me lift it!"

Reluctantly, the man took the far end, and together they wrestled the lid off the box.

"Aw, shit." The attendant flinched away, swallowing hard.

Inside, Jansen saw a fully clothed man in T-shirt and jeans with paint spots on the shirt front. Blackened blood matted his hair and streaked the side of his face. He was perhaps fifty, heavyset, and stank of beer and early decay.

The crematorium attendant shook his head. "I didn't know this was here. I didn't do this. It ain't right. I'm calling a lawyer." But he merely swayed on his feet, his arms hanging uselessly at his sides.

Jansen closed the lid gently, flipped open his cell phone and called the station. "Send a crew to Morgan Crematorium. I think we found Kenny Bristow, Karin Preston's landlord." He pocketed the phone and said, "Now, this looks like a full-blown murder case. You'll give us full cooperation."

The man nodded, cowed completely.

"The Alders kid first."

"These papers are all in order and I've got a schedule to keep here." His words were brave, but his voice quavered.

Jansen glared at him. "You're not going to keep anything. Get that end of the box. Now."

They lifted the lid, and the cloying smell of early decay rolled out. The crematorium attendant blanched, dropped his end of the lid and backed away, breathless. "My God!"

Jansen thought he'd seen it all, but this was new. And repulsive. As Jansen looked at the poor boy, he knew why Sissy hadn't been allowed to see her brother. Johnny Ray lacked eyes and was missing his leg and arm bones. Patches of his skin had been removed. His chest had been cracked open and his belly slit.

Johnny Ray had donated his all.

Chapter 38

The road up the canyon twisted through some of the most beautiful scenery in Colorado, yet Karin barely saw it. Her gaze stayed straight on the road ahead, taking each curve at just over the posted speed, to avoid a speeding ticket. Still, she nearly blew past the low-lying single story saloon with the large sign, Moose Lake Bar and Grill. The rear end of the car slid in the loose gravel at the road's edge when she braked. The same name as on the matchbook cover they had found under the foot of the kitchen table at Mellie's. This had to be the place. She rounded the next curve and saw a rambling log building, a large sign on the facade: Moose Lake General Store.

Karin pulled off, parked, and checked her phone for messages. One was from Joe.

Joe's voice was warm, almost jubilant. "You were right. Mr. Galt had a mountain place. I got the address and I'm on the way." He rattled off a long address, then added, "I pulled directions. You go west out past Rocky Flats, take the highway up the canyon and look for the Moose Lodge Bar and Grill or something like that. There's a general store right by. Wait for me there. I'll be there in about forty-five minutes. Melanie is dangerous. And Karin," his voice turned husky with emotion, "I don't want anything to happen to you."

He had left the message almost twenty minutes earlier. She turned her phone off again and headed toward the little store.

Inside, in the dim light, she headed straight toward an elderly man stooped over a magazine at a side counter. "Hi there," she called out.

He raised his head and squinted at her. "Eh?"

"Do you know where the Galt cabin is? Old Gracefield Road?"

He rubbed his hand over his balding dome, lips pursed. "Not sure. Maybe ask her." He nodded to the side.

Karin turned, surprised and saw a tall, gaunt woman in a worn plaid-flannel shirt sitting quietly at a cash register.

"Who wants to know?" the woman said.

"I do. I'm trying to . . . to look at it. Maybe buy it."

"Didn't think it was for sale."

"Maybe, maybe not." The terse, no-comment mountain lingo came back to Karin so fast she barely recognized herself.

"Your name?"

A trap. Maybe they'd been warned already. "Betsy Banderow. I'm a distant relative of old Mrs. Galt."

"Mmmm."

"So where do I find Old Gracefield Road?"

The woman took a long draw on a cup of stale-smelling coffee, telegraphing *more information needed, please.*

Karin obliged. "I'm looking for a woman named Melanie Allen. She may be living there. She has a five-year-old child, blonde, blue-eyed, angelic-looking. She may have another child looking similar, almost like a sister to that one."

"She might have been here." The woman glanced out the window over boxes of cereal in a display. "She might be coming across the street right now. That her?"

Karin spun around as Melanie pushed open the door to the store. For an instant she and Mellie locked gazes. Then Mellie bolted, running back toward a van.

Karin burst out of the store, crossed the short distance to the road, shouting, "Haley! Haley! Mellie, stop!"

A car horn sounded. An SUV came straight toward her, the driver's mouth open in a silent scream. Karin leaped backward. The SUV skidded and swerved away, horn blaring, and came to a rocking stop. Karin dashed around the end of the vehicle as Mellie, in the van, careened down the road away from her.

Ignoring a shout from the SUV driver, Karin ran to her car. Far ahead she saw Mellie's van take a curve too fast, the back wheels skidding, then straightening.

Dear God, she thought, *the girls must be in the van.* They were too young to be left alone. *Oh, Mellie be careful,* Karin prayed as she slid behind the wheel, started the car and floored the gas pedal. Could she risk racing up to Mel? Would she be pushing Mellie to drive even more recklessly? Could she risk a wreck and injury to the girls? No, but when she was so close, she couldn't let Melanie get away.

Karin took the same curve as Mellie, also way too fast, her rear wheels sliding dangerously close to the edge of the road. It had been years since she'd driven mountain lanes and she had forgotten the tricks of slowing and accelerating, riding ridges and avoiding low spots.

She would follow without getting too close, she decided. Where had Mellie got a van? The only thing she'd seen Mellie drive was an old Chevy sedan. Panting, Karin steered as carefully as she could, but Mellie was clearly a better driver on this road. She drew quickly away from Karin and disappeared around the hairpin turn, the van swaying.

Karin floored the gas pedal. Her car leaped ahead. Around a blind curve Karin swerved in toward the mountainside, her car straining to hold to the road. Then came a sickening sideways slide, the wheels slipping on the slick surface. She braked. A mistake. The car skidded. She let up on the brakes.

The edge of the road rose in front of her. She jammed on the brakes again, turning into the skid. Too late. The car flew sideways on a mud slick, tilting as the wheels slipped over the edge.

The air bag deployed. Just as quickly, something pierced it.

The car tumbled down the mountainside. Karin's head hit the door at window level. A sickening thud. The car stopped and rocked on its side. Terrified, Karin clung to the steering wheel. She dangled from her seat belt, which was cutting across her chest as she struggled to clear her head.

A thin trickling sound came from close by. Water? she wondered. Or gasoline?

Chapter 39

Haley strained against her seat belt. She had heard Mommy's voice. "Mommy! That's my mommy!"

"It's not Mommy. It's some other woman."

"It's Mommy! I want Mommy!" she cried, and tugged at her seat belt.

Melanie didn't stop. She just shouted, "Sit still. Do you want us to have an accident?"

The van swerved. Mommy never drove like this. Mommy never looked so mad, either. Mellie was different now. She wasn't nice anymore. She was scary. She'd hurt that man that came to the cabin. She got real mad and hit him with the big black skillet. He didn't move after that.

Haley looked at Jennifer. She looked scared and reached over and grabbed Haley's hand. She didn't speak, like she was afraid to make a sound. It made Haley feel scared, too. Her tummy hurt, but she hadn't eaten anything 'cause nothing looked good.

Tears came into her eyes, all hot and stingy. She couldn't see very well because of them. She tried not to cry, but the wet just kept coming. "I want my mommy. When is she coming?"

Mellie didn't turn around, but her voice came back, kind of scratchy. "Soon, honey. She has to work today. We'll meet her later."

But her voice didn't sound like the truth. It sounded like too much sticky-sweet stuff, like the cotton candy Mommy bought Haley at the fair last summer. It got too sweet and made her tongue hurt.

Mellie was like that. Too sweet, and made you hurt inside. Haley worked at her seat belt to get loose. It cut across her neck. She looked out the window. They were bumping over a bad road, and the trees were close enough to the van that some of the branches hit the window.

Haley looked down.

It was a long way. The trees were growing down the mountain; only the tops were showing up now. "I don't like this road."

"I don't either, Mama." Jennifer sounded like a sick cat. Haley'd heard one once and it was a terrible sound. It made her skin get all creepy.

All of a sudden there was a loud screech and a crash.

"Dang it!" Mellie stopped the van so fast it rocked back and forth. Mellie looked worried, real worried, and it scared Haley even more than her angry face had. "You kids stay here and don't move. I'll be right back. Don't move or the van could start to roll, you hear?"

Mellie was scaring them. Jennifer started to cry.

Mellie ran back down the road where they had come.

Haley scowled. She pushed the latch on her seat belt and this time it came loose. She crawled from the car seat to the front seat.

"What're you doing?" Jennifer whined.

"I'm gonna see what happened."

"The van will move!"

"No, it won't. The brake is on."

Mommy had shown her about hand brakes. Mommy always pulled on the hand brake. "The van won't move."

She pushed open the door and slid down out of the van. Mellie was way down the road, running away from them. Watching, Haley saw her stop at the edge of the road.

This was her chance. She'd go find her mommy. She'd heard

her, so she was somewhere around here.

Haley turned away and ran up the road. The down side of the mountain was too scary and steep, so she ran close to the side that went up. She ran as fast as she could, making her legs move as fast as possible.

After a little while her side hurt. She stopped and looked back. She couldn't see Mellie anymore and only the front of the van showed. She looked up the mountain. There was a tiny little path leading upward through the trees and rocks. She started up.

The ground was soft, sort of spongy from pine needles and the rocks were big, but she could crawl over them.

It smelled good here, like something clean. But it was a little cold. And her head hurt more now. Riding in cars always made her sick.

Still, she'd show Mellie. She'd go home all by herself.

Chapter 40

Joe drove steadily into the mountains, ignoring the speed limit. When he was at the station to let them scan Haley's picture, he had seen the charts Jansen posted. And the address in the mountains. Moose Lake, where the Galts had another property. He pressed harder on the gas pedal, passing a semitrailer truck struggling up the highway. Faster. His speedometer touched ninety.

So many things had gone so wrong. His good intentions, all lost. His questions about Karin, all wrong. She had told the truth. His letters, all kept by Linda Eberhard. No wonder Karin thought he had dumped her.

She had grown into a fine, independent woman who could take care of herself and her child. Without him.

Would she even want to try to make a relationship? Managing all this time, would she even want help? Or would what he had to offer even interest her?

He was an oil engineer. That meant time away from family. Even at his high level, he lived a solitary life. And if he were married, she would still face time alone. He could, he would, insist that she take money to support little Haley, but he realized he wanted to be a part of his child's life. More importantly, he wanted to be a part of Karin's life.

The muscles of his back and neck flexed as a wave of anger spread over his shoulders. Melanie Allen and whoever was helping her would pay. But when the heat of his anger faded, cold fear chilled him.

What was happening to that beautiful little girl whose picture he had in his pocket? He'd let the officers scan the photo, but he had kept the original. He pulled it out of his breast pocket and glanced at it while he drove. Haley and Karin. Where were they both now? Had Karin got his message?

Until a few days ago he was single, unattached, lonely once in a while, but overall okay with it. Now here he was, aching for a child he'd never seen and desiring the woman he thought he'd left behind. Could a person genuinely change that quickly? Could he?

Then he shook himself. He was getting ahead of things. First, he had to get Haley back.

Joe looked at his watch. He'd been on the road for forty minutes already. The general store should be coming up soon. Karin should be there, waiting, if she got his message.

The only other place he could think of that she could conceivably go was her father's. She'd gone there when she was accused in the Eberhard kidnapping, but soon afterward she'd left and disappeared. Something had happened to drive her away, and for some reason she went to Saint Louis where she had Haley, according to Jansen.

He had spent all that time with her six years ago, loving her, but never really getting to know her. He realized now that she had never talked about her family. The more he thought about it, the more he realized she had always turned the conversation to him, or to something current, anything, just not about her.

And her brother, Sam, had been the same, always in the present day, nothing of the past. And he, Joe, always thinking himself so smart, just loved being with them and never questioned a thing.

He pulled into the little parking lot in front of the general store. His rental car wasn't there. Where was Karin? Surely she wouldn't have gone on alone after Melanie.

Chapter 41

Karin lay totally still, waiting for the next roll, the next terrible sinking that would send the car pitching down the mountain. A rock clattered by on its way down. Then silence for at least four seconds, testimony to the distance of the fall. The car rocked on its side, the passenger side down, the door swinging open over empty space. A bird's call broke the quiet. Followed by the sound of metal scraping against stone.

Shock and terror left her trembling, but otherwise she was miraculously unhurt, except for a growing headache and pain in her arm where Roger's bullet from before had grazed her. Slowly, she assessed the damage. She touched the side of her head tentatively and found a swollen, tender spot about the size of a duck egg.

She tried to look up out of the driver's side window, but all that was visible was a frighteningly steep hillside of rock and brush. The road was way above her. No one would ever see her down here, and it was only a matter of time before the weight of the car sent it tumbling down the mountain. All that was needed was for the boulder or tree holding the car to loosen.

The driver's side was uppermost. Cautiously, she tried the door. Jammed.

She would have to slide out of the downward side of the car and hope it didn't roll on top of her. A huge risk, but if she stayed where she was, she would be killed with the next roll of the vehicle when it plunged down.

Drawing a deep breath, she released the seat belt cutting across her belly. Immediately she slid across the console, onto the passenger seat, toward the open door. She came to a stop, her head dangling outside the car.

The car rocked ominously. Only the slenderest of trees and a small boulder appeared to hold it back. From what she could see, the car had stopped on a crest. Two feet below it was a slender ledge then a drop-off of some fifty feet. The car teetered forward, seeming to hold there, perched against a thin young sapling. A low, creaking noise came from the little tree as though it was ever so slowly losing its battle to cling to the mountainside.

The oily smell of gasoline filled her nose. She had to get out. Fast.

Inching forward, she put her hand over her head to break the fall. If she angled it just right, she'd land on the little ledge when she fell out of the car. If she went too far, disaster. Gulping air, she hesitated. So far down.

The screech of metal against rock sounded. The car shuddered.

She shoved. Hard. At first she slid slowly, then the weight of her body carried her out in a slipping roll. Down, bumping, scraping. She landed with a crunch, blessedly on the ledge, her legs slipping down to lie on the narrow outcropping. For a moment she lay still, thankful to be alive. Then she belly-crawled forward, the rock scraping her arms. Above her the car tilted, leaning out farther until it seemed to hang in midair.

Only a few feet and she would be safe. She wriggled forward. Then her jeans caught on something. Above her, the car teetered. If it went over, she would be dragged along with it.

She tried to pull leg away from the snag, but couldn't.

Reaching back, she found the rear bumper had cracked and a strip of it had stabbed through her back pocket. She scooted backward and worked at the material, trying to loosen it.

The car shuddered again, as though it sensed what was to come.

She felt the ground beneath her leg rise as a root of the little tree started to pull loose.

She thrust herself backwards further to free her jeans. Again the car teetered. Her jeans loosened from the ragged piece of bumper.

Terrified, she scrambled forward over rock and gravel to a large boulder. She wrapped her arms around it and curled up with her legs tight to her body and then watched, mesmerized, as the little tree leaned farther and farther until it bent out of sight.

A low groan from somewhere: the tree or the car, she didn't know which. Then the car moved in slow motion. The earth under her legs seemed to rise. Dislodged rocks clattered down the mountain. The tree roots ripped loose from the rocky earth.

The car nosed over, engine first, and plummeted. Gone except for the resounding crash as it bounced off boulders, down, down, to the final, splintering crash.

For minutes after it reached the bottom, Karin lay with her eyes closed, willing her heart to stop tripping and her hands to relax their grip on the boulder.

"Karin?"

Was someone calling her name? She twisted to look up. At first she couldn't see who it was. Then, far above, she spied a thin, shaking figure. Melanie. Karin raised a hand and waved. She had no strength to shout.

Melanie turned and saw her. "Oh God, Karin, I'm so sorry. I didn't mean for it to go this way."

Karin's voice was a croak. "Mellie, help me!"

"I'll send someone."

"Mellie, help!" A mere whisper, no more. Head spinning, Karin laid her cheek against the rocks.

CHAPTER 42

Mellie clutched her stomach as she ran back toward the van, pain roiling inside. She shouldn't have stopped, shouldn't have taken the time, shouldn't have called out to Karin. What was wrong with her? Why did she care?

Her mind was a jumble. Something had to be done about Karin. And then there was that cop. That had been a nightmare. She pulled out her cell phone and pressed the numbers for Roger. "Rog, it's me. Are you back in Colorado yet?"

"I left the plane in Capstone and I'm about half an hour away from the cabin now, why?"

There was an edge in Roger's voice. *He's still pissed about the cop and getting more nervous,* she thought. He wouldn't like this, but she said it anyway. "Karin saw me at the store when I went to get medicine for Haley. I got away, but I didn't get any medicine and she followed us and on that last big curve her car went over the edge."

"Probably better she's dead."

"But she's not dead. We've got to get her."

"What do you mean?"

"I couldn't just leave her there, Roger. I had to see if she was alive."

"She saw you?" He was biting off his words. Bad sign. Really bad.

"Yeah, I know she's alive 'cause she answered me."

"You called to her?" His voice was incredulous.

"Sure, how else was I going to know if she was alive? I couldn't crawl down there."

"You could have left well enough alone."

That's what she should have done, but she couldn't. He wouldn't understand, though. "Roger, that's not so. You know it isn't. We might need her."

"You can't put an adult kidney into a kid!"

"Yes, you can. There are ways. If the kid's big enough, and Donny is."

"You don't know if she's a match."

She hesitated. She'd never told Roger who Donny's biological father was, just told him that Zeb was Donny's adoptive father, which he was sort of, well, not really, but almost. Never confessed how she'd loved Zeb and thought he would leave his wife and marry her. Or how he'd lied to and threatened her until she gave Donny up to him. And to that wife he'd said he would leave, but wouldn't.

In fact, if Roger knew Zeb was Donny's father he'd never, ever go through with any of this. Worse, if he knew, he might start thinking too hard about Zeb. He might start wondering just how long she'd been away from Zeb. She couldn't risk it. Couldn't dare let him start wondering about Jen. She said softly, "Yes, I do. She's a match."

"How do you know?"

"I typed her." Good thing she had worked out that lie ahead of time. "I got a blood sample by lying to her and typed her at Wetford's lab. And if Haley isn't going to work, then we need Karin."

"Shit! How many people are we going to line up, Mellie? You can't have the whole world standing by to snatch kidneys from."

"Just these two, that's all."

Silence. Then, in a strained voice that grew harsher as he spoke, Roger said, "Mel, Karin will be missed. Maybe no one saw her kid, but Karin is different. Remember, that's why we didn't take her in the first place. The cops have figured out who she is. That's why that one came up to the cabin. We don't have time to mess with her. Let her die out there on the side of the mountain, looking like an accident. You never should have gone back."

He was almost shouting by the time he stopped. Mel imagined his expression, the two little frown lines dividing his brow, the glint in his deep-set eyes. "Trust me, Rog, if I could get her up the mountain into the van myself, I would. You know I'd give Donny my kidney, but I'm not even close as a match."

Roger still made no comment, so Mel rushed on. "I had to wait until I saw her crawl out of the car. God, it was awful. She just barely got out before the car rolled over and down the mountainside. She was nearly killed."

Mellie turned, watching the van. No movement inside. The girls were fine. Safe.

"Too bad she couldn't've—" He muttered something else under his breath, then after a brief moment he asked, "Where is she now?"

"Lying about thirty feet down the mountainside, off Old Gracefield Road, a little over two miles from the highway. You'll see the tracks where her car left the road. She's got to have help."

"She saw you, Mellie. You know what that means."

"We'll work it out. Just get her," she said and started walking back up the road toward the van. "We can hold her, take her to Mexico and we can let her go there. Look, Rog, I gotta get going or I'll never make it there."

Silence. Then, "Okay. I'll take care of it."

His tone brought her the old feeling of a snake gnawing at her insides. "Promise me you won't hurt her. We may need her. If things don't work out with Haley."

"What do you mean, if things don't work out."

"If Haley's too sick. Or we need another kidney for some reason."

"Oh. I'll keep that in mind, right when I'm burying that damn cop you killed," he said, but his voice was sarcastic, like he was just saying it for her sake and going to do exactly what he wanted to do.

"Promise me!"

"Yeah, sure. Promise."

The feeling of unease didn't go away as Mellie walked quickly to the van. She picked up her pace, hurrying so she wouldn't feel so bad that she'd go back and try to help Karin.

She reached the van, put a hand on the door, and stopped. She'd left the door closed. Wrenching it open wide, she saw the empty car seat. "Where's Haley?"

Jennifer shook her head. "She runned away."

"Where? Where'd she go?"

Jennifer's frightened eyes were huge in her face. "That way." She pointed up the road.

"Don't move, baby. I'm going to get her." Mellie slammed the van door. "Haley! Haley, come here. I've got news!"

She ran forward up the road, then around the bend. Nothing. No sign of the child. "Oh, God, no!"

How long had she been gone? Looking over the mountain talking to Karin couldn't have been more than a couple minutes, or maybe five. Then the call to Roger another minute or so . . . how far could a little girl go in that time?

"Haley!" Mellie ran on up the winding road, shouting, "Haley, there are mountain lions out here. Haley, come here. You'll get lost. Come on honey, we'll have some cocoa and cookies. Your mommy will be here soon."

The only sound was a camp robber jay screaming in the treetop.

Would Haley go up the hillside, or down? Mellie ran to the far edge of the road and peered over. A sheer drop. She shuddered. If Haley went over the edge there . . . but she wouldn't. Mel couldn't bear to think of that.

She ran back across the road and looked up along the rising side for footprints in the soft earth. Doubling back toward the van, she looked again, examining each moist spot for signs of a little foot. Nothing.

"Haley!"

Back again farther along the road, looking upward. At this altitude spring had only begun to green the brush and the hillside. Haley had been wearing a little red jacket. It should show up among the still-bare bushes.

Finally she struck up the mountainside at a place where the earth looked slightly disturbed. Could it be Haley? Or some night-animal's track? Oh pray God it wasn't some awful wildcat.

"Haley! It will be dark soon. Come here, honey. We'll find your mommy."

Just as she was about to turn back again, she looked up. Some twenty yards ahead and above she spotted a flash of red. In this area at this time of year, nothing in nature was red. It had to be Haley.

Mellie moved quickly, the chill air closing in on her. The red color disappeared from sight briefly, then came again. It was Haley's jacket. But Haley wasn't in it.

"Haley! Where are you? Why don't you answer me?"

Barely visible in the softened earth, Mellie spotted little footprints. A tiny rivulet fed by melting snow from above ran nearby, tinkling over rocks as it cascaded down the mountainside.

Surely Haley wouldn't have fallen into the water.

Mellie pushed through a stand of prickly brush. The sound of the snowmelt was closer. "Haley! Oh, my God, no!"

Haley lay on the bank of the stream, her hand dangling in the freezing water.

Chapter 43

Jansen's gut was still in an uproar when he reached Dr. Wetford's office, still in revolt from the sight of those poor bodies at the crematorium. At least the three boxes in the cooler from other sources had held bodies untouched by even a postmortem examination.

Only Wetford's cases had been harvested. Johnny Ray, young and healthy until his death from a head injury, had provided the most parts. It might be legal, depending on whether the organs were donated or sold, and harvesting certainly saved lives, but the way Wetford had left Johnny Ray was nothing short of desecration. And the story, of how Johnny Ray had suddenly gone from healthy but injured to dead, was suspect. It was one thing to harvest from donors, another to make someone dead so they would become a donor. Jansen suspected Johnny Ray may have been "selected" to be a donor.

However illegal it was to sell human cadaver organs, bones, skin or anything else, Jansen knew there was a market. The very notion of that repugnant commerce made his blood boil. If Oak Manor, or Ethan Morgan, or this Dr. Wetford, any one of them, was making money by helping people along, by God, he'd find out.

Even if the harvesting was done legally and the organs were given to people legitimately on the waiting lists, Jansen suspected that Oak Manor was making money in some way. What kind of physician was Wetford, that he could harvest bodies in that manner? What made this man tick? And then Jansen thought, he didn't really care what made Wetford tick. He just wanted to stop him.

He cut the engine, stepped from the car and breathed deeply to calm himself. A memory flashed. He'd been in Oak Manor for rehab briefly after his accident and had appreciated the surprisingly low bill. He himself might have benefitted from this very practice. The thought left him a little sick.

Wetford's office was in a neighborhood of staid homes, old trees full of birds singing, a total contrast to the scene he had just left. Jansen wondered, fearfully, what he would learn from Wetford's office and what it might mean for Haley Preston.

He rang and pushed open the door when the electronic buzzer sounded. The doctor's offices showed only a single light in the hallway.

Inside a small, well-groomed woman sat at a clear desk, a flat screen of a computer the only sign of activity.

Jansen approached her. "I'd like to see Doctor Wetford."

"Do you have an appointment?"

He held out his badge. "The doctor."

"I'm afraid he isn't available just now."

"Is he here?"

"I can't answer that."

"You can answer it here, or at the police station, which will it be?"

"He isn't here now." She ducked her head, then spoke again. "He cancelled his appointments for this afternoon."

"I see. What about his nurse, Melanie Allen?"

"I'm afraid I don't know who you mean."

"The one who assists him at the nursing home."

"I can't help you on that."

"Again, it's here or downtown. You choose. Think it through carefully."

"I don't have to answer that."

"I believe you do."

"There is no one else here now. I'm the only one in the building."

"I'll wait for the doctor. And while I wait, I'll exercise this warrant. I need to see his office. His date book, his calendar, his patient list."

"That's confidential. Your warrant won't cover that."

"I believe it will. It's a subpoena *duces tecum.* It will cover two of his patients. Haley Preston and Johnny Ray Alders."

Twin red spots appeared on her cheeks, belying her cool composure. Jansen pressed on. "I just came from Morgan's Crematorium and it wasn't pretty. Now, I'm looking into a missing-child case. Do you understand why I'm so concerned?"

Her right hand shook mildly. "Do you realize what you're implying?"

"I certainly do. Do you want to aid and abet Doctor Wetford or do you want to assist the police?"

Her lips parted slightly, then pressed shut tight. She rose abruptly, then stood hesitantly. "Those names again?"

"Johnny Ray Alders and Haley Preston or Haley McGrath."

"Preston, McGrath?" The receptionist grew pale. He had finally reached some human decency in her. She rose and marched to a small room filled with medical records stuffed into file shelves. She returned with two slim files. "The McGrath file isn't here."

Jansen scanned the brief notes. The date was nine months ago. Haley Preston, then nearly five years old, presented with a sore throat, vomiting and small fever but otherwise in no distress and in good health. Tests ordered, prescription for amoxicillin noted, follow up at mother's request. The good doctor could easily have told him he'd seen Haley.

Then, familiar with medical records after the hospitalization and death of his wife and little daughter, he flipped to the lab pages. As he read these pages, a hollow pit grew in his belly. He reread the lab results. Haley had come in for a question of strep throat, but Wetford had ordered several blood tests, typing and matching tests.

He reached for Johnny Ray's chart. The first contact was nearly six months earlier when Johnny Ray was in the hospital, being treated for his original head injury.

From his cell phone, Jansen called Johnny Ray's sister.

Sissy's voice was breathy when she answered. "No. I'm positive. The first time Doctor Wetford saw Johnny Ray was about a month ago here at the house when he came to assess him for rehab. I'm sure."

"Did you sign for Doctor Wetford to have copies of Johnny's hospital chart?"

"Probably. I signed for so many things, it was probably in there too."

But in the chart it clearly noted that Wetford had seen Johnny Ray in the hospital six months earlier. And Johnny's lab sheets, duplicates of the hospital chart, were here and included blood type and other identifying tests, identical to those Wetford ordered for Haley Preston. Wetford had identified Johnny Ray as a potential donor at the time of his original injury, not later, when he was back at home recuperating. So he was a "selected" donor. And it looked like Haley also had been identified as a donor.

He stormed back to the receptionist. "How many patients does the doctor have lined up for transplantation?"

"I can't . . ."

"Answer me now!"

"Several adults." She wavered under his glare and added, "Maybe ten."

"Is it possible to use a child-sized kidney for an adult?"

Her voice was low as she spoke. "It can be done, but size matters. It's always best if the size of the donor kidney is approximately the same as the failing one. So, an adult kidney can be used for a large child, but not an infant."

Jansen felt his heart speed up. "And a child's kidney? Would it serve for an adult?"

She shook her head slowly, her lips barely moving as she answered. "For an adult, you need to use both of the child's kidneys together."

"How many transplants can a person have?"

Her voice remained low, throaty, as though she was now speaking around a sizeable lump of pain. "It depends on why the kidney is rejected and/or the health of the patient. If the patient is sensitized, rejection of a transplant is more likely." Her eyes seemed to focus across the room. "If the patient is a sick child who has had at least one transplant fail, then the child will do best with a very good match, like a relative who is a perfect match."

It made an ugly picture in Jansen's mind. "You mentioned a McGrath chart that isn't here. I need to see it. Where is it?"

"Doctor has it."

"What is the name, the first name of the McGrath patient?"

"I can't tell you that."

"Is it Zebulon?"

"Oh, no."

"Then his son."

Tears sprang to her eyes, confirmation. "You have to understand. Doctor Wetford is a wonderful doctor." She locked gazes with Jansen. "There are over twenty-six million Americans with chronic kidney disease, one in nine of us, and some twenty million more at risk. Some eighty-five thousand people are on waiting lists for kidney transplants, probably even more. Doctor

Wetford does transplants on people who can't get them otherwise."

"A very dedicated man, I'm sure."

"He is. His wife died of kidney disease because there wasn't a kidney for her. He's pioneered a special technique and he's an expert at doing living transplants, taking them from a living donor to give to a dying person. He has saved so many lives." She rose from her chair. "So, you might be lucky enough never to need a transplant, but thousands of people have needed them because of accidents, disease or whatever."

Jansen's head snapped back. He had had bone graft following his accident, and never given a thought to where it came from. He looked at the woman's pale, intense expression. "This is very personal for you." It was now personal for him, too, but he wasn't going to get into that.

Her lips trembled. "I'm one of the eighty-five thousand."

"Where does Wetford do his transplants? What hospital?"

"Mexico," she breathed. "He has a clinic there."

A clinic in Mexico, for private surgery. Private for cash, for people who wanted or needed to skirt the listing process. "Where he is now?"

"He also has a clinic in the mountains where his patients recuperate. In Capstone. He's on his way there. He plans to fly to Mexico from there."

"How long ago did he leave?"

Her voice was a broken whisper. "Half an hour, no, maybe an hour, but he had some stops to make."

No time to waste. Once little Haley Preston was on the plane for Mexico, she'd be out of his reach. At the door Jansen glanced back at the receptionist. She had buried her head in her hands.

Chapter 44

Mellie dried Haley's hand, then carried her whimpering back to the van and bundled her into the front seat, wrapped in the blanket they always carried in the back of the van. "Wake up, Haley. Got to drink a bit of water."

Haley's forehead was hot, but she had just been sleeping, not unconscious, as Mel had first thought when she saw the child lying on the ground. Carefully, she trickled a bit of water into her mouth, massaging her throat to get it swallowed.

Haley stirred, her cheeks red from fever. "Mommy!" she whispered.

Melanie was near tears. Whatever relief she had felt finding Haley merely asleep and feverish now dissolved. If Haley had an infection, she couldn't safely undergo the surgery. Further, her kidney wouldn't be safe for Donny. Any infection when he was so weakened would be fatal. "Take some more water, hon. It'll make you feel better." Mellie stroked her forehead, then her cheeks, just as she'd seen Karin do and hoped Haley would be comforted.

Jennifer piped up from the backseat. "What's the matter with Haley?"

"Shhhh, honey. She's got a bad cold, that's all." But it didn't look like a cold. "Here Haley, hon, take some more sips of this."

They'd go as soon as she got enough water in Haley to break the fever.

From experience, she knew that two more miles into the

mountains and she'd have no reception on her little phone. Almost panting, Mellie opened the cell and made a call. She had to get away, but she couldn't bear to go until she'd checked on Donny.

A single ring and the familiar voice answered, harsh from tension. "H'llo."

"How's Donny?" Mellie urged the last of the water into Haley as she listened.

"Not so bad." His voice dropped to a barely audible whisper. "Wetford says he's got to do the surgery in Mexico. He doesn't have the staff or the equipment to do it here, but he can take the kidney from the kid, so get her here. Where are you now? You sound anxious."

Mellie brushed her hair out of her face and started the van. "We're going to need Karin."

She heard him catch his breath. "Why's that?"

"Haley's sick. Donny will catch whatever she's got and he might not make it. She might not survive either."

He spoke heavily. "When will you get here?"

"Be about an hour and a half. Meet at your place?"

"No. Stop at the clinic and get the doc. Meet at the airport. We've got to get off the ground before the weather deteriorates. There's a spring storm coming in."

Melanie's gut clenched at the sound of the abrupt hang-up, tightening the coil in her stomach to a knot of hot, heavy iron. The weather always deteriorated at night this time of year up at Capstone. Something about the altitude, Roger had said. But that meant the flight could be delayed if she didn't get up there.

Gunning the motor, she steered the van over the ruts as it shot down the road. She had taken this backcountry lane that would bring her over Mule Head pass and down into Capstone faster, if she could just keep the van on the road. It was such an unwieldy vehicle.

The wheels hit a pothole. The steering wheel jerked out of her hands as the van slid, the rear end swinging out toward the edge of the road. She braked. Turned into the skid. Inches from the edge of the road the van halted.

Frustrated, she pounded the steering wheel. If she couldn't manage even this lower part of the road easily, then there was no way she could make it over that pass. It was mud season. The pass would be mired in melt-slick clay. She glanced at the gas gauge. Close to empty. She winced. That was the other thing she had meant to get in town. Gas. She'd have to take the highway, and she'd have to stop for gas, but at least with Karin down the mountain she wasn't as pressured as before.

She sucked in a deep breath and glanced at Haley. Resting calmly now, Haley slumped against the door, the seat belt cutting across her neck.

Mellie reached across and pulled it away, slipping it under Haley's arm, then turned the van around and carefully eased back and forth until she was headed back toward the junction with the highway.

She had to admit, she was feeling better since she'd seen Karin was alive. One way or another, Roger would get her. He was that way. He got things done. As soon as Donny had his surgery, life would be good again. One way or another, all the rest of the problems would work out, once Donny was well.

Chapter 45

Karin shivered. The sharp edge of a rock bit painfully into her cheek. She glanced up and saw a cloud drift slowly over the late afternoon sun, and felt an immediate drop in temperature. How long she had been unconscious, she didn't know, only that ground cold had seeped into her bones leaving her thoroughly chilled. And, oh yes, Mellie—her professed best friend—had kidnapped Haley.

She closed her eyes again, breathing in the resin and mineral scent of the air, hearing the soft breeze rustling in the tops of the pine trees below her on the slope. It would be so easy to just go back to sleep, but she couldn't. There was Haley. Everything ached—muscles, head, especially her arm—but she could move her fingers and toes. She pushed herself to sitting, waited a few minutes until dizziness abated.

The sun hung just over the high granite peaks to her right, soon to dip behind them. Sunlight dimmed earlier in the mountains, somewhere around four-thirty, five o'clock. Then hypothermia would become her worst enemy. She must move soon, must reach the roadside and hope to get a ride back to the little store to use their phone.

She was used to mountain terrain, but this was a steep slope, the rock surfaces smooth and slippery, her legs unsteady. She crawled, easing over waist-high granite outcroppings, held her breath stepping over boulders that threatened to spill her down the mountainside.

Shaking, she finally reached the roadside and steadied herself against a boulder. Karin looked back down the mountain. A thin wisp of smoke curled up from below in the canyon. Ahead in the road were the tire tracks where her car had slid off.

Patting her pockets, she found she had also lost her wallet. All she had left was a wadded old tissue and two name cards, extras she carried to give clients. *Useless,* she thought and tossed them aside, stumbling forward as fast as she could. She had no money, no identification. And no time to waste. She had to get to the store before it closed. Before Mellie got even farther away.

The thought drove her forward until she stumbled and had to rest. This didn't happen just because she'd trusted Mellie, it happened also because she had wanted a free night all to herself. Her selfishness had entered in. That and her pride in Haley. Her bragging about how perfect she was. Mellie had always agreed, pointing out how like Jennifer Haley was.

Nicole Eberhard had been a perfect baby, too. The only imperfection had been a strawberry mark on her inner elbow. Small, bright red, and completely distressing to her mother, who wanted it gone. Linda was so proud of Nicole, so determined that she would be the perfect child. Even Karin had been taken with how beautiful Nicole was.

The first week Karin was Nicole's nanny, Edward Eberhard had arranged for the mark to be removed. Karin slowed. Dr. Wetford! Why hadn't she remembered that birthmark surgery before? Dr. Wetford had removed the mark at his private surgery.

Karin tripped over a rock at the side of the road. She fell, but scrambled up, racing forward now even as her mind raced ahead, chasing one wild, terrifying thought after another.

Edward could have met Dr. Wetford at the nursing home when he was there visiting his aging mother. Wetford could have been the elderly Mrs. Eberhard's doctor. And, just as he'd offered a professional courtesy to Karin, Wetford might have offered to do the surgery on Nicole. Edward never would have suspected Wetford could have a darker reason for offering. He probably figured it was a wonderful opportunity. Cheaper, quicker.

And Mellie could have been Wetford's surgical nurse. Maybe that was when she began to be Mrs. Eberhard's private-duty nurse.

It seemed so clear now. Mellie kidnapped Haley, and before her Nicole, whose body was never found. Had she kidnapped other children too? But why would she do this? And if she took other children, where were they?

Karin tried to run, her lungs burning in the thin air, her chest working, her feet leaden. She stopped to catch her breath and realized her left arm ached. The sleeve of her coat was soaked in blood at the elbow. Closer examination showed a long tear in her sleeve and under it a shallow but bleeding cut. She hadn't even felt it with all the adrenaline in her system.

In the distance she heard a motor, a vehicle winding fast up the twisting road. Mellie might be coming back. Karin stepped down off the edge of the road near a tree where she could hide if she needed to.

The growl of the engine came closer. A flash of red through the trees below. Red. An SUV, a sturdy four-wheel-drive car. More importantly, not Mellie.

Karin stepped back up onto the road, waving her arms. She had to get the SUV to stop.

The vehicle rounded the last curve, approaching quickly. Karin stepped into the middle of the road. The driver would have to stop that way.

It came faster. Dust rising behind it as the wheels dug in. It was accelerating! Coming toward her. The driver didn't see her.

She dodged back to the edge of the road and slid on loose

rock, tumbled and rolled down the hill, coming to rest against a downed log, her fall cushioned by the rotting wood. Shaking, Karin rose and staggered forward. The rough ground caught at her feet; undergrowth and foot-high boulders hindered her progress. Desperate, she shouted and waved her arms. She had to get his attention.

The engine whined as the driver downshifted, then stopped. Wheels bit into the grit on the road. Dust rose. The engine idled, and a door slammed.

"Karin! Sorry! Didn't mean to scare you."

Her name, but an unfamiliar voice. She hesitated. How did he know her name? She slipped behind a tree, hoping it hid her.

"Karin, I didn't see you at first. Come on. We've got a lead on Haley. Get on up here."

She didn't move.

He started down. "I'm with the Ridgewood police. Come on now." His footsteps came closer. "I can see you. Your jacket is covered with dust and pine needles. Now come on. You're wasting time here. Time Haley doesn't have."

Did he really see her? She called out. "What's your name?"

"Snyder. Detective Wendell Snyder. Ridgewood police."

The smoothness of his voice, his seeming reassurance, didn't quite ring true. Still, she was too exhausted to run, too defeated to resist, and there was the hope he was telling the truth, that they really did have a lead on Haley's whereabouts.

"Come on up here. We got a tip where to find her. Only you need to hurry. We either get to her now, or they'll get her away."

"Away where? What are you talking about?"

"They're going to take her to Mexico."

Karin's skin crawled. Mexico? Then how would she find her daughter?

She was so paranoid at this point, she didn't know who to trust. But he said he knew where to look. She couldn't afford to refuse. Slowly, Karin came out from behind the tree.

Above on the shoulder of the road stood a tall, lean man with broad shoulders and a narrow face. His rumpled jacket lifted in the light breeze, the edge of it revealing a small holstered handgun. But he hadn't drawn it or threatened her. Maybe the quickest way to get to Haley was to let him take her there. At the least, she'd go along until she knew for sure. "Where's Haley now?"

A shadow seemed to flicker across his face. Then he raised his head and laughed. "They're up at the old Galt place. That's what you suspected isn't it?"

Her breath coming so quickly she almost choked, she whispered, "Yes." She climbed the last several feet, her legs aching and weak.

He reached out. "Give me your hand. I've got water in the car. You look like you could use some." He pulled her up the last few steps, his hand gripping her right forearm. "Get in. We're not far from where she is."

Closer now, Karin saw that he had deep-set eyes and a long thin nose. Her feet could barely move and as she tripped on the last step her gaze fell on his feet. Boots, muddy. Like the ones she'd seen on her attacker at Kenny's place. She tried to wrench away, but he held fast. In that moment she saw the long scratch at the right side of his face, running from the corner of his eye down his cheek. "You!"

CHAPTER 46

Joe sped up the canyon as fast as he dared.

He was both furious with Karin and amazed at her resilience. This was a definitely different woman from the smiling, innocent young thing he'd known and loved before. He admired and desired her. She was independent, strong, intelligent and utterly determined to find their child.

At the same time, she didn't know, couldn't know, how ruthless these people could be and that left him very fearful for her safety. Despite everything Mellie had done, Karin didn't seem to really fear her.

He did, though. He believed Karin when she said she'd seen Kenny Bristow dead. He'd seen the fellow blow out the windows of her car. No matter the police had not found a body, the shooter probably took it away. Then, when he'd stopped by the police station that morning with the photo of Haley for them to copy, he learned Jansen was out on another call. An old woman, a neighbor to the house where Karin had left Haley, had been attacked. It looked to Joe like the kidnappers were getting rid of witnesses.

The pine trees at the side of the road were a blur as he accelerated on the straights.

That the kidnappers would have a secondary place to stay near Denver made sense. He just couldn't figure out how they could live in someone else's place without being caught. But then, maybe they didn't stay only there. Maybe they had more places and moved often.

The side roads here weren't marked so far as Joe could see. He finally turned around and drove back to the little general store he'd seen. They'd know where the road was.

They did. Or, she did. She only grudgingly told him where the turnoff could be found. If he hadn't asked, he'd never have found it, since Old Gracefield Road split off from the North Creek turnoff, a good half mile in.

He rounded a sharp bend, caught sight of the rubber marks on the pavement. Someone had gone over the edge. He skidded to a stop at the side of the road, jumped out of his car and ran to the edge where the guardrail was broken. Peering down, he saw the trail of broken saplings and rutted earth where a car had evidently fallen. He hoped it wasn't Karin, but he had to call out. "Karin! Karin! Anyone!" No answer.

"Hello! Anyone?" No answer. He was turning away when he caught sight of a small, bright white rectangle of paper. Reaching it, he saw it was a business card. Karin's card.

Refusing to believe the worst, he got back into his car and pushed onward, telling himself it could have been anyone who lost it, maybe earlier, not today at all. He had to get to the Galts' mountain place. Despite all his efforts, he felt sick.

A couple miles up the road, he found the mailbox marked *Galt* at the side of the road. The drive disappeared sharply down and around the side of the mountain in a narrow and deeply rutted track. Walking would be the safest way in since he wasn't familiar with the terrain. Years ago when he'd lived in Colorado, he'd been over enough mountain tracks to know that when they were unused and unmaintained, they could be treacherous. He pulled several yards ahead to park at a wide shoulder.

He jogged down a track so narrow he doubted a car could safely pass through, but then in the softened earth of a low spot he saw the fresh tracks. Someone had come through recently.

Twenty yards farther on he came to a dip in the road where a stream, running with snowmelt from above, trickled over, gradually washing away the soil. Tracks led in, running on the upside of the mountain. A car would tilt dangerously passing through.

On the other side of the washout, shoes soaked, he rounded a corner. Almost before he saw the house itself, he saw a large wraparound porch that hung out over the steep hillside, and over a stone patio below. The cabin was a simple structure, basically two stories, the ground level and a large walk-out basement level. Before it, in a widened area, stood a red Chevy Tahoe parked in front of the steps leading to the porch and the front door.

Joe ducked to the side of the vehicle, using it as cover, and approached the house from the hillside. He peered through a handy window, only to find he could see nothing. A black shade covered the glass. He listened, but heard nothing except the breeze in the aspen trees uphill.

Moving around the house, he crept along to the next window. A slit at the side of the shade let him see a slender form on a narrow bed. Karin. She was lying down, one wrist fastened to an iron bedstead. She was thrashing, fighting, trying to loosen the binding on her wrist. The same lean, thin man he'd seen at Karin's apartment house stood next to the bed, cell phone to his ear, facing away. He could hear the man's voice, but the words were muffled.

The look of fear on Karin's face brought fury, almost blinding him. Joe's first thought was to smash the window and beat the man to a pulp, but he forced himself to calm down, think. He needed to get the man where he couldn't use Karin as a shield or threaten her.

Ducking down, Joe hustled on around the house, down to the lower level, sliding in a rush of loose soil. The sliding door off the stone patio was locked tight. The only way in would be the front door.

He stole back upslope to the front, sneaked across the porch boards and eased in the door. He was in a large living room, fireplace in the center back wall with a couch, two wicker chairs and a swivel desk chair, looking very out of place. He started across the floor. He sensed movement to the side and ducked as he turned, his right fist hard and quick. The blow crashed into his assailant's neck as a flash of pain shot through his shoulder. He had just enough time to catch his balance before the next blow landed straight in his gut.

Joe staggered back.

Brass knuckles flashed as the guy lashed out again. Joe danced to the side, took the glancing blow on his raised left arm and drove a hard punch to the man's unguarded middle. It landed heavily on the point of his sternum, enough, Joe thought briefly, to drop the guy in his tracks. But instead of losing his breath, his bright, icy blue eyes seemed almost to blaze as though the pain only heightened his senses.

Joe backed up farther, bumped into the desk chair and stumbled. A blow hit his head so sharp and bright it turned everything orange as he hit the floor.

CHAPTER 47

Jansen drove up the canyon. He glanced at his wristwatch, saw that it was three-twenty and flipped open his cell phone. The sergeant at the station said Frost was still out. "Haven't seen him since ten-thirty this morning. Must be onto something big."

Jansen cursed to himself. "Well, tell him to call me. I'm going first to the Galt cabin, be there in about fifteen minutes. They're probably not there, but I'll check it. From there I'm going up to Capstone. Would you alert the sheriff's office up there, request warrants? You can e-mail them to me on my phone. I think they'll head for the airstrip in Capstone."

The sergeant replied, "Better check the weather. It can get dicey, especially at that altitude."

"I think these guys will take off in a blizzard," Jansen said. *And we wouldn't be in this spot if I had believed Karin sooner.* He'd been blinded by the Eberhard case, just as the kidnappers had planned. And exactly as Karin had said would happen.

Quarter of an hour later, he flashed past the Moose Lake Bar and Grill and slowed. Fifty yards on, he ground to a stop in front of a small general store, perched on the main road in the village of Moose Lake.

Inside, he approached the woman behind the counter and showed his badge and identification. "Ridgewood police. I'm looking for a woman about five eight, slim, dark-gold hair, gray eyes. She may have come in here to ask about a slightly built woman with two kids?"

She peered over a pair of reading glasses at him. "Lotsa folks looking for that gal. Must be important."

"It is."

Shaking her head, she said, "She asked about a woman with a kid, or maybe two, that looked alike. Then she spotted the woman outside and took off after her. Nearly got hit by a car, she was in that big of a hurry."

"You've seen the woman she was asking about before?"

"She's been here before, only with just one girl."

"How long ago was that?"

"About a week ago, I guess."

Jansen turned to leave, then stopped. "What about the others asking about her?"

The woman seemed to think about whether she'd answer. Finally she said, "Guess I don't know why you're asking."

"There's a little girl been kidnapped. I think these people can help us find her."

"Well, there was a fella in here not long ago asking if I could tell him where the Galt place was, just like the woman before him."

"Did he give a name?"

"Joe something. Don't really remember."

Maybe she just didn't feel like telling him, Jansen thought, but it didn't make sense to get into a battle over it. "Can you describe the car the woman was driving?"

"The one with the kid drives a Caravan, but they both pulled out going like hell up toward Old Gracefield Road.

Jansen left, driving steadily and as fast as he dared. The melted snow on the road forced him to take each curve with caution. He'd begun to wonder if he had passed the Galt place or missed the turn when he saw skid marks on the side of the road and a broken guardrail.

He parked on the soft shoulder, climbed out, and peered over the edge. A gash in the tundra led down. He called in an accident report, then sidestepped down the hill, half slipping, to a spot where he could see a car might have rested before tumbling over. Below, a barely visible wisp of smoke drifted, coiling in the still air, dissipating before it reached him. That was all he could see.

Hoping, yet dreading to hear a response, he yelled, "Karin! Melanie!"

Birds quieted. Stillness spread over the hillside, smothering his shout. Sickened, he scoured the hillside for signs of a survivor. Nothing. As he climbed back to the tarmac at an angle to ease the pressure on his knee, he discovered drag marks in the moist soil leading upward, as though someone might have crawled to the road. Following along the edge of the road, he spotted a white card lying almost hidden. He picked it up. A business card. Karin Preston's.

Some eight miles further, Jansen spied a rusted mailbox at the side of the road leaning as though it had been rammed by a car on the skid. Faint lettering spelled the name *Galt.* The road in was narrow and heavily rutted, leading to a cabin built into the side of the hill, with a wide balcony hanging over space. His car was standard-issue cop car, worn and low-slung. On that road, he'd be high-centered and possibly stuck for hours. He pulled around the curve ahead and discovered another car parked on the side of the road. Jansen parked and jumped out. He touched the other car's hood. It was warm.

The last rays of sunlight glinted over the top of the mountain, lighting the cabin rooftop. Time was slipping by too fast. He jogged along, resenting every minute it took, wondering with each step if someone in the cabin was watching his progress, planning to pick him off when he got close. Sweat beaded his forehead more from nerves than heat.

He stepped carefully through a cold, melt-swollen creek, icy water soaking his feet. Within seconds they were numb as he moved forward until he reached the cabin nestled among pine trees, the windows dark and deserted-looking. The wide sun-porch that wrapped the cabin faced west toward the higher, snowcapped mountain range. Snug to the porch stood a mud-spattered, red Tahoe. Barely visible tracks in the soft earth led from the vehicle to the porch, as though someone had been forced along.

He could see no sign of anyone. Reaching the side of the SUV, he put his hand on the engine hood. It too was warm, but barely.

Jansen considered going to the rear of the cabin first, then noticed the front door was ajar. Not a good situation. Drawing his nine-millimeter Glock, he crept up the porch steps and stole inside.

The front door opened into a simple, large room sparsely furnished with a wicker couch and two chairs, which faced an empty fireplace. The air was warmer than outdoors and the scent of old wood smoke and ashes lingered, as though someone had been there and had a fire earlier.

He crossed the floor, thankful for the old braided rug that muffled his footsteps. To the right, he found a fairly modern kitchen, clean, but the stove had a scorch mark on the surface that might have been milk, boiled over and hurriedly cleaned up.

A muffled sound like a sob came from the rear of the cabin.

Jansen cat-footed to the door, halted, then swept in. Karin, lying on a thin mattress, her wrists tied to the iron headboard of a small bed, uttered a croak of stark terror until she focused on him and saw it was Jansen.

Blinking with pain, she choked out, "Have you found Haley? Mellie?"

He put a finger over his lips to quiet her, saying, "Not yet. We will. Are you all right?" He cut the ties that held her wrists, which were scored with blood, and noticed the left sleeve of her jacket was bloodstained as well. Her left cheek was reddened with fingerprint bruises. "You went off the road?"

"Yes. I'm bruised, but nothing's broken."

"Good. Now, who's here?"

"Roger. Mellie's husband. He's in the cellar. I think he killed Joe," she said in a whispered sob.

"Anyone else up here?"

She shook her head and stood unsteadily.

"As soon as you can, move outside. Hide. I'll call when it's safe. Take the cell. Use redial. It will get you to headquarters. Ask for backup."

Stealing back to the central room, then off to the left, Jansen found Joe Canan, furious, blood trickling down the side of his head where he'd been hit, mouth taped shut and bound to the leg of the iron claw-footed bathtub. He cut Joe loose, signaled silence and softly told him to go to Karin, then moved to the stairs leading down to the lower level. Sounds of a shovel scraping earth and someone panting heavily came from below. How far from the foot of the steps, he couldn't tell.

If he went down, he'd be seen. He ducked to the far side of the cellar opening, the side Roger would turn away from when he cleared the steps. He positioned himself and weighed the possibility of surprising Roger with a blow to the head that would knock him out. It worked in theory, but from his experience theory was a starting place, not an ending.

He needed to immobilize Roger, if possible with no fight, because in hand to hand, Roger would probably have the advantage. Jansen had to depend on surprise and his Glock.

He heard the clang of a shovel hitting rock, then a softer thud as it dropped to the ground. A grunt of satisfaction, then the sound of plastic rustling, probably being hefted, came up the stairwell. Roger had come back for his stash, no doubt planning to leave the country permanently. But where was Frost?

Footsteps started up the stairs.

The top of Roger's head showed.

Half hidden in the shadows, Jansen shrank back against the wall. He wanted Roger clear of the cellar, too far up to turtle back into the depths and safety.

Roger reached the top of the steps, his back to Jansen. He was holding a black plastic bag and a briefcase. He started to turn toward the living room.

"Police! Freeze!"

Roger stopped in mid step. "Who . . . ?"

Jansen jammed the Glock into Roger's back to prove he had the gun. Then, as he stepped back out of reach in case Roger decided to resist, he stepped on something. His ankle rolled and pain shot through his knee. He gasped, his knee collapsing, and barely caught himself before he fell.

Roger spun and got off a roundhouse kick.

His leg nearly paralyzed, Jansen scrambled to the side.

Roger plowed forward, knocking the wind out of him. A chop at Jansen's gun hand sent his Glock spinning across the floor and onto the deck. Roger circled, then grappled with Jansen, trying to crush him. Younger, stronger and in better shape, Roger dodged in close, hugged Jansen and lifted him. Carrying him backwards, like a crazy dancing bear, they staggered together toward the deck. The man was in top shape. Far better than Jansen with his bum knee.

Jansen jammed a thumb into Roger's throat, forcing his head back. A forearm across Roger's nose and the cartilage crunched. Roger howled as his grip loosened. Then his elbow smashed into Jansen's chin.

Sagging to his knees, Jansen thrust his arms around Roger's knees and reared back, using his weight against Roger's stance. Roger collapsed on the deck, momentarily breathless and stunned.

Jansen scrambled to his feet.

For an instant Roger sucked in a breath. Then he sprang whole into the air, his foot lashing out.

Grabbing for support, Jansen fell backward. There was nothing to break his fall and he crashed on his back onto the deck.

Roger's knee rose.

Jansen twisted away just before the boot came down. Roger's heel caught Jansen's hip bone, bruising, but missing his groin.

Jansen grasped Roger's boot and threw himself sideways in a desperate roll. Roger's knee twisted. He grunted with pain. Still, Roger managed to spin away onto the deck overhang.

Trap, Jansen thought, but scrambled after him. The vast hazy landscape flashed before his eyes, spreading away in a panorama of pine-clad mountains and valleys.

Roger's arm whipped through the air and landed square on Jansen's cheek, spinning him around in a bolt of pain. Stumbling, he fell flat on his back.

Roger snarled and lunged forward. Dizzy, Jansen raised his feet, planting them squarely on Roger's chest as he rushed forward. The momentum thrust Roger up and over. He smashed down on the porch railing.

Tearing wood screeched as the nails ripped from the beams.

Roger's arms windmilled, his weight tipping him over. And down. A fifteen-foot drop.

Jansen lay flat out on the wooden slats, for a moment unable to pull in enough oxygen. He was alive only because Roger had overshot. He rolled over and looked below. Straight into the cold, open eyes of Roger Allen.

Jansen dragged himself to his feet and forced himself to go down where Roger lay.

In the dim half-light of the basement he found Detective Frost. The side of his head was swollen beyond belief, bruising apparent. He'd been hit, hard, then stabbed to death.

What a waste, Jansen thought. If Frost had just waited, he would still be alive. How many people were going to die?

Outside on the stone patio, he checked to make sure Roger was dead, then pulled Roger's wallet from his rear pocket. Inside were two driver's licenses and a pilot identification card.

"You won't fly anymore," Jansen muttered.

CHAPTER 48

Joe's arm circled Karin's shoulders as they walked out onto the deck. She fit in the curve of his arm just as wonderfully as she had six years ago, only now she had an added strength. "Are you sure you want to see this?"

"I have to in order to believe it." She moved to the broken railing and looked down. "Seems too easy. For him, I mean."

Joe, standing on the deck and looking below, hated Roger Allen for what he had done. He would have liked to be the one to send him over the edge onto the rock paving beneath, and realized he felt diminished by having been thumped by Allen without so much as a moment to swing at him.

He glanced at Jansen, standing by the body, and knew the older man had fought for his life and nearly lost. Jansen's knee was bent and obviously painful. "You all right?"

Jansen merely nodded, his expression grim.

"You know this guy?"

Again he nodded. Then he wiped his face and pulled his cell phone out of the casing at his side. "Pretty sure I know him from when I worked Denver. He's no good, but I had hoped to keep him alive. To talk."

Joe moved back to stand next to Karin, his arm supporting her. Her face turned almost ashen as she stared, mesmerized, at the crumpled body below.

Joe's head throbbed as he stared at the man who was a pilot and who no doubt had planned to fly out of the country Haley and the people who stole her. "This is the guy who shot at Karin yesterday."

Karin straightened. "We have to find Haley. I saw her with Mellie."

Joe nodded. "We're going to. At least now their pilot's dead." Joe reached for the Glock at the side of the porch, put the safety on and dropped it down to Jansen. "You need to call it in, I suppose."

"Did that before I came inside." Jansen nodded again. "Should be here in minutes. Sheriff's just down at the crossroads next to the general store."

Joe tightened his hold on Karin. "The sheriff's going to be here any minute." He took Karin's hand. "We've got to get out of here. This is a crime scene. Jansen will have to stay until the sheriff arrives. If we're here, we'll be held for who knows how long."

"Right." She led the way, tiptoeing along the balcony and down the steps to the SUV.

Next to Roger's Tahoe, Joe stopped. Keys dangled from the ignition. "We'll take this. Safer." He swung into the driver's seat. "I'll drive. Get in before Jansen gets back up here and arrests us."

She settled in the passenger seat, saying, "Out this track, to the left. Head for Capstone. Wetford has a clinic there." Karin's face was grim. "It'll take at least an hour to get there."

He started the engine, saw Jansen in the doorway, waving and shouting. He tapped the horn, backed the SUV and swung around to head up the narrow track. If they could get through the spot where the stream had washed out the road, they'd be safe.

A shot rang out.

"Keep going. It's Jansen. He's just shooting in the air. Hoping we'll stop."

They slid going through the washed-out place, but the four-wheel drive kept them on the track. Once they were on the road above, Joe glanced at Karin. How much did she know? He spoke carefully. "Why do you think they took Haley?"

"I don't know. Because I said how perfect she is, because I didn't protect her, because I've always feared it." She fell silent. Finally she lifted her head and said, "Do you know, after my car went off the road, Mellie came back to see if I was dead or alive. I guess she felt guilty because she stood there in the road and had the gall to claim she 'didn't mean for it to go this way,' then left me to die out there."

"She probably figured you'd fight her and she couldn't handle you and the kids together, so she sent Roger to come get you."

"You think she sent Roger to get me?"

"Yes, I do." Joe shifted in the seat. "When you think about it, Roger had several times when he could have killed you. For that matter, they could have killed you at the outset. But they didn't. Any idea why?"

She shook her head. "I fought back. He didn't get the chance."

"Oh, but he did. When you were running down the alley away from him, he could have shot you in the back, but he aimed at your car instead. For that matter, he could have been at the house when you first dropped Haley off and just taken you then. And again on the mountainside, why did he come to get you, tie you to the bed? If he'd meant to kill you he would have done it there on the mountainside. He could have made it look accidental. Think about it. I think he didn't mean to kill you. Or was told not to."

"Then, why not kidnap me in the first place?"

"You'd be missed. Work would notice, a lot of people know you and the search would have started at once. Haley's different; you kept Haley hidden. All they had to do was take all the evidence of her and that would give them enough time to get away. And Haley must have something they need or want. It must be something important, because they went to a lot of trouble to get her and to throw blame on you. Look at the time they gained."

"That part I saw right off." Karin fell silent, her cheeks gray with strain.

Joe continued. "Doctor Wetford is connected to Nicole, to Haley, to Melanie, to Johnny Ray, and Doctor Wetford is a surgeon who—"

"—who specializes in kidney transplants," she interrupted. "I know. Where are you going with this?"

"I've been thinking this thing through, just as you have. I think they want Haley for a transplant."

"Transplant? Oh, my God, that's crazy."

"Is it? Your brother is listed for a transplant."

Waving her hands in protest, Karin said, "What are you saying? He doesn't have anything to do with this."

"No, I know he doesn't. But I've learned a lot about kidneys in the last couple days, and the need for them. Think about it. What if our child needed a transplant and couldn't get one. Wouldn't you do about anything to find one?"

"I sure as hell wouldn't snatch children off the streets for one. Besides, you can't just put any old kidney in somebody."

"That's what I'm getting at. Suppose Doctor Wetford has someone in mind?"

"Who?" she asked, then gasped. "You're thinking Mellie? Mellie trolling for a kidney for someone."

"Maybe a child you haven't met." Joe waited for a moment, to let Karin think, then he said, "Think about the possibility that Haley was identified somehow."

"But she couldn't have been. Oh, my God." Karin stared at Joe. "There was that one time when I took her in to see Wetford for a possible strep infection."

"I'm just supposing here. But if Haley is a match to some special child, aren't you likely to be one too? If Haley's kidneys are a match, yours probably are. That's why he didn't kill you. Karin, maybe they want yours too. And I just thought of this. Maybe they wanted you all the time and figured this would lure you there."

"That, I think, is a stretch."

He pressed harder on the gas pedal, taking the curve a bit too fast. The SUV slid, then straightened out. "Or maybe they figured your kidney was too big."

"Guess it's just good luck for me."

Joe looked quickly at her. "Why is that?"

"I only have one kidney."

"What? Where's the other one? What happened to it?"

"A long story." Karin's face regained some color, but she still looked shaken.

How had he ever thought she was a simple, easy to understand, dependent girl? Just as he thought he knew her, she changed again and another aspect came into view. As he drove, waiting for her to speak, he realized that in fact he could wait a lifetime for her. "Tell me."

She turned away from him, gazing out the window at the pines whose roots clung to the side of the mountain, anchoring them against the elements. He sensed she was looking back into painful territory and as much as he hated to put her in pain, he wanted to know what had happened. If he was going to spend a lifetime with her, and he realized he very much wanted to, then he needed to know her.

Her voice was barely audible over the hum of the tires on the pavement. "I always thought Mom was weak, at least I did when I was in my teens. She seemed to go along with Dad, even when it was clear his thinking was weird. Of course, I know now that she was sick. Her cancer was eating at her, but by the time I was a junior in high school, I realized that she tried to buffer things between Dad and Sam and me, at least as best she could. She pushed me to do well in school and to think about nursing school. When she finally went to the doctor and was diagnosed with very late stage cancer, I took care of her and discovered I was good at it. She died just after I graduated from high school and there was no money for me to go into a nursing program. Since Dad forbade it, I had no help from him and he wasn't all that well himself. He has polycystic kidney disease, too."

"Sam said he inherited it."

"It's a genetic thing, the family curse. Dad, Sam and Dad's twin, my uncle Zeb, the sheriff of Capstone County, they all have it."

"We should call Zeb, by the way. We'll need his help up there."

"Jansen said he's been called. The whole Capstone police force should be alerted. Capstone's force consists of Zeb and three deputies."

Joe glanced at the speedometer and lifted his foot from the accelerator, letting the car slow to eighty miles an hour, his mind going at least as fast. Her uncle had PKD. She had only one kidney. He put it together and risked a guess, "You gave your uncle a kidney."

"No." Mixed emotions struggled across her face. "I sold it to him. I sold him my kidney for money to go to nursing school. To get out of Capstone." She sighed. "It isn't legal to sell your own body parts, there can't even be an exchange of money or goods in any form, but he desperately needed a kidney and I saw it as a way to escape. He'd been listed for a long time and while he was near the top of the wait list, he was in very serious failure. He and my father are truly identical, which is why I was an ideal match. And why Haley would be a good match, too."

"This is a complicated surgery," Joe said. "Extensive blood

tests, matches, and the donor often has a tougher time than the recipient. You weren't even old enough to consent."

"I was nineteen. I knew the facts. And I desperately wanted out of Capstone." She glanced at him, her cheeks flushed. "Look, people can live just fine on only one kidney. The healthy remaining kidney just takes over. Uncle Zeb knew of a clinic in Mexico, a good one with a specialist and so off we went."

"Didn't your father protest?"

She was silent for a minute, then said, "I told him I was going with Aunt Mary for a vacation. She backed me up."

"Damn!"

"Look Joe, the success of the transplant is frequently related to the goodness of the match, the health of both the donor and the person receiving the kidney. Living, related good matches have an eighty-percent success rate. And this was back when transplants weren't all that common."

He was silent, trying to contain the rage he felt toward this man.

She continued. "Think on this. In two thousand five, there were four hundred eighty-five thousand patients, almost half a million, who had end-stage renal disease and that same year there were fewer than nineteen thousand transplants. That's not even four percent. Four percent! Think on that!"

"You made a study of kidney disease?"

"Wouldn't you? My brother was diagnosed with polycystic disease in two thousand five. The ultrasound showed he has large cysts on both his kidneys and his liver. Young for a diagnosis, but he was already having back pain, nausea, high blood pressure."

"How long does a transplant last?"

"Gets better all the time. Some can last twenty-five years or more, others fail sooner. It depends on a lot of factors."

"What about your father?"

Her knuckles blanched as she clasped her hands. "I would guess he's either in end-stage renal failure or close to it. The last I knew for sure he was refusing medical treatment, doing his own faith healing and some weird herbal infusion regime."

"When you had that surgery in Mexico, who was the surgeon?"

"I don't know. I never saw him. I was prepped by nurses, and recovered with nurses. I never heard his name and didn't want to know." Karin drew in a breath. "But, knowing what I know now, I've begun to think Doctor Wetford had a hand in it. What if six years ago when Doctor Wetford removed a strawberry mark from Nicole Eberhard's elbow, he typed and matched her at the surgery? When I started as her nanny, Nicole had a bandage on her arm and I had to put cocoa butter on it to help the stitches disappear. The Eberhards would never know he had typed her. Why he would have targeted Nicole, I don't know, but the more I think about it the more certain I am that Nicole was taken for her kidneys."

She bit her lip, then spoke again. "And I'll bet he's got Haley. It's all tied together."

"Jansen told me the police looked into Wetford, but he was out of town at the time of the Eberhard kidnapping. At the time he was a semiretired doctor handling geriatric nursing-home patients. No one knew about his surgical practice. The police turned the Eberhards inside out looking at them as possible suspects. Parents are always the first."

Karin's expression turned bleak. "Parents. And nannies."

Joe watched the expressions moving across her face. "I wish I'd been here."

"I didn't know how to reach you."

"Couldn't you have got help from your uncle Zeb? As sheriff he'd have all kinds of contacts."

Her voice had a flat tone to it. "When I told Dad I was

pregnant, he and Uncle Zeb together said I had to give the baby to Uncle Zeb and Aunt Mary. I packed and left that night."

"Karin, you have to believe me. I wrote to you. I wrote daily at first."

She stared out the window. "And you sent them all to the Eberhards. I wish I had got them." Her voice sounded choked. "So much time has gone by."

"Do you think we can make up the time?"

"I don't know. There has to be more than the memory of past love and . . ." Again she let the sentence hang in the air.

Joe smiled gently. "And great sex? I wish it were more than a memory. I thought I'd got over you, but I haven't."

"You don't know me now."

He looked at her stubborn chin, the slight tilt of her nose and the set of her lips, tight with stress now, but so soft. "I want to. More than you can know."

They drove in silence for a while, as Joe tried to put everything together. "Did you know this housepainter? The one who killed himself?"

She shook her head. "My memory of that time is in chunks with whole periods missing. I've done my best to blot out the police, the hours of questioning, the desperate search for Nicole and the terrible feeling of loss. I loved that child as though she was my own."

Joe shook his head. "You never talked about yourself. I guess it's because I was so busy talking about myself." He looked over at her.

"I didn't want to think about my past. It was enough to just spend time with you. And I thought we had so much time ahead."

"You were so young." He almost said, *and I was so in love with you, and full of myself, I yakked on all the time, never listening to you.*

"You know, Joe, I was doing just exactly what I swore I'd never do. I was living the same head-in-the-sand life my father has always lived. His zealotry is an excuse to stay away from tough choices. And my under-the-radar life was the same. I was always running away. I simply never saw it that way before. When this is all over, if you still want to know all about my family and me, I'll tell you." She glanced at the dashboard clock. "Right now, we need to take the shortcut. It'll cut fifteen minutes off our run, but it may be rough because it's mud season. Take the exit and the next left after that."

He turned onto a two-lane tarmac road that wound steadily upward around the side of the mountain through lightly forested terrain. Against the fading light of sunset Karin's eyes were deep and shadowed, her expression impossible to read. She was quiet, thinking.

Joe mulled over all that she'd said. There was more she hadn't said, he thought, much more that she hadn't even touched on. He waited for the smothering feeling that he used to get when he thought about committing to one person. It would tighten around his chest, making him feel suffocated. It didn't come.

Cresting the pass, he maneuvered the SUV through a narrow passage and then headed down the other side, which was much more sharply twisting than the ascent had been. Once below the tree line, the grade grew less steep.

He slowed, then accelerated gently, steering through a hairpin turn.

Karin gasped.

A huge buck elk stood in the middle of the road, statuesque, unmoving.

Chapter 49

Melanie wheeled through the town of Capstone, her cell phone to her ear, listening to the unanswered ring. Where was Roger? Why didn't he answer?

Panic rose like acid in her throat. Roger had a powerful satellite phone, he should have reception wherever he was in the mountains, even at ten thousand feet.

Beside her in the passenger seat little Haley's head nodded as she slept, her cheeks reddened. A slight fever, a sign of infection? Or just chapped skin?

Mellie's hands trembled on the steering wheel as she thought how close she had come to losing this child. Thank God she had found her. To lose her in the wild would have been terrible. And with mountain lions prowling the spring mountainsides for food, the thought nearly gagged her.

When she had first seen the child at the streamside she'd thought Haley had drowned, but it was only her little hand trailing in the icy water. If only Haley hadn't tried to run away. At least she had fallen asleep the last half hour of the drive.

Mellie punched in a button again. When she heard the solid, heavy voice of Donny's father, she said, "I'm in town, I'll be at the clinic in five minutes."

He answered, his voice thick. "Wetford's waiting for you at the clinic. Pick him up and get out to the airstrip."

So Roger must be there. Relief coursed through her. "When did Roger get there?"

Silence.

Relief drained away leaving a cold, hollow feeling between her shoulder blades. "Have you heard from him? He doesn't answer his cell."

"I talked to him. He's got Karin. He'll be along."

Mellie shoved her phone into a pocket and gripped the steering wheel. Where was Roger?

Chapter 50

Joe jammed on the brakes. The SUV slewed sickeningly.

The buck bounded off, disappearing down the mountainside.

The rear end of the SUV swung forward into the oncoming lane. Joe steered into the skid. The vehicle veered back toward the edge and the sheer drop-off.

Joe wrenched the steering wheel. The tires bit into a patch of dry pavement, and the car jumped back from the edge. Then the tires hit a mud slick, and the SUV spun fully around.

The rear fender caught a boulder, and the front end slid along the rock wall of the mountain. It stopped with a jolt against an outcropping.

Joe's heart was pounding in his chest. The air bags hadn't deployed. "Karin?"

She didn't answer immediately. He jerked around to see her panting and holding her arms tight across her chest. "You okay?"

"Yes. I can't believe you held it to the road. I thought we were gone." She looked at him, reached for him and buried her head in the crook of his neck.

Joe held her until she stopped shaking. His gaze fell on the tire marks at the edge of the road and he thought that it was a miracle they were alive.

Karin sat up. "We better get going. Are you okay to drive?"

Joe caressed her cheek. "If you're ready, I sure am, but I'd better check the damage."

He climbed out and saw a thin line of green ooze dripping

from the radiator. The front fender was scraped and dented, the left rear fender mashed against the tire. The left headlight and taillight were shattered.

He slid back inside. "How far to Capstone?"

"About three miles."

Joe nodded and keyed the ignition. "If the car starts, it will probably go that far before too much antifreeze is gone." The starter whirred, but the engine didn't catch. Joe cursed silently. The SUV had to start. On the third try the engine started. Joe eased the vehicle forward. A shriek rose from the rear wheel well.

Joe braked. "If we run with that we'll shred the tire." He eased out of the car. Together they pulled the bent fender free.

The car rattled and the wheels, out of alignment, pulled to the right but it went forward. Carefully but fast, Joe nosed the car down the narrow road in the failing light. One thing only lay in his mind—what was happening to Haley.

Karin leaned forward against the seat belt as though urging the vehicle onward. "Just ahead," she said. "The road divides. It runs above and below the clinic. I think we should stop at the clinic. I think Wetford will be there."

"Can we get to the clinic from above?"

She pursed her lips. "Probably. But it's quicker to go straight to the front door."

He hesitated, then said slowly, "We might want to have surprise on our side."

"Uncle Zeb will be there. He should have it all under control."

"Hmmm."

"What? You don't trust Uncle Zeb?"

"I don't like guys who take advantage of young girls for their kidneys."

"That's totally different."

"All the same, let's not take a chance. We don't know what

we'll run into."

Reluctantly, Karin agreed. "Go to the right here, uphill."

Two hundred yards farther on, Joe pulled to a stop beneath the low-hanging branches of a gnarled old pine. Below they could see the square box shape of the clinic and the puddle of light spreading out from the eaves of the roof.

They stepped out of the car, closing the doors only to the first click to avoid an echo. The only sound was the breeze in the pine branches and the ticking of the cooling auto engine.

Karin crouched by the fender. Joe joined her. She pointed down.

Joe scanned the driveway, a ribbon of concrete that wound around the building from the front to a garage in the back. There were no parked cars. "Your uncle isn't here. At least I don't see his car or any car."

"Maybe it's in the garage."

"Would he or the officers park in the garage?"

Karin bit her lip and stood. Then below, a dirty white van turned into the lower road, racing for the clinic. "It's Mellie!"

Joe grabbed her arm, afraid she was about to run down the mountainside.

The van rocked to a stop before the clinic door. Immediately a rounded figure carrying a thick black case bounded out of the clinic, opened the side door of the van and got in.

"Doctor Wetford!" The cry slipped from Karin's lips as the van backed up, turned and pulled away. "They're getting away!"

A small, almost iridescent pool of green antifreeze stained the road.

"Hurry." Joe threw himself behind the steering wheel. "This thing won't go far."

Joe let the car roll downhill, keyed the ignition and was relieved to hear the engine cough to life. From where they were on the mountain, he could see that the road curved around to a junction. As he watched, Mellie slowed, then turned to skirt the town.

Capstone huddled at the head of a long, narrow valley. Far down he could just make out a strip. He pointed to it.

"That's the airstrip," Karin said.

Joe maintained a steady speed, staying carefully back and driving without headlights. "Looks like they're headed to it. I'll go as fast as I can, but we have to go without lights. Watch for deer. We don't need another animal attack." A long-buried memory rose. "Dad always called them range rats."

She didn't comment. Her hands were fisted in her lap.

He handed her his cell phone. "Try your uncle's office again. There should be backup from the sheriff's office."

"There's no signal. You need a satellite phone to get reception up here. Mellie is heading away from town toward the airstrip now. It runs along the valley floor, roughly north to south."

"If we go into town, we can stop at the sheriff's office and get backup."

"No. You're right. Mellie's headed to the airport. And look at the sky. The weather's clearing. We can't take the time. They could take off in minutes. Uncle Zeb's probably out there anyway. He must be."

Joe bit back his concerns. He turned down the flat road, the van's taillights already mere pinpoints ahead. Mel was making tracks. "They don't have Roger to pilot them. They can't go anywhere." But even as he said it, he realized they could have a backup plan. "Tell me about the airport. What are we dealing with?"

"It's just a high country airstrip. There's an old, rusted-out, sheet-metal hangar and a blacktop runway." Karin's teeth chattered from nerves. "There's very little air traffic. I'll bet Wetford's is the only plane that flies in here. There used to be an elderly fellow, Gus Lightner, who would crank up lights when someone was coming in, but he was so old when I knew him, he couldn't possibly still be there."

"The FAA should know about the strip, if for no other reason than watching for illegal drug traffic."

"Zeb always used to keep an eye on it for drug traffic, but nothing ever happened."

So Zeb was in control of yet another thing, Joe thought, and caught sight of the dashboard heat gauge. The engine was hot and getting hotter. "Much farther?"

"A quarter of a mile. It's just beyond that rise." She pointed ahead where the van seemed to rise in the air; then it disappeared over the hill. "When I was in high school, I used to sneak out here sometimes, wishing I could just fly away. There was a split in the metal wall at the side of the hangar. I'd crawl in and just look at the little plane that Lightner used to keep there. An ancient Piper Cub. He sometimes gave flying lessons."

"Did he ever give your uncle Zeb lessons?"

Karin paused, thinking, then said, "He taught Zeb to fly the Piper Cub. I remember Zeb buzzed Dad's compound once, just to enrage him."

"Your dad and your uncle didn't get along?"

"I don't know whether you'd describe them as two individuals tied together or one person divided and fighting itself. Zeb took the opposite position from Dad on just about everything." She hesitated, then said, "The more inward Dad got, the more outgoing Zeb got." She brushed her hair back from her face and leaned forward, as though it would help her to see ahead. "Despite everything, I'd sure feel better if we could make contact with him."

At the top of the small hillock, with the heat gauge at the end of the red zone, a dull glow showed from under the hood of the

SUV. "Engine trouble. Get ready to bail. Soon as I stop."

Joe steered to the side of the road, braked and cut the engine. "Roll out. Quick!" He waited two seconds until he saw Karin go out, then he rolled out of the driver's seat and scrambled to his feet. "Over there."

They ran to the top of the rise, then stopped in the lee of a short, thin pine to catch their breaths and survey the area below. A stiff wind blew, whispering through the boughs, and ragged clouds scudded across the inky sky. Light from a three-quarter moon, dappled by the wisps of cloud, reflected off the last of the spring snow. Joe faced into the wind and saw a bank of clouds gathering on the northwest side of the valley above the mountains.

Karin pointed downhill to a building of weathered, corrugated steel that seemed to lean away from the northwesterly winds. "That's the hangar, office, everything."

"Looks like there's a little observation tower."

"Lightner used it for storage."

Joe considered the dark, windblown ribbon of runway stretching out from the hangar. It cut straight for something over half a mile, maybe three quarters, before it reached the bottom of a sheer granite rise. "That's one scary, short runway. They'll have to take off like Alaskan bush pilots, almost straight up."

Karin looked at him in surprise. "You fly?"

He shook his head. "No, but I've been in a lot of little jets in the last five years. Most of the places where I've been required a fly-in to get to. Hate those short runways. You feel like you're just dropping straight down. And taking off, like you'll never get the belly of the plane up in time."

Joe pointed to the side of the hangar. "There's the plane. A Cessna Citation Mustang, or maybe a CJ1, can't quite tell from here."

Didn't really matter, he thought, because either one was a

supremely capable jet and perfect for these conditions: high altitude, cold weather, short runway, oval bowl-shaped valley. Stopping the jet would be nearly impossible once it got underway.

"We'll work our way down from here in short bursts, keeping to the trees."

Karin nodded. "I know how to do this. Meet you at the back of the hangar."

Forty yards from the hangar in the last stand of weather-stunted trees, Karin stopped. "There's Mellie's van," she said. "She's just pulled in and there's another vehicle, parked. I'll bet it's Uncle Zeb's." She turned to Joe. "I'm going for Haley."

Joe's fingers clamped onto her arm. "Wait! We'll go straight to the back of the hangar together. We don't know for sure it's your uncle's car. There's no mark on it. It could be anyone, even a second pilot. We have to count on surprise."

He put a hand on the side of her face, to make sure she was listening. "First we'll disable the plane, so they can't possibly get away. Then we'll get Haley." Joe slowly released her arm. "We'll go in for Haley together. We may have only one chance at this. If Zeb is there, great, but if he isn't—you remember, you're a target too." He looked straight into her eyes. "Promise me, we go in together. You'll wait till I get back."

"I'll wait."

Thank God, he thought. Karin hadn't asked for specifics on how he would stop the jet, because he didn't know himself. The Mustang and the CJ1 were relatively new models. If he could get at the fuel lines he might be able to do some damage, but if access was sealed off, he didn't know what he'd do.

CHAPTER 51

Mellie cut the van's engine, glancing around the parking place in front of the old hangar again. She couldn't see any sign that Roger was there. "He should have been here long ago," she grumbled. "And he should've answered his cell phone."

Instead of getting out, Wetford frowned at his side-view mirror. "I think I saw something."

"Where?"

"Just now, back there on the hill."

"A car?" Was Roger just behind them?

"No. A shape, running down the hill."

Mellie scanned the hillside. "Probably coyotes."

Wetford peered out the back window, then squinted again at the side mirror. "I don't see anything now, but I thought maybe we were followed. Could have been a car without lights. It's not there now, though." Wetford reached for the door handle.

"Wait." Mellie switched off the overhead light so it wouldn't shine when he opened the door. "Now you can get out."

Wetford slid out of the van and strained to see up the road behind them until a cloud closed over the moon, dimming the light. He shook his coat into place. "I'm heading in to check on Donny."

Irritated, Mellie watched him walk away toward the rusted hangar, carrying only his case. He could have offered to help carry in the girls, she thought. Then she sighed and again scanned the dark road over which they had just come. The only sound was the rising wind and an occasional eerie clatter of falling rock from the top of old Capstone, the giant granite mountain at the far end of the runway.

Dammit, where was Roger?

Mellie threw one last look back up the road, then turned her attention to the sleeping girls, snug in their car seats. Her breath caught in her throat. *They could be sisters,* she thought. She reached for Haley, lifted her out of the car seat and carried her to the waiting plane.

Inside the cabin Mellie paused, considering the best placement. She finally decided Haley and Jen would share the second seat on the right, the seat next closest to the cabin door. Wetford had modified his Cessna CJ1 jet so that a recliner replaced the two seats on the left side. She would sit in the jump seat within easy reach of Donny in the recliner. The original two passenger seats were on the right. Wetford would get one of those. The two girls would have to share the other. The cabin would be crowded for such a long trip, and a bit overweight, but the girls and Donny didn't weigh much. Roger had said it would be okay, and he should know. They just had to be careful how much jet fuel they loaded.

She put Haley into the seat and raced back to the van. Carefully she lifted Jen out of her car seat, carried her to the plane and tucked blankets over both of the girls, then straightened and moved to the doorway. The girls would be fine here for now. The medication would keep them asleep. She could spend a little time with Donny.

The hangar was a simple rectangular metal structure set on a concrete pad with two doors, one leading into the building from the blacktop parking area and one on the other side leading out. Hurrying around Lightner's old Piper Cub, she saw a still, blanketed figure bundled on a gurney. She ran to the door of the office. "Donny!"

Chapter 52

Joe breathed heavily from running in the thin, high-altitude air, a sharp pain stabbing in his side. He saw that Karin was also gasping, doubled over at the far side of the hangar trying to catch her breath. He joined her.

She straightened and pulled on a protruding edge of metal siding.

Joe placed his hand on hers gently, feeling its softness. "Give it up. You'll only make noise and let them know we're here. I'm going to try to disable the plane and I want you to wait for me. I won't be long. Don't go alone, promise?"

When she nodded agreement, he moved to the back corner of the hangar. Waiting for cloud cover, he peered around the corner of the building. The jet was tethered to two blocks and rocked gently in the rising wind. Joe estimated its twin engines would need about three thousand feet of runway, and so far as he could see the runway itself was barely a mile long, probably more like three quarters. Enough that they'd have sufficient thrust to lift out of this bowl-shaped valley easily with the cold, so long as they weren't overloaded.

He had to keep it from taking off. If he remembered right this little beauty had a range of some one thousand nautical miles, sufficient to nearly get over the Mexican border without refueling. Even at this altitude, ten thousand feet plus, it would handle like a bird. With this cold air and wind, even fully fueled and loaded, if the plane got off the ground it would soar. Once airborne, there'd be no stopping this plane.

He dashed across the intervening space and found, as he had feared, the fuel lines neatly encased within the shell of the wing. No way to sever them.

The tires were new. Slashing them might be the only thing he could do, but it wouldn't be easy. And there was very little time.

He crept up to the plane and jammed his gloves into the jet engines' air intakes. Then he pulled out his knife and slashed at the nearest tire.

"Hold it!"

He rose and turned slowly, holding his hands high.

A bulky man whose eyes were barely visible beneath a heavy browridge held a pistol pointed lethally at Joe's chest. In a quiet, cold voice that seemed to come from deep within him, he said, "Drop the blade."

Joe released the knife. It clattered to the ground. As the man came forward, Joe noted his slow movement and readied a roundhouse kick. If he could send that pistol flying, he'd even the playing field. Could he stall him? Get him closer? "Sheriff?"

A smirk, then the man said, "Don't do it," and stopped short of the reach of Joe's foot. "Turn around. Put your hands on the plane."

Joe heard the crunch of frozen ground under the man's heavy foot, a whisper of fabric, and ducked. Too late. Pain seared from his head to his heels. He lost consciousness.

In the distance a coyote howled, joined by a second, sending chills of foreboding over Karin's scalp. Where was Zeb? Why wasn't he here? Jansen said he had been called.

How long had it been since Joe disappeared around the corner of the hangar? It seemed an hour ago, but it was probably only minutes. She tried to see the time on her watch, but it was too dark. She'd promised not to go alone, but she hadn't promised not to try to pry open a gap in the siding. Gripping the thin metal edge, she pulled until it opened enough for her to see in. On the far side of the structure light poured out of a glassed-in office. Just in front stood Melanie, bent over a small someone on a gurney. The rounded figure of Dr. Wetford stood across from her on the other side.

Breathless, Karin could only think, was it Haley? Had they drugged her, preparing her for surgery already?

Mellie moved aside. Bathed in the light from the office, the child's face came into view. Relief washed over Karin. Not Haley. An older child, pale, with swollen cheeks. Judging from the puffiness of his face, he was in profound kidney failure.

But where was Haley? Joe was still not back. Karin quietly eased the panel back into place and crept to the far corner where Joe had disappeared.

Once there, she stopped, peered around the edge and saw the plane rocking in the strengthening breeze. In the next second, she saw a huddled figure on the ground near the wing. Joe!

She stole forward, dropped to her knees at his side. "Joe! Wake up!"

She checked him quickly. Blood matted his hair. He'd been hit; from behind, judging from the location of the blood. She glanced over her shoulder. No one.

Joe breathed, but slowly, his heartbeat light and rapid. She shook him again, but couldn't rouse him. The plane's steps were only a few feet away, the door open. Light from inside streamed out of the door and windows. They were clearly planning to take off soon. Had they loaded Haley? She couldn't see anyone inside.

She kissed Joe's forehead, then rose, ran to the steps and clambered aboard. The plane had looked so large outside, but inside looked efficiently small and sleek. Originally configured to seat four passengers, a large reclining seat had replaced the seats on the left side while on the right were two leather-cushioned chair seats. At the very rear was a small curtained-off compartment, presumably for equipment, or luggage.

She stepped forward. In the second seat on her right, both girls were buckled in together, sound asleep and blanketed. "Haley!"

Karin's heart felt like it might burst. Blinking back sudden stinging tears of relief, she bent to her daughter. Haley murmured, but didn't wake. Mellie must have drugged the girls to be sure they slept.

Karin started to unbuckle the girls' seat belt. Then she heard voices outside. Through the window she saw Dr. Wetford backing out of the hangar, pulling a gurney. Beyond Wetford at the other end of the gurney was Mellie. They were perhaps twenty feet away and closing.

She scanned the plane. She could never make it out of the aircraft and down the steps with Haley. Even if she got down, she could never outrun them. Better to hide. Surprise them, like Joe said.

The storage area. She threw herself toward the end of the cabin and crawled into the gap there, adjusting the curtain across it. She had just enough room kneeling. Working to quiet her breath, she listened for sounds that Melanie and Dr. Wetford were coming aboard. The wind gusted, rocking the plane.

Wetford grumbled. "Damn awkward. Think we'd get some help with this."

Metal clanked against metal. Wetford grunted. "I'll carry him up from here. You take the gurney back to the hangar."

Melanie's voice. "Put the lights on low. The light hurts his eyes." The gurney rattled fiercely. Karin imagined Mellie pushing it roughly back to the hangar.

She peeked out, one eye at the curtain's edge.

Wetford's step was heavy, lumbering. He staggered into the

plane and deposited the ailing child in the recliner. The boy's face turned toward her. In that moment Karin noted the light yellow tinge in his cheeks and realized with a sinking heart that he was suffering liver as well as kidney failure. The way the blanket bowed up over him told her his stomach was distended; ascites had set in. Fluids were accumulating in his belly, indicative of complex organ failure. This poor child was near death. No one's kidneys would help him.

His eyes opened, then widened, and a slight frown slowly crossed his brow. Karin drew back. Had he seen her? Would he speak out? Holding her breath, she listened carefully.

He murmured something. Wetford's voice seemed almost to boom in the quiet. "We'll be underway soon."

Mellie's tread on the plane's steps was light, hurried. "Donny?"

Peeking out from the crack in the curtain closure, Karin saw Wetford disappear into the cockpit area as Mellie came to stand next to Donny's head, so close Karin could have reached out and touched her leg. Mellie stroked his forehead. "Donny?"

Donny returned Mellie's gaze. "Who . . . ?" he murmured. His voice was weak. His lips were cracked and dry.

Mellie wet his lips with a damp cloth and stroked his brow. "How're you doing, kid?"

"Hurting."

Mellie bent over him, tenderly tracing the child's face with her hand, her finger lingering on his pale, puffy cheek, then smoothing his brow as she crooned, "Oh, Donny!"

Donny lifted a hand. "Mommy?"

Mellie curled over him as though she might forever protect him from the disaster that waited. "Yes, it's Mommy." She caressed his face.

"Want Mommy."

Mellie held his hand. To Karin, her voice sounded as though

it had tears in it. "I'll be your mommy for right now. Is that okay?"

He continued to frown, his eyes leaking tears. "No . . . surgery."

"It will make you well."

"No." The child looked steadily at Mellie. "I want . . . to . . . go to Mommy in heaven."

Tears streamed down Mellie's cheeks as her whole heart showed in her face. At that moment Karin knew Donny might be near death, but Mellie would do whatever possible for him as long as he drew a breath. Karin's heart beat a tattoo against her ribs. Haley wasn't safe, not even with Donny dying. She had to get Haley out of the plane. Somehow. And fast.

A heavy-shouldered man, bulky in a down parka, stepped onto the plane. He seemed to fill the cramped interior and his voice thundered in the cabin. "Right. Listen up."

Uncle Zeb! He was here after all. And carrying a gun, waving it at the doctor and Mellie.

Karin lunged out from behind the curtain. "Uncle Zeb, thank God you came! I didn't think you were ever going to get here."

Her uncle's face registered shock. He pointed the gun at her.

"Uncle Zeb? It's me, Karin."

Zeb's face cracked into a grin, the pistol lowered but still ready. "Well, what do you know!"

Karin stared at her uncle. This wasn't the response she expected from him.

He rocked on the balls of his feet, the grin spreading across just half of his face.

Realization sank into her like a stone in a pond, right to the bottom. "You're not here to save Haley."

His expression mutated into a wolfish leer, mocking her. "No, I'm here because I'm Donny's father." He laughed, a dry, mirthless sound. "Your aunt Mary and I always called him

Danny to you. I'm surprised you didn't figure it out sooner."

Zeb straightened, rubbing his back. The gloating leer twisted off his face. Beneath the bravado he was pale, sweating. The same signs Karin had seen in her father. "You're sick. Your kidney is bad." The thought stretched out, sickeningly, to its logical conclusion. His transplant was failing, just like Donny's was.

Everything snapped into place: the reason why Roger had not killed her, the reason Mellie had come back to check on her at the accident. Zeb also needed a kidney. Her mouth dry, her words came out in a croak. "Why don't you just get listed, Zeb? You and Donny?"

His eyes narrowed. "We are listed. We've been waiting for over a year. We've done everything you're supposed to do. There just aren't enough kidneys, Karin. And Donny needs one now, there's no waiting. You know damn well what that means."

"Donny won't last long enough to get one from the list." *Which is why he needs the best possible match,* she thought. *Haley.*

Wetford sidled up. Karin's breath came fast and harsh. "Doctor Wetford, how can you do this? You're a doctor!" Even to her ears, the words sounded naive and laughable.

"You don't understand," Wetford said.

Zeb waved his gun at the jump seat folded against the side of the cabin. "Sit down, Karin, shut up. I've got film to blackmail him from now to Armageddon." He coughed, wiping his brow, his cheeks pale. "In fact, it's film of the good doc, here, taking out Nicole Eberhard's kidney. So he doesn't have a choice. None of us do. That's the irony of it all. None of us has a choice at this point."

Karin felt the blood drain from her face. "I want to sit with Haley." Without waiting for objections or permission, she picked Haley up. Holding her daughter tight against her chest, Karin squeezed into the front seat by the cabin door, as close as possible to the only means of escape.

Chapter 53

Mellie breathed a quiet sigh of relief as Karin appeared to comply and sat quietly by the cabin door. Now, she thought, if only Roger would show up.

Things were seriously out of control. Zeb was waving a gun around, looking like he was about to faint and Wetford was shaking in his shoes. But worst of all, Donny looked like he was in real trouble. She covered Donny with the blanket, smoothing it up to his chin. His ascites, the terrible swelling and water retention from organ failure, was bad, bloating his little tummy out painfully. They had to get airborne as soon as possible, but not without Roger. Roger had to be there.

Karin snarled at Dr. Wetford. "You call yourself a doctor. You're a murderer."

Wetford raised his hand as if to fend off a blow, but mercifully, didn't answer. Donny shouldn't be disturbed. Mellie stepped toward Karin, her hand out. "Okay, lower your voices. Nobody dies," she said in a lowered, throaty voice.

"They have, Mellie. You know they have." To Wetford Karin said, "How many people have you murdered for their kidneys?"

Wetford's face flushed an ugly red and he blurted out, "I don't kill people. I save them. Nobody dies."

"What about Nicole? And how about Kenny? And what about Johnny Ray?"

Wetford blanched. "Johnny Ray died of head injuries."

"Caused by Roger, when he went out to Johnny's trailer.

You've been putting your head in the sand if you think you haven't caused death. And Kenny. Roger killed him, too."

"It's not true!" Melanie said and started toward Karin. "Roger didn't kill anyone. Don't you say things like that. You're just causing trouble."

"Hey!" Zeb called out from the pilot's seat in the cockpit. "Wetford, get in here."

Wetford cringed and slid forward into the cockpit, taking the second officer's seat.

Zeb leaned into the middle space and waved his pistol. "Mellie, take a seat."

"We don't go without Roger. He's the only pilot."

"You don't give a shit about Roger. You've been using him from day one." He waved the pistol at Karin. "She's here, he's not. That means he's probably dead."

"No, he's not!" Mellie's voice came out louder than she intended as she leaned over Karin. "Where's Roger?"

"He's back at the cabin. I got away and left him there."

Mellie felt like she'd been hit. How could Karin manage to get away from Roger? He was tough, he'd kill before he let someone get away. Her knees weakened and she sat down in the seat behind Karin. Without Roger, how would they fly? A deep, sharp pain twisted in her belly. Her breath came fast and tight. Surely Zeb wouldn't risk piloting. But he always thought he could do anything. And he didn't listen. To anybody. Even if Roger had begun to teach him, chances were Zeb never even listened.

She had to be very careful, Mellie told herself, or Zeb would take off and they'd all be killed. Donny, Jen, Haley . . . nobody else much mattered, but the kids did. The pain in her stomach grew. She bit her tongue and tasted the pungent, coppery taste of fear.

Zeb would respond to criticism like a bee-stung bear, so she had to say things just right. Working to keep her voice steady, Mellie stood and started toward the cockpit saying, "Cessnas are difficult. Let's just wait a little bit. Roger'll be here. And Zeb, you're in no shape to fly."

"Yeah, well, I bet Roger isn't in any shape to fly either, or he'd be here by now."

"What if your cyst goes while you're flying?"

Zeb stepped from the cockpit. "Autopilot, bitch." He jabbed Mellie in the shoulder, sending her hard down the short aisle and against the last seat. In two steps he was beside Donny. He picked up Donny's hand, holding it gently in his large one for a long moment. Mellie watched as he bent over Donny, the only person in the world he gave a damn for. "Hold on, son. We'll be there in a flash."

Donny fastened his gaze on his father and mouthed, "No surgery."

Poor Donny, poor baby. Mellie's heart ached to see him suffering so. And his eyes were getting yellower, and real puffy. She knew what that meant. Zeb was right. They had to get going, whether Roger was here or not. And Zeb probably could fly, she rationalized. He was a natural with machines.

Zeb leaned close to the boy. "This surgery will work. You'll see. It'll last a long time."

Donny turned his head away. "It hurts bad."

"I'll give you a little more pain medicine. It'll work in about three minutes." He pulled out a loaded hypodermic, uncapped it and pressed the air out of it.

Mellie frowned. The needle's reservoir was full. Way too much for a small boy, even one who had been on painkillers long enough to be accustomed to them. She put a hand on Zeb's arm, trying to restrain him. "Zeb, that's too much."

"I know what I'm doing."

"Of course you do, but let me give it to him. You can get the engines going." Mellie heard the fear in her voice and knew instantly it would irritate Zeb further.

He brushed her off. Leaning forward, he uncovered the child's skinny arm and pressed the needle into the thin tube that ran into his little vein.

"Zeb, stop!" Again, Mellie tugged on Zeb's arm. "That's too powerful."

Zeb sent the plunger down. Donny's lips moved silently.

Zeb turned to face Mellie, his brows drawing a heavy line across his face and nearly hiding his eyes. In a low, menacing voice he leaned over her and said, "I know what I'm doing, dammit! Don't contradict me." Turning back to Donny, he said in a softer, warmer tone, "Just a little bit, you'll be feeling better."

Donny nodded ever so slightly.

"Try to sleep, son. It'll make the time go by faster."

"Yeah," the child whispered. His eyelids fluttered shut.

Zeb turned to Mellie, his expression twisting back into scorn. "Put on a happy face for the kid, God dammit!"

"That was too much painkiller."

"He needs it." Zeb walked heavily to the cockpit. Over his shoulder he said, "Leave him be. He'll sleep now."

Melanie's jaw clenched, the pain in her stomach blooming, expanding. Donny was pale, too pale. His lips opened as he drew breath, light feathery puffs of air that slowed as the pain medication took hold. It took hold fast. Too fast. She stroked his hot, dry forehead, feeling the fever in him.

At the entry to the cockpit Zeb stopped and looked down at Karin and Haley. "How's the kid?"

Karin answered quickly. "Got a fever."

"She does not," Mellie said. "Karin's just trying to fool you."

Zeb sucked on a tooth, then said, "Looks to me like she's got a fever." His gaze went to Jennifer. For a long, speculative moment he eyed her, then turned, went to the cockpit and slouched into the pilot's seat.

Mellie's knees started to shake. She had planned all this, risked everything, used Roger, all to gain access to Donny and prevent exactly what she had just seen: Zeb considering the possibility of using Jennifer's kidneys. Jennifer was the other match for Donny.

Desperate, she called after him, "Haley *will* be well enough for Donny."

Sick and scared, she bent over her son, smoothing the hair back from his forehead, feeling a cool, damp film of sweat on his forehead. His fever had broken.

She held her breath. It shouldn't have, he should still be hot. She grasped his hand. Limp. She put her cheek to his mouth. No breath. She pressed her fingers against his neck, over his carotid artery. There was no life-affirming pulse.

Fingers shaking, she raised first one of his eyelids, then the other. She waved her hand in front of each one. No response. Both pupils were fixed and dilated.

Frantic now, she fumbled for and grabbed a stethoscope from the bag at her feet and pressed it to his chest, over his heart. To the side, then back over his heart. No heartbeat. The pain medication had been too much for his poor little body.

Her throat constricted in grief, Mel could only whisper. "Donny, oh Donny."

Her heart began to break. All her energy, her life, had gone into saving Donny, the son she had denied. She had given everything. What did she have now? Ashes.

Instead of giving him temporary comfort, in a moment of arrogance and stubbornness Zeb had killed their son.

Chapter 54

A blast of icy air hit Joe's face. He roused, his thoughts scrambled, his ears filled with a roaring noise that might have been the strengthening storm but turned out to be the blood pounding in his ears. He raised his head, only to see flashing lights and feel a bolt of pain so blinding he had to wait for it to subside. The first gusts of wind-borne snow stung his face, clearing his mind a bit. How long he had been out, he didn't know.

A second later he discovered he was lying against the wall of the hangar, some thirty feet from the wing of the Cessna Citation CJ1, which was waiting on the apron. Ignoring the blast of pain, he pushed himself to sitting and ran a hand over his aching head. It came back sticky with blood.

Low-hanging clouds closed across the blackened sky, covering the sliver of a moon. He glanced at the runway, a straight single ribbon of blacktop running from the apron behind the hangar straight toward the massive granite mountainside. Even without the strengthening storm, it would be a very difficult airstrip for a takeoff.

Joe struggled to his feet and stumbled forward to the shadow of the gas pump. The smell of fuel was heavy from a small puddle staining the tarmac. He touched the nozzle. Wet inside. Zeb had already topped up the plane. Would the added fuel weight be enough to thwart the takeoff?

In summer at ten thousand plus feet, aircraft could lift off safely only half to three-quarters full of fuel and a light cargo load. More weight than that and even with extra runway, they'd lift a bit, then drop like a stone. Cold air had more density, which would allow more load. His gaze ran over the sleek lines of the CJ1. Powerful enough to carry five passengers plus two crew, fuel and baggage and still be maneuverable. He had to do something to stop it. He didn't know what, just that he had to make sure the jet didn't leave the ground.

The wind caught the collar of his jacket. Tiny wind-driven snowflakes stung his skin. The airstrip had no deicers. Ice on the wings would add terrific weight once it started to accumulate. Then even this muscular craft would need a skilled pilot and a load of luck to get off safely. If he could delay them, and if the storm brought more precipitation—snow, rain, sleet, anything of the sort—it might be enough to abort the flight. Joe had jammed his gloves into the engines' air intake, hoping they would cause the jet's sensitive instruments to cut the engines. Instead, the engines sounded fine. He felt sick. Where was Karin? Was she on the plane? Had he come this close only to lose her?

A shadow blackened the cockpit window briefly and he saw Wetford seat himself in the copilot's seat. Zeb sat down in the pilot's seat. The jet's engines fired, ran up. Deafening, powerful.

Joe staggered toward the CJ1, already untethered and bouncing lightly in the wind. The cabin door was still open, the steps down. He tried to run but fell, his knee an explosion of pain. Rising again, he thrust himself toward the sleek sides of the jet, his head pounding. His legs strengthened with each step. The powerful air intake was so close he felt the draw, and leaned away as he ran.

A thin woman in jeans and a down jacket came to the door and saw him. Mellie, he thought, and launched himself at the side of the plane. As Mel reached to close the door, he saw

Karin. The door slammed shut.

His fingernails scraped the skin of the Citation, inches below the sealed door.

Chapter 55

Karin, having glimpsed Joe stumbling toward the plane, thrust her shoulder into Mellie. Hampered by the sagging weight of Haley, still sleepy, she only hoped to keep the door open long enough for him to get there.

Mellie staggered but recovered, shoved Karin roughly back into her seat and slammed the door shut. Karin clawed at Mel's sleeve, but it was too late. Through the window, dimly, she saw Joe, arms raised, reaching for the plane, for her.

She lunged forward. "You can't do this!"

Karin's face was so close to Mellie's she saw the streaks in her pale-blue irises. Her expression was haggard beyond anything Karin had imagined, as though she were stricken and grieving. Did Mellie have a conscience? Could she even feel guilt?

Then she gasped. She understood. "That's the only thing that would drive you to do this, isn't it? Jen isn't Roger's kid. She's Zeb's, just like Donny is. That's why Zeb said you used Roger. Jen is Zeb's child. You took Haley so he wouldn't take Jen's kidneys."

She shoved Mellie back, hard, furious. "You are only thinking of your children. You're sacrificing others for your mistakes!"

Mel shrank back.

Keeping her voice low, Karin let her fury speak. "Zeb never once tried to help you, Mel. He used you. He uses everyone. He has no conscience. No guilt. The only person he's ever loved is Donny. If anything goes wrong with Donny, you'll be blamed. He will never blame himself for anything. You know it. Now, let us out."

Wild-eyed, Mellie shook her head. "No!" Then softer, "No."

"Mellie, think!" She had to make Melanie see reason. "I saw Zeb eyeing Jennifer like she was an object, or a piece of meat. You can't protect Jen from him." Karin grabbed her shoulders and shook her. "We're taxiing. He's going to take off. If you don't do something it'll be too late. We'll both lose our girls."

Mellie looked away, tears springing to her eyes, and wrenched away to sit on the jump seat next to the recliner where Donny lay.

Panting from anxiety, Karin peered out the little window in the cabin door. Snow was starting to fall, driven by winds buffeting the plane. Her gaze dropped to the side of the door and the instructions for opening it. Zeb was taxiing to the far end of the airstrip, planning to take off toward the town. He would have to slow to a near stop in order to make the turn on the narrow runway. There was still a chance.

The plane's landing lights bounced over patches of ice and the rough weeds at the edge of the blackened runway. Snow, growing heavier and blown nearly sideways, streamed past the windows, but on the horizon it was clearing.

In the cockpit, Zeb hunched forward studying the displays and switches, his hand hovering over the console. His lips moved as he concentrated on the instrument panel. She shuddered. He couldn't fly this plane. He couldn't possibly handle the crosswinds, the weight, the power of the engines. They'd crash.

Karin hugged Haley to her. If they didn't get off, they'd die for sure. There would only be one chance. They had to be ready when he slowed to turn.

"Haley, honey, wake up. Look at me."

Haley's eyes were dopey-looking, but she smiled lightly and

whispered, "Mommy."

"I'm going to wrap you tight in this blanket," Karin said, winding the flight blanket around and around, tucking a pillow around her daughter's head. "Now Haley," she whispered, "Don't say a word. Listen to me. Stand right there by the door."

Groggy, Haley nodded, clutching the aircraft blanket. Karin started to set Haley down.

Zeb's voice boomed through the cabin. "Donny okay?"

Karin heard a gasp from Mellie. She whipped around to see Mellie's face drain of color. Why didn't Mellie answer? She simply sat looking stricken, tears streaming from her eyes.

"Hey! Donny okay?" Zeb called back again. "Mellie! What the hell are you doing?"

Mellie stared straight into Karin's eyes, then turned slowly and gazed at Jennifer. "Donny's an angel."

"Told you I knew what I was doing," Zeb gloated.

Mellie's eyes narrowed, the drying tear tracks glistening on her cheeks. She rose, kissed Donny's forehead, then drew the blanket over his face.

Donny had died! Clutching Haley to her, Karin shrank toward the door. That was why Mellie was so stricken. Her only reason for all she had done was gone. Now would Mellie let them off the plane? Karin searched her face, finding her eyes dark and unreadable.

"Mellie!" Karin whispered even though she knew she couldn't be heard. "Let us out. You must!"

Slowly, as though awakening from a deep sleep, Mellie pointed at the cabin door. Then in a sudden movement she quickly lifted Jennifer from the seat and wrapped a flight blanket around her and a pillow around her head, as Karin had done.

The plane slowed for the turn. This was their last hope.

Mellie thrust Jennifer next to Haley at the door, then positioned herself in the cockpit doorway, blocking Zeb's view.

Her lips were bloodless. "Okay. Jen has to go too," she said to Karin.

Karin grasped the bar handle and pulled up. Alarms sounded. Together, Karin and Mellie pried the bar back. The door opened a crack. The wind caught an edge and ripped the door out of their hands. Alarms screamed. The craft wobbled.

"What the hell's going on?" Zeb shouted, furious.

"Door wasn't quite shut! Wind got it." Mellie yelled back, "Stop, for God's sake. I can't get the door!"

He slowed further.

"Stop the damn plane, Zeb!" Mellie shouted. She wedged herself in the opening to keep the door from flapping shut if he turned to face the wind. The plane came to a near stop, its alarms deafening. To Karin she said, "Go."

Karin gripped Haley in both hands and dropped her out. Wind whistled into the cabin.

Karin dropped Jennifer out.

Zeb shouted, "Shut the fucking door!"

"Just a sec, Zeb," Mellie shouted over the alarms. She put her mouth to Karin's ear. "Keep Jen. Promise."

The plane was turning. Zeb must not have suspected what was happening.

"Shut the damn thing!" Zeb shouted.

"I'm trying. The wind's got it."

Karin gripped Mellie's wrist. "You have to come."

Mellie pulled back. "Go, now!"

Zeb straightened the plane on the runway and ran up the engines. "We're going."

Mellie put a hand on Karin's back and shoved.

Chapter 56

As the plane glided away from him, Joe wiped his hand across his eyes. He watched helplessly as the marker lights on the plane grew smaller and smaller, the plane rolling to the far end of the runway. Zeb was going to take off into the wind, flying back over Joe and the hangar, then over the little town of Capstone, making as wide a circle as possible to rise above the granite massif that gave the town its name. Joe's gaze rose, climbing the sharp pile of stone until it disappeared in the snow and clouds. Could even a skilled pilot calculate the wind shear of this storm correctly?

An empty spot in his breast grew, hot and leaden. He should have held Karin. Loved her. Should have had the chance to love his daughter, too. He'd never even looked in her little eyes, never held her. He had come so close to having everything that he now realized meant the world to him.

At the far end, the aircraft appeared to stop. Then the lights flicked out of sight as the jet began its turn. Did it stop? Joe strained his eyes trying to see. He started walking, following the plane down the runway, then ran clumsily.

The plane resumed its turn. Its landing lights flashed across the rough field, glowing through the quickening snow. Another seeming flicker of lights, another possible pause in the turn. A shadowy form flickered through the glow along the side of the runway.

Joe held his breath as the lights of the plane swung abruptly away. The plane seemed to swing from one side to another. Was it the wind? Was Zeb losing control? He blinked, clearing the images from his sight and ran toward the plane even as it moved.

A shadow again appeared, then disappeared. Was it human? Deer? Could a deer be on the runway? Was it possible a deer would keep the plane from lifting off?

He squinted into the distance. Another slight, shadowy movement. Then the plane's lights brightened as it faced him. Just as suddenly, the lights flashed away, leaving him momentarily blinded. What was Zeb doing?

The shadow moved again. Not a deer. A person. Someone was out there and the plane was pursuing them. Zeb was a madman.

Legs pumping, Joe raced down the runway.

The lights of the plane swung back again, blinding him. Chin down, eyes fixed on the ground at his feet, Joe ran, one foot after the other. It seemed to take forever for his eyes to adjust. A rational corner of his mind told him this was hopeless. He couldn't possibly stop the plane. But if there was even one chance in a million that either Karin or Haley was alive, he had to try.

A strange coughing sound from the plane.

Still he ran on, lungs burning, toward the last place he'd seen the shadow move. Over the roar of the wind in his ears he was sure he heard the engines stutter.

His hopes rose. He pushed himself faster down the tarmac. His gloves that he'd shoved into the engine intake were finally causing trouble. Then, maddeningly, the engines smoothed out. He could no longer see where he was, just that he was closing the distance to the plane.

A wail rose from behind him. A siren. He glanced over his shoulder. A police cruiser screamed down the runway. It slammed to a stop beside him. A Ridgewood cruiser. The door swung open. Joe threw himself into the car.

Ahead, bouncing in the wind gusts, the lights of the plane grew larger, its wings catching the crosswind, tilting back and forth.

Detective Jansen floored the accelerator. The wheels screeched against the frozen runway. The car slewed forward. Its tires slid in the snow slicks. Jansen steered into the skids, his grip on the wheel firm. Finally rubber gripped the pavement.

The noise was deafening. Jansen mouthed something and ducked. Joe couldn't drag his gaze from the approaching aircraft. It seemed to explode in size, so fast it came toward them.

No time. The jet and an explosion of noise burst over them.

Screeching metal. The car was thrown into a spin. Around and around down the runway, toward the place he'd seen the shadow that he now prayed was Karin.

CHAPTER 57

Wind tore at Karin, stinging her face. Gripping one little hand of each girl, she ran hard, stumbling, straightening, pulling the girls nearly off their feet. She ran straight off the runway into the rough ground. Racing for her life, their lives. She dragged the girls away from the madman in the plane. Away from crushing death.

A glance over her shoulder. A figure outlined in the lights. Mellie? Had she fallen from the plane?

The ground fell away suddenly. Karin's foot went down, her ankle twisted. Pain shot up her leg. She fell. The girls landed on her. Karin's hair rose, sucked off her head as the jet flashed by, the wing tip overhead.

Gasping, Karin clung to the girls as she watched the jet roar down the runway. Then the jet's rear lights abruptly pulled up. It seemed to stagger into the air. Astonished, Karin saw the plane's right wheel catch on flashing red and blue lights on the roof of a car. A police cruiser.

The plane rose, its wings tilted. It struggled upward. The cruiser, its headlights flashing, spun across the runway, whirling out of control, sliding straight toward them.

Exhausted, breathless, Karin couldn't move. Couldn't drag the girls to their feet. No time. No way to run, no way to move.

Karin curled up, covered each girl's head, and waited for the impact. All this they had gone through, now to be killed by a police cruiser spinning out of control. So much flashed through her mind. She should have told Joe she loved him. She should have fought Zeb, should have recognized his rotten core. So many things she should have done. And now it was too late.

She waited for the tearing pain, the scorch of the spinning car ripping through her body.

Light as bright as day rolled over them. A roar followed, crashing like an ocean breaker in a hurricane, rattling their bones. Then searing heat broke over them. The girls pressed against her sides, shaking and screaming in the echoing sounds of the explosion. But no car smashed into them.

Slowly, Karin lifted her head. She saw a huge flaming scar on the runway. Through the rising flames, she could see the black metal skeleton of the plane. A strange, unearthly moan rose from the crash amid the crackle of the flames. Karin told herself it was the sound of melting metal, but she cried, all the same.

A trail of smoke and the searing smell of burning fuel filled the air. She couldn't move. Zeb, Dr. Wetford, Donny and Mellie, all gone in that instant. Nausea rose in her throat, choking her.

Turning, she saw the cruiser had stopped a mere fifteen feet from them, headlights futilely pointing out into the field. Steam rose from its wheels like fog, almost obscured a figure staggering toward them.

"Oh my God," Karin breathed and struggled to her feet, pulling the girls tight to her. She was shaking from nerves, cold and shock. Who was this? Joe? Jansen? Or one of Zeb's paid minions?

Jennifer tugged on her arm, her face glowing in the light of the flames from the crashed jet. "Mommmmma!"

Karin reached for her, tried to hold her back, but she wriggled away. "Jen, wait!"

Jennifer dashed forward, straight toward the heat.

Karin and Haley tried to run after her. "Jenny!"

"I'll get her," Joe shouted. In seconds he had reached her,

scooped her up and brought her, sobbing, back to Karin. Still holding Jen, he reached for Karin, drew her close, then pulled Haley in close as well. Tight, his arms wrapping them all to him. "I'm never letting you go again. Never."

The rumble of his voice was indistinct, but oh so wonderful. *Whatever it takes,* she thought. *Whatever it takes,* we'll make this work.

"Jenny?" A thin voice called from beyond where the police cruiser stood.

Jansen stepped out of the car, disappeared into the dark down the runway and returned, half holding, half pulling Mellie. "She must have jumped too. Here's your mama, Jen."

Jen wiggled free of their grip and ran to Mellie.

Karin saw Joe's gaze fastened to Haley's face. "Haley, this is your daddy."

Joe knelt. "Haley, so wonderful to meet you."

For several seconds she stared at him, her face somber. Finally she said, "Are you dead?"

"No. I've come back and I'm not leaving, am I?" He looked up at Karin, his eyes asking for confirmation.

"Are you sure about that?"

He rose. "I'm very, very sure about it."

Slowly she felt the fright and tension leave her body. "Welcome home." And she sank against his chest as his arms wrapped around both her and their child.

CHAPTER 58

Karin and the girls waited in the shelter of the rusty hangar while the volunteer fire crew finished controlling what was left of the fire. Jet fuel had spewed across the tarmac, the fire melting gashes in the surface. Black smoke rose, wind-driven and visible throughout the valley. From the hangar office Karin watched Deputy Sheriff Pascano lead Mellie to his car. Jansen walked outside with them.

"Where's Mama going?" Jenny wailed.

"Mama has to go with the sheriff for a while. You'll stay with Haley and me until she gets everything worked out." Karin drew the child closer.

Joe knelt at the child's side. "Mama has business to take care of."

The silence was awkward as they watched Jennifer try to work out what all this meant for her. Karin held her breath, wondering if Jenny would ask about Roger, but she didn't. She simply went over to the sagging couch where Haley had fallen asleep and sat down. Exhaustion took over and by the time Jansen returned, she too had fallen asleep.

Karin looked from Joe to Jansen. "What will happen to Mellie?" she asked.

Jansen leaned against a scarred wooden table, fatigue written across his face in broad streaks of grit. He was slow to speak. "Deputy Pascano and I have a lot of things to work out, but for now, she'll be held in the Capstone jail. There's a lot to sort out. You, Joe and the girls are free to go home, or stay the night here in a hotel."

Free. Would they ever be free of these memories? She raised her gaze to the little girls snoring softly on the couch. What would these little ones remember of all this? "What about Jenny? She can stay with me, can't she?"

Joe moved closer. "With both of us, she means."

Jansen looked thoughtfully at first Joe, then Karin. "Well, for right now, Mellie begged to have Jenny stay with you if you would keep her. Longer term, social services will have to make these decisions, but up here, there's no crisis placement for kids. According to Deputy Pascano, they use your dad's place as a sort of emergency placement. In fact, since the hotel burned down last year that's where anyone goes who needs a place when they get stuck here."

"Dad's? Not really."

"Yeah. He even has a license for emergency child placements."

"Since when?"

"Zeb licensed him about four years ago, according to Pascano."

"But he's in terrible health. He can't possibly manage children."

Jansen held up his hand to interrupt her. "I'm told a Mrs. Leland out there does all the care. She has a daughter and a foster daughter."

"I've never heard of her," Karin said, running through the people she could remember from the community. "Of course I've been gone for years now."

Jansen nodded. "And, she's not from around here. Apparently this Mrs. Leland came here with the girls about four or five years ago. Pascano said he'd call out and tell her you were coming. You and Joe aren't in any shape to drive back to Ridgewood, the roads are bad and it's the only place available for all of you."

Karin looked at Joe. "What do you think?"

"We'll go there," he said. "It'll give me a chance to meet your father."

Lucky you, she thought. "Will you stay there as well, Detective?"

"No," he said. "I've got paperwork to do."

"Will Mellie face . . ." Karin couldn't say *prison.* "She saved my life, and Haley's and Jen's."

Jansen's expression turned grim. "Roger's wasn't the only body at the cabin. I found Detective Frost's body in the cabin cellar. It looks like she killed him. He went up to the cabin early, evidently thinking he'd get a jump on things."

"Oh, dear." Karin felt dizzy.

Joe wrapped an arm around her and smiled down into her eyes. He seemed to know what was going through her mind. "It's okay. There's too much to think about just now."

"You're right," she said and forced the ugliness to a far corner of her mind. "I'll concentrate on the girls for now."

He smiled wider. "We both will."

Five miles south of Capstone, Karin braked and let the car roll over the metal rungs of a cattle guard. The moon overhead shone bright on the drifted, crusty snow, lighting the countryside. The bare branches of the aspens stretched out like so many dark fingers casting long shadows on the ground. Just at the edge of the car's beams she saw the glint from the eyes of a raccoon seconds before he scurried into the brush.

Joe shifted in the front passenger seat. "Was this a religious compound?"

"Not really. Dad believed passionately in a simple life, sort of a Walden Pond existence. It wasn't about religion so much as it was about his ideas and his leadership. He ruled the place, dictated how things should be, but he didn't work to keep anyone there. People just came and stayed and talked about truth and justice and all kinds of ideological things. It was more like a communal way of life, but with him as king. If that makes any sense."

"It sounds like control to me."

"He would share anything and everything, but on his terms. Control was the issue. His way or no way. He always seemed to find people who wanted a strong leader."

The road wound through a stand of pine trees that had grown tall in the six, almost seven years since Karin had fled the place. She wondered how many other changes she would find.

A quarter of a mile farther, the road rose gently up the side of the mountain, then turned in toward the residential part of the compound. Ten houses ringed the central circle, each dark. The clerk at the sheriff's office had said that many of the people had left the compound in the last two years. She certainly could understand. Still, it was a shock to see how many of the little cabins appeared deserted. Her father would not have accepted that easily.

She parked in front of the sprawling central house with its wide, welcoming porch. Light glowed warmly out the front windows and door; the place almost looked wonderful. Almost.

She and Joe carried the groggy girls into the warmth of the house as Mrs. Leland, whose gray hair was worn in the severe drawn style of women at the compound, opened the door and ushered them inside. Mrs. Leland led them past the cavernous living room warmed by a dying fire in the grate of the stone fireplace. The temperature inside was warmer than outside, but not by much.

Mrs. Leland said, without elaborating, "Father McGrath is already in bed. He's been poorly."

For her father to be in bed before midnight meant he was very ill indeed. His kidneys, no doubt.

"I'm cold," Haley whimpered.

"You'll warm up with soup," Mrs. Leland said, ushering them into the barn-like kitchen. It was unchanged from when Karin had lived there, except perhaps a bit more worn.

Mrs. Leland pointed to a long, rough wooden table and a basket of home-baked bread. "I fixed you a bite to eat. Soup and some fresh bread. Not much, but it's hot."

"Looks great," Karin said and settled the girls in chairs.

Mrs. Leland served them big bowls of vegetable soup with the bread. "As soon as you're finished I'll take you upstairs." She seated herself in a large rocker. "It's the Lord's work that sent you here now."

Karin read worry in Mrs. Leland's face. "Is Father in a lot of pain?"

She nodded. "My daughters, Gracie and Colly, are with him now. I never like him to be alone. Can't know when the good Lord will come to collect him." She rocked steadily while they ate.

When they finished, Mrs. Leland led them up the wide stairs, the fourth and tenth step still creaking loudly when stepped on. Mrs. Leland offered Karin the large room her parents had shared, but the memories were too raw to sleep there. Karin smiled at Joe and asked for one of the guest rooms at the north end of the hall. "We'll be comfortable there."

"Your father is in the south bedroom. The sun comes in the window in the morning. He says it warms his bones. Colly is there if you want to see him."

Karin watched as Joe put the girls into the large bed, pleased at his tenderness with both of them. Once tucked in he started a story, but they were asleep in minutes.

He turned to Karin and took her in his arms. "When the

door of the plane slammed I thought my life was over. I saw you in there, struggling and all I could think was I so nearly had the one person who would make my world and I couldn't do a single thing. I thought I'd lost you forever and I couldn't breathe." He lifted her chin. "I love you and I need you. Please, please say you'll have me."

"I want to, Joe, but we have so much . . ."

"Shhh, we have all the time in the world to work things through. Just let me hold you for now."

When the children snored with heavier settled sleep, Karin pulled away from Joe. "I have to see him." Together, they went down the hall, her heart thudding in anticipation. "I have to talk to him."

"I know."

"Come in with me?"

"Of course."

Before the door of her father's room a young girl perhaps nine years of age stood in the shadows, her head tilted shyly to the side, eyes downcast, her hands clasped in front of her. Her dark hair curled out of a severe bun resting at the back of her neck. The same hairstyle Karin had worn as a child. Joe's brow drew together in a silent question.

"Father's rules. The subservient pose," Karin explained in a murmur, to avoid embarrassing the girl.

The girl opened the door for them, her gaze tight on Karin's face as though memorizing each feature, intense as though she could not quite believe her eyes.

Karin's father was propped up on pillows, his fierce eyes sunken beneath his prominent brow. Home dialysis equipment filled the far corner. So his kidneys had ceased to function. His breathing was labored. Not yet the deep chest rattle that would declare the end, but close. This husk of a man with hollow cheeks barely resembled her father. Where was the strong man she remembered, with the broad shoulders and the long arms with whipcord muscles?

The sight of her father obviously at the end of his life shook her. From all that she saw, he had little time left. Or perhaps it was she who had little time left. She had expected at least a man of similar size and health to Zeb, but her father looked twenty years older than Zeb had. The shock stunned her despite the fact that she knew her father had refused to consider a transplant.

Surprised by the pain she felt at his plight, her gaze flitted away from him to examine the room. She had expected to feel rage and fury when she saw her father, but this shadow of the man she had so feared only engendered pity. He was so close to death; what should she tell him, and how? He and Zeb had been tied to each other through the years, hating and loving each other so fiercely they could barely stand to be in the same room. How would her father take Zeb's death?

Karin's gaze drifted further around the room, stark in its few furnishings. The walls were covered with crosses of all sizes, shapes and materials. The logs comprising the walls were dusty and in need of cleaning and oiling.

Karin struggled with a thousand warring emotions as the girl, Colly, came to the bedside and leaned forward, saying in a clear, firm voice, "Father McGrath, you have a visitor."

His eyes opened slowly, rheumy and pale, finally focusing first on Colly, then drifting to the foot of the bed where Karin stood. For several seconds he looked at her, taking in her face, his gaze traveling slowly from her eyes to her mouth and back.

"It's me, Father. Karin." She felt Joe's warmth reaching to support her, strengthening her. "I want you to meet someone."

"I see." His glance ran over Joe, rested on his face, then switched to Karin. His voice was dry, rattling in his chest as he spoke. "You look like your mother, Karin. A good woman."

"I have a baby. Her name is Haley."

"So I heard."

She had specifically told Sam not to tell him. "Who told you?"

"Zeb. He kept track of you."

Karin felt her spine stiffen. Her chin came up, angry. What part had her father played in this? "Why was that?"

His tongue, dry and pale, tried to wet his lips. "I thought it was for me, but now I know that isn't true." He reached for a glass of water. Colly bent to help him, the sleeve of her dress riding up on her arm. "That's enough, Colly. Thank you." He wiped his lips with a tissue, his hand shaking with the effort. "I need to tell you something. Terrible. About your uncle."

Karin waited.

"I know he's dead. I thought I felt it and Mrs. Leland got a phone call confirming it. She said Zeb crashed the plane. He was going to Mexico to get a transplant for Danny, again. Should never have done that."

Joe gripped Karin's hand. A mix of feelings rose in her throat until she could barely speak. "Do you know where the kidney would have come from, Dad?"

"I learned Danny was failing and I could see Zeb was, too." He closed his eyes, a thin blue vein at his temple pulsing. "I figured it would be like before. I know what you did to get away from here."

From you, she thought and felt her heart thud in her chest.

Her father continued. "I started thinking about Danny, how Zeb always came up with a kidney for him." He turned to Colly. "Girly, show Karin your scar."

Colly's face flushed red.

"Do it. It's important."

Karin watched the girl come to her side. Small, delicate and young. Too young to be the daughter of Mrs. Leland, a woman obviously in her sixties. "Please don't be frightened. I just have a few questions for you. I'm trying to understand something. Are you Mrs. Leland's daughter?"

The girl stood before her, her hands dangling at her sides, her gaze glued to Karin's. "Mother Leland is my primary mother. My parents were killed when I was two."

"When did you come here?"

"I think when I was four or five." She looked at the old man whose gaze now rested darkly on her. "I lived in Mexico for a while."

"With Mrs. Leland."

"Yes."

"How old are you?"

Colly smiled in return, a slow grin that grew until it lit up her face. "I'm seven, but I'm big for my age."

She leaned toward Karin and said softly, "Sometimes I feel older."

Slowly, Colly unbuttoned the front of her dress, letting it drop. Then she turned her back to Karin and raised her little woolen undershirt. There it was. The scar left by removal of a kidney.

Karin said, "Thank you, Colly. Here." And she moved forward. "Let me help you get that dress back on." She lifted the dress and slipped it over her right arm, then held it as Colly slid her left arm to the sleeve. "Wait."

Karin took hold of Colly's forearm, holding it gently but firmly, a chill crawling across her scalp. She pointed to a small round scar in the soft hollow of Colly's inner elbow. "How did you get this?"

Colly shook her head. "I've always had it."

Karin pulled the dress over her arm and buttoned the dress up. "Thank you for showing me your scar. You know, I have one just like it on my back, too. But yours is much nicer than mine."

Colly brightened. "Gracie has one, too."

"Does she? Tell me about her."

"She's a little older than I am. She came to live with us in Mexico when I was five. She was sick for a while, but she got better." Colly leaned in close to Karin. "She can remember her mother."

"Can you remember yours?" Instantly Karin regretted asking her because Colly's face clouded over. "No. But Gracie says my mom probably had blue eyes like mine, because her mom had brown eyes like hers."

Karin glanced at her father. His eyes were still closed, but his mouth worked silently as though he was about to speak again.

He raised his head. "Colly, girl, please leave the room for now."

He waited until he heard the door close softly behind her. Then he spoke, his voice low and choked-sounding. "Zeb took their kidneys, like he took yours. I know now about the way you sold your kidney to get away from here. I didn't want to believe it of you or of Zeb, especially Zeb, but I'm sure of it. Now."

Karin leaned into Joe for support, struggling to contain her feelings. "It took you a long time."

His gaze shot to her, hard and angry, a look she had seen too many times in her childhood. "You judge me."

"As you judged me, many times."

"Then you are doomed to make the same mistakes I made. Is that what you want?" His voice rose. "Blindness takes many forms."

Joe tightened his arm around her. "What made you see Zeb differently?"

The old man stared hard at him. "I'd like to say I figured it out all on my own. It would be a lie. Mrs. Leland told me. She used to be a nurse for the doctor Zeb uses. She told me I'm dying and I'd better face the truth." He sighed. "Karin, I was hard on your mother. And on you."

"And on Sam. Even more on Sam."

"I thought it would keep you both on the right path."

"You were wrong."

He was silent for a long time, his gaze locked on an old photo of her mother, framed and hanging on the wall opposite. After several minutes he turned to look straight at Karin. "I'm sorry." Then in a soft voice he added, "I missed you."

CHAPTER 59

Joe wondered that Karin didn't burst into tears. He placed a hand on her shoulder to tell her he was there if she needed him, but her eyes stayed bright, joy shining over any sorrow she felt. And he knew with a certainty he seldom had, that she had endured sorrow from this ancient, dying man whose features so resembled her brother, Sam.

He'd seen the tangle of medical equipment in the corner and the oxygen tank next to the bed. This man would live only a short while. Little sympathy lay in his heart for the man who had cast out his only daughter, pregnant and penniless. He wanted to shout at him, to call him down, to punish him for the cruelty he suspected Karin had suffered at his hands. The rigidity, the unforgiving wrath, the hints he got from Detective Jansen about the life Karin had endured made him rage against the old man.

Instead, he drew a deep, deep breath and watched as Karin leaned toward the little girl who had moved to her side. Puzzled he watched as Karin brushed the child's cheek. What was her name? Colly?

"I call myself Nicole."

Karin bent and wrapped the girl in her arms. "Are there other girls like you here?" she asked, her voice a bare whisper.

Colly nodded. "Just Gracie. We have the same scar. I told Father McGrath about it two months ago. That's when he changed. He got real sick afterward." Her voice faltered. "He got real upset when we showed him the scars." Her voice dropped to a whisper. "It's my fault he's going to die."

"No. It isn't your fault, Colly. He has been sick with his kidneys since I was a little girl. He got upset because he learned the truth when you showed him your scars. He knew then that he had made a terrible mistake."

Joe saw twin tear tracks trace the old man's cheeks, and still he felt no softening toward him. *Let him have pain,* he thought. *He's earned it.*

Colly's chin quavered. "I didn't mean to hurt him."

"You didn't hurt him, Colly. You told him the truth. I'll bet Father McGrath has told you many times just what he told me when I was little."

Colly blinked away a tear. "The truth will set you free."

Karin swallowed. It wasn't what he'd told her, but it was better than anything she could think of. She smiled. "And the truth has set him free, too. Now, would you show me your left arm? The inside of your elbow again? Please?"

Colly slowly rolled up the sleeve of her dress. "Am I sick like Father McGrath is?"

"No, sweetie, you're not sick. I just want to see this other scar again."

The light slanted over the child's pale skin, illuminating a faint silvery line of scar tissue with tiny white dots where stitches had been. Exactly where there had been a wound after Dr. Wetford removed the strawberry mark. Karin felt a rush of adrenaline, her heart beating a tattoo of happiness. "You're healthy and fine. Everything is fine. Absolutely fine."

The girl slowly leaned into Karin and circled her with her arms.

Of course there would have to be a DNA test, but Karin was sure. Absolutely sure. Colly was Nicole Eberhard.

ABOUT THE AUTHOR

C. T. Jorgensen is the author of the successful Stella the Stargazer series, and most recently a stand-alone, *Calling for a Funeral.* A member of the Rocky Mountain Fiction Writers, Mystery Writers of America and International Thriller Writers, Jorgensen is turning from humorous amateur sleuth novels to the harder-edged suspense-thriller genre.

Jorgensen grew up in the Midwest town of Monmouth, Illinois, where her family has roots back to the early days of the town. She moved to Denver where she worked for years as a social worker at the Children's Hospital. An avid traveler, she lived in London for three years, taught in China four different times, and has traveled to China, Mexico, Europe, Egypt, Kenya and most recently Russia.

Jorgensen lives in Denver with her husband, the most patient person in the world, and her dog, Tyranus Rex, so named for his household status.